Something Sinister Within

By
R.G. Johansen

Shades Creek Press, LLC
Hiawassee, Georgia
Birmingham, Alabama

First Edition
First Printing, 2022

Something Sinister Within

By

R.G. Johansen

Cover Design by Chyna Tyree
Final production cover by Anna Harmon
Cover images created by Gabrielle Alejandra Rosell
& Ebru Sidar
Licensed through Arcangel Images, Inc., NY
Edited by Candice Lawrence, Athens, Georgia, &
Nancy Brown, Bessemer, Alabama
Content reading by Rosann Hearn, Savannah, Georgia

ISBN: 9798986843421
Copyright©2022 James Randall Gober
Copyright©2022 R.G. Johansen
Shades Creek Press, LLC
First Printing, 2022
Printed in the United States of America

All rights reserved. No part of this book may be used or reproduced in any manner, including internet usage, without express written consent of the author or publisher.

Disclaimer

This is a work of fiction. All the characters and plot situations are totally fiction and are not based in whole or in part on any known or related person(s), situations or circumstances. This work of fiction is a total artistic creation of the author based on imagination and thought. Any similarities created are purely fiction.

Dedicated to the Walkers Chapel Boys

Tommy, Larry, Henry, and Jimmy

A bond of friendship that has lasted over sixty years and still counting. Thank you for letting me be a part of your stories.

CONTENTS

PROLOGUE – WHY ME?..1

PART I – DARK SIDE OF PARADISE

1. A PLACE FOR EVIL...5
2. HEAVEN CAN WAIT..11
3. RED WORMS OR NIGHTCRAWLERS....................17
4. THERE IS SOMEONE AFTER ALL..........................25
5. THE SUN IS COLD AND..29
6. HELP WHEN YOU NEED IT.....................................33
7. A QUARTER HERE, A QUARTER THERE...............39
8. AN UNHOLY ALLIANCE...43
9. NO ESCAPE...45
10. GOLDEN RULE DAYS..53
11. NO ANSWERS..61
12. FRIDAY NIGHT LIGHTS...69
13. MAW TO THE RESCUE...75
14. IN A COLD SWEAT..79
15. HOT TEMPERS...87
16. ANATOMICAL RIDDLES..91
17. YOU MAKE LEMONADE..97
18. THE LONE RANGER..107
19. UNDERSTANDING...113
20. UNDER THE STARS..121
21. DID THIS REALLY HAPPEN?................................129
22. IT'S NOT OVER..139

PART II – AN IRREVOCBLE CALL

23. A PLAN IS HATCHED..153
24. A WITCH'S BREW...157
25. MIDWAY MAGIC..175
26. A DIRE WARNING..189
27. LIAR, LIAR, BIBS ON FIRE...201
28. A BAD FEELING..217
29. THIS CAN'T HAPPEN..223
30. WHY?...229
31. SORROW IS INDIFFERENT..237
32. "HAYELL" AND BACK...241
33. COMPELLED BY DESTINY...249
34. THE GAME IS AFOOT...257
35. SUMMER OF CLUES...265
36. LOOKING FOR ANSWERS...279

PART III – A MIGHTY FINE PLAN

37. CAN'T GET NO REST..291
38. DEAR LORD IN HEAVEN...305
39. WE GOT HIM?...315
40. A RESTLESS SPIRIT..319
41. PLAN B...329
42. WHAT A SURPRISE..335
43. KEEP LOOKING BACK..347
44. THE ANSWER..355
45. YOU'RE RIGHT!...359
46. NIGHTFALL...363
47. AT CLOSE RANGE..383
48. EPILOGUE–WHAT WE BECOME................................393

Prologue

WHY ME?

Jamie Thompson didn't fit the mold of a typical teenage girl in 1967. She was smart and pretty, and of course, she did all the usual teenage things. She was a good student at Belmont High, had a stable job working part time at the Food Stop and had even fallen head over heels for a handsome young boy. But her life was a test in many ways. She never chose to be thrown in the middle of a mystery in Gaston County, a one-hundred-year-old riddle of unsolved murders that had baffled every law enforcement agency in North Carolina. No, her involvement wasn't by choice, but perhaps by destiny. The sequence of unexplainable events left only questions; "What evil had deemed her worthy of its attention, and why was she left to solve the unsolvable on her own?" There was a measure of comfort knowing she had identified the killer, but it was a shallow victory given the price it cost to uncover the truth. This is the story in the life of that special sixteen-year-old girl. A sinister tale of unimaginable deceit, brutal murders, and the incredible answer cops refused to believe.

PART ONE

THE DARK SIDE OF PARADISE

One

A PLACE FOR EVIL

It's not the way you want to start the weekend. The call came into the Gaston County Sheriff's Office late Friday afternoon around six o'clock. The caller sounded confused, his words garbled and disordered. The man kept saying something about finding two bodies on the bank of Ramsey Creek off Lake Norman. The location was just north of Mt. Holly, about a thirteen-mile drive for Deputy Sheriff Joe Griffin. With the deputy's shift ending in ten minutes, it was an untimely interference of a big weekend planned with his wife. He knew the trip and the preliminary investigation would likely last through the night and into the next day. But with a small department and two officers on vacation, the deputy had no choice in the matter. Reluctantly, he climbed into the black-and-white Ford cruiser and drove east on Highway 74. Twenty minutes later, he arrived at the Gulf filling station in Mt. Holly to meet the caller. Griffin immediately recognized the individual walking with a bowlegged stride toward his patrol car.

His name was Doug Dutton, but everyone called him Puck. No one knew how he got stuck with that moniker. The handle certainly had no connection to anything dreamed up by Shakespeare, although he looked very much like a hobgoblin...especially if you had consumed a jar of his high-octane moonshine. Puck was creepy, very creepy. He was a scrawny man in his forties although he looked every day of sixty. And he was about 110 in weight, with a frame like the Hunchback of Notre Dame. His pockmarked face with the hook nose of a witch and the prick-ears of an elf were features best suited for a Halloween mask from Walmart. His only teeth were two lateral incisors on the bottom with an in-between gap just wide enough to wedge his hand-rolled cigarette. All his ugliness aside, it was comical to see him talk with an extra-long smoke bouncing in his mouth. The up and down and all-around motion looked like a music conductor waving his baton, only Puck never had to use his hand.

"Shuriff! I'd be the one that called. I's found two dead peoples when I's wus fishin' up yonder on Ramsey. Looks like they'd been campin' out." Puck seemed agitated as his voice grew in pitch.

Deputy Joe knew this man, and his reputation. And it certainly wasn't for catching trophy largemouth up on Ramsey Creek. No, Gaston was a dry county, and he was famous for making illegal whiskey and stealing pigs. Puck figured when you have no education and you can't read nor write, you do what you must to make a living, even if it's against the law. The deputy's gut told him that Puck was most likely scouting out a new location for one of his stills when he stumbled upon the campers.

"Mr. Dutton, why don't you get in your truck, and I'll follow you to a point where we can park our vehicles and walk to where you found the bodies," he instructed.

It wasn't difficult to follow Puck's 1955 Ford F100 pickup. The beat-up truck was missing both bumpers, had a cracked back window, and sported multi-colored fenders that were discernible a half mile away, not to mention the trail of smoke belching from the exhaust. And if the deputy should by chance lose eye contact, he could still find his way to Puck by listening for the overloud noise from his absent muffler.

Fortunately, both men stayed together as they drove to the remote location past a local boat launch and down a chert road for almost a mile. Finally, they arrived, parked in the tall weeds along the roadway and got out of their vehicles. Puck wasted no time waving Griffin over to begin the journey—and a journey it was. The trip to the site would have been easier by boat as the deputy struggled to force his way through a labyrinth of briars, low trees, and thick bushes while Puck walked through the vegetation as though his skin were made of leather. Meanwhile, the deputy was getting angrier with each snag on his tan and brown uniform and prick on his exposed arms from the blackberry thorns. Beyond his ire, without the protection of thick leather boots, he was even more afraid a mean copperhead would add to his puncture wounds. He suspected Puck was leading him on a meandering path to make sure they weren't within eyesight of his whiskey stills and Deputy Joe was fighting mad about the deception.

"It's just up ahead, shuriff. We'd be almost there," he answered while waving his arm for the deputy to continue to follow.

And then without notice, the heavy foliage opened to a sandy area where two canoes were pulled up on the creek's bank. Deputy Griffin stepped into the opening beyond the narrow boats, whiffed the foul air, and scanned left to right at the camping site, wishing he could just wake up from this grotesque nightmare. The scene was surreal, and the fading sun and dark shadows added to the twisted visual. The wind moaned, calling from the tops of the towering oaks and thick pines which made the deputy even more jumpy and anxious. That bad feeling was confirmed when the shocking scenery revealed something sinister had, indeed, happened.

A young man with ash-gray skin was in first stage rigor mortis. He was on the ground in a defensive, fetal position near a small triangular tent some fifty feet from the water's edge. His clothes, along with the tent, were torn and ripped as though they had been shredded by the claws of a wild animal. Dried blood somewhat concealed numerous slashes on his face, torso, buttocks, and legs. That same caked blood helped cover the stab-like wounds deep in his throat around the jugular. There was no need to check for vitals. The deputy instantly knew that this horrific crime scene would need the professional expertise of a medical examiner and lab technicians.

"Don't get close to the corpse, Puck. I don't want anything disturbed. Where is the other body?"

"It's over yonder, next to that honeysuckle bush," Puck answered and pointed to an area some thirty feet away.

As the deputy cautiously walked closer, he noticed what appeared to be an animal track in an area of bare soil among the floor of pine needles and leaves. Or at least he thought it was the mark of an animal. The print also carried some unusual characteristics that appeared to be human. As he continued to move toward the tall honeysuckle, he gazed left and right at the camping supplies and unopened food items strewn about the site. He thought it odd that there were no sleeping bags or cots. He carried on with his search until his eyes found the blood splatters on the bush next to the body. It left a baleful warning that evil of the worst kind had been at this place, and Joe struggled to keep his emotions and visceral reactions under control. The early scent of decomposition mixed with the fragrance from the honeysuckle made him dizzy and twisted his stomach. But he knew he had to keep his composure, especially with Puck looking on, so he fought back the unwanted sensations.

After wiping the sweat from his face, his eyes widened to view a woman in her mid-twenties lying on her back among the leaves. Daylight had mostly disappeared, so Joe needed a double take and a flashlight to make sure this was not an illusion. The violence imposed on the woman seemed beyond human comprehension. Her limbs were grotesquely contorted as though every bone in her arms and legs were broken, her mouth agape from screams for help that no one heard. Her nude body made the deputy wonder if she had been sexually violated. And her lack of clothing exposed the postmortem lividity which was present across her entire body. Unlike the male victim, there were no slashes, just the massive bruising and a set of circular wounds on her neck. And worst of all, her pale green eyes were open, suggesting that she had a first-hand look at the killer before she died. Joe, a fifty-year-old father with a daughter about the same age as the deceased woman, couldn't help but think that this was someone's baby. He had seen death before, but nothing that wounded his soul like this.

"Do you think a black bar attacked these folks?" Puck's question sent the deputy's heart rate in overdrive. He knew Puck wanted this to be an animal attack so the investigation would be brief, so law enforcement wouldn't be traipsing through the woods looking for evidence and stumble upon his stills.

Red faced and livid, Griffin responded, "This was no damn bear attack. A black bear would never do anything like this! Now, let's go. It's getting too dark, and I need to get back to my car to use the radio. We can mark the trail on the way back if the techs want to walk instead of getting here by water."

"But I's seed a bar the other day when I's fishin'," Puck retorted.

"Just shut up and let's go." The deputy had the look of a man in fear, a man who knew that evil had arrived in Gaston County. He could only wonder why.

Two

HEAVEN CAN WAIT

"Momma, get up! You've got to go to work." Jamie pulled at her mother's shoulders attempting to wake her from a deep slumber, a lethargy prompted by too much Smirnoff the night before.

"Let me sleep a little longer. I'm not feeling well and may need to call in sick," she mumbled.

"They said you'd lose your job if you did that again. Get up," Jamie demanded.

Slowly, Ann Russell slid to the side of the bed while rubbing the sleep from her eyes. Still woozy from the booze, the dull throb in her temple signaled an oncoming headache and the churn in her stomach warned of an impending case of diarrhea. She was about to make her way to the bathroom to relieve that uneasy stomach, but her daughter stopped her before she could make the trip.

"The commode is backed up. It's the septic tank again. It overflowed last night, so you'll have to use the outhouse. I'll call the landlord about getting it fixed," Jamie snapped.

Such was the life of the Russell family in Paradise Point in the late summer of 1967. A life that was anything but a celebration in the Promised Land. How else would you describe a dirt-poor existence in a dilapidated, aluminum mobile home on the Catawba River? Purgatory Point? Maybe, but it damn sure was no paradise. It was a strange community—a fish camp with no restaurant, with Raymond's Bait and Tackle store serving as the hub for this unusual neighborhood. A melding of plank board shacks, old house trailers, and a converted RV here and there was an odd backdrop against the surrounding beauty. The nearby flowing river and the banks thick with flowering dogwoods, Carolina phlox, loblolly pines and American Beech must have been God's reward for having to look at a mold-stained ceiling every time you woke up in the morning. On this day, God's hand would have been more appreciated had Ann's vantage point not been the inside of an outhouse.

"Fine, I'm gettin' up. And don't talk to me like you're my momma," Ann shouted.

"Well, you act like a ten-year-old with no responsibilities when you make excuses every time it's time for you to go to work," Jamie retorted while taking note of the bags under her mother's eyes.

"Just get off my ass, and hand me my cigarettes and my bathrobe while you're at it. And make me some coffee," Ann fired back. At forty, Ann already had the look of someone on Medicare. Her face was pinched and hard-bitten by too much booze and too many smokes. She was once an attractive woman, but a rough life had left her gaunt and misshapen from her head to her toes. Her only redeeming physical feature was a shag of natural blonde hair cut in uneven layers around her face. As for her emotional wherewithal, it was Ann against a world where everyone was out to get her. Her mistrust was mostly irrational, but it was a fine crutch to lean on when she had no other excuse. That kind of impoverished life can do that to a person. When your choice of a home is the one with the cheapest rent and you have to move from place to place like a band of gypsies, it can grind you down to the point where you are filled with bitterness. An existence where alcohol feels like the only medicine for your damaged soul, and drugs seem like your only escape from reality. You work harder and sacrifice more, yet the good life always seemed reserved for the privileged class in Belmont. Of course, Ann had only to look in the mirror to identify the main cause of her misery.

It was a litany of bad decisions that brought her to Paradise Point, that and a pea green Chevy Corvair that was broken down more often than the toilet in the mobile home. It was heartbreaking that Ann seemed unable to find serenity by choosing a divergent path. Instead, she always found herself in a storm, always in bondage to men who had no respect for women other than something to abuse and impregnate. Jamie never understood why her mother stayed with men who treated her so badly. The genesis of Ann's vacant mind began at a young age when she dropped out of high school her senior year and fell in love with a disreputable reprobate named Karl Thompson. At eighteen, no one is above dumb decisions, but leaving school so close to graduation and marrying Karl had to be at the top of the "Stupidest" list. Ann saw him as a twenty-four-year-old rebel when, in fact, he was nothing more than an abusive husband fueled by a temper as hot as the devil's hell itself. Karl was a man prone to violent outbursts and Jamie had spent many nights in hiding, listening to the sound of slaps and her mother's crying. The next morning always confirmed the night's horror when she saw the bruises on her mother's swollen face. That was life in the Thompson household. Carl with a "K" would get drunk, beat on Ann, and then join up with his gang of thugs to go about burglarizing homes, stealing cars, and selling any hallucinogenic drug that would take you on a magic carpet ride. Prison for Karl was as inevitable as the sun rising in the east, but not before he sired Jamie. Fortunately, he left her only his surname and a bucket full of mournful memories instead of all the contusions her mother had to endure.

Never to learn from her first mistake, Ann married again. This time to a piece of crap named Billy Russell. Russell's claim to fame was a resemblance to Elvis, but only if you had 20/500 vision. Just the same, he used that far-flung likeness and those gyrating hips to thrust himself into an addiction of infidelity. His knavery was the source of bawdy whispers among the church ladies at First Baptist Church. The gossip was rampant even beyond the church pews as most of the town folks agreed Billy never saw a mini skirt he didn't like. Ann forgave him for his first adulterous fling with a big-busted hairdresser, and then again on two more occasions with two lonely housewives. But the fourth indiscretion with Ann's best friend was beyond her heart's forgiveness. He tried to talk his way out of that tryst as well, but by that time, Ann knew that if his lips were moving, he was lying. She kicked Billy and his blue suede shoes out the door, saved enough money to hire a lawyer, and divorced her second mistake. But not before she was impregnated with Tommy. Much like Jamie, Tommy never knew his deadbeat father. And much like Jamie, it was best that his only burden was to carry his name.

Ann's mastery at being a single parent was as bad as her judgement for picking husbands. She would've been better at raising two beagles than a son and daughter. As a matter of fact, Jamie was more of a mother to Tommy than Ann. Changing diapers, preparing meals, and cradling her little brother when he was sick with fever were just a few of the responsibilities Jamie assumed at ten years of age. And the worry and fear that something would happen to him was constantly shading her mind. It was a price that should've never been paid by a young girl who was a child herself. It was as though her innocence had run past her and she could never get it back. But that was her life. A life that demanded overnight maturity. There was, however, one upside to her instant adulthood. It required an intimate closeness between the siblings, an unbreakable bond that was rare at such a young age. It infused Jamie with a sense of love and self-worth, and she cherished the connection.

Ann returned from the privy just as the timer sounded on the coffee maker. After lighting a second Marlboro, she poured herself a strong cup, plopped down at the kitchen table and watched as Jamie searched the cabinet for something to eat.

"Don't fix me anything. My stomach's too upset to handle any food right now."

"I'm seeing what I can find for Tommy. We're going fishing today, so he needs to eat before we head out," Jamie answered.

"I don't like the two of you on the water by yourselves, and I don't like you going by that bait shop either."

"We live next to the river. How the heck are we going to avoid it?" Jamie refused to let her hungover mother steal her good mood. During the night she had a wonderful dream about sitting next to her brother on an old dock under a sprawling tree. Both were reeling in one fish after another, and she was certain that today held promise. Appalachia's mountain folks called it "dreaming true" and she had experienced those type visions in the past.

"Well, as soon as I find a better paying job, we're moving out of this hell hole," Ann replied followed by a deep drag on her cigarette and a sip of coffee.

"Sure, Momma."

Ann was like a broken record and Jamie had heard that song many times before, although moving to Belmont within walking distance of the schools would save on gas for the car. The only problem was that it cost money to move up in the world and her mother was more adept at holding a tumbler filled with vodka than holding a job. It would have been nice living in Belmont, but it was only an inconsequential benefit given the grand scheme of their predicament.

Three

RED WORMS OR NIGHTCRAWLERS

The brother and sister duo shared the second bedroom in the 14x60 mobile home. The small space looked as though it was furnished by a decorator who loved to shop on the last day of a garage sale. The unmatched furniture and strange accouterments consisted of a light brown, six-drawer dresser on one wall, a platform bed on another, and a bare mattress on the floor. A red bean bag served as an inexpensive chair and a single bulb hanging from the ceiling supplied the light for the picture of *Dogs Playing Poker* hanging on the wall. You have few options for sleeping quarters when you live in a two-bedroom trailer, so Tommy slept on the mattress next to Jamie's bed. The location, however, had one advantage. It was an easy jump onto his big sister's bed when a nightmare interrupted his sleep. And last night had been a sleepless night, but not because of a bad dream. His nighttime was consumed with dreams of catching a whopper on the river. It was Saturday morning and Jamie had promised to take him fishing on the Catawba; the excitement was palpable.

"Good morning," Jamie laughed as she sized up her little brother standing in the doorway to the kitchen.

Tommy holding two Zebco 33 combo rods and reels in one hand, while rubbing the sleep from his blue eyes with the other was a funny sight indeed. His sandy blonde hair, a compromise between his mom and Elvis, was tousled and his frame could be described as slight for a six-year-old. And he was adorable. A disarming grin and an impish face brought a smile to anyone he encountered.

"You need to eat something before we head out. Sit down and I'll fix you some cereal," Jamie insisted.

"I'm not hungry," Tommy objected to the delay.

"Just eat a bowl of Cap'n Crunch and we'll be out of here in a jiffy. I promise." Jamie's mouth curled in a smile.

Eating a cereal named after a boat captain was apropos for the day ahead so, grudgingly, Tommy complied. He finished the sugary bowlful in record time, hopped from the chair, grabbed the tackle box on the floor just inside the screened door, and yelped, "Let's go!" Meanwhile, Jamie gathered the remaining gear and headed out the door with her little brother closely behind.

Once outside, the two anglers began a fast-paced walk down the dirt road known as Bullfrog Lane. It would have been a depressing trip had Jamie and Tommy not been so fixated on the beauty of their destination. Both avoided staring at the front yards of the shotgun shacks covered with worthless litter—junk car and leaky boat carcasses, jettisoned refrigerators, rusty 55-gallon drums that were filled with who knows what, along with broken kids' toys and an above ground pool covered in algae. Needless to say, cutting the grass was an impossibility. Of course, river rats never cut their grass anyway since their broken-down mowers were usually mixed in with all the other junk. River vermin, however, were good at drinking and cursing the government. But never too drunk to run a trotline or cash a welfare check from Uncle Sam. Jamie hated being called a river rat by the city folks. A redneck or hillbilly would have been a preferable label to being called a rodent. Even white trash would have been better. She knew it was a derogatory term and didn't think she deserved the slight, especially since she never considered herself part of the river community. Nonetheless, being born into an underprivileged class was a terrible disadvantage, yet she was determined not to die with nothing more than a Zebco reel. She was also keenly aware of the commitment it would take to get out of those circumstances. This sixteen-year-old was too smart and driven to be doomed to that way of life.

Within a minute, Jamie and Tommy arrived at Raymond's store. The freestanding building had an understructure of cinderblocks and mortar coated with a white masonry paint that had been washed out by the sun. The weather had been equally harsh on the high-pitched tin roof. It was covered with rusty splotches that looked like a cancer trying to meet in the middle. Raymond's Bait and Tackle was painted in crooked, red block letters on the triangular gable at the entrance. One could only surmise that the workmanship was done by someone who had imbibed the moonshine or smoked the marijuana that Raymond sold out of the back of the store, or most likely both.

All that aside, the physical look was unimportant to the siblings. Both dropped their fishing gear at the entrance, stepped inside, and split up in pursuit of two very different outcomes. Tommy headed for the candy rack in the front of the store while Jamie moved to the back where Ramond kept the bait. On her way to the rear, she walked toward the Guin twins who were thinking about taking a five-finger discount on a Zara Spook fishing lure. The identical boys, whose imaginative parents named them Terry and Jerry had just turned seventeen and Jamie's fetching appearance had interrupted their sticky intent. Both turned to give her a long stare as she hurried by.

She had a natural beauty about her, a face that was well-favored and needed no makeup to improve her attractiveness. Striking dark eyes and page boy bangs that touched her brows complemented her shiny raven hair. And the coloring of her skin, high cheek bones and full lips, made her wonder oftentimes why she looked so different than Karl and Ann. Of course, Ann was pretty fed up with her rebel husband back then, so Jamie's real father could have been a one-night stand. If true, there must have been a Cherokee limb or two in his family tree. As Jamie continued to look for bait, the twins continued their indecent gawking, making comments loud enough for her to hear. Wisely, she chose to ignore their sexual innuendo. Nonetheless, the boys continued to stare at her blue jean shorts and loose-fitting t-shirt that covered a willowy body with narrow hips and developing breasts. Although she was still going through puberty, her body had all the signs of a beautiful young woman, and the boys whispered obscenities about how they would rock her world if given the chance. She refused to make eye-contact with the hooligan brothers and kept moving along.

At the back of the store, Jamie noticed Maw Bates, Raymond's eighty-year-old mother standing next to the cooler that stowed the nightcrawlers. She also caught a glimpse of the sign on the wall above the fridge that read, *Jesus don't steal worms!* Jamie felt certain the sign was Maw's handiwork because her son had assigned all the minnows, crickets, and worms as her domain. And Maw believed in the Bible, and she could quote it cover to cover, especially that eighth commandment about not stealing stuff that belonged to other people. Apart from her God-fearing ways, keeping Maw in the back of the store was a win-win for Raymond. He had a bait cop to minimize pilferage and she wasn't within earshot to hear him talking about distilling another five gallons of whiskey. Maw could recite the verses in Galatians that preached against the sinful act of drunkenness. As a mother, she may have looked past her son's indiscretions, but she never approved of drinking whiskey.

Maw took notice of Jamie coming her way. "Hey, baby girl," she said in an upbeat voice.

"Hey, Maw. How are you doing?" Jamie asked with the same excitement.

"I's got a little bursitis goin' on, but otherwise, I feel as fine as frog's hair!" Maw flashed a crooked smile, exposing a pinch of snuff above her lower lip. "Is you goin' fishin'?" she asked.

"Yeah, I'm taking Tommy. We stopped by for some bait," Jamie's answer was followed by an affirmative nod.

"That boy sho' nuf' love to fish, don't he?" It was a rhetorical question. Maw knew Tommy loved to fish, but she also knew that he loved to fish even more with Jamie. "What kinda bait you looking for?"

"Well, he gets impatient if he's not catching anything, so I'm thinking we'll have more luck using worms?" Jamie said while lifting an inquisitive brow.

Maw, the little four-foot-ten-inch prodigy, took another pinch of snuff from her Bruton can while lighting an unfiltered Camel. With perfect vision and hair yet to turn gray, she was a miracle of nature. How else could you simultaneously dip snuff and smoke cigarettes for sixty years and only have fingers stained yellow from the nicotine and a little stiffness in the joints to show for it. In between puffs, she explained in detail how you can catch pretty much anything with fins with red worms—bluegill, shellcrackers, bass, catfish and even an occasional crappie would bite an earthworm. So, worms were the best bet. But she also warned Jamie not to swear while fishing because that was bad luck, and to give thanks to the first fish caught so she and Tommy would have good luck the remainder of the day.

Maw may have been a friend of Jesus and knew how to echo Scripture, but she was reared in the Appalachian wilderness on a summit called Devil's Nest near the Big Ridge Mountains. She still spoke with a mountain-talk dialect, and she still believed in the old ways of medicine versus a pointy-headed doctor with a syringe of tetanus vaccine. When Raymond was a baby with an earache, she would blow tobacco smoke in his ear to ease the pain. And when he accidently lost two of his toes at the sawmill, she poured coal oil on the wound, wrapped his foot with strips from a bedsheet and told her twelve-year-old son that God would take care of the rest. In her mind, coal oil and The Almighty could cure anything. She also believed that reading a palm or using a little elderberry tincture to treat the flu were tried and true practices. And naturally, a little saliva-soaked tobacco worked well on a wasp sting and the oil from earthworms cooked over an open fire would take care of arthritis. Maw had grown up in the ways of the mountain, and folklore and superstitions had always been part of her life. And no amount of modern-day science would make that go away.

Jamie had grown very close to Maw since moving to Paradise Point. This little Scottish-Irish woman had taken to her as well. "I'll get you some worms from the cooler and meet you up front," Maw said.

"Thanks," Jamie responded. As Jamie neared the front, she could hear a voice growing louder with each step.

"Put that candy back, boy, unless you're gonna pay for it!" The protruding veins in Raymond's neck looked like a tangle of cottonmouths as the hateful words spewed from his mouth. "You need to git if you don't have any money!"

"Leave him alone, asshole. He's just looking at the candy!" Her tongue was sharp and direct. Jamie was as mad as a sack of rattlesnakes and had her own set of fangs to back up her animosity. She would fight a grizzly if it meant protecting her little brother, so going tooth and nail with a bony old moonshiner was an easy draw. As she was getting ready to gouge out his eyes, she noticed that Tommy was wide-eyed and terrified, unable to understand what was taking place. Out of fear, he dropped the candy bar on the floor and disappeared behind his big sister's legs, hiding like a scared puppy. It was a pitiful sight. Fortunately, Maw appeared in time to intervene before the situation got out of hand.

"Leave that boy alone, Raymond. He ain't hurtin' nuthin'!" Maw demanded.

"He picks up those candy bars every time he comes in here, and he never buys nuthin'." Raymond's face transformed to a deep red hue and his voice grew mean as he turned to confront Jamie. "And you don't buy nuthin' half the time you're in here either. Y'all need to git."

Maw stepped between Jamie and Raymond to diffuse the rising tempers. "Jamie's buyin' sum worms. I's take care of her. You go check on the Guin boys in the back. They're acting suspicious. Better yet, go outside and see if anyone wunts to rent a flatbottom. I's sold Booger sum minnows a few minutes ago and he said he needed a boat for the day. He's probably waiting on you out there." After Raymond walked away, Maw motioned Jamie to follow her to the cash register.

To Raymond, Jamie had no name, no feelings. She was just a thing, just a source of money. Nothing more. And Tommy was someone to be bullied. Maybe it was because as a kid in school, Raymond was small in size and presented an easy target for the bigger boys. Perhaps he felt compelled to exact his revenge on a six-year-old given the bitterness he carried all his life. Or maybe it was because he had been labeled a coward by his friends since he wouldn't trade fists with anyone. His so-called buddies tagged him with a suitable, albeit offensive, nickname. Chicken, they called him. Chicken Bates. The moniker stuck for decades given his beak-like nose and his inhumane Saturday night business of cockfighting. Maybe that's why Chicken yelled at Tommy. Or maybe, he was just an asshole. But to Maw, Jamie was a child of God, someone to be cared for and loved. And Tommy was an innocent boy who needed that same affection and tenderness, along with a dose of protection. Maw had the heart and backbone to deliver on all counts. Having dispensed of Raymond, she stepped outside the store entrance and stopped the brother and sister before they could walk away.

"Hey, Jamie, wait's a minute. I's wunts to say I's sorry for what Raymond did in there," Maw said.

"It's okay. It wasn't your fault," she answered. Jamie knew that Maw's sympathy wasn't just because of an uncaring old man. No, when you can't scrape together enough extra change for a candy bar, you feel helpless, and you lose hope. It was heart-breaking for Jamie to watch Tommy beg for things he couldn't have, and that despair made her feel angry at everyone. The clash with Raymond was a terrible reminder of that reality and it could have become a permanent scar for Jamie were it not for a little old lady with a heart of gold.

"Here, I've got something for you and Tommy." Maw reached into the large side pocket on her baggy dress and pulled out two Milky Way bars. Her eyes grew warm, and her smile turned sweet as she handed them the candy.

It was a simple act of kindness, but to Jamie there was something sacred about the gift. It was the first time anyone cared, and it was the first time she didn't feel helpless and defeated as though separated from the love of others. She gave Maw a big hug as she fought back tears. "Thanks, Maw. That means a lot to me and Tommy—knowing that somebody cares about us."

Four

THERE IS SOMEONE AFTER ALL

At one time, the Catawba River was a wild waterway unencumbered by hydroelectric dams. The river, rich in history, provided a home for the Catawba Indian Nation for thousands of years until explorers and early America settlers made it to the shoals and left their indelible mark on the basin and the tribe that lived there. Many of the tributaries were still raw and supported fish, wildlife, and unique flora along the river's two-hundred-mile journey. Jamie and Tommy found one of those beautiful headwater branches, and by mid-morning, had set up their fishing location. Their lucky spot was exactly as Jamie dreamed it would be. An abandoned boat dock shaded by an impressive water oak tree was waiting on their arrival. After settling in side-by-side on the creaky pier, Jamie baited Tommy's hook with a juicy wiggler and watched as a smile found his face as he dropped the red worm into the water. Before baiting her own line, she dangled her legs off the dock and swung them back and forth as though walking on air, pausing to think how her life had been so dark compared to the bright panorama around her.

It had been a rough start to the day, and she wondered if anyone other than her mother and Maw really cared about her. She was never raised to believe in a higher power, never knelt before an altar or been baptized in the Holy Spirit, nor had she ever sought God because if His job was to watch over her, he must have been distracted or off the clock. Yes, Jamie understood what cruelty looked like, how the unkind places can wound your soul. But on this day, the warm breeze had washed her resentment away and she learned that nature's beauty has no boundary. On this alluring morning, Jamie was stirred by a sense of goodness, not evil, a sense of wonder as she watched the water's surface sparkle like diamonds. Upward she looked through the wispy clouds hoping to find her missing God smiling at her, speaking to her through the songbirds among the bright green hillsides. And she did see and hear Him. She caught a glimpse of divinity in the blue sky, the flashing waves, and the Carolina wildflowers. It was a lovely thing, listening to His voice in the birds and the wind that whispered through the pines. Yes, she sensed that He was there, delivering this beautiful gift just for her, telling her that everything was going to be all right. For the next four hours, the darkness had ended.

"I've got another bite," Tommy squealed as Jamie watched his rod tip bend toward the water.

Jamie was an expert in fishing but was a novice when it came to catching. Today, however, was different. She reeled in, unhooked, and released her third bream of the morning. And she wasn't the only one who found magic in the day. Her little brother had whipped her soundly in their fishing contest. He had caught and released four bluegill and a small bass before his plastic float was broken on one of the pilings supporting the pier. It was a fortuitous mishap. The accident forced him to drop his bait all the way to the river bottom instead of being suspended by the bobber. The presentation of fat worms to the channel catfish was irresistible. He yelled with excitement as he reeled in another scaly victim.

"Okay, you've caught enough for today. Besides, we're out of worms. We'll take the fish by Raymond's and see if Maw will clean them for us," she said while adding the last cat to a makeshift stringer. She then gathered their remaining fishing gear while Tommy insisted on carrying the fish.

Tommy hopped, skipped, and jumped down the dirt trail and all the way to the bait store. Maw was thrilled they had such a favored day. Of course, she assumed that Jamie and

Tommy had heeded her advice and not taken the Lord's name in vain. And naturally, she happily agreed to clean their fish. That smallish woman could filet an alligator, so five catfish took all of fifteen minutes. She placed the filets in one plastic freezer bag and a chunk of lard in another. She then gave Jamie instructions on how to best cook their fish...fried. It was the only recipe Maw had in her cookbook because she deep fried everything in an iron skillet—corn on the cob, watermelon, even butter sprinkled with sugar for dessert. She would even cook pig ears in the pig's own rendered fat. How ironic.

"I can't wait until Momma sees all the fish we caught!" Tommy exclaimed.

Given Ann's indifference to her motherly role, it could have been a dark time for her kids. Her absence could have left deep emotional scars, but that didn't happen because of days like today. Jamie and Tommy seemed to buffer each other from their mother's inner turmoil. Besides, Jamie rarely resented filling her mother's role, and fishing with Tommy was just one way she created their own special world.

Five

THE SUN IS COLD AND....

In 1967, most people described the burgeoning decade as a time of rebellion and counterculture. A time when young people questioned and revolted against everything. Fads played an instrumental role by reflecting society, but music—music was the language that expressed it all. From civil rights to a war most people opposed, from psychoactive drugs to sexual liberation, and from important women's causes to the environmental movement, the diversity of the music spoke to all those trends, and it was unparalleled. It was a smorgasbord of talent from pop singers like Chubby and Fats to the British Invasion led by the Beatles and Stones. The vibe of that music was upbeat and fast. But the rhythm and blues tones from Motown were different. Those sounds filled your soul, spoke to your heart, and moved your feet. Who didn't love Aretha, Smokey, and Marvin? And filling in all the gaps were the rocks...surf rock, country rock, southern rock, progressive rock, funk rock, and any other rock you could imagine. Given all these cheerful musical options, why would Ann choose a song of lamentation?

Jamie and Tommy left Raymond's and headed back to the trailer around three in the afternoon. Tommy was still beaming about his day on the water and Jamie was excited about having a dinner of catfish and hush puppies ready when their mother arrived home from work. When they came within view, Jamie noticed the Corvair parked on the rock-covered driveway in front of the trailer. As they drew closer, she could hear the sound of music through the screened door and wondered why her mother was home so early. She felt uneasy and nervous, sensing that something was wrong and that something bad had happened. Her suspicion was confirmed when she recognized the song blaring on their stereo console in the living room. Ann only played the 45-rpm record of *I'm so Lonesome I Could Cry* when she wanted to wallow in self-pity.

There she was, lying on the sofa, drinking out of a sixteen-ounce tumbler filled with vodka while singing along with B.J Thomas between gulps. Ann liked B.J.'s mournful rendition much better than the original by Hank Williams. She also thought B.J. was better looking and had pretty hair.

"What happened?" Jamie asked while a confused Tommy stood nearby. It wasn't a life-or-death situation, but it was bad.

"I got fired at the diner today. I caught hell for coming in late and then Old Man Crowder said the customers were complaining about how I was treatin' 'em. He told me I was a shitty waitress and that I had to leave," Ann stammered.

"Well, great. Now we can't pay the bills." Jamie couldn't understand how anyone could get fired from a job serving plates filled with greasy food and apple pie. Ray Crowder owned and operated the diner that was known around town for deep frying any animal on Noah's Ark. He was normally a patient man, but he had been pushed too far by an irresponsible employee.

Ann extinguished her cigarette among the mountain of butts in the glass ashtray. She took another swig and started back with the karaoke routine. The vodka had attacked her brain and her eyes were blind to the dilemma she had put her family in—or maybe she just didn't give a damn. Jamie knew the kind of damage caused by the alcohol, and she was keenly aware that her mother's drunkenness was only a temporary condition that went away after a night of sleep. She also knew that Ann wasn't just a Saturday night social drinker. No, her mother was more faithful to Russian vodka than to her son and daughter and she never missed a day of numbing her mind. Without a doubt, the evil spirit in the bottle was the problem and it demanded her mother's attention. But she was also aware that there was something much worse than getting tanked from the booze. The long-term impact of depression, irritability, and social withdrawal was taking a piece of her soul every day. Ann's ragged employment record at six jobs in three years was just one example of the toll on her life. The euphoric day for Jamie and Tommy had turned into a nightmare. All Jamie wanted was something better.

Six

HELP WHEN YOU NEED IT

With a bare cupboard and empty refrigerator, Jamie and Tommy made it through the remainder of the weekend on breakfast cereal and leftover catfish. Ann, however, was on a completely different diet. She was sustained by Smirnoff, cigarettes, and the incessant moaning coming from the Magnavox record player. Having grown tired of B.J., but still needing to feel sad and mistreated, she opted for a vinyl recording of Roy Orbison singing *Crying*. Hour after hour, the Big O cried and cried, and hour after hour Jamie grew more and more sick of hearing him wail. She loved music more than hushpuppies, but the irritation of Roy's voice reverberating through the thin plywood walls was worse than being keelhauled under one of Raymond's rental boats. At one point she broke the plunger while forcefully trying to clear the stopped-up commode. Jamie pretended she had a suction cup seal on Roy's face in the bottom of the bowl and was giving him something to cry about, something other than getting dumped by his girlfriend (pun intended).

"It's Monday and you haven't moved off that couch. When are you going to start looking for another job?" Jamie's voice was filled with frustration.

"I don't know. I just need to get my head on straight before I start lookin'," Ann grumbled.

Jamie could see all the signs of surrender; her mother had given up. But Jamie also knew pity would not feed the family. She would need to act on her own if they were going to stay ahead of the landlord and have food on the table. Besides, school started in a few weeks and Tommy only had one change of clothes and a pair of worn-out sneakers. Jamie knew how cruel kids could be and she didn't want her brother to be branded a river rat because of his donation-box clothes. A little extra money meant a three pack of underwear, and a new shirt that wasn't threadbare from being worn every day. Come hell or high water, she was going to take care of her little brother.

"Where are the car keys, Momma?" Given the tone in Jamie's voice, this was more of a demand than a question.

"In my purse on the end table. Where are you goin'?" Ann asked as she sat upright, twisted the cigarette butt in the ashtray and lit another smoke.

"To the Food Stop to ask Mr. Morton if he'll let me work full time until school starts," Jamie grunted while digging for the keys.

"You don't need to do that. I can go to Belmont tomorrow and sign up for welfare. That'll get us by until I can find another job."

"It takes too long to get approved for that. I'm going to Belmont. Stop drinking and look out for Tommy until I get back."

The Corvair shook, sputtered, and left a smoke screen all the way to the Food Stop grocery store. The steering wheel vibrated badly, and the car seemed possessed by a ghost determined to make a right-hand turn when she wanted to go straight. Jamie felt as though she was in a wrestling match with Gorilla Monsoon as she struggled to keep the car between the lines. New tires and a front-end alignment would have solved the problem, but those were luxuries the Russell family could not afford. And forget about a tune up. That kind of service was only available to people with money. Jamie was relieved when she finally pulled in the store's parking lot. She tried to kill the engine, but the car's evil spirit kept the motor running for a few seconds after the key was pulled from the ignition. It was embarrassing, but at least the little car didn't die on the side of the road.

Jamie entered the store and headed straight for the elevated office located just off the check- out lanes. It was an area set off by four low walls with glass partitions that allowed Mr. Morton keep a watchful eye on the shoppers in line, although backed-up lines were not a problem on Monday mornings. The start of the week was a slow time for grocery stores, a time for unloading the delivery trucks with goods and produce, and re-stocking the shelves and freezers. It was also a time for handling necessary paperwork, so Jamie's timing was perfect. Mr. Morton was sitting at his desk and completing order forms when he saw her coming his way.

"Hi, Mr. Morton. Do you have a few minutes?" She asked.

"Sure, Jamie. Come on in and have a seat," he said with a smile on his face.

Jim Morton was a handsome man in his early forties. His hair was dense and neatly trimmed with a little wisdom gray around the temples. A wide friendly smile, and an ocean of love behind his deep blue eyes were eye-catching features that would stand out in a room filled with faces. And beyond his fine looks, he had a wonderful rapport with the teenagers who worked at the store. Oftentimes he was called Coach because of his encouraging words and willingness to listen to and support them when they needed help. His philosophy was not to micromanage the kids, but to give them room to fail, and then teach them how to overcome that failure. Those kinds of experiences were immeasurable for teenage boys and girls. It helped the kids understand the meaning of hard work and being rewarded for that effort. Jamie loved Coach. His words never failed to lift her spirit. Her words, however, were a different story. All the dirty details of her family's circumstances flowed from her mouth like a broken hydrant, including her missing jailhouse father and alcoholic mother. It was enough to make Norman Vincent Peale crestfallen and depressed. No amount of positive thinking could erase the harsh reality of her day-to-day existence.

"We're in a bind now that we don't have enough money coming in. It seems like our landlord, Mr. Nuby, is always at our front door asking for the rent. And we could use some cash to buy groceries." Jamie was wearing a wry smile as her eyes ranged from left to right while waving her finger at the aisles stacked with food. "I was hoping you'd let me work full time, or at least put in some more hours until school starts."

The coach picked up on Jamie's attempt at humor. He laughed and then began asking her questions about the days and hours she could work. She found herself wondering what her yesterdays would have been like if Mr. Morton had been her father instead of Karl. Coach didn't drink, didn't steal, didn't do drugs, and he loved Jesus. He would never abuse or cheat on Ann, and he had a steady paycheck coming in every week. And, most importantly, he would protect Jamie and Tommy from harm. It would have been a grand life, but unfortunately, Mr. Morton snapped Jamie from her spellbound dream.

"Jamie? I think I lost you there for a minute. Are you okay?" he asked.

"Oh, yes sir. I'm fine. I just didn't get much sleep last night," she answered.

"Well, can you come in at eight in the morning and work full time until school starts?"

Jamie never prayed for help from above, but sometimes we find compassion even when we don't petition a higher power. Unexpectedly, Coach also asked her if she needed a fifty-dollar advance on her paycheck, a little cash to get by until Friday. Of course, she said yes. It was as though the weight of the world was lifted off her shoulders. She wasn't Jean Valjean with no options other than stealing bread for her family, but to a sixteen-year-old, her situation seemed dire. And she had been thrown a lifeline from the most wonderful man in the world. Those fifty bucks would buy enough groceries to last a week and fill up the Corvair with gas.

It had been a good day until Jamie saw Lenny Robinson on her way out of the Food Stop. Lenny, a teenage friend who worked at the store seemed thrilled to see her. He extended a warm greeting, but then his face was painted with worry. "Did you hear about the people who were killed up on the river? It wasn't too far from where you live," Lenny said. "It was a couple who just got married. People are sayin' a bear killed them."

Jamie's good day had just turned bad.

Seven

A QUARTER HERE, A QUARTER THERE

It was a blue 1959 Rambler American two-door Club sedan powered by a flathead inline-six-cylinder engine with a three-speed shifter on the column. Jamie had never driven a three on the tree manual transmission and would have to learn, but that was just a minor inconvenience. The car also had high mileage, bald tires, and dented fenders, but it was priced right at one hundred dollars, and it was waiting for her at a used car lot in Belmont. That Rambler meant independence to Jamie and that's all she could think about as she hurriedly filled another bag with groceries. It had been three weeks since she started working full time at the Food Stop and she had been setting aside every extra dollar she earned to buy that baby blue dream. And she was close, real close. Her regular pay had been steady, and a little overtime had helped, but her tip money had been exceptional. She had been making a killing bagging groceries and hauling them one buggy after another to the customers' vehicles. Standard tip was twenty-five cents a trip, but Jamie was smart. She learned she could double that fare by complimenting a woman's hair or asking men about the horsepower in their muscle cars while walking them to their automobiles. On one busy Saturday, both pockets in her hip-huggers split from the weight of the coins.

Ann was bringing in a little cash on her own after starting a trial job. It was night shift work as an in-home caregiver for an eighty-one-year-old matron with Alzheimer's. The money wasn't great, but the schedule meshed well with Jamie's daytime hours, so Tommy was never left alone. Jamie was pleased that her mother had escaped the grip of alcohol long enough to pass the probationary period but feared her mother would return to her bad habits when the old woman's mind would go away. For now, there was enough money coming in to pay the bills, and with a few more bucks, Jamie would be behind the wheel of the most beautiful car in the world.

The Food Stop was closing in twenty minutes, and normally, activity would be winding down. But Mrs. Sorenson was in the store and her buggy was almost full, so the check-out lines were abuzz with movement. The kids were aware that Mrs. Sorenson went to church and talked to the Lord, and they knew that she lived a life of generosity by thinking of others. Of course, her presence threw them in a frenzy as they jockeyed to be the fortunate one to bag and cart her groceries. Her family was respected and as they say, "well off", and she was known for handing out one-dollar tips. Jamie needed that money, but she needed a rabbit's foot and perfect timing to get it. Unfortunately, she was in the middle of bagging another customer's goods when Mrs. Sorenson made it to the check-out cashier next to her location. Jamie was downcast until she saw the lottery winner, Lenny Robinson, motion her over to take his place. Luck was with her, although it didn't hurt that Lenny had a big crush on her as well.

"Swap places with me, Jamie," Lenny suggested while waiving her over.

Jamie had a quizzical look on her face. "You sure?" She asked.

"Yeah, I'll take care of your customer," he insisted.

With an engineer's precision, Jamie bagged Mrs. Sorenson's groceries making sure the frozen foods were in separate bags from the boxed goods, and the detergents separated from any edible items. For good measure, she double bagged the milk and sodas to avoid an accident. She completed her first-class service by complimenting Mrs. Sorenson's beautiful complexion, engaging smile, and silky dark hair. Jamie also asked her how she found time to stay in such good shape. Mrs. Sorenson saw right through her pandering but chose to reward the effort just the same. Jamie wanted to scream in celebration when she wrapped her hand around two one-dollar bills. Two bucks would buy her more than three gallons of gas and five barbecue sandwiches at the Jiffy Check convenience store, or two packs of cigarettes and a bottle of vodka at the liquor store which meant she could never tell her mother about her good fortune. For just a moment in time, she felt rich.

When she re-entered the store, Lenny was waiting, hoping that Jamie had hit the jackpot, praying that he would be rewarded with a hug. He was. There was something about that girl, a shimmer that played with his mind. And Jamie felt the same way about him, but it had nothing to do with an aura or glow. Lenny, a year older, had an angular build like a basketball point guard. Jamie was attracted to his athletic frame, but she also loved his steely blue eyes and closely cropped blonde hair. That along with his dark jeans and rah-rah shoes rounded out his pleasing appearance. He was a handsome boy by all accounts. And the other girls loved his little-boy side and cuteness as well. Most of his admirers said he looked like a young Steve McQueen. And even though he didn't own a High Green Mustang GT with a 390 V8, he did drive a badass Granada Gold Chevy II Nova SS with a 327. Close enough to Frank Bullitt's street rod to grab the girls' attention and make the boys green with envy.

Jamie couldn't imagine a better day until Lenny explained that he was updating his under dash eight-track tape player with a Craig Pioneer. He offered to give his old Lear Jet to Jamie, and even volunteered to install the player in her new car. She was beyond words.

No crises at home for three weeks, extra quarters in her pocket for the laundromat, and a music maker for the new car. Jamie pinched herself to be sure she wasn't dreaming.

Eight

AN UNHOLY ALLIANCE

Since the early 1900's, there had been a number of unexplained deaths on and around Spencer Mountain. Perhaps that was to be expected since it had a reputation for being a remote and lawless place where wickedness thrived among the hills and hollers. The steep rocky bluffs and green mossy balds were an illusion that hid the handful who preferred to live in the blackness of the endless woods. The few troglodytes who lived there held a deep religious curiosity, but not in wonder of the Good Shepherd, but in worship of the Prince of Darkness. Here they practiced black magic among the shadows of the oaks and made outlaw whiskey as an offering to the dead spirits for favors and to fund their devilish endeavors. On those isolated Appalachian hills, you could shout obscenities to Heaven and praises to Hell with only Jesus and Lucifer hearing your voice. And up on that same mountain, there was a witch woman who had sold her soul to the devil for the power to conjure up the unthinkable. But there was also another wicked soul, someone who stooped close to the ground and sprinkled a handful of graveyard dirt on the most unexpected place. The follower declared that the Scriptures were a book of lies and chanted incantations, hoping to wake a spirit from slumber that would cross over and play a role in the most horrific acts. The price to be paid was a blasphemous renunciation of God.

"Ever and ever for, glory and power, the kingdom the is thine for. Evil from us deliver but, temptation into not us lead and. Us against trespass that those forgive we as, trespasses our us forgive...."

The words were read backwards and delivered with a vengeful purpose. The evil had been awakened.

Nine

NO ESCAPE

It was the dead hour of night, and they were in a deep hollow shrouded by a canopy of white oaks covered in dark green ivy. The kudzu covering the trees and ground was known as the vine that ate the South. And for good reason. The creeping plant grew a foot every night, and for most folks, it was a pain in the ass, especially if it invaded their backyard. But for the three brothers busy at work around the makeshift still, it was the perfect cover from any moonlight that might expose them to the ABC revenuers that patrolled these parts.

Buck, the married brother, was the oldest sibling at sixty-one and he was busy gathering wood and filling the sixty-gallon barrel with water from a narrow stream off the Catawba. Meanwhile Beaver, the middle boy at fifty-three who had never come out of the closet for fear of getting shot by his brothers, was pouring in sixty pounds of sugar. And Bodean, the youngest at forty years of age, well, Bo was single and had a reputation for being a hillbilly playboy. This wannabe Hugh Hefner was keeping an eye out for any leaks in the copper piping while stirring the mash with an old wooden boat paddle. At that time, there were only two flavors of grain alcohol in Gaston County—legal and illegal. The boys were making the 140-proof illegal kind. The Sugg brothers were also known for cooking the cheapest moonshine in the county and each man played a specific role in distilling the hooch. Unfortunately, no one was assigned the job of quality control. The low-cost price for their rotgut meant they paid no mind to any bacteria, contaminants, or poison additives that might find its way into the drum. Nor did they properly drain the methanol from each batch of shine. Buck liked to say that they made mean whiskey, panther's breath. But Beaver said their brew was a skull bender that could fry your brain and leave you blind and paralyzed or take you on a trip to the Promised Land. Either way, this operation was anything but a Jack Daniel's distillery.

"Damn, Bo. Don't stop stirring the mash!" Buck barked at his baby brother.

"I jest needs to smoke a cigarette and I'll start agin'. 'Sides that, I'm gettin' hungry fur somethin' to eats and I needs to stop anyways," Bo retorted in an Appalachian brogue.

"I's hungry too, Buck," Beaver concurred as he dropped an empty bag of sugar on the ground.

"All right, dammit. We'll eats some of the pie that Ludean made for us, and then we'll gets back to putting the corn in the still," Buck reluctantly gave in to his famished brothers.

Ludean, Bucks wife, was known for her culinary skills in the kitchen. Of course, you had to be a backwoods rube to appreciate some of her dishes. The boys, as expected, precisely fit that bill. All three had grown up eating squirrel stew, carp hash and swamp cabbage, so naturally they were big fans of her cooking. Their only problem was their lack of gnashers to do the job. With only five teeth among the siblings, dinner was quite a spectacle for the Suggs. Of course, in keeping with his nickname, Beaver claimed two of the five with a malocclusion that was impossible to ignore. His two upper incisors stuck out in front of his lips and were colored orange from chewing tobacco and the lack of dental care. And Bo, he was blessed with the remaining three choppers, one up top and two on the bottom. As for Buck, he had a set of dentures he refused to wear, so he depended on gums that were rock hard from years of chewing his wife's possum fricassee. Fortunately, tonight's specialty required few teeth, if any, to consume. It wasn't four and twenty blackbirds, but earlier in the week, Buck had shot a couple of crows with his 12 gauge and Ludean had whipped up one of her specialties...crow pie. The brothers sat in a semicircle around the campfire and began passing around the pie plate. Lacking any eating utensils, each man scooped out a handful of the scrumptious bird, filled his mouth, and moaned with gastric delight.

"Hot damn, that's some good pie right there!" Beaver exclaimed as he wiped his mouth on the front of his sleeveless T-shirt and unveiled a buck-toothed grin.

"Damn straight it's good. We jest need a little likker to wash it down," Buck chuckled, exposing a toothless mouth filled with crow and gravy. Being the eldest, Buck was much more refined than Beaver. After chasing the pie with a big snort of hooch, he withdrew a stain covered rag from the front pocket of his redneck tuxedo and cleared the dripping whiskey and pie gravy from his scraggly chin. No, he wasn't about to wipe his mouth on his worn-out shirt or raggedy overalls.

Never to waste an opportunity to sample their product, the other two boys joined in by passing around the liquor filled jug and black bird pie as though having communion with the devil. All three continued to eat and drink while making jokes about how John Law would never find them so deep in the woods. And for the next hour, it was truly a fine evening of good food and hillbilly revelry until Bo started acting strange, looking uneasy, and acting squirmy as though he was about to sit on a porcupine. It was obvious that the combination of the alcohol and crow pie had inflamed his bowels and a colon attack was on the way. The noisy gurgling sound from his distended abdomen sounded like a Maytag washing machine and confirmed his discomfort.

"Whut's wrong with you?" Beaver blurted, "You look like shit."

"I needs to take me a dump," Bo declared with a distressed look on his pale face.

"Well, hell. Git the lantern and git fur nuff in the woods so we can't see or smell you," Buck commanded.

Like a good soldier, Bo followed Buck's orders by grabbing a kerosene lantern and a half-used roll of toilet paper. Meanwhile, Buck and Beaver continued to pass the jug as they watched the light from the lantern disappear among the timbers. Oddly enough though, within seconds, Bo hurriedly returned to join his brothers. Buck was the first to notice that Bo had done the unthinkable. He had soiled his new pair of Levi jeans he recently purchased from the Sears catalogue.

"You can't waits to git yourn britches down before you takes a shit? That's gots to be the world's record for the fastest crap any ones has ever took," Buck said. The whiskey had muddled Buck's brain so much that everything seemed obscenely funny, including his brother's terrible predicament. He guffawed like a donkey causing him to lose his balance and fall backwards off the stump where he was sitting.

Beaver was ribbing his brother and doing a lot of hooting himself until he noticed that Bo had something more important on his mind than his nasty pants. His eyes seemed transfixed in the direction from where he came out of the woods on his way back to the campfire. "You looks like you've seen a ghost, Bo." Beaver thought that maybe the booze had affected more than Bo's intestinal tract. Maybe his faculties had gone haywire, and he was having illusions.

"I seed somethin' when I wents to take a dump. Jest take a look over yonder, over by that biggust tree," Bo nervously said as he pointed his finger.

"I don't seed nuthin'," Beaver said as he squinted, attempting to see what had spooked his little brother.

"Look agin, a little more to the right!" At this point, Bo had risen to his feet in a position of alarm, as though the fight or flight response had gripped his body.

Beaver may have been nearsighted, but Buck had not missed the ominous eyes watching them from the tree line—eyes that were red, glowing like two hot coals in the night. Wide-eyed and slack jawed, Buck snatched his double-barrel Mossberg, loaded it with two slugs and sprang from the stump. Then, in preparation to shoot, he spread his feet apart and sighted down the twin barrels. Buck had killed many a deer for Ludean's iron skillet while hunting illegally from the road at night, so he was intimately familiar with the night-shine from those four-legged animals. And this was no Bambi. At this point, his heart was in tachycardia, beating completely out of control. Nevertheless, he wasn't going anywhere. His reaction was to stay and fight! "Right over thar, it's two shiny eyes over thar between those trees."

Whoever or whatever it was mattered little to Buck. He wasted no time by madly firing both barrels in the direction of the unwanted visitor. Meanwhile, Beaver, blind as a bat, pulled the old .38 revolver from his waistband and emptied the six rounds in the cylinder in the general direction of nothing. It would have been an okay defense, but the boys were dazed from the loud blasts of the guns. More importantly, both forgot to consider the muzzle flash that occurs when you fire eight rounds on a dark, cloudy night. Both men were sightless, temporarily blinded and unable to quickly reload. Their eyes could only see vague images of the monstrous evil that was rapidly coming toward them. And then it began. Clawing and biting, the tearing of flesh from their throats, and the slow disembowelment of their bellies.

The attack was violent and deadly. Buck and Beaver's screams echoed off the hillsides and drifted upward through the treetops as they cried for help. But there was none to be found. Certainly not from Bo. The rush of hormones and fear that filled his body spurred him to leave his brothers behind to fend for themselves. So much for compassion and brotherly love. No, he had hit the gas pedal and was running as fast as his two skinny legs could carry him. Normally, Bo couldn't outrun a three-legged possum. But tonight, wildly and fast, he ran. Frantically and out of control, he ran. A face plant into the hard bark of a maple produced a field of stars that momentarily left him stunned and bewildered. But that couldn't stop him. Nor could the thick wall of blackberry briars that tore at his arms and face. The surge of adrenaline in his body took care of that by subtracting pain from the equation. By the time he reached their pickup truck hidden in the pines, he had soiled himself repeatedly, his shirt was soaked with sweat, and his mouth was filled with blood from a busted lip and two missing teeth. A broken nose that made breathing more difficult simply added to his confusion. And his arms and face looked as though a mountain lion had used him for a scratching post. But he made it.

After lunging into the cab, he was heaving for air and could feel his heart hammering in his chest. He could also taste the blood flowing in his mouth as he spat to clear his airway. Hopeful that a cigarette would calm his nerves, he lit an unfiltered Pall Mall and took two long hits and stared anxiously out the window. The tobacco didn't help. His physical agitation was far from over as his body had another unexpected response... an unpleasant loss of bladder control that added to the nasty odor that permeated the truck.

And he had another problem, a much bigger problem. Buck had the truck key in his overalls and Bo was damn sure not going back to retrieve it. If the monster that attacked his brothers didn't kill him, a heart attack from the strenuous exertion would. Besides, the cab and Bo were rank from sweat, urine, and feces. A person with terminal sinusitis could track him if he left and continued fleeing in the dark. The decision was an easy one. He would take his chances and stay put. Bo slid to the floorboard and tried to quieten his noisy breathing and slow his heart rate as he inhaled another drag from his cigarette. And for a second his mind drifted to the sky, wondering if the Lord's Prayer would save him from this terror. Probably not since he had used the Lord's name in vain every day in every imaginable way.

Since he couldn't recite the prayer anyway and only said things that made Satan happy, he gave up on that option.

He thought of option two. If today was the day he would meet his maker, why not bargain his way through the pearly gates. Who knows, maybe God was running a garage sale on redemption, and he could buy his way in. That possibility was dismissed as well. It's hard to bribe The Lord of Lords when Beelzebub is your best friend and lives in your mind. Plus, Bo had already struck a bargain for his soul with the devil by living a life of sin. As a last resort, he tried to remember a Bible verse or two he had heard in passing when he was a kid. But nothing came to his shattered mind. The closest words to heaven he remembered were a simple "God bless you," and that blessing came from Pastor Holland when Bo sold him a quart of white lightning in the shadows of the back door to the preacher's house. Bo figured the blessing was probably from Lucifer anyway since he had to try so hard to be invisible during the transaction. It's not like the Bible condones getting drunk on Saturday night when you have to preach about abstinence the next morning.

Taking his chances on the floorboard of the truck was it. It turned out to be a fatal decision. He was about to be doornail-dead and washed in the blood, but the blood would be his own. If only he had noticed the deer rifle in the gun rack mounted across the cab's back window. If only he hadn't been found. But he had been discovered and nothing could give him more time on Earth. Satan was going to take him home.

At first, he heard low-pitched snarls that seemed to be circling the pickup, as though he was being stalked. And then, he felt a thud on one side of the truck. A minute of silence, and then a louder thud on the other side. Next came an awful sound, the screeching sound of something like a hand scraper being dragged across the rusty hood. This thing, this monster was tormenting its prey while Bo was still praying for help. Finally, the driver's side door was yanked off the hinges and he saw the thing face to face. It was much worse than his friend the devil.

It was a long and agonizing death.

Ten

GOLDEN RULE DAYS

Jamie pulled at the back of Tommy's high-waisted jeans to keep them, high-waisted. With a tight budget and an eye on the future, she had purchased pants a size too large to accommodate his growing body. It was a wise decision for a sixteen-year-old, but for now, it required a lot of snatching and pulling to keep him decent.

"You may have to keep pulling up your britches until I can get you a good belt," Jamie instructed.

"I want to wear my old pants. These are too big." Tommy complained.

"You can put on your old pants when we get back. You need to look good this morning. Hop in the car and let's go," Jamie said with authority.

After loading into her new Rambler, she started the engine, shifted the car into first gear, and began the fifteen-minute drive with Tommy in tow to Belmont Elementary School. The school required aptitude testing for kids starting the first grade and last week Ann and Jamie had taken Tommy to complete the standardized exam. Unfortunately, last night Ann had slipped back into the bottle while at her caregiver's job and was still drunk this morning when the sun rose on the horizon. Not surprisingly, the responsibility fell on Jamie to fill in for her wasted mother.

Jamie was taking Tommy back to the school to learn the test results. She was very optimistic. She had educated her little brother on many subjects since he was three and was confident that his IQ was well beyond the mental mastery of a six-year-old. Adding to her good mood and positive attitude was the eight-track tape player and four speakers Lenny had installed in her Rambler when she purchased it a few days earlier. That was the day she got out of mobile home jail and gained her freedom. Feeling good and in need to express her good cheer, she popped in a tape of The Doors and pretended she was playing the Vox organ on the steering wheel while grinding through the transmission gears. And then she began belting out *Light My Fire*… with a little impromptu twist of her own.

Jamie looked to the right to find her brother wearing a sheepish grin. "What do you think of my singing? Pretty good, huh?"

"No, you're terrible," he emphatically answered, his smile now ear to ear.

"You don't think I sound better than Jim Morrison?"

"Who's Jim Morrison?" Tommy asked.

"Never mind," Jamie ended the conversation and wrapped up the song with a final, "try to set the night on fi-uuur!"

It hit her hard when she pulled the little car into a visitor's parking space and caught sight of the elementary school. Suddenly, her joy turned to anxiety. Her baby brother was growing up and would be starting first grade. It reminded her that she would no longer be able to keep him small and dependent. But more than that, this transition meant Jamie could no longer keep Tommy as close as in the past. A sadness filled her heart and she wanted to cry, but knew she needed to hold it together. Instead, she bit her lower lip, exited the car, and walked hand in hand with Tommy down the sidewalk while giving the schoolhouse a thorough viewing. As it turned out, finding the entrance was a bit of a challenge. The one-story building lacked any hint of logic. It was a rambling affair of fingerlings clinging to a central structure covered by a siding of concrete blocks, gray stucco, and a horizontal roof. It was dull and uninteresting, more the look of a prison instead of an institution for learning. The only thing intriguing in the vicinity was the cemetery adjacent to the teacher's parking lot. At least the neighborhood of the dead was markable if you had to find your way in or out.

Jamie finally spied the double doors to the entrance and guided her little brother inside. After moving a few feet past the doorway, they were greeted by the echo of empty hallways, along with the unmistakable smells of musty books, disinfected floors, and lead-filled pencils. Jamie ignored the resonating sound and the unusual mix of odors and scanned her surroundings for any clue that would lead them to the counselor's office. Her eyes came to rest on a white poster board taped to the tile wall. The temporary sign was marked with a crooked arrow, the kind of symbol a first grader would draw. The arrow appeared to be pointing to the Student Support Office.

Again, Jamie grabbed Tommy's hand and walked down the long hallway until they arrived at a door with a stenciled window that confirmed they were at the right place. Both entered the reception area with Jamie checking in with the registrar at the front desk while asking Tommy to take a seat and wait. Within minutes, Linda Foster, a first-grade teacher and part-time guidance counselor arrived, acknowledging Jamie with a warm smile and friendly greeting. Her words were delivered with an unusual tone and dialect. It was soft and pleasant, spoken with a gentile hypnotic effect that made you stop and listen. A little Southern lilt, perhaps, from a bygone time when those of privilege wanted everyone to know that they were aristocrats. Her words were a little syrupy, not the harsh twang or slow drawl from the Appalachian or Black Belt regions of the country. Maybe the articulation hailed from Charleston or Savannah, where a lady could be offended by an impolite young man, and yet be flirtatious when she told him that her daddy was going to hang him from a tree behind the barn.

"How are you, Jamie?" Mrs. Foster asked.

"I'm fine, Mrs. Foster. How are you and Lisa? I haven't heard from her in a while."

The rumor around school was that Linda Foster's daughter, Lisa, was born out of wedlock. And even though she and Jamie had been schoolmates and good friends since their freshman year at Belmont High, Lisa had never spoken about her father. Unsurprisingly, Jamie never asked, given the embarrassment of her own daddy residing at Central Prison in Raleigh. The two girls, however, had more than missing fathers in common, so Linda gave Jamie a quick rundown about Lisa spending the last month of the summer with relatives in Charlotte. She continued by saying her daughter would be returning home to Belmont the week school started.

"She asks about you a lot, you know, whetha I've seen you at the grocery store lately. I told hur that I've missed you the last few trips but would let you know that she's askin' about you if I saw you."

"Well, tell her I said hello and that I miss her," Jamie said.

"I sure will." With the chitchat winding down, it was time to get down to business. "Is your mutha here with you?" Mrs. Foster asked.

"No, she's not feeling well." Jamie reasoned her answer to be a half-truth, not a whopper told by a brazen liar. Her mother had thrown up in the early morning hours and complained of a severe headache from the toxic alcohol when she rose from bed. So, she certainly wasn't at the top of her game.

"Well, your mutha is supposed to be here to review the test results."

"I know, but will you please just tell me how Tommy did? I can let my mother know," Jamie implored.

"All right, but you'll need to get hur to return a signed copy of the report before the first day of school," she said with the authority of a school official.

Jamie happily agreed to the conditions and followed Mrs. Foster down a narrow side hallway off the main corridor, tagging close enough behind to smell the trail of her perfume. It must be roses with a touch of vanilla, she thought, wondering what it would be like to smell so sweet. But there was no deliberating Linda Foster's image. As though she had found the fountain of youth, she appeared to be maturing in reverse. This woman looked more like a high school cheerleader than a forty-two-year-old mother. Jamie found herself staring at her most striking feature, mesmerized by her pale blue eyes accented by the dark winged eyeliner. Glowing skin, shapely lips and a straight nose with a delicate upturn added to her attractiveness. Her hair was flaxen with a short, bob-like cut that flipped out at the ends. Really cute. The kind of look you get from innumerable trips to the beauty shop. And her clothing and adornments spoke to the family's affluence. Linda was taller than most, but the pricey, mod shift dress that hung loosely around her body couldn't hide her curvy figure.

Ms. Foster's jewelry was a combination of a stylish necklace, Tiffany earrings, and an expensive Omega 14K white gold watch. Without question, Linda Foster was a high stepper who belonged to a wealthy family. Unlike Paradise Point where people lived in shot-gun shacks with wandering chickens, the Fosters lived in a neighborhood of pretty brick houses and inside dogs. Subdivisions with names like Alexander Woods and Magnolia Estates that declared their exclusivity with tall stone columns and bronze lanterns at their entrances—private communities that wanted to keep the riffraff at bay by erecting wrought iron gates with guards. Jamie stared at her dime-store necklace, thread bare top and worn-out sneakers and felt embarrassed by her lack of importance. The only cotillion she would attend would be a dance at the high school gym. That's how insignificant you feel when you are at the mercy of those with power and money.

The office was down a narrow side hallway. The door was open, so Jamie and Mrs. Foster stepped inside and took their seats. The room was windowless with dim lighting given several fluorescent ceiling bulbs that needed replacing. Jamie thought the office felt a little spooky as she sat in a straight back chair that fronted a desk covered with books, file folders, strewn papers, and a cup filled with pens and pencils. The wall behind the desk was dominated with the usual diplomas, certificates and letters of verification while filing cabinets and bookcases filled in the space on the remaining three walls. Linda took the chair of authority at the desk and opened the file containing Tommy's test results.

"Well, Jamie, fust I want to say that Tommy is very bright. Really exceptional for a six-year-old startin' elementary school…."

Mrs. Foster began by complimenting his critical thinking skills and spent the next ten minutes talking about his numerical competence in math. Jamie was elated at the positive affirmation. She had always made excellent grades in her subjects and surmised that some of her problem-solving skills and smarts had rubbed off on her little brother.

"Yes, Tommy's aptitude is above a child his age, but we discovered somethin' of concern in the testin'."

"What's that?" Jamie asked, thinking that the world was about to deliver another blow to keep her family down.

"Tommy has some early warnin' signs of dyslexia. He oftentimes confused letters that looked similar like b and d, or p and q. And he wrote letters like r and f backwards when he transcribed simple words. It could be an issue of poor central vision, that his eyes see certain letters and words at an abnormal angle. Has he been to see an ophthalmologist in the last year or so?"

"No, we can't afford to take him to an eye doctor. Besides, he'll probably grow out of that anyway," Jamie emphatically replied.

Mrs. Foster recognized that she had hit a nerve but continued with her excruciating explanation. "I can help you and your momma find a way to have his eyes tested. We even have eye doctors that come to the school and examine the kids for free. But if it's a neurological dysfunction, something to do with his brain, he'll need to be seen by a medical doctor."

It would have been less painful if Jamie had been punched in the gut by Muhammad Ali. Her mind searched for someone to hold accountable, and her memory immediately fell on her mother's irresponsible behavior when she was pregnant. If all that hard drinking could ravage Ann's liver, just think about what it was doing to an unborn child. And the chain smoking surely played a role. Her mother was an easy target for all this bad news, but Jamie needed a solution, not a scapegoat to blame for Tommy's disability.

"Does this mean he can't start to school?" Jamie asked, thinking of the worst possible outcome.

"No, he can start next week with all the other kids. He'll just need to be placed in a special needs class to help him cope with the disorder. I actually teach that class and can get him signed up. I can also help him get signed up for the free lunch program too," Mrs. Foster said, thinking she was helping solve the family's impoverished state of affairs. And to make matters worse, she kept repeating her same words for another ten minutes.

To cope with the disorder...to sign up for free food. Jamie was livid at what she considered to be belittling remarks from an intellectual snob. To her, the meeting with Linda Foster simply confirmed what she already knew. This was just another chapter in the book of the haves and have nots, and she was the poor and disenfranchised main character. Tommy would be segregated and cast into a system with the other so-called "dumb kids." That's what some of the well-to-do smart kids would call him anyway. Dumb. Jamie was feeling like an overheated pressure cooker. She imagined a small tribe of schoolyard bullies intimidating and maybe even physically harming her defenseless brother. She was about to explode when, wisely, she clenched her teeth, took the paperwork, and calmly thanked Mrs. Foster for her time. She hurried down the hallway, stopping only to pick up her brother who was still waiting at the Student Support Office. Both briskly left the building and headed back to Paradise Point. Not wanting to scare or confuse Tommy with the bad news, Jamie was silent as she stared out the windshield. But Tommy still sensed that his sister was upset, so he did the only thing he knew that would lift her spirit.

"I love you, Jamie," he softly said.

There was no singing on the way home, but his loving words did soften her anger.

"I love you too, Tommy," she responded.

Eleven

NO ANSWERS

Ludean had contacted the Gaston County Sheriff's Office the morning after Buck failed to come home, but she was unable to provide specific information regarding his latest whereabouts. She knew he was cooking moonshine all right, but Buck trusted no one and had only shared the still's general location with his untrustworthy wife. Buck knew that Ludean had two areas of exceptional know-how: her unique hillbilly cooking and her love of rumors. She was the top gossip-hen in the county and would babble to anyone about anything, including her husband's secrets and private matters, so Buck had only given her a general notion of where he and his brothers would be doing their thing. She shared that information with the sheriff's office, although she was advised that nothing would be done until twenty-four hours had passed from the time of her phone call.

The next morning, Bobby "Ole Man" Sims met Deputy Sheriff Joe Griffin and Sheriff Harley Myers at a remote location north of Lowesville, about half a mile down a dirt road that led to Ramsey Creek. Ole Man's gray hair was cropped short and hidden underneath a raggedy John Deere cap, and his bony knees had worn holes in his threadbare denim overalls. In total, he was a five foot, one-hundred-pound bundle of nervous energy and he was there for a reason. He was known throughout the county for his bloodhounds. Folks said that Maddie and Belle could track anything on four-legs, even in a thunderstorm. Deer, wild hogs, bobcats, you name it. If it walked on land, those canines could sniff it out. The sheriff's department, however, had another animal in mind. The officers wanted to use the dogs on a search and rescue mission for the two-legged humanoid kind of creature. Ole Man knew his sleuth-like hounds could find anyone lost, dead or hiding, and he knew his babies would be relentless once they were on a scent. He dropped the tailgate on the Ford pickup, unloaded the leashed dogs, and ambled over to meet the deputies.

"Howdy, shuriff. Hey, Joe," Ole Man greeted the officers while straining to hold the tall black-and-tans in check. Sims had the frame of a sixth grader, and the big hounds were jerking him around like an angry mother correcting her five year old. "Looks like my girls have already picked up on a scent."

"We had a report yesterday morning from Ludean Suggs that her husband and his two brothers never came home night before last. She thinks something has happened to them and she told us we should begin our search here," Joe explained.

"Hell, everybody knowed the Suggs have a still or two off the Catawba. They probably jest got drunk testin' out their shine and couldn't find their way home." Ole Man grinned, exposing a set of store-bought teeth covered with Red Man tobacco juice. He then spat a brownish missile between Maddie and Belle as an overflow of saliva ran down his scruffy chin.

"Could be, but we need your help to see if we can locate them. After the two campers were killed near the Ramsey a couple weeks ago, we want to be sure nothing has happened to the Suggs," Deputy Griffin responded with a touch of apprehension in his voice. He was still unsettled by his earlier discovery of the young couple's bodies.

"Well, let's git goin'," Ole Man said with confidence.

His two girls at one hundred pounds each were drooling, trying to taste the earth and air when they exploded on the trail with their paws digging in the ground as though they couldn't wait to find their quarry. It looked as though Ole Man might lose his grip on the reins as he yelled for the dogs to slow down. But he held on for dear life. Joe and Harley were amazed as they watched that seventy-one-year-old munchkin run. It would have been easier if Ole Man had slapped a saddle on Belle and rode her like a pony. She was certainly big enough to support his child-like body.

As for the cops, Joe was muscular and fit, in good shape for keeping pace. But Harley had a fondness for anything sweet, and he was hauling an extra forty pounds in his oversized belly. That added weight had him wheezing while yelling for his partner to wait up. Joe would never say it aloud but pulling that fat man around was like dragging a boat anchor buried in sand. Both yelled for Ole Man to slow down, but he never heard them over the yelping dogs. Maddie's and Belle's long ears flopped like wet noodles as they kept their noses to the leaves while pulling their master along at breakneck speed. The old man's voice calling out encouraging words to his girls as their mournful barking drifted along the hillsides was haunting.

About a half-hour later, Sims and the hounds arrived at the still's location near a creek bottom surrounded by a dense stand of oaks and black gums encircled by ivy and wisteria. A murder of grounded crows took flight, and instantly the baying faded to silence as the dogs became restless, as though they could smell an unnatural presence. The deputies were concerned when they could no longer hear the howling, but a quick upward look through the treetops made it clear that the howling was no longer necessary. Against the clear blue sky, both men could see a spiral of buzzards soaring on the thermal while descending forebodingly toward the forest floor. It was a bad omen.

There would be no tomorrow for the Suggs brothers. Buck and Beaver were unable to wake from their nightmare; they no longer needed to fret about growing their whiskey business in Gaston County. Perhaps Satan would give them a liquor license and allow them to reopen along the Lake of Fire, but on Earth, their lawless business was over. They had been discovered two days after their horrific deaths and whomever or whatever killed them had done so without mercy. Ole Man was struggling to keep Maddie and Belle in check as both hounds pulled hard to leave the site. He securely tied their leashes to a small sapling, spit out his chewing tobacco, and hand rolled a cigarette to calm his nerves. Within minutes, Joe broke the cover of the woods and the tension and anxiety returned to his psyche much like at the first murder scene. Sheriff Myers, the last one to arrive, doubled over and immediately lost his breakfast of johnnycakes and syrup. The combination of the mangled corpses, the stench of decomposition and his abnormal breathing was more than his full stomach could handle.

The sheriff and deputy didn't know where to start. Both were in a haze of confusion. Buck's and Beaver's lives had been drained from their bodies. Both had been stripped of their clothing and were tethered by nylon ropes, hanging upside down from a lower branch on a large hickory tree. There was an odd purple coloration to their torsos, arms, and heads, most likely due to the gravitational movement of blood in their dangling bodies.

The implication was clear. Both men were most likely alive when they were hung from the tree. Even more grotesque, both had been gutted as though someone was butchering a hog. And both had been savagely bitten on their necks and clawed on their backs and legs. Their mouths were agape and their eyelids wide open as though their last vision was one of eternal horror. The terrifying picture of the brothers was compounded by the foul odor swirling in the wind. The gases from the corpses' active decay had Joe and Harley covering their mouths and noses with handkerchiefs while attempting to assess what had happened. Ole Man just stood in silence, staring at the brothers' abhorrent features.

"Why would anyone do something like this?" the sheriff asked.

"I don't know, sheriff. If I had to guess, I'd say this was some kind of revenge killing, something personal between the Suggs and whoever did this. The strange thing is that their wounds look similar to the two campers who were killed about a mile from here off Ramsey. Remember the report I filed after those murders? I included the coroner's assessment as to the cause of death and he said the gashes and massive loss of blood is what killed them," Joe answered. "Same gashes here, all the way down to the bone. And look at the whiskey still. It's destroyed and all their stuff is scattered everywhere. And there's a shotgun and pistol on the ground over there, so you'd have thought they could've protected themselves from whoever attacked them. Had to be more than one person who did this."

"Weren't thar supposed to be three brothers?" Ole Man joined the cop-to-cop exchange. "I don't seed the third one. You think he coulda kilt his brothers?"

"Not likely," Joe replied. "Those boys had a reputation for being as thick as thieves. Do you think the dogs could pick up a scent and help us locate the other brother?"

"Hell, my hounds can smell a storm comin' from two counties away. They'll have no trouble trackin' another Suggs brother. Let me untie 'em and we'll git goin'," Ole Man spoke with a mixture of fear and agitation, worried about what the dogs may find next.

A minute later, Mattie and Belle were tracking in a zigzag path as though they had a road map to Bo Suggs. But this time the dogs seemed wary, restless about what they might discover by following a similar smell. No excitement, no baying cadence, just the muffled sound of their noses sniffing the rustling leaves. There was one difference, however. Harley and Joe had withdrawn their firearms from the holsters on their utility belts. Both allowed their handguns to swing by their sides as they followed Ole Man and the slow-moving hounds through the dense woods. Within minutes, the entire search party arrived at the pickup truck partially camouflaged by a thicket of smallish, sweet gum trees.

If the brutal slayings of Buck and Beaver had been done by some deranged individual, the gruesome murder of Bo screamed of an unnatural malevolence. The youngest Suggs brother was on his back some twenty feet from the pickup. Even though the falling leaves partially covered his rotting body, the swarming blow flies gave away its location. The massive injuries were obvious. Although not disemboweled, his head had been corkscrewed from his spine and was at the mercy of several crows that had pecked out the dilated eyes. The light cotton shirt had been shredded apart, exposing what looked like a mannequin that had been sliced with a Samurai sword. Joe was certain there was purpose in this killing. Someone wanted to immobilize Bo and take their time torturing him. There were shallower, non-life-threatening slashes in his chest and arms where the flies had begun laying their eggs. And the feet were contorted outward at ninety-degree angles as if the ankle joints had been snapped like twigs. It was as though someone was playing a gruesome game with him, much like a cat would torment a mouse. Harley was unable to keep his composure and examine the corpse up close and personal, so he backed away, holstered his weapon, did another queasy bow and lost the remainder of his breakfast. Both officers wondered what evil shadow had fallen on their peaceful county.

"You aw-right, sheriff?" Ole Man asked while standing away from the body, but within view of the truck cab.

"I'll be all right, Mr. Sims. I just need a minute to catch my breath," the sheriff murmured.

"Well, when you does, you and Joe needs to come take a closer look at this truck," he said.

All three men gathered at what would have been the driver's side door had it not been yanked off the hinges. With eyes bulging, the men peered inside to see blood splayed all over the ripped seats and headliner. Given the massive amount, it was obvious that much of the damage to Bo's body took place inside these close confines. The steering wheel was also damaged. It was bent upward toward the dashboard as though the killer used supernatural strength to gain better access to Bo hiding on the floorboard. And the truck's exterior had its share of defacement as well. All four tires were flat, the windows shattered and every panel including the hood appeared to have been scraped by a garden rake. And although not apparent to the deputies, the high-powered rifle and gun rack had somehow disappeared.

Horrified, shocked, and sickened. That was the only way to describe how deeply the surreal view had affected their souls. Ole Man turned away so the officers couldn't see the tears in his puffy eyes. Harley was dry-heaving, and Joe, well, he was in early-stage hypoxia. He appeared confused and had a splitting headache caused by the shortage of oxygen filled blood in his body. None of the men could think clearly and all needed help from someone who could.

"Sheriff, we need to contact the Medical Examiner's Office to get a forensic pathologist out here as soon as possible. These murders are more bizarre than anything I've ever seen. We don't have the expertise or resources to dig into what happened. Plus, we need some lab techs to gather and preserve the evidence properly," Joe said in a solemn voice.

"I'll make the calls, Joe. Would you stay here while Mr. Sims gets me back to the cruiser? I've got some orange marking tape that I'll use to spot the trail so we can find our way back in," Harley quietly responded. "And I'll notify Ludean Suggs about her husband."

"I will, sheriff. I'm not going anywhere," Joe answered with authority. He was trying to look calm, remain strong, and not show any sign of weakness to his boss or to the old man. After watching Harley's and Mr. Sims' emotional and physical breakdowns, he felt an even greater need to be the rock. After all, that's how the public expects a police officer to act when confronted with the worst impulses of humankind. But any man or woman who has worn the badge will tell you that witnessing a murder scene always leaves an imprint on your spirit—that sometimes evil does beget evil. Joe sensed that his heart could turn dark if he waited too long to feel the warmth and love of his family. Yet, all he could do for now was find a gap in the treetops and let the sunlight soothe his inner being.

As the sheriff and Ole Man methodically walked back to their vehicles, Harley could only think about the look on Ludean's face when he delivered the terrible news about her husband. The sheriff may have looked and acted tough to those in his presence, but he was really a softie at heart. The badge and sidearm could never conceal that side of his soul. He always felt a measure of sadness when he had to knock on that door to say that life's harmony would never be the same. He knew that Ludean would be broken and filled with sorrow when she heard his words replete with grief, and he knew that he would look away to hide his own sadness. After years with the Sheriff's Office, he knew that there are some things people don't want to know when they tragically lose a loved one. But he also knew that Ludean, like others, would ask the inevitable. Did Buck suffer before he died? It was an inescapable question from any grieving relative who wanted to lessen their anguish. And Harley would answer in the same way he had many times in the past. He would lie and say no.

And that's how the day ended—tearful and mournful for Ludean Suggs with no understanding why. For those at the crime scenes, the deep woods were holding a secret. The professionals were left with no logical answers to their questions, no valid theories to postulate and not even one reasonable guess as to what happened.

Twelve

FRIDAY NIGHT LIGHTS

School had been in session for a week and Jamie's anger had eased about Tommy's placement in the special needs class. Her brother seemed thrilled with his first-grade teacher, Mrs. Foster, and talked about her constantly: so much so, Jamie felt a tinge of jealousy. But she withheld criticism of any kind given how well Tommy had adjusted to his new life.

Moreover, she was on a positive high herself. She was smart and loved the stimulation of the classroom environment, especially being challenged to think on her feet by her instructors. After all, she had won a spelling bee in the fourth grade by delivering on the word *enormous*. Although not intentional, Ann helped develop Jamie's winning vocabulary and reading ability by frequently dropping her off at the public library on her way to work. You learn a lot of obscure words when you spend every day in a building filled with Shakespeare and Dostoevsky. And why wouldn't Ann leave her there? The library was a free babysitter, and when you're broke, you have no other options. Beyond teaching her to be an excellent speller, the treasury of books was a place where she could hide and dream, and live in a make-believe world of wonder. The unexpected benefit just happened to be a ten-year-old with college-level reading skills. Sometimes things just turn out for the best.

As for Jamie, embracing the pressure had always felt natural and it stuck with her over the years. The only downside of school had nothing to do with getting an education. Her hours at the Food Stop had to be significantly cut back given her eight to three o'clock commitment at Belmont High. Fewer hours meant less money and with her mother's inconsistent job record, she worried about paying the bills. Just the same, life was going well at home and within the protected borders of the schoolhouse. Meanwhile, the outside world was growing more and more paranoid by the minute.

The North Carolina newspapers had exploded like a powder-keg about the brutal murders. Every chief editor at their respective publication tried to out script the competition when it came to the sensationalism and hyperbole. *The Post* headline read *The Catawba Assassin*, while the News referred to *The Ramsey Creek Ripper*. And the supermarket tabloids were going with *Neurotic Alien Serial Killer*. Not to be outdone by the papers, the church ladies at First Baptist swore that the Devil was responsible. The labels would have been humorous had the crimes not been so horrific. There was one thing the rags did get right, however, and that was the cause of death.

With an inside source at the medical examiner's office leaking information to her favorite reporters, every article referenced that the victims died from trauma due to the loss of blood from the wounds, and that the analysis and ensuing reports on the blood and tissue samples could take up to three months. The murders and frightful circumstances would have prompted any reasonable adult to lock their doors and stay home. But Belmont High teenagers had something far more important on their minds than the shocking headlines. The Friday night roars of the opening football game, and the music on Saturday night at the big dance had the school abuzz with excitement. Other than the boys and girls who had traded rings and were going steady, everyone needed to find a date. Given all the sex hormones bouncing around in those young bodies, priority number one was stealing a kiss, not staying safe from some unknown menace in the woods.

Lenny wasted little time asking Jamie to the game and dance, and Jamie wasted little time in accepting. Her mom wasn't needed in her caretaker's role for the weekend, so Tommy had a built-in babysitter, albeit a capricious one. Even though Jamie agreed to the date, she wanted to have complete flexibility in case her mother did something stupid, so she insisted on meeting Lenny at the stadium on Friday night.

Jamie wasn't a big football fan, which in and of itself was a paradox. In the South when you are born, you are christened in the holy water of your parent's favorite college football team. It is simply a mandatory rite of passage. In North Carolina, you must pledge allegiance to either the Tar Heels or the Wolfpack when the nurse cuts your umbilical cord. As for your high school days, you are a fan for the four years you're in attendance and again for the twenty-year reunion when you can still remember the glory days of your youth. At the fifty year get together, however, you can't recall the name of your mascot and wonder who the hell are all these strange, old people?

No, football wasn't important to Jamie. Yet, in watching the players and interacting with the fans, she understood that the caste system of the ruling elites and blue-collar workers didn't mean diddly squat under the lights. The boys on the field didn't care either. The linebacker didn't ask if you were a banker's son or a mechanic's boy when he tried to knock you onto the second row. Jamie liked the atmosphere, the neutrality and unity of it all. A high five from the mayor on your right and a waitress screaming that's *my boy* on your left. It just seemed like one big happy family sharing a lot of love. But more than all of that, Jamie really liked being with Lenny. He never stopped looking at her, cheering, and smiling until Belmont was up by twenty points late in the fourth quarter. At that point, it was time to beat the post-game traffic jam.

"You ready to go, Jamie? I was thinking we could go by the B&W to get a hamburger and root beer. That is, if you're hungry," Lenny asked. "We can come back to the parking lot and get your car later, if that's okay?"

"That sounds great; I'm starving," Jamie smiled.

The B&W Drive-In was one of the hot spots where the kids gathered on weekends. The root beer floats, shakes, and burgers were part of the attraction, but most of the teenagers simply needed a place to congregate and be teenagers. The main building had a colorful roof shaped like a multi-decker flying saucer capped by a low-level spire with just enough room for the restaurant's neon name. Surrounding that building was a circular drive with parking spaces which included individual menu boards and intercom systems so customers could park their cars and place their food orders. If you chose to eat in your ride, a car hop donned in a white shirt and black bowtie would deliver your order on a plastic tray which would be attached to a partially rolled up window. And if you wanted some room to move about and socialize, there were several picnic-style tables and benches just outside the restaurant's side door. That's where the kids hung out in groups based on their common interests. Boys mostly clustered to talk about their street rods, how to get their hands on a bottle of Southern Comfort...and girls. Girls primarily gathered in social cliques to discuss the latest styles in clothes, hairstyles, makeup...and boys.

There was no need for Lenny and Jamie to announce their arrival. The sonic boom from the glass pack mufflers on his Chevy II took care of that. With his left arm hanging out the driver's window, Lenny drove two slow loops around the B&W building with intermittent presses on the gas pedal to race the engine. That 327 V8 sounded like thunder and his muscle car looked as fast as lightening with its Cragar chrome wheels. It was all part of the *I'm Mr. Cool* ritual.

The football game may have been the feel-good unifier for Jamie, but Lenny was her great equalizer. Being with him made her feel important; there was something about the way the girls stared and gossiped about her presence with the most popular boy at Belmont High. Meanwhile, every time the Nova drove by growling like an angry lion, the boys paid their respects with jealous gazes and reverent declarations. Lenny would leave Richard Petty in his wake in a drag race, they whispered. And Bobby Allison, he would tremble if he had to run side-by-side with Lenny at Rockingham. Their final prayerful act was yelling his nickname every time he looked their way. Like choirboys in concert, they called out "Roscoe" while giving a thumb's up approval with each pass. It was a rite of passage for teenage boys to give other boys nicknames. It was a far-reaching way in which the high schoolers related to each other, a way in which they expressed their friendships. The names made the teenagers feel like they were members of a special brotherhood. As for Lenny, there was no deep deliberation about his alias. At the time, there was a popular soul singer among the kids named Roscoe Robinson. Given Lenny's surname, "Roscoe" seemed like a good fit and easy choice. The boys gave more thought to their choice of car wax or cologne versus someone's byname.

After backing the Nova in, Lenny and Jamie enjoyed their burgers and shakes while the guys who didn't own a car asked him to pop the hood so they could gather around and marvel at the engine. There was nothing stock about Lenny's Nova. All the wannabe rebels admired the Holly Four Barrel Carburetor and Hooker Headers and dreamed about holding the reins to that kind of boundless horsepower. Lenny loved the attention with one exception. He had to keep reminding the onlookers not to scratch the waxed finish with their belt buckles while hanging over the fenders.

It had been a wonderful evening for Jamie, and an hour later, Lenny returned her to the school parking lot, stole a kiss, and watched as she closed the door on her Rambler. Being the perfect gentleman, he stood by to be sure the six-cylinder engine cranked with no hitch. It did, although it sounded like the high-pitched whine of a broken sewing machine. No need for high performance headers on this baby blue clunker, he thought as the Rambler disappeared in the darkness. It was a good night for them both.

Thirteen

MAW TO THE RESCUE

Jamie awoke and rose to a Saturday morning of unusual weather. The rain would show up for a fifteen-minute soak followed by fifteen minutes of sunshine. The odd pattern felt like a day in South Florida as the air was thick and steamy. It was as though the clouds and sun were taking turns controlling the sky creating their own outdoor sauna. Jamie was unaware of the humidity, although she did notice that Tommy was missing from the mattress next to her bed. She found him in the kitchen, woofing down a bowl of cereal.

"Why are you up so early?" she asked with a drowsy yawn.

"You promised to take me fishin' this morning. Remember?" Tommy answered.

"Oh crap, I forgot. Why don't we go next weekend?" Jamie made her appeal as she peered out the window, looking for an excuse. "It's raining outside anyway."

"You promised. You can't take back your promise." Tommy was pleading for his morning on the water.

"Promised what?" Ann appeared hungover and her voice was barely audible. She had overheard part of the conversation while standing at the kitchen door.

"I promised to take Tommy fishing today, but I forgot that I've got to work. I'm sorry, Tommy. I can't take you. Momma, why don't you take him?" Jamie knew the answer to that question before it was asked. She also sensed that the conflict was about to begin.

"I've never been fishing in my life. I don't even know how to bait a hook or where to go to fish. Besides, I've got a lot to do before I sit with Mrs. Evans tonight."

"You told me you were off for the weekend," Jamie could feel the emotional tension rising in her gut.

"Her son called me last night and asked if I could stay with her. He said he had to leave today to catch a late afternoon flight to New York. Said it was a family emergency. I told him I could do it."

"I made plans to go to the sock hop with Lenny tonight. If you can't keep Tommy, I can't go," Jamie's voice was growing louder in timbre with each passing second.

"Well, that's too bad. Someone has to keep your little brother." Ann's voice sounded snarky, as though having someone join her misery club brought her pleasure.

"I can't believe you're doing this. The one time I ask you to watch Tommy, you somehow just happen to bail. I shouldn't even be surprised anymore," Jamie's voice had reached a new level of agitation.

"Please stop fighting. I don't need to go fishing." Tommy hated the hostility every time it happened, and it happened a lot. Even when out of the room, he could always hear the quarreling through the paper-thin walls, and it made him feel insecure and unwanted.

"You're such a terrible mother—always have been. You've never cared about us. It's always been about you," Jamie screamed as the tears found her eyes and her lips began to quiver. On her way out of the mobile home, she slammed the front door so hard it split the frame. She hated being subjected to the authority of a dysfunctional alcoholic, even if she was her mother.

Her mind was in a fog of anger, and she was as mad as a hornet. As she tearfully walked down Bull Frog Lane, resentfulness flooded her heart. It made her think about running away to find a new life without her washed-out mother. It would solve all her problems, she thought. Maybe Lenny would take her away from all this unhappiness. But there was one problem her volcanic response could not reconcile. And his name was Tommy. Inexplicably, even before Ann knew she was carrying a child, Jamie at ten years of age told her she was pregnant and would have a baby boy. All her life Jamie had thought only of him, and their bond was unbreakable. The name calling and mother-daughter conflict aside, she would never leave her little brother. As she approached Raymond's store, her mind returned to rationality, and she thought about a solution to her dilemma...Maw. That sweet kiss from Lenny was still on her mind and finding a sitter for her brother was the only way she could enjoy an encore. Maybe it wasn't first love, but she had a crush on a dashing blonde-haired Adonis, and she liked the intense feelings that had been triggered in her body.

Her only true friend was Maw Bates. She was the only person Jamie knew she could trust, and while she hated to ask, she knew this was her only option. After arriving at Raymond's, Jamie made a beeline to the back of the store where she found Maw on patrol.

"Hey, baby girl. Whur have you been? I haven't seen you in a while," Maw asked while taking another dip of sweet snuff and a long look at Jamie's troubled face.

"Well, I've been working more hours at the Food Stop and I started school about a week ago. Tommy started the first grade, and I've been taking him to school every day too and trying to help him with his homework at night. So, I've been really busy."

Maw studied Jamie's flushed face. "You look like you've been cryin'. What's wrong?" Maw asked.

"Momma and I had a fight 'cause she's got to sit with a lady tonight, so she can't stay at home with Tommy. She was supposed to be off, and I was counting on her being home. I had plans to go to a dance at school with a boy I know, and now I can't go if she has to work," Jamie said beseechingly.

Maw smiled exposing a set of false teeth covered in a moistened layer of brown snuff. It was the most beautiful smile Jamie had ever seen. "Why I can keep him. You know I love that boy."

"Thank you, Maw! I can't tell you how much this means to me." Jamie grabbed and hugged Maw so hard she thought she heard a brittle bone or two snap in her thin body. The hardness in Jamie's heart softened as she sensed something she had never felt. It was an overwhelming emotion. A realization in her soul that you can't buy love and friendship, that you can't bargain for kindness nor blackmail someone to have it. It must be freely given. She didn't feel like she deserved such adoration from this little woman, and yet there it was in the most unexpected way. She wanted to cry again. This time for joy.

"Glad to hep out. When do you need me?" Maw asked.

"Can you come by our trailer around six-thirty? Lenny is coming to pick me up about seven."

"I's have to stay at the store here until eight. Can you bring him by here? He can hep me sell some fish bait 'til we close. Then we can go to your place," Maw answered.

"Yeah, Maw. That's no problem. He'd love to learn more about fishin' anyway."

"You wun't me to fix him somethin' to eat?" Maw asked.

A picture of Maw serving Tommy a plate of her famous salted hog jowls and pickled pig's feet entered Jamie's mind like an unwanted nightmare. Tommy was a finnicky eater and if the bread crust wasn't sliced from a peanut butter sandwich, he wouldn't touch it. Without a doubt, swine parts were not on his menu. Pigs in a blanket might work but forget about any pork belly cracklin's.

"No, no. It's okay, Maw. I'll fix him something before I bring him by." Jamie's problem was solved, and her return home was a complete reversal from her departure. For now, Lenny was back at number one.

Fourteen

IN A COLD SWEAT

The rumble of the car's V8 and the crunching sound of the driveway gravel signaled that Prince Charming had arrived early. Jamie would never ask Lenny to pick her up at home, but the Rambler was acting up with a sputtering engine, grinding gears, and a fan belt squealing like a stuck pig. She wanted to keep Lenny from seeing their run-down mobile home, but she couldn't risk a breakdown in her Rambler on a drive to the high school, so a souped-up Nova would have to be their chariot to the ball. Still in the bathroom drying her long hair, she never heard the knock, or her name being called when Lenny stepped inside the doorway.

"Jamie, are you here?" he asked in a loud voice as he scanned the den for any sign of Cinderella.

"Oh, crap! Just a minute—I'll be right out," she yelled.

Jamie had planned to be out the door before Lenny could enter the mobile home. In her mind, allowing him a close-up view of their living quarters was something to be avoided. She understood that he wasn't someone of privilege, that he knew what it was like to stand in line. She was also aware that he came from a hard-working middle-class family. Nonetheless, the Robinson's owned a nice house and drove cars that didn't breakdown. So, Lenny's blue-collar family was like the Rockefellers to her.

Jamie's roots were deep in the tilled soil of her criminal father and philandering stepfather. The scumbag men in Ann's life had made sure that their social scale would be somewhere between poor white trash and trailer park crackers. And given her mother's indifference to wearing either label, the cosmetics inside the mobile home were a disaster, especially for a sixteen-year-old girl wanting to impress her date. Of course, Jamie didn't help with the aesthetics either. The front door was still hanging off the hinges from her anger fit with her mother. And from the moment Lenny arrived, he was surprised and taken aback when he surveyed the surroundings.

Outside, the trailer's white siding had turned mildew green, and the window shutters were on the ground in the tall uncut weeds. Inside, the sofa appeared dirty with a pattern of Bloody Mary stains caused by the drunken hands of one Ann Russell. And the carpet, the travel path from room to room was worn so badly a blind armadillo could follow it at night. As for photographs, there were none. The walls and furniture tops were bare as though the family were ghosts, concealed from the world of baby pictures and family portraits. Fortunately, before Lenny's arrival, Jamie cranked up the window air conditioner and sprayed the rooms with air freshener to cover the smell of burnt cigarettes and a stopped-up toilet. Not a great first impression, but all was forgotten when Lenny saw Jamie enter the den.

Her tapered hip-hugger jeans were complemented by a cotton top with thin horizontal blue stripes. The top was difficult for Lenny to ignore since it fell short of covering Jamie's mid-drift, giving him an occasional glimpse at her flat tummy centered by a cute belly button. With sleeves rolled up, a blue jean jacket that belonged to her mother was the final piece to her ensemble. It was a warm evening, but she needed to cover a noticeable hole in the back of her middy and the jacket served that purpose quite well. When you are in the grips of having nothing, you do your shopping at a backyard rummage sale or the Goodwill Thrift Store and then try to hide the fact that you're wearing other people's clothes. Of course, Lenny's attention was on anything but her wardrobe. Even the wretched condition of the mobile home couldn't distract from her appearance.

When you're seventeen and love finds your heart for the first time, it's a wonderful thing. And for Lenny, it was euphoric. He just stood speechless and stared at her face made more radiant by a touch of makeup and some Coca Cola flavored gloss that added luster to her lips. And her hair was no longer cinched in its usual ponytail which allowed the tresses to flow loosely on her shoulders. Adding to her presence were dark eyes, lively and bright, and skin as smooth as a rose petal. She had a raw, untamed beauty about her. A face sculptured by a heavenly hand that wanted to show off his handiwork. And it had not gone unnoticed by a googly eyed boy.

"Wow! Jamie, you look great," Lenny said as his heart raced from the surge of hormones.

"Thanks, Lenny. You look pretty good yourself." Jamie responded in a voice dripping with honey. She was excited that he found her so attractive.

"You ready to go?" he asked.

"I can't wait," she answered.

The drive to the school gym took about fifteen minutes although it seemed like fifteen seconds. Lenny and Jamie were enjoying each other's company, talking, and laughing about the silliest things. And after Lenny slid in an eight-track tape of *No Mountain High Enough*, they did their best rendition of Marvin Gaye and Tammi Terrell while making dance moves with their arms and hands. It was a grand time.

After parking, Lenny and Jamie exited the Chevy and held hands as they walked to the gym entrance. Once inside, Lenny paid their one-dollar admission which was a donation to help fund new uniforms for the marching band. The band was grossly inept when it came to reading music notes, so it was best to look like a million bucks when you sounded like fifty cents. After kicking off their shoes, they placed them in the sea of teenage footwear, a multi-color mix of flats, go-go boots, t-straps and square-heels for the girls, and mostly brown penny loafers for the boys. The guys weren't exactly followers of the latest fashion in footwear.

They gave more thought to the best engine oil for their Camaros and Chargers than wearing the most stylish shoes. However, the kids did have one thing in common. After shedding their hard soles, most wore a pair of smooth socks or sneakers to prevent damaging the gymnasium's varnished floor. Once inside, the loud music from the disc jockey playing vinyl records had the place hopping as Lenny and Jamie made their way through the crowd of bell-bottoms and bouffant hair. Lenny's many pals were paying their respects by shouting his nickname while Jamie's one friend softly tapped her on the shoulder.

"Lisa!" Jamie cried in a high-pitched voice when she turned around and saw her best friend.

"Jamie!" Lisa Foster returned the greeting with the same enthusiasm.

The girls grabbed each other in a warm embrace while jumping for joy. Both acted like twins seeing each other for the first time since being separated at birth. Lenny just stood and watched, listening to Jamie and Lisa talking over each other, asking question after question while not bothering to answer any of the inquires. The reunion continued for a half hour as though they were the only ones on Earth. Meanwhile, Lenny who was patient at first started getting a little jealous and very irritated by being excluded from all the revelry. At that point, he left the girls, drifted into the crowd, and found the company of Della Myrick, a drop dead gorgeous perky blonde cheerleader he had dated on several occasions. Lenny was no playboy, but he was good looking and had a fast car—dating every cheerleader on the squad felt as natural to him as driving that Chevy II ninety miles an hour. And Della, one of the many who liked his vibe, gave him her full attention and more. She was within inches of his face trying to talk over the sound reverberating from the speakers when Jamie saw them together. Knowing she had made a mistake by being inattentive, she assertively grabbed his arm and pulled him away to an opening on the floor around center court where the kids were slow dancing to *My Girl* by the Temptations. She pulled him close, wrapped her arms around his waist and pressed her body against his. Lenny exhaled a sigh of relief knowing he had not been forgotten while both swayed to the melodic beat. *Della who?* Whether it was lust in his unmentionables or first love in his heart really didn't matter. It was different. She smelled of jasmine and felt like heaven.

In typical DJ fashion, a slow number is always followed by an upbeat tune so the kids can cut loose and release some of that pent up sexual energy. It was perfect timing for Jamie. This girl had beauty, but she also carried two more special gifts from above. She was highly intelligent, and music was a big part of her inner being from the day she was born. It was an unexplainable love since Ann had never bothered to rock and sing even one lullaby to her infant daughter. But that's what makes music so special. It's as though it has a spirit of its own. And where that spirit finds a home can be a hit or miss proposition. There are some who are tone deaf, many who have a favorite song or two, and the few who have the beat deep in their bones, who can invite music to be part of their soul and translate it to smooth energy on the dance floor.

As for the handful who have that gift, the musical tones become as much a part of their bodies as their hands and feet. Jamie was one of the few who could feel the harmony from head to toe and the back-to-back songs by James Brown were the perfect choice... *Papa's Got a Brand-New Bag* and *Cold Sweat*. The heavy beat combined with a slick pair of cotton socks had her gliding and spinning on the waxed floor like she was on air. With eyes closed and hands in rhythm she danced to the lively music as though she had no control of her body. So limber were her hips, she made the Godfather of Soul look as stiff as Frankenstein. This was the Jamie Thompson version of the Boogaloo, and all Lenny could do was feign a few awkward moves while staring in a cold sweat much like the godfather—as did all the other leering tomcats that had encircled Jamie to watch the show and whisper about her allure. Of course, Della and her cheerleader friends finally joined the onlookers to see what was drawing the crowd. As the song came to an end, the squad jealously watched and openly mocked Jamie's thrift store outfit and made fun of her river rat reputation. Everyone else paid their respects by complimenting her ability to bust such an effortless groove to the beat.

"Wow, Jamie. You can really dance!" Lenny wiped his brow and smiled with approval.

"So can you," Jamie returned the adulation, albeit more out of courtesy since she never really noticed his footwork. She had been in her own little world and her eyes were mostly closed while Lenny was dancing, sweating, and dreaming about a kiss.

"Why don't we go by the B&W and get a shake so we can talk without having to yell over the music?" The chocolate malts were a ruse. Lenny really wanted to get away, hoping he could take Jamie parking after a quick trip to the drive-in.

"Sure, let's go," Jamie agreed, but in truth, she was starting to feel the magic at the gym and would have preferred to stay for a few more dances. But she still felt guilty and wanted to make it up to Lenny for his exclusion from her homecoming with Lisa.

The planned stop at the B&W for shakes turned into a quick in-and-out. Lenny had dashed inside the restaurant and climbed back in the car with a couple of cokes. He was in a hurry to do some smooching and it took way too long to suck down a cup of ice cream. He had the perfect place in mind to park the Nova, have a little conversation, and steal a kiss, and it wasn't under the bright lights of the B&W Drive-In. No, Lenny was like all the other teenage boys at Belmont who thought their cars were invisible to patrolling cops after the sun went down—like he had a stealth button on the dashboard and need only push it. A secluded parking area behind the elementary school was the perfect spot to hide out. The locale was bordered on one side by the school while a heavy stand of mature hardwoods fronted two other boundaries. And the final perimeter was the Hope Baptist Church cemetery. Added together, the hovering trees, empty school building, and eerie graveyard made for a very spooky venue that kept the fraidy-cats away. But not Lenny. He was brave at heart and had one goal in mind. Tell the scariest story he could conjure up hoping the hair-raising yarn would frighten Jamie into his arms seeking protection. And Lenny was good at telling stories. After all, he had taken many girls to this spot before and the tactic never failed to work. Not on anyone. Including Della. So, he began by describing the trees as cover for the Carolina axe murderer, the schoolhouse as the ghostly home of a teacher killed by the axe murderer, and the cemetery as the location where the axe murderer was buried after being caught, convicted, and electrocuted by Old Sparky. Lenny was completely invested in the story, using sound effects, hand gestures and words filled with tension. Jamie just stared at his worried face and sipped on the straw until, finally, she finished the last drop in her drink. The loud slurp was quite the conclusion for his whopper tale. Instead of leaping into his arms, she grinned and giggled at his lame attempt to scare her. Not exactly the response Lenny was looking for.

"Lenny, please don't tell me that girls fall for that kind of stuff. Do they?" Jamie asked with a playful smile.

Lenny sheepishly grinned. "Well, believe it or not. Most of them do."

Lenny was still after that kiss, and he always had a backup plan. After witnessing how much music inspired Jamie on the dance floor, he popped in an eight-track tape of Aaron Neville's *Tell It Like It Is.* In Lenny's desperate mind, if the greatest love song of all time didn't buy him a measure of affection, nothing would. It worked. He leaned across the console separating the bucket seats and completed the mission. Jamie's lips felt wet and soft, still holding fast to the sweet taste of the lip gloss and soda. And for a tender moment, time stood still.

Fifteen

HOT TEMPERS

On Sunday mornings, Maw always attended the Church of the Holy Ghost. It was the way she sought forgiveness for her weekly sins and sang praise to The King of Kings. Her non-denominational church was located down a long dirt road through the piney woods not far from Raymond's store, and it was the rock on which she stood. Even though this cinder block chapel had a tiny congregation, they sang and shouted with a thunderous roar, even louder than the big brick churches in Belmont. However, there were a few noteworthy differences between these houses of worship. On the Lord's Day, Pastor Dewey at the Church of the Holy Ghost angrily pointed his finger and spoke about Hell and damnation waiting for the unsaved. With that same zeal, he assured the believers that even in the guise of a serpent, Satan could never harm them. The preacher would even hold a canebrake rattlesnake to his bosom to demonstrate the protection found in a New Testament Book in the Bible. Of course, he never told the trembling flock about how he helped prove the Scripture of Mark by milking the snakes prior to the service. He just thought that sometimes God needed a little help revealing His power. As for the pastors in Belmont, most would be filled with the joy of the Spirit, preaching about love and heavenly relationships, and using fluffy kittens for props. Certainly not venomous snakes. Unfortunately, today, Maw was not to be found at any place of worship. Her blood was stirring, and she was at the bait shop arguing with her son.

"I told you to never do that, Raymond. I told you that you'd stir up a hornet's nest if you did." Hot tempers were fueling the conversation and Maw shouted loud and clear to make her point.

"It wusn't my fault, Maw! One of my runners was stealin' some of my shine and sellin' it to Cooter Jones over near Lowesville. And Cooter was reselling it to folks who live on the river. I told Bobby Ray that he wuldn't be runnin' for me no more," Raymond attempted to explain the predicament, but his words were a bold-faced lie to his momma. In truth, he never fired Bobby Ray. His runner was the perfect cat's-paw for his whiskey business, and he was willing to let him off with a reprimand. Raymond knew Bobby Ray was knee-deep in debt to the finance company for the Chevy pickup he purchased from Leroy's Used Car Lot in Ranlo and most likely needed the extra money to catch up on his payments. Aside from that, Bobby Ray was as mean as a junkyard dog and never failed to collect any outstanding moonshine debts owed to Raymond. No, a mild rebuke would work just fine.

"It dun't matter who or why, trouble's on the way and you know it," Maw's eyes narrowed.

"You just stay out of my business. I can handle any trouble that comes my way. I's not 'fraid of nobody!" Raymond tried to sound tough, like he could win a bare-knuckle brawl with a prize fighter. In truth, Maw could have knocked him into next week. All the short tempers aside, Raymond knew she was right about one thing. You had to be as dumb as a box of rocks to disrespect another moonshiner by breaking their unwritten code. His operation had crossed the boundary by drifting into the territory of another, by selling dew to a competitor's customers. And the repercussions had started, and a day of reckoning was on the way.

"Son, you're on your own. I love you, but hate whut you do. You're in bed with Satan and I's can't hep you if you wunts change your ways." Maw could sense that her son was in danger and her lips were trembling for a reason. Those in the church said that Maw had been marked by

God, that she had "the sight." That she was a "teller "and had the gift to sense things others couldn't feel and, on some occasions, she could see what would happen in the future. She knew her son wasn't right with the Lord and walked in darkness. And she had prayed many times for his salvation, hoping he might catch a glimpse of Oral Roberts while changing channels on the RCA and turn to honest work. She thought it would be a fine miracle to save someone so much in love with the devil's lies, to have him see the light and give up making whiskey and selling drugs. It just never happened.

"Don't worry, Maw. I's be awright. Don't worry." Raymond walked away with the Prince of Darkness perched on his shoulder like a pet Macaw.

Sixteen

ANATOMICAL RIDDLES

The morning tension was thick as Deputy Joe Griffin and Sheriff Harley Myers made the twenty-mile trek in search of answers. Joe was tight lipped as he nervously tapped the patrol car's steering wheel while Harley talked non-stop about the Belmont High School football team. Silence or chatter, it really didn't matter. The men were attempting to fill the time with anything other than discussing the homicides. It had been frustrating since the discovery of the bodies, not having any real leads or theories on what happened. Both men felt as though they were living in a make-believe world of goblins and monsters, but both were hoping that a meeting with Ron Hinkle at the medical examiner's office in Gastonia would restore some level of sanity to the chaos. Any clue, any evidence, anything to help the officers unravel the mystery would be a win.

The M.E.'s office was inside an oblong two-story professional building that was indistinguishable from the other white stucco structures in the office complex. Joe and Harley had been there before, so locating the building and finding a parking spot took only seconds, leaving them plenty of time to make their ten o'clock appointment. One would think it odd to consult with a pediatrician about an investigation into the horrendous murders, but in North Carolina, the medical examiner system is made up of a network of local doctors practicing in various fields of medicine. These various disciplines could be anything from family medicine to dermatology to orthopedics. These physicians worked for the county on an as-needed basis and were paid to determine the cause of death in the most straightforward cases. If the cause was natural or accidental, the doctor would issue a brief report, and a death certificate, followed by releasing the corpse to the family. If the demise included suspicious, unusual, or violent circumstances, the body would be transported to Mecklenberg County where a board-certified forensic pathologist would conduct an autopsy. Since all the recent deaths were homicidal in nature, Dr. Hinkle followed standard procedures and sent the bodies of the two campers and the Suggs brothers to Charlotte after he finished his initial examinations.

Normally the meeting would take place in the county medical facility that accommodated the morgue on the ground floor, but Dr. Hinkle had a waiting room filled with screaming kids who needed attending. He thought his everyday clinic would be a more expeditious meeting place. A nurse escorted Harley and Joe to a side office where the doctor was waiting at his desk.

"Good morning, Dr. Hinkle," both men said in a very deferential fashion.

"Good morning, Harley. And you too, Joe. And skip the formal doctor stuff. I've known you both for over thirty years; it's not necessary. Take a seat," the doctor responded and smiled while peering over his reading glasses. Ron Hinkle was in his early sixties but had two distinct features for a man his age. Hours in the gym had paid dividends by giving him the body of a youthful athlete. Bull-necked and broad-shouldered with muscular arms and narrow hips, he looked as though he was ready to play middle linebacker for N.C. State. Contrary to his sturdy build, however, the exaggerated lines that fringed his mouth and furrowed his forehead told a more accurate story. His snow-white hair that stood on end was another witness that spoke of his true age. The spiky coiffure made him look as though he had just seen a ghost. In truth, Dr. Hinkle had seen something much worse. His first patient of the day was a four-year-old boy throwing an uncontrollable tantrum, fighting him like a wild animal when he tried to use a tongue depressor to examine his throat. And that was where Ron's other unique talent came into play. With the crazy personality of a circus clown, he handed the unruly youngster two balloons made from latex gloves, delivered on three funny doctor faces, and finished the bribe with a cherry sucker. Without a doubt, he was a jokester at heart.

"Thanks, Ron. Joe and I just wanted to see if you could help us in our investigation of these recent killings. We're at a complete dead end right now," Harley said, hoping for a nugget of information.

"Well as you and Joe know, I was at both crime scenes and had a close-up look at everything. I tried to make sure no trace of evidence was destroyed and that the bodies were handled in a way that would keep them in good condition. Hell, I even helped prepare the corpses and put them in body bags. And I'll tell you, it spooked the hell out of me. I mean, I wish I could tell you who did it, but I don't have a clue as to what happened to them. I inspected the bodies again when they arrived here at the morgue. And given the seriousness of the wounds, all I did was put them in the cooler for preservation and had them transported to the forensic doctors in Charlotte."

"Have you heard anything from the pathologist in Charlotte?" Joe asked.

"He called to ask me some questions about what I observed at the crime scenes. He was a little surprised by the lack of blood on and in the bodies and wanted to see some of the photos that were taken. I reminded him that Buck and Beaver Suggs were hung upside down from a tree and he told me he was aware of that. But he said the dried blood inside their chest cavities was a relatively small amount. He thought the massive trauma caused their bone marrow to absorb a lot of the blood when they were being killed. He also said there were some unusual hair fibers he found on their clothes and bodies. All the samples were sent to the lab for identification. That's all I can tell you right now. As you know, the lab results will take a while."

"When you initially examined the bodies of the campers and the Suggs' brothers, did you get any impressions on how they were killed?" Joe continued to probe for answers.

"Other than Bodean Suggs having his head unscrewed from his torso, the loss of blood from the wounds caused their deaths. I looked closely at all the cuts, and I certainly don't think any of the slashes were caused by a knife. The wounds were too wide and jagged to be caused by a sharp-edged instrument. And the wounds on their necks were savage, like they were caused by the jaws of a spring-loaded trap. The young lady's broken bones had to have been done by someone or something incredibly strong. I x-rayed the areas of the breaks, and the fractures were splintered like a dry stick that had been snapped in two. And listen to this. I don't know how it was done, but Buck and Beaver had been dunked in that big drum of moonshine. Either that or they were using the tank as a hot tub. I didn't need a lab tech to tell me that they had a coating of whiskey on their bodies. It was strong enough to clear my sinuses for a week. But you know what, the alcohol may have helped slow down their decomposition. And that's a good thing that's going to help with the autopsy. Bottom line, I'm telling you that whoever did this is evil, and they need to be found. I can't sleep at night without having nightmares about it."

The deputies continued asking questions, recounting how they searched the areas outside where the bodies were discovered by crisscrossing the land through every briar patch, stand of trees, and bog. Even Ole Man Sims and his two bloodhounds returned to offer their assistance. No one found a trace of anything other than another moonshine still about a mile away from where the Suggs were cooking their brew. Several State Highway Patrol Officers participating in the search took care of that smoker by smashing it to pieces.

Finally, after twenty more minutes of questions, Dr. Hinkle told Harley and Joe that he needed to get back to work. Too much delay in doing his job usually made the parents more ill-tempered than their kids.

"Thanks for all the feedback, Ron. Just one more question. Was there anything else that struck you as out of the ordinary?" Joe asked while he and Harley rose from their chairs.

Ron removed his reading glasses, placed them on the desk, and cracked a smile followed by a chuckle. "Yeah, well, there was one thing," he answered, ready to deliver on another joke.

"What?" Harley urged.

"Well, Bodean, the youngest Suggs brother, had a very unique appendage that got my attention."

"What was it?" Harley asked.

"He had a huge penis. I mean enormous! So big it hung well past the mid-point of his femur! I mean, it was halfway down his thigh! My bet is that Bodean had lots of girlfriends. You may want to interview some of the women he was seeing to find out if they knew about any enemies he may have had." Ron seemed pleased he had broken the anxiety.

All three laughed with envy. Given the seriousness of their work, they needed the levity.

Seventeen

YOU MAKE LEMONADE

It was Sunday. A week had passed, and life had settled into a somewhat comfortable routine for the Russell family. Tommy loved going to school every day and his big sister was enjoying her classes, especially after getting an A on each of her reports in English and American history. Jamie had no delusions about a college fund waiting for her when she finished high school. She knew her only way out of poverty was a higher education and she was keenly aware that it took high-level grades to qualify for an academic scholarship. In the past, staying focused on exceling at school had been as easy as ABC, but after a couple of dates with Lenny, her mind was distracted, racked with thoughts about seeing him again. Working so closely together at the Food Stop only made her heart flutter even more, always thinking about that next kiss. No, their feelings for each other may not have found its way to love, but they were beginning to live in a world of their own. As for Jamie's world at home, it was improving. Even Ann had slowed her drinking and wasn't being swept up in a tidal wave of booze each and every day. She did, however, ramp up her smoking to compensate for the drop-off in Smirnoff. She had been wheezing, coughing incessantly as though her lungs were filled with a cloud of dust. It bothered Jamie that she was struggling so much but having her momma bone-dry and conscious was a better option than dog drunk and passed out. In a perfect world, Ann would give up the Marlboros and start attending AA meetings. But the world is imperfect and messy. And this would have to do. At least the tension had eased between mother and daughter and that was reason enough to celebrate.

It was Lenny to the rescue that morning and he didn't come alone. He feared that Jamie was swindled when she bought the Rambler, that the slick used car salesman fast talked her into buying a lemon. But like a knight in shining armor, he was there to save the day and he arrived with something much better than Excalibur. You don't need a sword's magical powers when you have a good friend like Johnny Steele. People said that Johnny was simple-minded but could take a wrecked car that had been laid to rest in a junkyard and bring it back to life. And today, Jamie's Rambler was the clunker incarnation of Lazarus, and it needed a miracle. Both boys arrived ready to do a little shade-tree engineering. Johnny's pickup was filled with mechanic's tools, transmission fluid, filters, hoses, and belts for the alternator and fan. Jamie met them in the front yard of the mobile home as they stepped from the truck. She had her hair pulled back in a ponytail and was wearing a light gray t-shirt and faded jeans. Lenny couldn't help but notice her cute tomboy look.

"Hey, Jamie. I brought Johnny with me to help work on your car. He works at his father's garage in Belmont and knows everything there is to know about fixin' a car," Lenny confidently said.

"Hey, Johnny. Thanks for helping out. I hope you guys can figure out what's going on with the Rambler," Jamie responded with a smile.

"Okay," Johnny answered succinctly. Unlike Lenny, Johnny wasn't known for being a smooth-talking ladies' man and he considered it a good day when he didn't have to say a word. But if his lips had to move to answer a question, his response was short and sweet. The teenager was good, however, at staring intently at his steel toe boots. He refused to look directly at Jamie, but she was close enough to smell his cologne of gasoline and burnt oil. And he was close enough to offer his hand in greeting.

Lenny didn't expect his friend to instantly warm up to Jamie or to be as affable as a Southern politician. And for good reason. Johnny was as shy as a church mouse and the only thing that would loosen his tongue was a discussion on how to rebuild a four-speed transmission. He was one year out of trade school where he studied to be an auto mechanic and he loved everything about cars, especially souping them up the way he did Lenny's Nova. Learning that vocation was a wise decision and working twelve-hour shifts at his father's auto repair business provided him plenty of time to practice his trade. Jamie couldn't help but think that his unusual appearance contributed to his timidity and awkwardness when around strangers. Yes, she thought being smallish in size with a moon face decorated with a flat nose and stick-out ears made him look like a troll doll. For certain, it made him self-conscious, especially around pretty girls. Jamie also imagined that his image had made him a target for name-calling and taunts from other kids, starting most likely early in childhood. It's easy to get beat down when you live in that kind of world. But Jamie took note of something more important than his outward veneer and struggles, something that spoke to his character and resilience. She had learned from her grandfather that you could tell a lot about what a man does by looking at his hands. Bruised knuckles, calloused palms, and fingernails manicured with axle grease made it clear that Johnny didn't have a cushy, white-collar job. There aren't many mechanics with creamy soft hands working at the end of a socket wrench, grinding it out in a smog filled repair shop every day. And she admired and respected who he was and what he did. He looked like a beautiful angel to her.

It was just before two o'clock that afternoon when Lenny and Johnny completed the resurrection. Both were hunched over the fender, running a final check by revving the throttle arm on the carburetor, pushing the car engine to its limit. They couldn't help but laugh a little at Jamie's puny six-cylinder engine, wondering if the high frequency squeal was scaring every dog in Gaston County. Jamie could care less about the shrill sound. The Rambler was back, and her freedom had been restored. After stepping out of the mobile home, she greeted the boys with a big smile and a plate stacked with bologna sandwiches. But before she could deliver their lunch, she was taken aback as they straightened from leaning over the car's fender. Lenny's face was grimy, streaked with dirt from installing the alternator belt. But Johnny had been crawling under the Rambler adjusting the clutch and changing the transmission fluid. The sweat on his freckled face caused the syrupy liquid and road grime to stick to him like glue. It gave him the look of an army commando covered in face paint. His hands were stained from grease deep in the pores of his skin. No amount of Goop Cleaner could make that go away. Recognizing their need to scrub their faces and hands, she invited them inside the mobile home and led them to the kitchen sink to wash up before eating. They accepted her offer and proceeded to use half a bottle of liquid soap. After settling on the chairs around the table, Jamie watched in amazement as the boys wolfed down the sandwiches and gulped down a pitcher of sweet, iced tea. She, then, thought it timely to discuss paying her debt. She was ready to horse-trade for the Rambler's repair, although she had nothing to offer in exchange other than bologna and bread.

"You know Lenny, I want to pay you and Johnny for fixin' my car, but it may take a little while for me to save up enough money," Jamie was hoping he would recommend the never-never payment plan, but since Johnny had invested so much in parts and labor, she knew Lenny couldn't waive the cost of the repairs. But he did anyway.

"No, you don't owe me and Johnny anything. We were glad to help. Plus, Johnny got all the parts at cost through the garage, so it really wasn't that expensive," he answered.

"But that's not right. You both did too much work for me not to pay you anything," she said with an *I can't believe you would do this for me* look on her face.

Lenny turned to gauge Johnny's reaction to the pro bono offer, but it was hard to get a read on his friend's face since he still had his mouth stuffed with tea-stained bread and bologna. With cheeks pouched outward and mouth half open, he looked like a starving squirrel getting ready for winter as he shook his head side-to-side indicating he would accept no payment for the labor or parts.

Being poor means you are always beholden to someone, that you don't have choices—not even to buy a little boy a five-cent candy bar. It means that you must depend on *good people*—as they are called in the South—to help you survive. And that means you can never lose hope. Hope that someone will care. Hope that you won't be judged. Hope that someone will protect you. Hope that you won't be mistreated. And hope that someone will fix your car. Jamie quickly rose from her chair and hurried to her bedroom to hide from view. She didn't want the two boys to see her crying. After regaining her composure, she returned to the kitchen and tenderly hugged each of them in an embrace of appreciation. For the first time Johnny looked at her eyes, feeling the warmth of a teenage girl who saw his tender heart, not his awkward appearance. "Thank you, thank you, thank you. Thank you both," she said, still trying to hold back the tears.

"Well, there is one thing we would like," Lenny said.

"What? What is it? Do you want another sandwich?" Jamie asked.

Southerners love to eat. A lot. And pretty much anything. But the boys weren't interested in another bologna sandwich smeared with mayo. "No. No more sandwiches. Johnny and I brought our rods and reels with us, and we were hoping you'd show us the place where you and Tommy caught all the fish. We'd like to do a little fishin' this afternoon. You and Tommy can come with us if you want to," Lenny answered.

"Oh my gosh, we'd love to. Tommy's going to be so excited!" Jamie immediately headed to the living room to tell her brother the good news.

If you're going fishing, you'll need some bait, and the four kids made the short walk down Bullfrog Lane to Raymond's Bait and Tackle to take care of business. Along the way, Jamie explained that she and Tommy had used wigglers on the day they were so successful, telling Lenny and Johnny the importance of sending the worms to the river bottom if they wanted to catch the big cats. And boys being boys, these two listened carefully. They were excited about wetting a line and would use bologna for bait if it meant catching a ten-pound catfish. Worms sounded good to them.

After entering Raymond's store, they immediately headed to the back to visit with the resident bait expert. She saw them coming, so she doused the half-smoked Camel in an empty Coke bottle and placed the leather-bound King James on the rocker where she had been sitting. She then offered up the sweetest ear-to-ear grin.

"Thar's my baby girl and my little boy!" Maw exclaimed. "How have youins been doin'?" she asked with a twinkle in her eye. But before they could answer, she grabbed Jamie and Tommy in a three-way hug, squeezing like she would never let go. But when she did release her arms, she immediately turned to size up the strangers with a quick once-over. Top to bottom she stared until she finally settled on their eyes. Well, she made eye contact with Lenny. Johnny was back to staring at his boots. "And who are these two handsome boys you have with you?" Maw asked.

"This is Lenny Robinson. And this is Johnny Steele," Jamie answered. "They've been working all morning fixing my car."

Like a true gentleman, Lenny greeted Maw with "It's nice to meet you, ma'am," while Johnny never looked up.

Instead, he extended his grease-stained hand for his customary salutation. Maw returned Lenny's smile, but immediately turned to Johnny and gently grasped his hand between the two of her own. And then she did the most unusual thing. She held it for a moment as though it was a delicate flower, like she sensed his pain and vulnerability, his hidden desire for someone to love on him. It was the most wonderful thing, to be told that your life matters without a word being spoken. To witness his heart melt and head lift upward to see Maw's face was a joy. And his smile, it was the most loving smile you could ever imagine. Lenny and Jamie stood by with mouths wide open, as Johnny gazed at Maw's affectionate eyes. It was as though everyone had caught a glimpse of heaven.

"We're going fishing and need some red worms for bait," Jamie said, causing Maw to return to business.

"Well, we can fix youins right up with some sure-fire special worms. Just remember not to do any cussin' while you're fishin', and you'll do jest fine."

Maw stepped over to the cooler and pulled out a plastic cup of worms. Lenny and Johnny stood by, wondering what spewing a bad word or two had to do with catching catfish. But Maw's new wall sign which read, *God is Listening, No Cussin' if a Big One Gets Away,* explained everything. It was clear that bad luck would hang over their heads like a storm cloud if they took the Lord's name in vain. So, the boys agreed straight up to follow the Third Commandment with a nod of their heads and a "yes ma'am" to Maw. Lenny took the bait and he and Johnny headed to the register along with a six-year-old tagging closely behind. Tommy knew where the candy was displayed and was hoping their generosity included buying him a Snickers bar. Before they could walk away, however, Maw grabbed Jamie's arm to prevent her from following the boys.

"I's need to talk to you for a minute. Let's go out back," she said in a low voice.

Maw led Jamie outside the store where they stood between the concrete tanks that held the live bullhead minnows. Her face grew solemn as she reached into the side pocket on her dress.

"I's need to give you and Tommy somethin' before you leave," she said.

Jamie expected to see another candy bar since Maw had given Tommy one on another occasion. Instead, she pulled what appeared to be two unusual necklaces from her pocket. The spaghetti thin cords were made from an animal skin that had been treated to prevent its decay. And the hoodoo ornaments were as odd as the cords. Two slender brown roots an inch or so long were attached to the necklaces.

"Here take these, baby girl. I's got one for you and one for Tommy," Maw said while handing Jamie the unexpected tokens.

"What are they, Maw?" Jamie asked.

"They're from an oak tree that was struck by lightnin'. They'll protect you and Tommy."

"Protect us from what?" Jamie appeared puzzled.

"There's somethin' evil goin' 'round here. All these people gettin' kilt and all. The devil is havin' his way and I worry 'bout you and Tommy. These roots will keep all the bad things away so nuthin' will harm youins," Maw said with an unsettled look on her face.

Jamie immediately thought that this must be something rooted deeply in Maw's backwoods education, some type of folk lore she learned in her upbringing. And maybe today, it was just granny magic that she was practicing. After all, granny witches were good and worked primarily with God, and Maw was certainly a God-fearing person. Moreover, she was from the Appalachian hills where legends were as common as a toothache, and she probably knew all about conjuring and charms. Jamie was aware of her unusual background and took that into account. But there was something else that chilled her to the bone. The look of concern on Maw's face frightened her. The heebie-jeebies had found her core and Jamie had no intention of turning down the gifts. Instead, she thanked Maw for keeping a watchful eye on her and Tommy, and then she left to join the others.

All-in-all, it had been a wonderful day that ended on a high note with a repaired Rambler and eight channel catfish. Tommy was on cloud nine and Lenny and Johnny were thrilled with their luck on the water. For certain, a terrific day in everyone's minds but one. In the soul of a teenage girl, there was an indescribable feeling of worry, a fear that, as Maw said, there was some malevolent force lurking about, and that she was the target.

Eighteen

THE LONE RANGER

A month had passed, and Sheriff Harley Myers and Deputy Sheriff Joe Griffin needed to be rescued. The sheriff's department was stretched thin just handling its day-to-day operations, and the added weight of five murder investigations was taking a toll on the two men. If the crimes were to be solved, the officers needed a helping hand now. The deputies had done their individual best, and for a while, gave the impression of an agency in control. But now their case was going nowhere, so they had reached out through the media for support from the public. And given America's obsession with serial killers and the need to make sense of the brutal murders, the media and public were glad to do their part. Leads came in by the dozens with sightings of every maniac from Jack the Ripper to Charles Manson.

And the media just added to the frenzy and made the citizens even more panic stricken with sensational prime time television reports along with newspaper headlines that grew wackier with every edition. It had to be a cold-blooded killer without a conscience, maybe the North Carolina version of the Zodiac Killer. Or maybe it was just a transient hobo possessed by some unclean spirit forced to unknowingly commit these brutal acts. Someone who would soon move on and no longer threaten the community. In truth, no one had a clue, so the fear and anxiety grew by the minute. No witnesses, no fingerprints, no motives, no evidence, no anything other than the unusual animal-like hair had left all parties confused and bewildered. Recognizing their dilemma, Sheriff Myers made the decision to contact the Gaston County Police Department to ask for assistance. Unfortunately, Chief Blankenship said the department was facing a personnel shortage of its own and had to apologize for his inability to provide the much-needed support. The sheriff's second call to the North Carolina State Bureau of Investigation, however, bailed him out of an impossible situation.

The Southern Piedmont SBI office in Harrisburg responded to Sheriff Myer's request by sending Special Agent Tim Hobbs and Special Agent Ellison O'Neal to the Sheriff's Office in Gaston County. The agents' priority was to help the deputies brainstorm about the killer's motive and interview those who were close to the victims and knew them well. They also needed help establishing a detailed investigative plan and a formal case checklist that would come into play once the killer was on trial. And finally, the special agents were given the green light to work with the forensic pathologist in Charlotte. The new cadre of deputies and agents also agreed to bring in the F.B.I. if needed. The four officers began their cooperation with an early morning meeting in Sheriff Myer's office. Harley was seated at his light gray metal desk in his non-descript quarters, while Joe and the special agents sat in chairs that formed a semi-circle around the desk. After pleasantries, the discussion centered on the crime scenes. Since Deputy Griffin was present at both locations, he reviewed the descriptions in his case file that matched the photographs taken at the scenes. From there the exchange evolved into ideas regarding possible motives that could help narrow their focus.

Special Agent Hobbs began the collaboration. "I guess the obvious question is, do you all think these homicides were planned or spontaneous?

"What do you mean, Tim?" the Sheriff asked.

"Any thoughts about whether the murders were just random, or maybe they were calculated killings?" Hobbs asked again while preparing to take additional notes.

"This is just my opinion given the condition of the bodies and the state of the crime scenes, but I think the Suggs' murders were personal, especially the killing of Bodean Suggs," Joe responded.

"Why is that?" Tim asked.

"Well, our medical examiner in Gastonia x-rayed Bodean's ankles and said that the talus, the ankle bone, on both feet had been snapped from the femur. That's something you would do to immobilize someone. Plus, the slash wounds were shallower than the other victims, like killing someone little by little. Death by a thousand cuts. And the decapitation, that was just a final touch of rage. Bodean was tortured, and that means he was killed by some insane wacko who feeds on power and control, or someone who wanted revenge," Joe paused to catch his breath.

"You mentioned the decapitation. Don't you think it would take unnatural strength to do that?" Special Agent O'Neal fearfully asked.

"I don't see how anyone could do that with just their hands. Maybe you could remove someone's head with a rope using leverage of some kind, but there were no bruises or burn marks on the neck nor anywhere else on the body for that matter." Reliving the crime scene had Joe feeling the anxiety building in his body. He tried to avoid the attack by taking several long, slow breaths.

"And what about the other brothers?" O'Neal asked, squirming in his chair as though someone had threatened to dismember his own body.

"I can answer that one, Ellison," Sheriff Myers responded. "I think it was a personal killing, maybe revenge or maybe someone was sending a message. You don't butcher two men while they're still breathing unless you have some kind of mental disorder, or you want to make a statement about how you've been wronged in some way. I believe there was a lot of hate in those killings; you could feel it when you were around that crime scene."

"And what about the young man and woman that were killed at their campsite?" Tim asked.

"I can answer that, Sheriff," Joe responded and turned to face the agents. "I was the first one on the scene with the man who found the bodies. I don't think this was a revenge killing. These murders appeared more random to me. It seemed as though someone stumbled onto their campsite and their deaths were more a matter of opportunity. I think the young woman was discovered first and was purposely disabled when her arms and legs were broken. Then the killer murdered the man, knowing that she couldn't get away. Without the lab results, our M.E. couldn't say for sure. But he did say the woman appeared to have been sexually assaulted which means the killer returned to rape and murder her as her boyfriend was dead or dying."

"What about the person who found the bodies? Do you think he could have committed the murders and was trying to appear innocent by reporting the crimes?" O'Neal asked.

"His name is Doug Dutton, and he weighs about a hundred pounds soaking wet. Plus, he's decrepit and bone thin and probably couldn't pick up an empty bucket of water without help. Unless he had someone with him, he doesn't have the strength and size to do something like that," Joe said.

O'Neal asked a follow up question. "Well, could he still be involved somehow?"

"It's possible. We just haven't been able to connect the dots to anyone yet," Joe answered.

"So, it sounds like you all haven't developed a list of suspects at this time?" Special Agent Hobbs asked rhetorically.

"Hell, we don't have a clue about even one person who could have done this let alone a list," Sheriff Myers answered while turning his head side-to-side.

"Well then, why don't we start over and interview the family and friends of the victims. Then we can contact anyone of interest we find out about from those interviews," O'Neal suggested.

The officers agreed to split up the interviews to expedite the process. The special agents would contact the relatives of the two campers, while Deputy Sheriff Griffin would start with Ludean Suggs and the high sheriff would oversee a general canvassing for witnesses with help from members in the department.

Nineteen

UNDERSTANDING

The cruiser left a trail of dust as Joe Griffin slowly made his way down a narrow dirt road marked with deep ruts and bordered by green hillsides dotted with pines, dogwoods, and junipers. Slithers of light from the morning sun flickered through the car's windows, reminding him that it was a beautiful day to be doing such unpleasant work.

Ludean Suggs had given him permission to come by to gather more information surrounding her husband's death. And he was still thinking about his line of questioning when the country road made a sharp turn and opened to a little stretch of bottomland that was hedged by an army of beautiful hardwoods and a scattering of Mimosas shoving their way through the heavy timber in search of the sun. In the middle of the property stood a small homestead made of whitewashed planks and a rooftop of tin that was breached by a stone chimney. As for the land, one side of the house was occupied by a three-rail fence holding about five goats used for milk and breeding, and on the other side stood a wire mesh enclosure that was home to about the same number of pigs. The Suggs owned a dairy cow at one time, but it became too expensive to feed, so they ate T-Bones and Prime Ribs for a year. In the rear of the house was a small chicken house and a quarter acre garden where Ludean worked mostly on her knees gathering tomatoes, purple hull peas, and okra for the dinner table along with the occasional off-guard rabbit she caught eating her vegetables. Buck always said she was a better shot than Annie Oakley with that .22 caliber rifle, and tomatoes and okra were always mouthwatering additions to her rabbit stew.

Joe parked the cruiser, got out, and zigzagged his way through the roaming chickens that were pecking the ground, unable to avoid sniffing the unpleasant odor wafting from the animal pens. He stepped up on the rickety front porch and was about to knock when Ludean opened the front door and invited him in. Once inside, the outdoor stench was replaced by the irresistible aroma of cathead biscuits in the oven, skillet sausage on the stove, and hot coffee brewing on the counter. After the introductions, Ludean, being a thoughtful host, asked Joe to sit down at the kitchen table and offered him a sausage biscuit and cup of coffee. It was too tempting to turn down. He was hungry after skipping breakfast at home, and it would be rude to rebuff her kindness. He wasted little time before he was gobbling down the biscuit and slurping the coffee. Ludean loved to watch others enjoying her fine cooking.

"When Sheriff Myers come by to seed me a few days aftur Buck's funral, he eat a half dozen sausage biscuits while we wus talkin'. That man sho' nuff loves to eat," Ludean said while smiling with pride.

"He sure does, Mrs. Suggs. But I have to tell you, that's the best sausage I've ever eaten," Griffin said as he took a sip of coffee to help wash down the delicious meat.

"You best call me Ludean. And I'm glad yous like it. It's the paprika and red pepper spices that heps it tastes so good. Plus, I add just a tiny bit of pork to the possum meat, and that heps with the flavor so it ain't too gamey," she said, feeling needed again. Having Joe enjoy her savory fare was helping her gain back some of her self-worth after her husband's demise.

Everyone knew that Ludean's specialty was cooking creatures of the forest, everyone but Joe. Of course, he never suspected that he was eating a big rat-like creature for breakfast given all the fat pigs right outside the front door. Considering the priceless look on his face, you would have thought he was eating a biscuit filled with goat droppings.

He wanted to immediately spit the sausage from his mouth but knew it would be extremely rude and would most likely end the interview before it started. Instead, with a wince on his face, he forced down the last bite, took a sip of coffee, and turned his attention on Ludean. For the first time, he closely studied her face and was surprised by her appearance. Given the ugliness of her dead husband's features at the murder scene, he expected to see someone of like kind and quality, someone ill-favored like an old humpbacked witch with a bent nose and scraggly gray hair. But she was just the opposite.

Ludean Suggs was in her late fifties, close to the age of her deceased husband, and unlike Buck, had cheated time. Her hair was long and as black as a crow's feathers. And her emerald eyes set below her dark eyebrows were impossible to ignore. Milky smooth skin as though never touched by the sun and fine-features defined her face, and a flat-chest with a willowy frame spoke to her fine physique. The only thing that looked aged was the patch-work dress that hung from her shoulders. It's hard to look like Jackie Kennedy when your monthly income is moonshine money and seventy bucks from welfare. Joe took another sip of coffee and began the conversation.

"To be honest, Ludean, we're not making a lot of progress on the deaths of your husband and his brothers and decided to circle back to see if there is something we're overlooking. Is there anything you can tell me about Buck that might help us find who did this?" Joe asked the open-ended question.

Ludean loved to talk, and Joe had just, unknowingly, opened Pandora's box of chit chat that contained the Suggs family history. But it was too late to close it. Her eyes softened and her mind drifted, talking about the day they were married.

"Well, I met Buck when I's wus in high school. I dropped out in the tenth grade and we's got married right after that. My momma and daddy didn't like him, but I wus in love and we did all right. He'd work odd jobs, you know, like repairing a roof or painting a barn. And I know'd that he made whiskey, but the money helped pay the bills, so I never told him to stop," she said with a nasal twang.

"Did he ever make any enemies; you know, when he was making moonshine?" the deputy asked.

"None that I know'd of exceptin' them revenuers, I guess. He was always tryin' to stay away from the law cause he'd gone to jail a couple times when he got caught. So, he wus always 'fraid the law would blow up his still and send him to prison cause he'd got arrested before. But he never hurt nobody I know'd of. And he never laid a hand on me when he got drunk."

In preparation for the inevitable, Joe refilled his cup with coffee and suggested they take advantage of the more comfortable furniture in the cramped living room. He sat on the couch while Ludean found the recliner and continued defending Buck's passion for making and drinking shine. There are mean drunks and happy drunks she said, and Buck was neither. Ludean smiled with fondness and went on to explain how he turned sweet when his bootleg whiskey numbed his brain. As affectionate as a little puppy, she said. Maybe that's why she never considered his drinking immoral. It was the only time he was openly tender with a wife that would do anything for him. But the sin was always in the shadows. So, from there, she delved into Buck's faith or, more accurately, his lack of it. She was a God-fearing woman, but Buck refused to go to church and wasn't one with the Lord. But she held fast to a whisper of hope, the hope that God was looking the other way and listening to someone else when her husband was cooking hooch and cussing the ABC agents. Only The Holy Spirit knew the answer to that question. So, on and on the recital went until an hour later when Ludean wrapped up the story with a one sentence summary of their life. Since they were married, all her attention had been focused on Buck. Cooking, caring, sacrificing, doing for him most of her life. And now that he was gone, the sadness had gripped her hard inside, leaving a big hole in her heart. She cried knowing he was never coming back.

"Ludean, again I'm so sorry about Buck. Thanks for being so honest and telling me about your life together. Can you tell me anything about his brothers? Did they have any enemies? Given how Bodean was killed, there had to be someone who wanted to brutally punish him," Joe prodded while taking one more trip to the kitchen for another refill of coffee.

"Well, I heard all kinds of stuff about Bo," Ludean revealed.

"What kind of stuff?" Joe asked.

"You haf to understand, what I's gonna tell you is things I heard from different folks, even some women in my Sunday School class at church. I heard them say these things when I talked to them on the phone, so I don't know if I should tell you. If they find out I told you this, they will get mad at me." Ludean failed to mention one minor fact. She had rather spread around other peoples' dirty laundry than win the Publishers Clearing House sweepstakes. If Granny Riddle's back was out, Ludean knew about it. If Malene Roberts just found out she was having a baby girl, Ludean knew about it. And if Bo Suggs was messin' around where he shouldn't be messin' around, Ludean knew about it. Yes, she was the broker for all the unconstrained tittle-tattle, not her friends. And with Buck deep in the woods making shine most days and nights, she needed something to keep herself busy. And spreading rumors about everyone over the phone was the perfect hobby to fill the time.

"Don't worry, Ludean. Anything you share with me will be kept confidential," Joe said in a reassuring tone.

Joe's question had opened a new box. Not one steeped in Greek mythology, but one of unrestrained human behavior and endless complications in the real world. Bo may not have been handsome, smooth-talking or Mr. Personality, but he was as endowed as a Kentucky racehorse and lived like the devil. And that led him to be as promiscuous as the rabbits Ludean murdered in her vegetable garden. She spent thirty minutes talking about the long list of Bo's concubines. Other than one, she referred to the women as full-figured or big boned which is the polite way Southerners describe someone who is overweight. But only three piqued the interest of Deputy Joe and made his short list.

The first was an abused and lonely forty-one-year-old housewife with big-hair named Dovena Rubley. Dovena's husband, Zelbert, was a regular customer of the Suggs Distillery and was the meanest drunk that walked the Earth. His pastime was drinking three-quart jars of white lightning that sharpened his tongue and loosened his fists. It was a predictable pattern of verbally abusing his wife and then knocking her around until he passed out. Having sex with Bo was Dovena's way of getting even for all the hurt feelings, black eyes, and missing teeth. And Bo was a willing participant to her scheme. He always timed his whiskey deliveries when Zelbert was on the job at the welding shop in Belmont. And it was a fine arrangement until Zelbert found out about his wife dancing with the devil. Being the self-righteous drunk he was, he threatened to send them both to Hell where they belonged. When Buck found out that Zelbert would no longer buy their shine, he threatened to send Bo to Hell himself. It wasn't that Buck disapproved of his brother's tryst, he just hated losing a good paying customer.

Mistress number two was squat and fat, about two hushpuppies shy of two hundred and fifty pounds. She had a five-foot frame and had a penchant for cowboy hats and boots, although no one knew why. And according to Ludean, she was the thirty-five-year-old wife of Puck Dutton when her affair began with Bo. She went by the name Dixie, although her God given name of Effie May Trotter was written on the inside leaf of her momma's Bible. As best as

Ludean could remember, Dixie and Bo met at a gas station over in Dallas. After fueling up the pickup, Bo went inside to pay for the gas and buy a pack of Winston's when he saw her at the register purchasing a sixteen-ounce RC Cola and three Moon Pies. He made his move with a promise about his unmatched manhood, which definitely aroused her interest. Maybe it was curiosity, or maybe when compared to her troll-like husband, Bo looked like Sean Connery with a hillbilly accent. Bo didn't have 007's money, however, and didn't want to spend a measly twenty dollars for a motel room when they got together, so they made sweet music wherever they happened to be at the time—in the bed of the pickup, on the ground, in the creek; it really didn't matter. And for six months, Dixie stopped wearing her wedding ring and became one of Bo's angels. Everything was going well until she started talking about divorcing Puck and getting married to him. Bo was too cheap to buy a wedding band made of lead, much less a band of gold, and he was growing tired of her anyway. And beyond his boredom with Dixie, he was really scared of Puck. That's when he ended the relationship. Ludean said that Puck was filled with hate after Dixie followed through on the divorce and moved in with her momma over in Bessemer City. Bo just moved on in search of a replacement angel.

  A large-breasted seventeen-year-old named Clystine Burgett was Bo's third angel, and she was Ludean's great niece. Ludean described Clystine as a big girl with dirty blonde hair, a face rounded with baby-fat and a bottom shaped like a pumpkin. She was a miserable teenager, always looking for a way to escape her all-controlling father who happened to be addicted to alcohol. And Bo had the solution for her need to get away in the guise of a dark blue 1959 Chevy Apache Pickup. Clystine would get in touch with Bo when her daddy, Otis Burgett, started drinking. Within an hour, Bo would pull around behind her house and wait until Otis was as drunk as Cooter Brown, and then she would slip out the back door. From there, the two would head to an isolated spot hidden in the kudzu on the riverbank, drink liquor, and go at it like two drunk raccoons. Bo knew it was wrong, but he didn't care. He was willfully ignorant of Clystine being a minor and her father being another good customer of the Suggs brothers' whiskey. Ludean told Buck about his little brother's indiscretions with her underage niece, and he was as mad as a wet bobcat. But not as mad as Mr. Burgett when he found out. Otis was insane with rage, publicly swearing to hang Bo by his toes from a tree and dismember Little Bo and the twins for defiling his innocent young daughter. The bold threat was enough to scare the hell out of Bodean, so a quick divorce from his unlawful relationship with Clystine was his best way out.

Joe Griffin felt like he needed to take a shower when Ludean finished spinning her entertaining stories about wild sex, hard drinking, and double-dealing deceit. As crazy as they sounded, most of her tales made sense, although Joe was certain she had selective recall when it came to Buck. No one could be that angelic. No one could live sixty-one years on God's earth and never befriend the devil at least once. The pigs outside had a better chance of flying than that being true. Ludean was clinging to his spirit and Joe didn't want to dig up the dead and cause more pain. So, he let it go. As for Beaver, he was a head-scratcher, an enigma. Ludean knew nothing about Beaver's history that would help the investigation, although she was aware that he was gay. She kept the secret from Buck knowing his reaction would have been emotional dynamite.

All in all, Joe had a productive morning. He had identified at least three individuals with motives to kill the youngest Suggs brother and sensed that Bo's killer would lead him to the answers he so desperately sought for the other victims. His patience had been rewarded. For now.

Twenty

UNDER THE STARS

Other than an occasional outburst, the past two weeks had been quiet and uneventful at the Russell household. A dustup between Jamie and Ann was the only conflict that led to spiteful name calling. Ann had been drinking heavily when she discovered Tommy wearing the unusual necklace given to him by Maw. The vodka had impaired her mind and helped ignite her anger and she threw the trinket in the kitchen trash can. Her tirade about never allowing her son to wear a voodoo necklet from a witch gave rise to Jamie absorbing the hurtful words and sending them back with frightful anger.

Whether or not the ornament had magical powers was immaterial to Jamie. It was a gift from a loving old woman who wanted to protect Tommy, and that was all that mattered. This rift created the hostility that ended any hope that a normal mother-daughter relationship could ever exist, much less some special lifetime bond created by love and understanding. Ann's words were mean spirited, maybe due to the booze. Or perhaps she was jealous of a daughter who had found a measure of happiness in a young boy that wasn't destined to be a wife beater or career criminal. You become bitter when you've failed at everything. And Jamie let her have it for her incessant self-destruction, her chain-smoking and willingness to drink anything alcoholic. She called Ann a horrible mother who didn't give a damn about protecting Tommy, and Ann retaliated by calling her a disrespectful brat who didn't care about shielding her brother from hoodoo magic. The words were palpable. From then on, they ignored each other as though they were invisible combatants. Unfortunately, there was a little boy trapped in neutral territory in the middle of their war.

* * * * * *

It was a cloudless evening showcasing a sky filled with scintillating stars and a beautiful crescent moon trimmed in gold. And the open-air Skyview Drive-In was the place to be if you loved movies, especially this weekend. The theater was debuting *El Dorado* starring John Wayne and Robert Mitchem, and everyone loved The Duke, especially at the bargain rate of fifty cents per car plus fifty cents per person.

Two boys in Jamie's homeroom at school had asked her for a date to the movie, but she declined them both. She and Lenny had made plans to go to the movie getting away from the turmoil at home. Jamie thought it odd, however, that Lenny asked her to drive until she found out why. He had promised three of his pals a free ride through the admission gate in the trunk of a car, her car. Lenny's Nova SS had a very small luggage compartment whereas the Rambler afforded more space to hide. In addition, when Lenny and Johnny repaired her car and brought it back to life, they rigged the upper section of the Rambler's back seat so it would pop on and off with the pull of a pinkie finger. The plan was simple. Lenny would remove the spare tire and his pals would entomb themselves on a blanket in the trunk until the Rambler had passed the entrance and parked in a remote location on the theater grounds. And then they would crawl through the back seat and burst from the car like a bunch of circus clowns. They would scatter to unite with their friends in other cars, leaving Lenny and Jamie some privacy to smooch and eat popcorn.

Beyond the intricate scheme to avoid a couple of dollars in admission fees, Lenny was very fastidious getting ready for their date. His attire was an easy decision. White Levi jeans, a light blue buttoned-down shirt, and a pair of black and white rah-rah shoes had him looking as trendy as

Anthony Perkins. The tough choice was the cologne he would douse on his face that would make him the object of her affection. Lenny spent most of his earnings from the Food Stop on his car, dates, and cologne. And in his eau de cologne inventory in the bathroom medicine cabinet, he had three options from which to choose...Jade East, English Leather, and High Karate. Only the mind of a love-smitten teenage boy could come up with his answer. If one cologne was an effective aphrodisiac with the opposite sex, why not mix all three together and be three times more attractive. It would be a powerful scent—so powerful it could knock a red bird from the sky. And if by chance it didn't make Jamie swoon, maybe the strong odor would make her eyes well with tears and he could steal a kiss when she wasn't looking. Meanwhile, Jamie's preparation consisted of hair styling, light make-up meant to look as though she barely wore any, and a touch of her mother's Chanel No. 5. She thought it would be just enough to accent her attractiveness. Her threads were faded jeans, a pink long-sleeved pullover, and a pair of black-top sneakers. In total, it made for a clean and simple look. The rendezvous location for their high jinks would be the high school parking lot where Jamie and the Rambler would meet up with Lenny and the clowns.

Lenny and friends were waiting on Jamie when she pulled into the parking lot. Lynn Moore and Danny Sylvester were first stringers on the school's football team, and Bruce Deason was an outstanding basketball star who would be playing at the collegiate level after graduation. Before Jamie and Lenny became a thing, these boys couldn't pick her out of a lineup of one. But now, as they piled into the Rambler's trunk, they called her by name and teased her like a little sister. Most importantly, they acted as though they had known her all their lives. It was exhilarating to be raised up in the eyes of these well-liked jocks, but it was more thrilling to feel wanted and respected. She knew she couldn't close the gap between herself and those of privilege, but for that moment in time, she felt like the most popular girl at Belmont High.

"Don't drive too fast, Jamie!" Danny said with a mischievous grin as he climbed inside the trunk.

"Don't listen to him. Drive like a bat out of Hell to get us there faster. I don't want to be jammed in the trunk with these two bozos any longer than I have to be," Lynn laughed and gave Bruce a playful shove on the shoulder.

"Get in, Bruce," Lenny said. "You guys just need to stay quiet. Jamie and I don't want to have the cops called on us if we get caught!"

"If I get caught, you're going to pay big time!" Jamie smiled, unable to believe that she had agreed to their harebrained scheme.

She was waiting in the Rambler when Lenny closed the trunk lid and jumped in, riding shotgun on the passenger front seat. He gave her a quick smile of reassurance, knowing that in her eyes anyone doing such a devilish thing must be awfully silly. After all, it wasn't as though the boys couldn't afford the cost of admission; they just had an impish streak in their DNA. Perhaps having coaches screaming, "Walk it off," in response to every injury, or being told to "Give one-hundred ten percent," despite that being impossible, created a need in the boys to push back against authority. The attendants at the drive-in were easy targets. Whatever the guys' motives may have been, Jamie was nervous when they arrived at the entrance. The three stooges in the trunk were snickering and elbowing each other, threatening to give away their hiding place. Lenny whispered for them to shut up while Jamie held her breath as the young attendant stared through the car's back window and glanced at the Rambler's trunk. Satisfied that there was no conspiracy involving teenagers hiding on the floorboard or in the luggage compartment, he accepted a buck fifty and let them pass. Within seconds, the Rambler parked on a back row in front of the border fence and Larry, Moe, and Curley burst through the back seat and gave Lenny and Jamie a series of celebratory high-fives.

Jamie and Lenny relocated the Rambler on a ramp about midway on the lot so they would have a better view of Cole Thornton and his upstart friend, Mississippi, shooting it out with the bad guys in the town of El Dorado. Jamie carefully parked the car, removed the portable speaker from the stand, and attached it to the inside of her car window. Meanwhile, Lenny slid over to allow her a better sniff of his lethal cologne. Unlike the Nova's bucket seats that were separated by a console and shifter, the Rambler sported a bench seat which gave him the perfect opportunity to get shoulder to shoulder for a little snuggling. Jamie was all-in for a little kissing and cuddling, but in that moment, she was more interested in the powerful aroma wafting from the concession stand than Lenny's cologne. She hadn't eaten since breakfast and the smell had her spellbound thinking about the delicious food. She made a subtle comment about the food smelling good, and Lenny took the hint. He made the short trip to the fast-food stand, and returned with burgers, fries, chocolate shakes, and a pack of Juicy Fruit gum. The gum was his idea. He was thinking ahead about how to tame the aftertaste from the hamburgers. It was never a good idea to have onion breath when you were trying to be romantic. The evening's meal and Juicy Fruit cost a whopping five dollars and twenty-five cents. A little pricey, but it seemed like a fair trade since they had bootlegged their friends through the gate.

The food solved the hunger pangs and the love-struck teenagers started working in a kiss or two between gun shoot-outs on the giant screen. Their date was going spectacular until they saw an early scene in the movie with John Wayne and Robert Mitchem. Looking for help from the local peace officer, Cole Thornton (John Wayne) had found Sheriff J.P. Harrah (Robert Mitchem) in a jail cell at the sheriff's office. The sheriff drunkenly incarcerated himself. His badge was penned to a nasty long-underwear top, which signaled that he didn't give a tinker's damn about his appearance. And his speech was as slurry as a two-year-old trying to say the alphabet. When Cole asked for the sheriff's help to fight the bad guys, like any alcoholic, J.P. Harrah's demeanor was apathetic and uncaring. The scene struck a painful nerve with Jamie. It was an unwanted reminder of her mother and the indifference she harbored for anything other than booze and cigarettes, a reminder of their latest fight that ended in animosity and division. The movie's dialogue killed the lovey-dovey mood as fast as Cole could draw his Colt revolver. Lenny sensed Jamie's frame of mind had changed and probed for what happened to dampen her spirit.

"What's wrong?" Lenny asked.

"That sheriff reminded me of a fight I had with my mom. She was snockered like him and she accused me of not caring about Tommy," Jamie answered.

"What do you mean?" Lenny appeared perplexed knowing how much she loved her little brother.

"She was mad because I gave Tommy a necklace from Maw. She wanted him to wear it. It was the day you and Johnny fixed my car. Remember when we went by the bait store before we went fishing?" she asked.

"Yeah, I remember. Why would your mother get mad about that?" Lenny was still confused.

"The necklace was kinda like a good luck charm, but my mom said it was voodoo and that Maw was a witch. And she said I was a brat who cared more about Maw than her," Jamie's response was less than candid. Maw was crystal clear that the necklet wasn't for good luck, but for protection against the devil. The rift with her mother wasn't the only thing that had left her anxious and confused. Maw's foreboding words were still imprinted on her psyche, leaving a shadow of fear on her heart she couldn't dismiss.

"Heck, you should just ignore all that stuff your mom said," Lenny offered a suggestion that was impossible to pull off.

"I can't ignore it. She's getting drunk more often now and can't take care of herself, much less me and Tommy. I feel like I need to do something, but if I report her to social services, they'll put us in a foster home. They may even split me and Tommy up. I can't let that happen," Jamie answered with sadness in her voice.

"Can you get rid of all the booze?" Lenny asked.

"I've tried that. I've poured it down the sink, but she goes and buys another bottle. Until she gets some help from something like Alcoholics Anonymous or maybe a doctor, I don't think she'll ever stop drinking. I don't know what to do."

"We can skip the rest of the movie and go somewhere else if you want to," Lenny offered a big-hearted solution to the dilemma.

Jamie welcomed Lenny's suggestion, thinking how thoughtful he was to leave early before the movie had ended. Of course, Lenny still thought he had a shot at getting a little sugar, so he volunteered to drive the Rambler and headed straight for the elementary school parking lot. He soon realized that necking was the last thing on Jamie's mind. She needed someone to talk to, someone to listen, someone to understand what it was like to have such unstable family relationships. Jamie couldn't help but think how grand life would be if she were part of a perfect all-American family. Like the families on television where no one was flawed. The kids would obey their parents like dutiful soldiers, the mother would wear a string of pearls and pumps while cooking dinner, and the father would dress in a suit and tie when he cuts the grass. But that was unrealistic and wishful thinking, a dream really, especially for Jamie. She lived with The Addams Family, not Ozzie and Harriet Nelson. She had become a permanent fixture in a life of disorder and negativity, and she told Lenny about all the dirty details. And being the perfect gentleman, Lenny dismissed any ideas about stealing a kiss and patiently listened. He listened with an understanding heart as Jamie purged the darkness from her soul. Little did she know that very soon her mother's demons would be the least of her worries.

Twenty-One

DID THIS REALLY HAPPEN?

The homestead was near Tryon, a good quarter mile down a dusty road that veered off the rarely traveled County Road 1474. Otis Burgett and his daughter, Clystine, lived at the end of that road among a grove of pines at the crest of a low-rise hill. Deputy Sheriff Joe Griffin had become the de facto lead investigator in the Suggs brothers' murders and needed to gauge the family's possible involvement in the homicides. It was early morning when he headed to their woodland home to interview them both. He slowly drove across a dry creek bed and made several lazy turns up and down some shallow ridges and valleys until the dirt road finally halted at an odd mixture of untidy structures spread across a grassy opening. After parking the cruiser, the deputy made his way to the house on a long footpath that passed by several burial plots that were overgrown with weeds. Not exactly the Bonaventure Cemetery with beautiful statues and live oaks dripping with moss. But the graves were marked by three decomposing crosses in keeping with the decomposed bodies in the ground. Home gravesites were common in the rural South given the high cost of being entombed in pretty cemeteries with year-round flowers. And although the Burgett's weren't penniless, caskets with gold hardware and granite headstones were not within their meager budget. So, the unkempt graveyard was the unremarkable home of Otis Burgett's wife, Hazelene, who died of cancer, and his momma and daddy who passed away from old age.

Joe continued down the path while sizing up the dwelling and shacks that huddled around it. The house was boxed-shaped with a dead center front door that was bordered by two casements with unrepaired windowpanes. The low-pitched roof was covered by rotting shingles and the clapboard siding was crumbling from the lack of maintenance and repair. On one side of the house was a pole-shed structure that covered an assortment of non-working farm implements and an old Massey Ferguson tractor coated in rust. On the other side stood a ramshackle shed with a lean-to roof and an outside wall accentuated with deer skulls. Otis was certain that the hunting laws were for other people because he preferred to kill deer out of season, on the road from his Dodge pickup, and in the dark. Filled with the pride of a prolific poacher, he would nail the skulls and antlers to the plywood siding and then lie to his hunting buddies about how he shot the animals at dawn from a tree stand. Joe thought the place was a disaster as he stepped around a Blue Tick porch dog sleeping near the front door. Reaching with his right hand, he rapped several times on the unpainted door and waited for the arrival of a Burgett family member.

"Who is it?" the deep voice loudly called from inside the home.

"Deputy Sheriff Griffin from the Gaston County Sheriff's Office," Joe answered.

"Jest a minute," the voice was deeper and raspy this time, bellowing with more force.

The deputy was shocked when the door opened, and he had his first look at Otis Burgett. Joe had imagined a behemoth of a man, something akin to the son of Godzilla when he spoke to him about their meeting. Instead, his eyes angled downward and found a short, pudding faced fat man that looked as though he were made from dough. Decked only in a pair of frayed Liberty overalls and low-rise boots, his body appeared hairless although he did have a long lock of dark hair that fell from his bald skull cap and covered his ears and the back of his head like a curtain. And given the rolls of fat around his neck, he also appeared chinless.

Chalky skin of a vampire, a slack mouth with thin lips, and bad teeth rounded out his unusual features. Joe didn't know Mr. Burgett's exact age, but he guessed him to be in his late thirties. However, Joe didn't have to guess about two things as he stepped across the door's threshold. Otis had dark disturbed eyes that darted about when making eye contact, a common tendency of those who have something to hide. And Clystine's blue eyes seem to be pleading, hoping to reveal the skeleton that was hiding in the closet, as she peered around her bedroom doorway.

"Come on in, Shuriff." Otis waved Joe inside.

"Thanks, Mr. Burgett. But I'm a deputy, not the High Sheriff," Joe said. "Harley Myers is the sheriff in Gaston County. You can just call me Joe."

"Well, come on in, no mattur whut you are," Otis spoke with a tone of annoyance.

"Thank you. I appreciate it," Joe courteously replied.

Joe entered the house and Otis motioned him down the hallway. The narrow hall split the four main rooms in the middle, with the kitchen and master bedroom on one side, and a second bedroom and den on the other. The men continued walking until they reached the living area occupying the last room on the right. Once they entered the den, Joe did a quick scan of his surroundings, noticing a room that was at one time very bright. One wall held most of the family pictures and archetypes of faith, and it had all the earmarks of a strong foundation built on a higher power. The room also whispered of the past when there was an unbreakable bond between the parents and their daughter. The picture of the Last Supper and the crucifix were powerful symbols of their relationship with God, and the many framed photos of Otis, Hazelene, and Clystine spoke volumes about the closeness of their family.

Otis pointed to a chair and instructed Joe to take a seat. Seconds later, the deputy and Otis were sitting facing each other on two fabric armchairs adjacent to a large light beige sofa. Unlike the past when Hazelene was still living, the room now appeared unclean and raw. The odd stains and foul odors emanating from the furniture caught the deputy's attention. And so did the lack of lighting. The lamps were off, and the window shades were drawn, making the room unusually dark as though it were hiding a secret. Meanwhile Otis was perched on the edge of his seat while Joe was playing it cool, leaning back in a relaxed fashion like he was drinking a beer with some of his golfing buddies. He calmly pulled a notebook from his portfolio bag and began the interrogation.

"First off, thank y'all for meeting with me this morning. I really appreciate it," Joe said calmly, hoping to soothe any anxiety.

"Well, I dun't think Clystine has anythin' to tell you, but I'll tell you whut I know," Otis said as he nervously lit an unfiltered Lucky Strike.

"As I told you on the phone, your name and Clystine's came up when I was interviewing Ludean Suggs about the murders."

"Hell's bells, I dun't know why Ludean would bring up our names." Otis had a look of disbelief on his face as he took a deep drag on his smoke.

"Well sir, your name didn't come from just Ludean. Several others confirmed that they heard you make statements about wanting Bo Suggs dead because he was having a relationship with your daughter. That's the main reason why I'm here. I need to follow up with you and Clystine about these allegations."

It took all of fifteen seconds for the cordial meeting to turn hostile. No fire drill was needed to launch Otis from his chair. Deputy Joe's finger-pointing comments triggered a loss of self-control from Otis as his back stiffened and his pallid face turned as red as a beet. His arms started flailing wildly and he began an angry tirade.

"That sun-of-a-bitch was rapin' Cylstine. It weren't no relationship. He wus sneakin' 'round here and takin' her from the house and rapin' her. And he wus gettin' her drunk. She'd come home so drunk she could hardly walk after bein' with him. I wanted that bastard dead and I'd kilt him myself if somebody hadn't kilt him already." Otis couldn't have served up a more likely suspect than himself. When the interview began, Joe was prepared to spend whatever time necessary to gain Otis's trust, to cajole him to get him to speak freely about any violent intentions. Contrary to the good cop/bad cop tactic, this was going to be Joe solely in the role of a good cop.

Even though Deputy Griffin had yet to speak with Clystine, he knew the age of consent was sixteen and if she willingly had sex with Bo, his hands were tied. Of course, if Bo plied her with booze and then raped her, he could face very serious charges. It was a moot point, however, since Bo had been dispatched to a special place in Hell where he was being tormented by the devil. Spending ten years in prison for a rape conviction was the least of his worries. So, there was no need to charge Bo for rape, and it was too late to calmly coax Otis to be forthright. Joe had only one dilemma. The meeting had gotten completely out of hand, and he needed a way to deal with the explosive emotions spewing from Otis' foul mouth. As a lawman, Joe was trained to remain peaceful when in heated exchanges with citizens since it was hard to think clearly when your mind was on fire. Cop training aside, he could feel the intense animosity rising in his own body and decided that there would be no more Mr. Nice Guy. Instead, the deputy abandoned all his training. He glared intently at Otis and went for the jugular.

"Mr. Burgett, why did you kill Bodean Suggs?" Joe snapped as he sprang from his chair and cast the blame for the murder directly on Otis.

The fury went out of Otis as fast as it arrived. He was stunned. The stark realization that his homicidal threats could be used to convict him of the murder hit him hard. Instantly, his voice dropped to a whisper, and he became as harmless as a newborn puppy.

"Shuriff, you dun't think I had anythin' to do with Bo Suggs gettin' kilt, do you?" Otis asked with the innocent look of an altar boy.

"I'm not the sheriff. I told you I'm a deputy. And you just told me you wanted Bo dead. Why wouldn't I think you killed him?" Joe asked with an incredulous stare.

"I've dun some bad things in my life, but I ain't ever kilt nobody. I may have hated Bo Suggs, but I damn shor didn't kilt him!" Otis answered.

Fortunately, over the next few minutes, their tempers cooled, and they returned to their seats. At that point, Otis opened up to Deputy Griffin about everything. Joe's heart softened somewhat as he gained an understanding of how Otis had become such a wreck of humanity. He was once a regular churchgoer at a Baptist house of God that practiced foot-washing and speaking in tongues on Sunday. A man who spoke to Jesus and believed in the Bible. He also loved and adored his family and worked every day at the lithium mine near Spencer Mountain to prove it. But then his wife, Hazelene, was diagnosed with lung cancer. Naturally, that's what happens when you smoke two packs of Lucky Strikes every day. She died about a year later after going through months of chemo and radiation. Her death left Otis devastated and heartbroken. He took to whiskey for medication which opened a door which should have remained closed. He grew mean and nasty like a cornered snake. And he created a living Hell by acting like a prison guard, trying to control every second of his daughter's life. He confessed to all those wrongdoings but pleaded again and again for Deputy Joe to believe that he was incapable of murder. Joe was uncertain. He knew that the best deceivers always mix a little truth with a lot of lies, so he needed some corroborating evidence. Speaking to Clystine was the answer. Her testimony might clear up some of the ambiguities in her daddy's tale of events.

"Mr. Burgett, I'm going to need to ask Clystine some questions about Bo. Would you get her for me?" Joe asked

"She'd be sick, shuriff. She's got a high fever and some kind of bug, so she can't talk right now," Otis answered.

Joe was tired of correcting Mr. Burgett about his rank, so he ignored his imaginary promotion to sheriff. However, he didn't ignore Otis lying about his daughter. "Well, I'm still going to need to talk to her. She can stay far away from me so I can't catch what she's got, and I can ask her some quick questions," Joe insisted.

"No, shuriff. She can't get outta bed, she's so sick. Can't you come back some other time?" Otis said adamantly as the ire started to reappear on his face.

Not wanting to reignite Otis' short fuse, the deputy agreed to call him in a couple of days to rearrange the meeting with Clystine. Otis apologized for his acrimonious behavior and seemed relieved when the two men shook hands, and he escorted Joe to the front door. *A prime suspect*—that's what Deputy Griffin thought as he left the house and walked down the footpath. *Given Mr. Burgett's temper and hatred for Bo, I've found a prime suspect in these murders.* When he made it to the cruiser and was about to open the door, he spied some movement to his left, about twenty feet in the woods behind a sizable white oak. It was the spread-out silhouette of a person who was unable to completely hide their body behind the hardwood. It was Clystine. She was covertly watching him while keeping a vigilant eye on the house for her daddy. Much like in the past when she would clandestinely meet Bo, she had slipped out the back of the house when her father and the deputy were walking to the front door. Of course, she wasn't sick and just wanted to give Joe her side of the story before her father found out she was missing. The deputy recognized her immediately given the description from Ludean and motioned her over to his car.

"Are you Clystine?" Deputy Griffin asked, although he already knew the answer. If seeing her gaze from her bedroom doorway didn't reveal her identity, her button nose, blonde hair, and shapely figure surely did the trick.

"Yeah, I am," she answered in a nasal voice.

"Your father told me you were sick. Was he lying?"

"Yeah, he didn't want you talkin' to me," she said while taking a quick look over her shoulder toward the house.

"Why not?"

"He didn't want me tellin' you what he does," she answered.

"And what's that? And while you're at it, tell me everything about your relationship with Bodean Suggs and why your father would want to kill him."

"Well, first off, since Momma died and Daddy started drinking, he acts like I'm Momma. He touches me in places that ain't right. And he won't let me leave the house for nuthin' cause he's 'fraid I'll tell somebody. Or maybe he thinks I'll leave and not come back. If he caught me tellin' you 'bout this, he might beat me. It's the moonshine. It moves him to do stuff he would never do," Clystine explained.

"What do you mean he touches you? Has he raped you?" the deputy asked with alarm in his voice.

"No, he can't do nuthin' when he's drunk. He just touches my private parts and wants to kiss me like I'm his wife," Clystine answered.

Whether or not Clystine's account of her father's obscene acts was truthful, embellished, or an outright lie didn't matter. Joe felt certain that Otis had a weird sexual predisposition in some manner given how hard he tried to shelter Clystine from speaking to him. He felt the anger rise again, along with a surge of disgust in his core. Having raised a daughter himself, he held a punitive bent for anyone who would breach the inviolable trust between a father and his daughter. It didn't matter if Otis drank all the bootlegged whiskey in the county, pretending that Clystine was his replacement wife was totally unacceptable.

"Clystine, would you be willing to meet with someone from Child Welfare Services and one of the female officers with Gaston Police and tell them what you've told me?" the deputy asked.

"No, I can't do that. They'd put Daddy in jail if I told them. You have to understand, I'm the only one he's got. The stuff he does is jest because of the liquor. He treats me real good when he's sober," she answered.

"What about Bodean Suggs? Were you intimately involved with him? Did your father kill Bo because he didn't want to lose you?"

"Daddy found out 'bout me and Bo all right, and he talked a lot about makin' Bo go away. But he wus jest talkin'. I don't think he would do anything like that. He still believes in the Lord and killin' somebody ain't in his heart."

"How did you meet Bo in the first place?" the deputy asked.

"Daddy was buyin' liquor from Bo, and Bo would drop it off at our house. When Daddy found out 'bout us, he stopped Bo from comin' 'round and he started buyin' it from some man named Puck. And then he bought it from Raymond Bates cause his price was the cheapest," Cylstine's voice trembled as she glanced toward the house for any sign of her father.

"Clystine, I can't help you if you won't stand up to your father. If you'll make a statement at the sheriff's office, we can stop your father from molesting you."

"No, I can't talk to nobody. 'Sides that, I don't think Daddy will do anythin' else now that he knows you're looking into everythin'," she answered.

Their conversation lasted only for a few more minutes. Clystine had fallen silent and again glimpsed at the house for any movement. She was spooked that she had dug up too many bones and needed to get back inside before Otis discovered her absence. Joe understood her predicament. He felt that he had fulfilled his duty by carefully listening to every syllable in every word she spoke. Offering to bring in expert help added to his confidence that he hadn't left Clystine without options to get away from her father. But for now, he had given up hope of getting any more information from her or Otis. He was still in a fog, baffled by all the moving parts in this strange saga. He slid into the cruiser and started thinking about his next move. Who would he contact next? Puck Dutton seemed like the right choice.

Twenty-Two

IT'S NOT OVER

Cooter Jones was not a man endowed with the business acumen of Henry Ford. In truth, a six-year-old kid running a lemonade stand had more marketing sense than Cooter. The moonshine business was a subculture with laws and punishments outside the decency of robed judges and impartial juries and reselling shine purchased from another moonshiner is never a good idea given bootlegger jurisprudence. Yet that's exactly what Cooter did. He had failed at making his own sellable shine, so he bought good whiskey from Raymond Bates, jacked up the price, and sold it to customers in another legger's territory. That kind of competition was dealt with swiftly and deadly.

* * * * * *

A phone call from the sheriff's office woke up Deputy Griffin at 6:30 in the morning. The dispatcher explained that all the other deputies were on calls and a civilian needed a police presence immediately. Alma Jones had discovered her husband's corpse on their property. Even though it was his day off, the deputy quickly rose, jotted down sketchy directions to the location, and dressed in his uniform. Before walking out the door, he woke his wife, told her he had an emergency call and had to leave. She faintly murmured "okay," pulled the sheet back around her neck, and told him to be careful. Joe then hurriedly left the house, jumped in the cruiser, engaged the roof-mounted flashing lights, and began the high-speed drive to a locale in between Spencer Mountain and the South Fork of the Catawba River. While driving on State Highway 74, the deputy couldn't help but think about how quiet things had been for the past several weeks. Sunny skies with no domestic disputes, no burglaries, no drug offenses, and no homicides. Even if the Suggs murders were never solved, he had wistfully hoped that the killer had moved on, that his life would get back to normal. After turning north on State Highway 29, a heavy rain started pounding the cruiser, forcing the deputy to ease off the pedal. The thunderstorm reminded him that his fanciful imagination about a world without evil was just a dream.

An exit off the state highway placed Deputy Griffin on a county road heading in an easterly direction. That byway led to three additional turns from unmarked crossroads that placed him in a remote area along the river. It was known as a territory of mystery where people ignored the law and acted as savage as the animals in the woods.

After driving up and down a narrow rise on an unpaved road, he finally arrived at the homestead of one of those wild animals. His name was Jesse Jones, although everyone called him Cooter. And Cooter had a reputation for dabbling in anything that would make him a buck and his property confirmed his entrepreneurial spirit. With a blackened sky and driving rain, visibility was poor at best, and Joe had to lean close to the car's windshield to gain a better view of the Jones compound. By squinting, he could make out a simple one-story dwelling centered on the open bottomland. The structure was built with logs chinked with a yellowish mortar and lacked any interesting features other than a squat chimney in the rear that protruded from a rusty tin roof. Looking on either side of the farmhouse, his eyes spotted a 6' x 6' smokehouse for curing meat, a chicken coop for eggs, and a brooder house for poultry. A pole shed covered an old John Deere tractor and tiller, and in the distance, he identified a gambrel-roofed crib barn made with unchinked logs covered by vertical planks that were falling to the ground from neglect. It was an ominous scene. The foul weather and the swirling live oaks that surrounded the log house and outbuildings appeared twisted and evil.

The sinister landscape sent a chill up the deputy's spine, a feeling he had experienced at the murder scenes of the young campers and Suggs brothers. He did feel a measure of reassurance, however, when he parked his cruiser next to another law enforcement vehicle driven by a friend he had known since high school. Officer Willy Freeman with the Gaston County Police Department had arrived about twenty minutes earlier and had spoken with Cooter's wife about the location of her dead husband. After Officer Freeman left Mrs. Jones in the cabin, he returned to his car and donned a bright yellow rain jacket. He then made his way to the barn and surveyed the area where the body was located. After making his initial assessment, he headed back to his patrol car to radio for backup. As he was walking past the log house, he saw Joe arrive and headed toward the deputy's cruiser. He found Joe digging in the trunk for his own rain gear.

"Hey, stranger," Willy emphatically said over the sound of the rumbling thunder.

"Oh, my gosh! Is that you, Willy?" Joe asked with a broad smile.

"Yeah, it's me. How've you been?" Willy asked as he shook his friend's hand.

"I'm doing well. How 'bout you?" Joe answered.

"Same. I can't believe we've run into each other. How long has it been?" Willy asked as the rain dripped from the hood of his jacket.

"Maybe since high school," Joe answered. "I heard you joined the police department after putting twenty in with the army. Given all the trouble we got into when we were young, it's hard to believe that we both ended up as police officers. Heck, I thought we'd be dead or in prison by now."

Willy rolled his eyes and laughed. "Yeah, I never thought we'd end up being cops."

"Speaking of being cops...have you talked to Mrs. Jones about her husband?" Joe asked as he closed the trunk lid.

"Yeah, I spoke to her about what happened," Willy answered. "She's pretty shook up. Said her husband got up in the middle of the night after hearing a commotion behind the house. He told her to go to back to sleep, that he'd take a quick look and be back in a few minutes. She said she fell back to sleep and didn't wake back up until this morning. That's when she noticed he wasn't in bed with her. She looked for him in the house and couldn't find him, so she started looking outside. Said she found him in the hog pen next to the barn."

"Have you been back there where the body is?" Joe asked while pointing behind the house.

"Yeah, it's bad—real bad. I was about to call for backup when I saw you park. I've seen dead bodies before, but I've never been on a call for anything like this." Willy shook his head in disbelief.

"I know what you're sayin'. I've seen more dead bodies in the last few months than all my years being a deputy. Don't worry, though. We'll figure it out."

As they walked to the old tumble-down barn, the officers welcomed the cessation in the rain, although both men knew that any evidence such as body materials and impressions were most likely destroyed, altered, or lost due to the heavy downpour.

Willy had seen the gruesome crime scene and fought back the nausea when he first witnessed the brutality in the pen. In his mind, it would be a sign of weakness for a hardcore cop to get sick, especially in the presence of another cop. So, as he led Joe to the hog pen, he was silent, trying not to think about the horrid sight and hoping he could keep his stomach in check. As they drew closer to Cooter's body, Willy looked to the sky as a distraction while Joe stared ahead, attempting to make a mental note of the structural integrity of the pen. Nine hog panels made with heavy gauge wire fastened to ten posts which created an enclosure that was attached to the east side of the barn. There was an exterior gate that swung inward and a separate doorway opening that allowed in and out access to the barn from the pen. Both the exterior gate and barn door were closed and secured.

Within the pen there were two feral boars averaging about two hundred fifty pounds each with prominent tusks. The two males were mixed in with five mostly feral females at around one fifty apiece. The blackish colored hogs were actively grunting, rooting, and eating. Doing what hogs do. Their stocky bodies, flat snouts, and large ears were their obvious characteristics. Incredible smarts, bad attitudes, and the speed of a jack rabbit were some of their not so apparent traits. These were intimidating creatures that would send the Big Bad Wolf running home in fright—and Joe and Willy too if they had a choice in the matter. They didn't. They were cops. Both men leaned over one of the fence panels to assess the surreal landscape. It was the corpse of fifty-one-year-old Cootie Jones lying face up in the mud. He was in the middle of the pen, wearing a pair of dark gray pajama bottoms and a sleeveless t-shirt. Both garments were significantly torn. Also visible was a large section of missing flesh on his neck near his carotid artery, a section wider than the bite radius of the hogs. In addition, there were many smaller plugs of muscle and tissue that had been removed over his entire body. It appeared that the aggressive swine caused the lesser bites. It seemed obvious that the hogs had been eating breakfast and Cooter was the entrée.

"I can't believe what I'm looking at," Joe said in shock.

"I couldn't believe it either. What do we need to do to protect the body from the hogs?" Willy asked.

"I'd rather get the hogs out and leave the body undisturbed if we can," Joe answered. "That way, we won't contaminate any evidence."

"That makes sense. I tried to go inside the pen when I got here, but the hogs charged me."

"There's an entry door from the pen to the barn. If we can herd the hogs into the barn and shut the door behind them, we should be able to secure the area until the crime scene folks get here," Joe said while pointing to the 5' x 5' entry door.

"Why don't I go in the barn and open the door to the inside stall? Then you can try to drive the hogs inside," Willy suggested. He had experienced the hogs' malicious intent and wanted no part in facing down these ill-tempered creatures. He was hoping he could open the door and quickly find cover within the barn before he could be attacked. Fortunately, Joe agreed to his proposal.

"All right, just to be safe, let's both draw our side arms in case we get in a tight spot," Joe said as he pulled the Colt Python from its holster. "Give me a shout when you're ready and I'll yell back when I start to push the hogs through the door."

"Will do," Willy confirmed.

Officer Freeman knew their primary responsibility was to stabilize the pen by isolating the body, so he turned and headed to the barn's front entrance. Upon arriving, he took a cautious look at the outside loft opening above the double-swing doors. William J. Freeman had served in the infantry in Vietnam and had felt the slipstream of an AK47 bullet whizzing by his head in a fire fight. Given his military experience, he wanted to be sure he wouldn't be ambushed by someone hiding in the upper part of the barn. He had a bad feeling, however, that the threat was anything but a sniper. A maniac, ghost, or monster perhaps. What else could have caused this mayhem?

Sensing something malevolent looming in the darkness, he drew his .357 magnum in his right hand and swung the left door outward to gain a better view. Once inside, he was immediately slammed by the stink of pig manure and decaying hay. Regrettably, his vision was not nearly as acute as his sense of smell. The cloudy sky prevented any measurable light from filtering through the gaping planks on the side of the barn. So, to aid his vision, he pulled his tactical flashlight from his utility belt and stepped into the dark shadows. At first, he felt clumsy, as though he were dizzy from a carnival ride. But after a few seconds, his pupils dilated as much from being afraid as from the lack of light. It helped his myopic eyes see more clearly and his uncoordinated feet gain their balance. Willy could now see a narrow corridor down the middle of the barn with a line of five stalls down the east wall, a tact room, and a feed area down the west. To his right, he spotted a stall that was larger and in the middle of the other four enclosures. It was the stall that opened to the outdoor pen. Glancing in every direction, he slowly made his way while looking for the best escape route once he opened the door. After arriving, he shined the flashlight beam at the ground inside the pen and was shocked at what he discovered.

"Heaven help us!" he whispered in disbelief.

Willy identified the carcass of a large hog lying on its side inside the pen. The sow had been slashed multiple times in its tough hide on the discernible side of its body and appeared to have a massive bite on its throat. Of even more concern, it appeared to be partially eaten. Within six feet of the carcass was a large pool of blood among the mire and waste on the ground. There was also a trail of blood from the pool to the doorway that opened to the outside pen. Willy surmised that the blood wasn't in the proximity of the dead hog which left only one explanation. It belonged to Cooter Jones.

"Joe, don't open the door. Get in here now," Willy yelled.

"Hang on. I'm on my way." Joe shouted back.

Within seconds, Willy could see the beam from Joe's flashlight shining left and right, and up and down, as though he was trying to gain his bearing. Willy flashed his own beam in Joe's direction, giving him a clear visual of where he was standing. After Joe arrived and investigated the pen, he was as stunned as Willy.

"Geez! What the hell happened here?" It was a rhetorical question, but Willy answered it anyway.

"There's something wrong with this picture. The wound on the hog's neck, and the way something has been eating its body, and the pool of blood—none of this looks right. At first, I thought that Mr. Jones had walked in the pen last night and was killed by the pigs. But if that's his blood over there, then it looks like he was assaulted here and dragged to the outside pen. I just wonder if he was still alive when the hogs started eating him." Willy's mind was all over the place, searching for a rational explanation as to what happened. "Had to be," he said.

"I don't know. Maybe. But regardless of how he died, we've still got to decide how we're going to preserve this evidence. We can't let the hogs in here, and we can't leave them in the pen either." Joe's face was filled with confusion.

"What about if we just turn 'em loose? Hell, they're mean enough to survive in the woods, so it's not like we'd be doing anything wrong," Willy said. "They'll probably hang around close by anyway."

"I don't know. If we let them out and they turn on us, or on anyone else who shows up from the M.E.'s office, we'll have a big problem."

"Hell, if they do that, we'll just shoot 'em," Willy offered his answer while raising the Colt from his side as though he were doing a show-and-tell demonstration.

"Willy, I just thought of something," Joe said. "Have you secured the barn already?" Joe asked.

"Oh, shit! No, I haven't." In all the ghastly haze, Joe and Willy had forgotten the first and foremost cardinal rule of law enforcement. Secure the scene and remove any potential threat.

"Let's search and clear the rest of the barn. Then we can move the hogs out of the pen," Joe said as he withdrew his service revolver from the holster in preparation to sweep the area.

"Let's do it," Willy agreed.

Thankfully, the search didn't expose a killer hiding in the shadows. Nor did the officers uncover any more dead bodies or pigs. The men did, however, discover a few more unexpected surprises. Cooter had a crystal meth lab in the feed area and had the initial makings of a crude moonshine still in the tack room. If nothing else, Cooter deserved credit for his attempt at diversifying and expanding his businesses, although it was unlikely that he had a protégé ready to step into his shoes and continue Cooter, Inc. Beyond the lab and whiskey still, the officers identified several asymmetrical boot-like prints on the ground in and around the pen that appeared too small for Cooter but could belong to his wife Alma. Regardless of the source, the men tiptoed around the area and cordoned off a large section of the barn with yellow crime scene tape to preserve the evidence. When finished with their inside work, they walked outside in time to greet two deputies who had arrived as on-scene support at the location. With removal of the hogs next in order, Joe and Willy were thrilled to see their fellow comrades.

"We got a call from dispatch that we were needed here. What's going on?" Deputy Sam Mizer asked while standing next to the new rookie on the force, Deputy Sheila Wilson. Joe and Willy filled in the two deputies about the crime scene and their plan of action. It was a frightful proposal that required courage and a belief that someone always had your back. Everyone agreed to their roles.

On any given day, police officers are asked to risk their lives by stopping an armed robbery, delivering a backseat baby from an expectant mother, performing CPR on a senior, or ending a domestic dispute among many other unbelievable and dangerous scenarios. But today, they had encountered a once in a lifetime situation they could tell their grandkids about. Today, Willy would straddle one of the wire partitions and open the gate allowing Joe to step inside the enclosure and herd the hogs out of the pen with a shovel he found in the barn. His service revolver would be on standby if needed. As for Sam and Sheila, they had drawn the short straws and were assigned the dangerous responsibility of clearing the hogs away from the pen after they were released. Both knew that they would need to cut down any animal that jeopardized their safety. Their Smith & Wesson Model 28's chambered .357 magnum cartridges and were powerful enough to handle that task, so they drew their weapons and stood anxiously nearby.

"Okay, Willy. Open the gate!" Joe shouted while lifting the shovel to his side.

It was chaos. Joe and the shovel were unnecessary. The pigs bolted from the pen like a herd of wild horses and headed straight for the two deputies positioned close-at-hand. Instantaneously, the booming sound from the firearm reverberated within the grove of trees that encircled the barn.

The ordeal was over. Two hogs outside the pen were on the ground and the remainder had scattered to the woods. Joe and Willy had pulled off their assignments without a hitch. But two boars had led the passel from the pen and charged Sam and Sheila with the malevolent intent of an axe murderer. Sam, a big man who was barrel chested with a brawler's reputation, tensed up in fear, unable to squeeze off a round. Sheila, a small woman who weighed 110 after Thanksgiving dinner, held steady and fired two perfect rounds into the brain cavities of the now dead pigs. Damn fine shooting, Joe and Willy thought. Damn fine courage too. Even Sam had to acknowledge the rookie's bravery, although he was ready with an excuse given his petrified behavior.

"Good work, Sheila. I would have fired my weapon, but I was afraid I might hit Willy over at the gate," Sam said as he gasped for air.

Everyone knew that Willy wasn't in the line of fire, but all held their tongues, knowing that they might panic the next time they were faced with a dangerous situation. No one was above their body's response when in peril. No one.

"Great job, everybody," Joe said, relieved that their duty to protect the corpse and any evidentiary materials had been successfully completed. And with that mission accomplished, he and Willy left the two deputies at the pen area, walked to their patrol cars, and radioed for assistance from the crime scene techs and the Medical Examiner, Ron Hinkle. Afterwards, both men met with Alma Jones and explained what the next steps would be regarding her husband's body and the investigation. Cooter's criminal character aside, it was a heartbreaking meeting.

At the end of the day, the only unanswered question was the location of the cookout. Someone had five hundred pounds of pork for a barbeque.

PART II

AN IRREVOCABLE CALL

Twenty-Three

A PLAN IS HATCHED

Belmont High School buzzed with anticipation. The football team was finishing a successful season and felt confident of making the playoffs. With the weekend in sight and Halloween only a few days away, the excitement felt as though it had a life of its own. The final classes of the day had just wrapped up with the ring of the 3:00 p.m. bell and students were flooding the hallways, talking about their plans while tucking away any unneeded books in their lockers. The girls were chit chatting about the upcoming football game, their Saturday night dates, and a trip to the department stores to freshen up their wardrobes. And the boys, not to be accused of having good sense, were fantasizing about street racing their muscle cars, how to get their hands on a fake I.D., and which cemetery or haunted house to visit with their girlfriends. The boys were certain that a spooky boneyard or scary ghost had to be part of the weekend entertainment. Not great judgment, but with all things considered, poor decision making wasn't exclusive to the boys. Both sexes were living mostly in oblivion, and both were susceptible to making questionable choices when being coaxed by or seeking approval from their young friends. And with the recent demise of Cooter Jones making the lead stories on all the local television stations, the students had a double dose of the heebie jeebies.

   Jamie was at her locker, stowing away all her books. She had completed her English and history assignments early, and the books would be no part of her Saturday and Sunday recreation. It was unfortunate, however, that her weekend entertainment included taking care of her little brother. Ann had agreed to sit with Mrs. Evans Friday and Saturday nights, so Jamie was the babysitter by default and any hope of seeing Lenny was impossible. Or so she thought.

Lenny, Lisa Foster, and Lisa's boyfriend, Chuckie Miller, were walking shoulder to shoulder down the hallway smiling ear to ear as though they couldn't wait to deliver the mysterious news. Jamie saw them coming and grinned as well, tickled by the mischievous looks on their faces. When they arrived at her locker, all three formed a half-circle and revealed their farfetched idea.

"Hey, what's going on?" Jamie asked, while looking for a clue to explain their impish behavior.

Lenny was the first to deliver their spiel. "Well, we're thinking about goin' up to that spooky house on Spencer Mountain on Saturday night. You know, the one where the witch lived before she was hung years ago?"

"You guys are nuts! That place is supposed to be haunted. Plus, it could be dangerous up there, especially with all the murders around that area. Besides, I have to keep Tommy Saturday night." Jamie rejected their proposal, although it was tempting. She grew up with a vivid imagination and was drawn to the stimulation and trepidation of anything frightful. Maybe it was the rush caused by the adrenalin skyrocketing through her body, or maybe the arousal from the chemicals that affected her brain. Regardless of the reason, it just seemed natural. After all, fear was as old as life on earth.

"You can bring Tommy with us," Lenny reassured.

"Yeah, you can bring him along," Chuckie piped in.

"Come on, Jamie. It'll be fun. We can go by the B&W when we get back and get Tommy a shake or a hamburger or something. He'll have a good time. I promise," Lenny begged.

"Yeah, come on, Jamie. It'll be our Halloween adventure. It'll be fun!" Lisa insisted.

Jamie couldn't resist the offer. Tommy had never been to anyplace like the B&W, and Lenny's proffer to buy him a shake and burger was too enticing to turn down. She knew her little brother would jump at the opportunity. "Okay, we'll go. But you'll have to pick us up. Momma's Corvair is broken down and she's using the Rambler."

"No problem," Lenny answered. "We can take my Nova. You and me in the front, and Chuckie and Lisa can sit in the back with Tommy."

"All right. Can you pick us up around seven o'clock?" Jamie asked.

"We'll be there," Lenny confirmed the plan with Chuckie and Lisa, and the three friends left Jamie at her locker, wondering how they had convinced her to do such an irrational thing. Minutes later, she was on her way to pick up Tommy at Belmont Elementary.

Jamie arrived late to the elementary school. She found Tommy sitting on the curb with his elbows resting on his knees and his head supported by his hands. He also had a big scowl on his face. He looked miffed for certain, annoyed at having to wait. After Jamie stopped the Rambler, Tommy got in and slammed the door in frustration. It had been a rough day for the six-year-old and his anger was the climax of many things, not just her late arrival. His class had a show-and-tell session earlier in the day when the kids talked about their fathers and what they did for a living. He felt embarrassed when his turn arrived. How could he talk about his father when he'd never known or seen him? Tommy was embarrassed standing in front of his classmates, so he made up a story about his daddy being a construction worker, making lots of money by building all kinds of pretty houses. He felt terrible about the lie but wanted to avoid the shame of telling the truth.

Jamie's Rambler, which sounded like a sewing machine on wheels, was another source of Tommy's embarrassment. Monday through Friday, his friends were greeted by moms driving shiny Buicks and Chevys while Jamie arrived with gears grinding, wheel bearings crunching, and a loud backfire when she turned off the engine. Tommy's buddies teased and ribbed him every day when they heard the high-pitched squeal and weird noises coming from his sister's car a block away. "Here comes Tommy's jalopy," they said. "Cover your ears, the blue clunker is around the corner," they joked. Tommy's immature schoolmates may have been unable to appreciate his feelings, but it was still cruel and unfeeling.

"Hey, hey!" Jamie said with admonition. "Why are you so mad?"

"Why are you so late?" Tommy retorted with the same sharp wit that his sister possessed.

"Well, I'm sorry. I was talking with Lenny about taking you with us on a fun trip Saturday night and then going by the B&W for burgers and shakes. But if you're so mad about me being late, maybe we should tell Lenny we can't go, and we'll just stay at home." Her dangling carrot was an offer he couldn't refuse. It took milliseconds for Tommy to bite and replace indignation with exhilaration.

"Can I get a hot dog instead of a hamburger? And I want a chocolate shake!" Tommy had heard all about the B&W and squirmed in the car seat with wide-eyed excitement.

"Yes! You can have a hotdog. And some fries too if you want them." Jamie smiled, a little surprised that Tommy had not asked any questions about their trip. Needless to say, when good things were out of reach, something as simple as a hot dog could seem like an extravagance.

With the mood now bright and sunny, the siblings kept to their after-school tradition with Jamie cranking up the Lear Jet with a Beach Boys cassette. An eight-track tape that included Tommy's favorite song...*Good Vibrations*. Both joined in the chorus, singing so loud you couldn't hear the whine of the engine.

Little did they know, the trip to Spencer Mountain would fill them with anything but good vibes.

Twenty-Four

A WITCH'S BREW

The little man stood outside in the nippy air, listening for a sign, knowing that he would hear it before he saw it. He tightened his belt another notch to hold up his oversized pants, and again, stared down Bullfrog Lane into the darkness. And then he heard the loud rumble and saw a flash of Granada Gold. Without a doubt, it was a familiar two door coupe, a Chevy II Nova SS. It was Lenny. Quickly hitching his jeans, he jerked the door open, ran inside the mobile home and summoned his sister.

"Jamie! Lenny's here!" Tommy cupped his hands around his mouth and yelled.

"All right. All right. I hear you. I'll be right out," Jamie responded.

"I'll be outside!" he shouted, then turned and raced out the door.

Tommy had been looking forward to the evening and was as enthusiastic as a frisky puppy. He was short of breath, bouncing up and down and waving his arms skyward. It appeared as though he was guiding a Boeing 727 into a terminal gate instead of Lenny's Nova up the gravel driveway. Lenny, of course, saw him and honked his horn in response to the little boy's excitement.

"Tommy looks like he's about to jump out of his pants!" Lenny said while pushing the car horn one last time.

"Yeah, he's really excited." Lisa said as she looked out the front windshield.

Chuckie was in the back and had to lean forward over the console between the bucket seats to gain a better view. "Oh man, you're right. He is about to jump out of his pants."

Jamie heard the commotion from her bedroom, and not wanting anyone to come inside and see their slum-like living quarters, she snatched her blue jean jacket and headed outside to greet her raucous friends. Lenny was the first out of the car, and like a man of honor, he held the door open while helping Lisa exit the tight quarters in the passenger front seat. Tall and slender much like her mother, Lisa needed help and appreciated the good manners and gentility. Once out, she started giggling, displaying her wolf-ears headband, a nose covered in black makeup, and her furry tail. Her werewolf act included making scary hand gestures at Jamie and Tommy, showing off her retractable canine fangs, and growling as though she was about to attack her innocent prey. With eyes fixed on Lisa, Tommy stood motionless while taking in the monster show, not knowing whether to laugh or run.

"It's okay, Tommy," Jamie said as Tommy looked to her for reassurance. "It's just a Halloween costume." Her little brother slid behind her legs just to be sure.

Chuckie, sitting in the back of the car, tilted the front bucket seat forward and struggled to climb out. His six-foot three-inch frame combined with the black eye patch he was wearing made it difficult to get out of the coupe's narrow back seat. Naturally, he had no say regarding his tall frame, but his Halloween costume was a different matter. The eye patch was a paltry attempt at pulling together a pirate costume, and it hindered his ability to clearly see. He grabbed the passenger front door to keep his balance and finally stepped onto terra firma. Given Chuckie's vanity, no one was surprised at his meager outfit. He thought of himself as a dashing swashbuckler whose face was crafted by the gods and should never be completely covered. His fastback Mustang, star quarterback position, and his back-to-back peer-elected Big Man on Campus role made it easy to get a head so big a pirate bandana wouldn't fit around it. All his self-conceit aside, he was a handsome young man with a magnetic personality. His glorious raven hair, according to Chuckie, and lively dark eyes were in stark contrast to Lisa's blonde tresses and baby blues. They would have been a convincing example of "opposites attract" were it not for their on-again, off-again relationship.

"Damn, Roscoe! You're going to have to trade the Nova in for a four-door if you want me to ride in the back seat again." Chuckie said while laughing at his lame attempt to get out of the car.

"Your Mustang has less room than my car. Besides, you had better get used to it; you and Lisa are going to have to squeeze in the back seat with Tommy until we get back to Belmont," Lenny retorted.

Lenny had never played high school sports and had never been chosen BMOC, but he was as popular as Chuckie. It was hard to explain given how the jocks were put on a pedestal, but the other kids were as attracted to him as bees to honey. Yes, he had the fastest car in the school, and his good looks played a role, but his classmates would have liked him even if he looked like Quasimodo, partly because he had a soft heart for others. But, without a doubt, his wonderful sense of humor was the main draw. He loved joking around with everyone, but he and Chuckie took it to another level. They loved ribbing each other as much as Abbott and Costello. So much so, they were often distracted by their foolishness.

"Don't worry. We'll have plenty of room with Lisa sitting on my lap," Chuckie grinned while slapping Lenny's palm in a high five.

"Yeah, well, Lisa may have something to say about that." Lenny laughed.

Jamie was glad that Lenny decided not to dress for Halloween. Chuckie's and Lisa's costumes were unexpected, and still wanting to fit in, she didn't want to be the one who spoiled the party. She was relieved that no one gave it a second thought. The gang piled in the car with Tommy sitting in between Chuckie and Lisa in the back seat while Lenny was at the wheel with Jamie riding shotgun. Tommy was still feeling a little apprehensive with a werewolf sitting at his side, so Lisa helped soothe his fears by treating him like he was her baby brother. And Chuckie, well he treated Tommy like his little brother as well. He won his favor not with affection, but with a fully loaded Supreme water pistol he pulled from the inside pocket of his windbreaker. He handed the loaded squirt gun to Tommy with one hand, and with the other, placed his index finger to his lips making a shush gesture. Leaning over, he whispered in Tommy's ear, instructing him to put the toy in the waistband of his pants and to promise to keep it a secret from the others. Chuckie had pilfered the water gun from his own six-year-old brother, knowing it would keep Tommy entertained until they could make it back to the B&W in Belmont. Jamie and Lisa were too busy talking about the new, good looking English teacher to notice the shenanigans. Once the Chevy was heading north on Highway 29, the conversation turned to their destination on Spencer Mountain.

"Okay, who has directions to this place? This was the lame brain idea of the three of you, wasn't it?" Jamie asked jokingly.

"Well, it was actually mine," Lisa answered. "We need a little excitement in our lives every now and then. I know how to get us there. And Chuckie and Lenny brought flashlights for us to use when we get to the house."

"Oh, shit," Lenny and Chuckie said simultaneously.

"Don't tell me you guys forgot to bring flashlights?" Jamie asked in disbelief.

Jamie's question triggered the finger pointing between Abbott and Costello. "Roscoe was supposed to bring flashlights for everybody!" Chuckie said, placing the blame on his friend.

"I was? You said your dad had enough lights for all of us," Lenny countered.

"That's just great!" Jamie exclaimed. "We may as well turn around and go back."

"No, no. I've got a big flashlight in the trunk of the car we can use. We can't turn back now," Lenny pleaded.

"All right. But I'm still not comfortable with only one flashlight," Jamie said in a loud voice. Even though she had given in to her cajoling friends, her little brother was anything but comfortable with their three-person tete-a-tete. Tommy was frightened by his sister's high-spirited tone and became as silent as a graveyard.

"Woo-hoo!" Chuckie exclaimed. "This is going to be awesome!"

Lenny found a station on the car's radio that played popular music and the mood turned from apprehension to exuberance. The four teenagers listened to their favorite songs and had a sing-along when WZOK played *The Monster Mash*. It was a pitiful, albeit fun, quartet. Lisa had the most atrocious voice of the bunch and sang the loudest. A hound baying at the moon was more on-key than her tone-deaf warbling. Thankfully, she occasionally stopped to give Lenny traveling instructions, and to spin a tale or two about the hags that lived in the haunted house going back for generations. Lenny, Jamie, and Chuckie listened to the hair-raising stories about witches who practiced black magic and made pacts with the Devil to eliminate their foes by resurrecting the unliving. Then the teens made jokes about bringing back the dead and talked with bravado of how they would burn any witch at the stake that showed up at the empty house. Meanwhile, Tommy remained in his shell of silence.

Lenny's final turn was on a dirt road that furrowed through a forest of oaks, American chestnut, and sugar maples. A mix of rhododendron and mountain laurel rounded out the low-level vegetation that carried on for two miles down the roadway. But then for their final mile, the majestic trees and beautiful plants disappeared, leaving only an odd brew of baneberry, jimson weed, and hemlock among some scattered pines. It was as though the hearty vegetation that was common to these hillsides had been eradicated by some strange disease and was somehow replaced by an anemic cast of vines and weeds. It was dark and the teenagers never noticed the change in plant life, but the singing did stop three miles down the single-lane road when they realized that the closest sign of civilization was in the rear-view mirror. And in the darkness, they did take notice of a heavy mist that seemed to appear from nowhere. The soupy fog and waning moonlight added a little ghostly drama to a bold nighttime plan that was cooked up when the sun was high, and the sky was blue.

"Hey, guys. Where the heck did all this fog come from?" Jamie anxiously asked. Even though she relished the thrill of being frightened, something in her core told her that this trip was a terrible mistake.

"We're up pretty high in elevation, you know, so it's not uncommon to see it up here," Lisa answered with the confidence of a schoolteacher.

"It makes it really spooooooky! Doesn't it?" Chuckie was trying to be funny, so his cohort chimed in with his own comedic response.

"Yeah, maybe we'll get lucky and find a cemetery with a few ghosts hanging around!" Lenny said in his best Dracula-like voice.

"Look! Just ahead. It's the house. Can you see it, Lenny?" Jamie asked while pointing her index finger at the windshield.

"Yeah, I can see it. I'm going to park over by that tree that's not far from the house," he answered. "It looks like it's an easy walk from there."

Sometimes people find more courage and engage in riskier behavior when surrounded by friends as opposed to standing alone. This was a prime example of that kind of behavior. They had landed in a place of superstitions, lost souls, and the Devil himself, and their brave frivolity had abruptly ended. But they pushed ahead with their adventure just the same. Lenny parked the Nova next to one of the only two trees on the barren property. Their eyes grew wide, and their mouths turned dry as they stepped out of the car to size-up the tree and survey their surroundings. Everyone but Tommy. He refused to depart from the safety of Lenny's Nova, so Jamie let him remain in the back seat with his eyes closed and water pistol drawn, hoping the monster would pass him by.

The old, abandoned house was a remnant of what it once was. What wasn't expected was its frightening appearance, considerable size, and the rancid odor that drifted from the gaping holes in its timberwork. It was the smell of damp dirt and death as if the house had risen from a freshly dug grave. And the large homestead, a long-ago mansion, seemed out of place in the poverty-stricken backwoods on Spencer Mountain. Even in the dense fog, the luminescence of the moon exposed a gray two-story edifice that had a rust-eaten gable metal roof, and a jutting balcony covered in vines attached to the front of the house. The odd parapet was supported by six columns and spanned about one-third of the house. It was located outside the upstairs sitting room and, most likely, served as a perch for the wicked to cast their hexes and watch over the evil spirits they conjured from the unholy ground below. Although not remarkable, the glass panes were missing in most of the windows, and the open casements were partially covered with rotten boards. As for the remaining span of the dilapidated structure, it was hidden under a thick network of snake-like vines save an outside batten door to the cellar. The ground level entryway to the below-ground room stood out among the undergrowth, free of any covering as though it was a thing, a badness, a beast inviting an unsuspecting victim into its lair. The teenagers couldn't have described a creepier house in a school essay.

"Holy crap, do we really want to do this?" Jamie asked with a look of incredulity.

"We've driven all this way. We may as well go inside and have a look around," Lenny answered as he walked to the back of the car, opened the trunk and pulled out a Ray-O-Vac three battery flashlight.

"Yeah, Jamie. It won't take us long to check it out," Lisa said. "Come on. Let's go inside."

"Are you a fraidy cat?" Chuckie asked while sticking out his tongue, grabbing his throat with both hands, and pretending to strangle himself.

"Damn straight I'm afraid. Forget about ghosts inside—just think how dangerous the flooring and stairs are in that place. What happens if one of us falls through some rotten boards and gets hurt? We're a long way from the hospital in Belmont," Jamie said adamantly.

"Come on, Jamie. You can stay next to me with the flashlight. I'll make sure it's safe wherever we walk inside." Lenny reached down, gripped Jamie's hand, and gently pulled her toward the house.

So, the adventure began. Lenny led the way, Jamie next, then Lisa, and Chuckie in the rear apart from the pirate eye patch he had stuffed in his pocket. Their jitters grew worse before they even entered the old house as the path took them beside an ancient graveyard that was marked by a scraggly willow tree that appeared to be made of stone. Unknown to the teenagers, burying your kin next to a willow was a common practice started centuries ago and the graves would have been dismissed as unremarkable had one gravesite not been so different. The tall weeds that covered the graveyard were missing from this site. And with no headstone pinpointing the tomb, the only sign that a grave existed was the freshly disturbed earth that was piled about two feet above the ground. It was impossible, but it seemed as though someone had recently been laid to rest. Or raised from the dead!

"Look!" Lenny said while aiming the flashlight beam through the fog at the ground. "It looks like someone has been digging up that grave."

"I don't like this. We need to go back to the car and leave," Jamie's voice was filled with apprehension.

"Come on, Jamie. We don't even know if that's a grave. Besides, we're almost to the front door. Let's just go inside, take a quick look around, and leave," Lisa begged.

"I don't know. There's something wrong with this place. It feels evil to me." Jamie stopped in her tracks and made a half-turn, pulling Lenny toward the Nova.

"Don't worry. I've got your back and Roscoe will be in front and won't let anything get to you. We'll be in and out really fast," Chuckie said as he moved to block her pathway to the car.

It was against Jamie's nature to take this kind of risk, especially with her little brother in the car. But her need to fit in was still in play, and she acquiesced to her friends. "All right, but just for a few minutes," Jamie said.

Speaking no words, the four explorers walked up the wobbly steps to the front porch. The veranda was uncovered other than the area below the unusual balcony, and the evenly spaced windows on either side of the front door were shuttered, preventing a look inside for any monsters. As the kids inched forward in an old man's shuffle, the sound of the rickety planks provided the first sign that the house was somehow alive, filled with a sinister spirit that was warning them to stay away. Filled with stupid confidence, they ignored the message and crept toward the front door, bumping into each other in an out-of-sync conga line.

"Damn, Chuckie. You're going to knock me down if you don't stop running in to me," Lisa complained.

"Well, you keep starting and stopping like you can't make up your mind. It feels like I'm doing a football drill," Chuckie fired back.

"I'm just following Jamie and Lenny! Just back off a little bit and give me some space!" Lisa fired right back with an annoyed look on her face.

Lenny ignored them, released Jamie's hand, and pushed the creaking door open. The cobwebs attached at the entryway pulled apart, causing an explosion of dust that had been accumulating over the years. Shining the flashlight into the entrance hall provided little help given the airborne dirt and the pitch darkness. Just the same, Lenny fanned the light in all directions making sure there was no human being, nor some nameless thing, lurking inside waiting to ambush his friends. Given the recent murders and the remoteness of the house, he couldn't help but entertain a terrible thought about the four of them being killed without the world knowing. He quickly dismissed the notion and reassuringly clasped Jamie's hand again. And then, he led everyone through the front doorway and down the narrow passage.

It was no surprise that Chuckie was the first who felt unworried enough to regain his humor. He just couldn't help it. He wanted to unleash a ghost so as they tiptoed ahead, making their way to the vacant living area, he leaned forward and blew a puff of breath on the back of his unsuspecting girlfriend's neck. Lisa reacted with a scream and a clumsy jump into Jamie that almost knocked her off her feet.

"Damn you, Chuckie! You scared the crap outta me," Lisa yelled and swatted Chuckie on his shoulder. The place was frightening enough without his ghostly comedy act.

Chuckie couldn't hold back the laughter, nor his personalized version of *The Monster Mash* to put an accent on his antics. "I did the monster mash. I was a graveyard smash," he sang with outstretched ghoulish arms.

"I'll monster mash your ass if you do that again!" Lisa threatened.

"What did he do?" Jamie asked, regaining her balance while sounding breathy.

"He blew on the back of my neck when I wasn't looking," Lisa answered, and then whispered to herself about how she would get even with him for his bone-chilling hoax.

Lenny was still focused on leading the way and ignored the commotion between Lisa and Chuckie. He stepped from the foyer into the large formal parlor which was, much like the entire main level, void of any furniture or personal belongings of any kind. It wasn't void, however, of the creatures that permanently lived there. Rats. They were everywhere. Lenny was shocked by the rapid movement on the floor. Squeaking, skittering, and scattering in every direction, trying to avoid the intruders and the beam from Lenny's flashlight. Lenny knew everyone would freak out if they could see the rodents, so he raised the light to eye-level and moved it back and forth which exposed another unsettling view. The four walls that surrounded them were covered with paint cracks and flakes caused by long-standing time and moisture. And under the artificial light it was spooky, as though the house was alive and shedding its skin. No, this wasn't a safe house in a gated community where the kids could be enjoying the warmth of the fireplace and drinking hot cocoa. This wasn't even a make-believe haunted house at the county fair. This place was evil, and it was real.

"Look," Jamie softly said. "Shine the flashlight above the fireplace over there, Lenny. I thought I saw something."

"Over on that wall?" Lenny asked while aiming the light in the direction Jamie was pointing.

"Yeah, that's it. Shine it above the fireplace," she said.

Jamie had spotted a timeworn portrait mounted above the fireplace mantel. Even though the framed oil painting was covered in dust and cobwebs, the image of an old matriarchal woman was visible when Lenny held the light steady so everyone could see. Half of the woman's slender face was as dark as the quilted surcoat she was wearing. It looked like an artist's rendition of someone trying to hide in the shadows. The side of her face that was visible was wizened with pitted skin, an upturned nose, and slits for lips. Her corpse-like complexion appeared to be splotched with liver spots, although the odd patches were probably caused by the painting becoming brittle and deteriorating over time. As for her snow-white hair, it seemed somewhat ordinary. It was neatly brushed back on the top of her head, yet it hung like broken straw on the sides of her face. But the dark cold eyes, they were anything but ordinary. Unkind and savage with a scarlet tint, she seemed to be the one watching, transfixed on what the kids were doing in her home.

"Do you think that's the witch that was killed here?" Lisa asked.

In unison, Lisa and Lenny answered, "Yeah!" The pointy hat, broom and black cat may have been missing, but they could see the wickedness in her face and feel the evil all the way down to their jittery feet.

"It has to be her," Jamie sounded sure of her answer. Whatever morbid curiosity she once had was gone. "I think we need to leave. Now!"

"Let's take a look upstairs first, Jamie. It won't take but a few minutes and then we can leave," Chuckie was feeling more and more emboldened with every passing minute and didn't give the painting a second thought. Having seen no apparitions, he was growing cocky, thinking about summoning another would-be zombie named Charles "Chuckie" Miller to scare his companions.

"All right. Let's hurry up. I don't like Tommy being in the car by himself." This time, Jamie grabbed Lenny's hand and pulled him and the flashlight up the creaking stairs. Lisa followed with Chuckie close behind, reaching upward, tickling her ribs with his fingertips. Her defensive reflex was to take a swat at his own flanks.

"Dammit, Chuckie. Stop! I don't like you aggravating me while we're in this house. I'm scared shitless enough without you doing stuff like that." Lisa made her point loud and clear and Chuckie backed off, pondering how he could isolate Lenny and, perhaps, play a prank on him.

The hall at the top of the grand stairway ran in a straight line with rooms attached like fingers on either side of the corridor. The first room they entered was the one on the right, the sitting room with the French doors that opened to the exterior balcony on the front of the house. Within seconds after going in, Lenny scanned the room with the spotlight and caught a glimpse of an old handmade rocking chair circa late 1890. It would have been ignored were it not positioned in the middle of the room. But more aberrant than its location was how the rocker was free of any dust and cobwebs. It was as though it was still being used.

"Watch out for the rocking chair," Lenny warned. "Everybody stop for a minute and let's get our bearings."

There was something else out of place in the room. It was an unnatural chill that wasn't present downstairs. Everyone noticed the change in temperature, but no one wanted to bring it up, thinking that ignoring the cold would make it not so. What couldn't be disregarded was the deep sound that echoed from below.

THUMP!

"What the hell was that?" Lisa nervously asked.

"It sounded like it came from below the house, down in the cellar maybe," Lenny answered.

"Okay, that's it. I'm leaving," Jamie said as she tugged on Lenny's hand.

"All right, all right. We'll go," Lenny agreed. "Lisa, where's Chuckie?"

"I think he's out on the balcony," Lisa answered.

"Okay. Jamie, you and Lisa start heading back to the car. I'll go get Chuckie and we'll be right behind you." Lenny handed Jamie the flashlight and headed for the double doors.

Sometimes plans come together, sometimes they don't. Chuckie had smuggled in a *Creature from the Black Lagoon* rubber mask in his jacket and had been waiting all evening for the right opportunity to use it. The balcony was the perfect movie set. He would don the mask and lie in wait until someone stepped outside, and then he would leap from the dark, growling and aggressively charging at his unwary patsy. It was a fine plan until he saw something in the darkness that stopped him dead in his tracks. Peering over the waist-high rail, in the distance he caught sight of a pair of glowing red eyes near the apple tree where the Nova was parked. He did a double take to be sure his mind wasn't playing tricks on him. It wasn't. His sanity was confirmed when the terrifying eyes turned to the balcony to meet his own. If a heart could skip a beat, his did. If someone could be overwhelmed in fear, he was—especially when Lenny walked up behind him, touched his shoulder, and asked what was holding his attention.

"Damn, Roscoe, don't scare me like that!" Chuckie's body jerked and his teeth clenched from the shock.

"We're leaving. Jamie and Lisa are waiting on us," Lenny pulled at Chuckie's bicep, but he refused to budge.

"Wait. Wait a minute! Look over at the tree next to the car," he said while pointing in the same direction. "Do you see the pair of eyes staring at us?"

At first, Lenny thought Chuckie was setting him up for another prank. But when he spotted the searing eyes, he felt the same initial shock as his good friend. And when he heard the muffled screams coming from inside his Chevy II, his body felt out of control as though he had no say in his own actions.

"Tommy," Lenny whispered. He heard the cry for help again. "TOMMY!" Lenny screamed.

Jamie and Lisa heard the same shrieks and had scrambled out the front door and were on the front porch when Chuckie blew by, skipping the porch steps by leaping to the ground, running like he was being chased by an angry linebacker. Lenny didn't possess Chuckie's athleticism, but a huge flush of adrenaline gave him speed enough to stay on his coattails. When the boys arrived at the car, Chuckie yanked open the driver side door and folded the bucket seat forward as Lenny reached inside and pulled the cowering boy from the back seat. Jamie appeared in seconds and wasted no time in grabbing her trembling brother, hugging him, and whispering reassuring words to calm his fears. "It's okay. It's okay, Tommy. Everything's okay. We're here. Nothing is going to happen to you," she whispered.

"What's wrong? What happened?" Chuckie asked.

"There was someone looking in the car, and they knocked on the window," he answered as he locked his legs around his sister's waist.

"Who was it? What did they look like?" Lenny asked the open-ended question knowing that he and Chuckie had seen something from the balcony that couldn't be explained by a rational mind.

"Did you get a good look at them?" Jamie frantically implored, hoping to understand what had taken place.

"It looked like an ole woman with lights in her eyes. She kept smiling at me. And she had real crooked teeth," Tommy answered. "I shot at her with the water gun Chuckie gave me." Tommy was so petrified he forgot about his promise to keep the toy a secret.

"Water gun?" Jamie asked with a quizzical expression on her face.

"Oh yeah, I gave him a squirt gun for Halloween in case he wanted to dress up like a cowboy," Chuckie offered up his defense, and a jury of his peers would have found him innocent of any wrongdoing. But not Lenny. He had noticed that the Nova's side window and inside door panel were drenched with water and was not amused by Chuckie's mischievous behavior. But given the tense circumstances, he remained quiet to avoid making matters worse.

"All right, everything's okay, but we need to leave now!" Jamie took charge. "Chuckie, you ride in the front with Lenny. Lisa, and I will ride in the back with Tommy."

In fast order, everyone loaded into the car, ready to leave until Lenny turned the ignition key and the car refused to respond. "What the heck is going on? The car won't start," he said.

"Oh, crap. This is just what we need! Give me the flashlight and I'll pop the hood and check the battery connections. Just keep trying to crank it, Roscoe," Chuckie's voice sounded urgent, knowing that he had seen the same monster as Tommy and Lenny.

A twist of the cable on the battery post solved the problem. Chuckie slammed the hood and jumped back in the front seat just as Lenny shifted the transmission into first gear and jammed the gas pedal to the floorboard. The V8 engine roared, causing the Nova to do an about-face while slinging a wave of dirt and rocks in every direction. Everyone was relieved to get away and, within minutes, felt at ease enough to talk when they viewed the first house that wasn't barren and dark. Chuckie began the conversation by providing details on what he and Lenny had seen from the balcony. At the time it happened, it seemed like madness. But in the safety of the car, doubts began to surface about all the abnormal phenomena. Perhaps the combination of the moonlight and fog created the illusion of a pair of eyes from the balcony, perhaps the sound from the cellar was just a tumbledown timber in a crumbling house, and the disturbed earth at the gravesite, well that could have been caused by a host of wild animals searching for food. All the hysteria was caused by a collection of immature minds that allowed their imaginations to spiral out of control. After all, when reasoned thinking was applied to the circumstances, there were explanations for everything, and those explanations would have made sense were it not for Tommy. As his lip quivered, he described with perfect clarity the woman in the painting over the mantel. Exactly, down to a recounting of her pitted skin, dark reddish eyes, and snow-white hair. She was the one peering into the car.

"Tommy didn't make up what he saw. He was terrified. My brother doesn't lie about stuff like that," Jamie was angry that the others were wishing away what she regarded as truth. "Do you all think he made that stuff up? Do you, Lenny?"

Regardless of what they really thought, no one was going to challenge a furious big sister. Especially Lenny. "No, of course he didn't make it up. Chuckie and I saw something near the car when we were on the balcony. And we all heard Tommy screaming," Lenny's answer was the measured response of someone who wanted to remain in his girlfriend's good graces.

"Who knows how long this is going to affect him." Jamie's mind was taking her down the path of long-term trauma for her brother and the need for childhood counseling. And so, for the next five miles the car fell deathly silent, as quiet as a tomb, until the so-called traumatized little boy decided to speak.

"How much longer before we get to the B&W?" Tommy asked with anticipation and a big smile, "I want to get a chocolate shake with my hotdog."

All it took was a hungry first grader to end the frightful mood and bring the house down. The car exploded with laughter!

Twenty-Five

MIDWAY MAGIC

It had been a ho-hum week at school other than word getting around about their frightful trip to Spencer Mountain. Chuckie wasted no time in telling everyone about his chivalry, his stalwart resolve inside the haunted house when confronted by the evil witch, the sorceress that threatened to take his friends' lives. To say he embellished their adventure was a gross understatement. His version of the story was relatively truthful when told on Monday. But at some point in time the truth seemed too boring, so by Friday, the story had morphed into an out of this world exaggeration of his Don Quixote heroism. In only five days, Chuckie's role evolved from a mere balcony sighting of a faraway specter, to battling hand-to-hand with the evil monster in the witch's castle. Lenny, aka Sancho, just laughed every time he heard the latest version. Being a good squire, he chalked up the hyperbole as the school's grapevine on steroids, not his buddy's need for attention.

Earlier in the week, Lenny had asked Jamie on a date to the county fair near the Charlotte Motor Speedway. Since they both were working at the Food Stop on Saturday, they agreed to drive over after work to enjoy the once-a-year event. Lenny was on his way to his biology class when he saw Jamie pulling a book from her locker. He stopped to make sure they were still on for the weekend.

"Hey," Lenny said. "You headed to your English class?"

"Yeah, we've got a pop quiz on *To Kill a Mockingbird*," Jamie answered.

"How do you know about the test if it's a pop quiz?" Lenny asked.

"I don't know. I just always have a strong feeling a few days before a teacher surprises the class."

"Are you gonna ace it?" Lenny knew the answer to his question without asking. This wasn't the first time she had predicted exams that were given without notice. Besides that, he was aware that she had a restless mind and felt the need to assign each moment of the day a specific task and was certain she had read the novel and was prepared even without the clairvoyance of a fortune teller.

"I loved the book and did some research at the library, so I think I'm ready," she smiled.

"On another subject, are we still on for tomorrow night?"

"Yes, we are! I'm looking forward to it. But I need to ask you about something else."

"What's that?" Lenny asked.

"I hate to ask you this, but something's wrong with Momma's Corvair. Sometimes it cranks, sometimes it doesn't. Do you think maybe you and Johnny could take a look at it whenever you have a little spare time?" Jamie angled her face down while giving Lenny an upward glance with her soft brown eyes. Her sad puppy dog look worked.

"Sure, we can take a look at it. I'll check with Johnny to see if we can come by Sunday morning. Maybe we can go fishing after we fix it. Johnny's been dying to go back and fish anyway," Lenny had the perfect answer.

"Thanks, Lenny. You're awesome to help us out like that. I'll see you at the store in the morning," she said.

******

Wanting the kids to look professional, Mr. Morton recently instituted a new company dress code. All employees had to wear uniforms consisting of collared white shirts and clip-on green bow ties. The teenagers hated the new rules and teased each other about working a second job scooping ice-cream at Baskin-Robbins. Fortunately, the boss wasn't picky about their lower extremities and allowed them to sport whatever britches they happened to be wearing that day. The Food Stop was competing with a newly opened grocery store in Belmont, and Mr. Morton was looking for a competitive edge. He even had a coin-operated kiddie ride installed near the store's entrance. After all, what kid wouldn't love a palomino named Trigger. These were big moves for a man who hated change, but all in all, his new strategy seemed to be working. The store was having an unusually busy Saturday which meant lots of tips for Jamie and Lenny, but only if the parents could keep their kids off the mechanical horse. Even with the delays, by closing time, Jamie's and Lenny's pockets were filled with change from hustling groceries from the checkout lines to the customers' cars. Lenny held on to most of his quarters instead of converting them to bills, not because he wanted to add them to some esoteric coin collection. No, he was motivated by something much less arcane than that. He merely wanted the quarters for playing games at the county fair and, hopefully, winning a stuffed animal for his girlfriend. As for Jamie, she swapped her coins for bills with pictures of George Washington and Abraham Lincoln. Ann had not been paid for two weeks and money was tight, and the cash was needed to help buy food and pay the electric bill. Since it was customary for the guy to pick up the check on a date, she knew her money would not be needed for the evening's activities anyway. After cashing out, the teenagers heard Mr. Morton announce the store's closing on the PA system, and employees scurried to the restrooms to change their clothes. Lenny ditched his uniform for a cotton shirt and N.C. State sweatshirt, while Jamie opted for the same white top and blue jean jacket she had worn on many other occasions. Both met at the store's entrance as Coach was about to lock the doors.

"See you, Coach," they said simultaneously as they shimmied through the sliding double doors.

"You two be careful and enjoy the fair," he responded with a big smile. "And don't eat too much cotton candy!"

Jamie had agreed to leave the Rambler at the grocery store and ride with Lenny for the twenty-six-mile jaunt to the fairgrounds. All in all, however, the trip seemed much shorter than the thirty minutes it took to get there. Perhaps the boisterous laughter and terrible harmonies had a lot to do with the brevity. It was their cringeworthy rendition singing backup for *Hit the Road Jack* that caused most of the hilarity. Thank heaven *Ray Charles and The Raelettes* weren't around to hear the caterwauling couple. Fortunately, the singing stopped when they caught sight of the bright carnival lights penetrating the dark night sky.

Upon entering the parking area near the speedway, Lenny circled the lot like a hungry shark until he found an end space with plenty of room. As any car aficionado would expect, he was strategic about where he parked the Nova. You must be if you want to keep your baby free of scratches and door dings. Jamie was amused, knowing that she would have squeezed her Rambler in between two Mac trucks if she could find a space near the entrance. After turning off the ignition switch, Lenny got out, opened the door for Jamie, and clutched her hand for the walk to the ticket office. This was not Lenny's first visit to a county fair. He had taken Della the prior two years and knew the best routine for entertaining and for smooching. He already had their evening planned out in his mind. Buying a stack of tickets for the rides was first on the agenda. Always do the ups and downs and spinning around before stomachs were filled with hot dogs and chicken bites. The ride is called whirl-and-hurl for a reason. Next came the deep fried anything you want to eat from the concession trailers. And finally, be the hero by winning a stuffed animal for your girlfriend by besting the games rigged in favor of the seedy carnies. And one postscript: get a big kiss for being the best boyfriend on the planet.

This was Jamie's first time experiencing a midway and the scene seemed surreal, almost like a parallel world filled with nothing but happy people. And enjoying that happy world with Lenny made it even better. She slowed their pace while letting the sights, smells, and sounds soak her overwhelmed senses. The colorful lights that seemed to stretch forever dazzled her eyes. The sounds of the calliope music, animated barkers and screaming kids on the amusement rides tickled her ears. The heat from the huge fryers in the food trailers warmed her body as they walked by. And the smell of the savory corn dogs and pretzels was so thick it seemed like you could reach out and touch it. It was magical. Jamie couldn't wait to experience even more, so she reached down, grabbed Lenny's hand, and pulled him down the midway. Along the way, neither teenager heard the loud barker wanting to guess their age for a dollar to win a rinky-dink prize, nor any of the other colorful raconteurs standing in front of the freak shows selling a view of the bearded lady, tallest man, or werewolf boy. All interesting biological peculiarities, but Lenny and Jamie had something else in mind. He had twenty tickets in hand, and they were talking about making a mental list of their top ten rides. And having attended this same fair since he was a little boy, Lenny was the perfect tour guide.

"Okay. What do you think about The Big Dipper roller coaster first, and then the Dodgem bumper cars? And then we'll do the Paratrooper, Tilt-A-Whirl, and The Haunted Mansion?" Lenny asked.

Jamie was feeling a little discombobulated from being shoulder-to-shoulder with so many people along with the loud noise from the rides, but not enough to distract her from what she really wanted, and what she wanted no part of. "All of those rides sound good but one."

"Which one?" Lenny asked.

"After last weekend, a haunted house is the last place I want to be," she said while squeezing his hand. "But I've never been on a Ferris wheel, and I don't want to miss out on riding that one."

"All right. We'll skip the haunted house and save the Ferris wheel for last. I promise. Is that okay?" Lenny asked, looking for confirmation.

"That's perfect!" Jamie said. She was thrilled with the new game plan.

Like the other riders, Lenny and Jamie had a death grip on the lap bar and were as quiet as a broken grandfather clock as the roller coaster climbed to its initial apex. It was as though the clickety-clack sound of the wheels signaled an impending danger and the need to remain silent to contemplate the hair-raising drop you were about to experience. But once the plunge began, the screams were loud and steady throughout the breathtaking ups and downs and riveting rights and lefts. The shrieks finally stopped when the ride ended, and Lenny and Jamie hopped off and made a mad dash to the bumper cars.

If the roller coaster was a thriller, the bumper cars were an all-out war. At least it was to Jamie. She climbed onboard and made two quick loops around the arena floor as the sparks flew from the top of the car's power pole as it scrapped across the wire grid overhead. Convinced that her bright yellow car could outmaneuver the other dodgems, she completely ignored the other drivers and focused her all-out assault on Lenny. Given the way she roughed him up, you would have thought she was The Intimidator, knocking around Bobby Allison at nearby Charlotte Motor Speedway. She rear-ended Lenny three times, T-boned him twice, and even maneuvered a head-on collision with his crimson red car. Being a smart boyfriend, he never bothered to ram Jamie in retaliation for the punishment he was taking. He simply let her win by making himself as available as a sitting duck while wondering if she was related to Dale Earnhardt, Sr. It was a hoot and the laughing continued when they left the Dodgem cars and arrived at the Paratrooper ride. After taking their side-by-side seats under the round metal umbrella, the ride and fun began as the suspended carriage went airborne, rocked side-to-side, and dived toward the ground. It was as though they were in a P-51 Mustang dropping bombs on a Japanese battleship. Even though the Paratrooper lacked the thrill of the roller coaster, it did allow Lenny to sit snugly next to Jamie and take pleasure in watching her big brown eyes flash with excitement. He was certain she was having a terrific time and he felt important knowing that he was the one who made it happen. He also realized that he had a serious question to ask, but the time and place wasn't right given all the screams and crazy motion. So, he decided to wait for a better opportunity.

Lenny wanted to head straight to the Ferris wheel and make it the last ride of the evening. After all, he was hoping to get Jamie by herself, and it was the perfect spot for a little privacy and a lot less noise. But he had four ride tickets left in his pocket and, even though Jamie didn't pinch pennies, she had learned when you grow up poor, you don't waste anything. So, she insisted on finding another ride before the Ferris wheel and Lenny picked one that seemed to defy the laws of nature. The Tilt-A-Whirl was like the other fast-moving rides with one major difference. Jamie and Lenny had to share the car with two other riders. Those riders were an aggravating eight-year-old boy and his smart-aleck fifteen-year-old brother. The two boys were on the ride for a fifth time and had become experts in cheating gravity by spinning the car non-stop at its maximum velocity. They were also accomplished at irritating the hell out of anyone who dared to be in the car with them. Initially, the centrifugal force had little effect on Jamie, but when she started feeling nauseous, she wanted to get off and regain her stomach. The last thing she wanted to do was throw-up in Lenny's lap.

"Hey, guys. I'm starting to feel sick, so would you please stop turning the wheel?" Jamie politely asked.

The two brothers ignored her plea by shifting their weight and turning the wheel even faster.

"Hey! Would you stop spinning the car? I'm feeling sick!" This time it wasn't a polite request, but a stern demand from Jamie.

Their indifference may not have risen to juvenile delinquency, but it was certainly inconsiderate and antisocial. "Screw you! You shouldn't have got on if you were sick," the oldest brother retorted.

"Please stop!" she cried. "I'm getting sick." Her strong appeal was again ignored.

Lenny was someone who had always been a prisoner of his emotions, always dwelling at the north and south borders whenever he felt passions rising in his body. Even as a young boy, people said he always wore his feelings on his face like a welcome or warning sign. One minute he would be full of love, and the next brimming with fury. He just never seemed to bother with the middle ground of indifference. Some said God had a little bit of personality left over from some of his creations, and just loaded it all up in Lenny's thin frame. Others said it was a gift because, at times, he just seemed to feel things more deeply than others. And this was one of those occasions. The disrespectful brothers had triggered a flash of anger, or more likely rage when they refused to cease and desist making his girlfriend sick.

"That's enough!" Lenny grabbed the wheel and held it stationary while staring savagely at the boys. He was feeling badger mean and the brothers were startled by the growl of his voice and the look on his face. So was Jamie. The boys yanked their hands from the wheel and leaned back in the bench seat to gain a little clearance. "She told you that she was sick. And asked you to stop. And you wouldn't. What kind of assholes are you anyway?" he asked rhetorically.

"We're sorry, Mister," the eight-year-old said apologetically.

"Shut up, Jimmy. We've got nothin' to be sorry for," the older brother interrupted and glared at Lenny, not thinking how unwise it was to badger a badger—especially one that was good with his fists in a fight.

"If you want to keep your teeth, you'd better keep your mouth shut, asshole!" Lenny's heart was racing wildly, and he aimed his index finger at the boy's derelict face to make his point. He was infuriated and sensed a wildness inside that felt impossible to control.

In his anger, Lenny had almost forgotten about the queasy girl sitting at his side. Upon pinpointing the carney that was controlling the ride, he yelled for him to stop as they zoomed by. "Hey, stop!" Lenny shouted while waving his arms. "We need to get off, now!"

This ride jockey had cleaned up hurled corn dogs and tacos on the Tilt-A-Whirl seats more than once, and he knew exactly what to do when he saw a ghostly white face. He brought the ride to an abrupt stop and ordered everyone off. Time had expired anyway, so no one complained except the troublemaker brothers, although they didn't hang around very long given Lenny's threat to send them to the dentist. As the boys disappeared in the crowd, Lenny helped Jamie off the platform and on to the sawdust-covered ground.

"Can you eat anything, Jamie?" Lenny asked. "That might help settle your stomach."

"Yeah, as long as it's not greasy," Jamie answered, feeling better already.

Other than cotton candy, finding something to eat that wasn't boiled in hot fat proved to be impossible. And Jamie was in no mood for cotton candy, so she asked Lenny to get her the Dixieland special—a banana pudding funnel cake and sweet tea. Lenny had a cast iron stomach and was a devotee of a balanced diet that contained the three essentials: high fat, high sodium, and high sugar. So, he opted for two Coney Island chili dogs, cheesy fries, iced tea, and a deep-fried brownie for dessert. Jamie, still recovering from her nausea, tried not to look at or smell the food Lenny was stuffing in his mouth. Her strategy worked and she felt instantly better after eating, so the two kids headed to the piece de resistance of the amusement park. The Ferris wheel was ideal for cuddling and stargazing and the ride was appropriately named The Top of the World.

Lenny gave the jock operating the ride his last two tickets, and he and Jamie climbed on a bucket swing without the company of any other riders. Being the first two to get on, the wheel stopped intermittently to allow the ride to transition to a new group of onboarding passengers. Given the slow process, by the time they reached the peak, Jamie had forgotten all about her queasy stomach and was snuggling next to her beau. It was a euphoric feeling, staring up at the sky as though she was counting the stars. It was quiet and peaceful too, as though they were floating in space and Lenny thought this was the perfect time to pop the question.

"Jamie, I've got something to ask you," Lenny said softly.

Jamie pulled away from his embrace to look at his face. "What is it?" she asked.

"Well, you know we've been seeing each other a lot lately, and I was wondering if you want to go steady? You know, just date each other?" It was a vulnerable moment and Lenny held his breath waiting for her reply.

Teenagers don't dream about the future because tomorrow seems like an eternity away. They just live in the moment because there is power in the moment. Sometimes it's hard for adults to understand that simple truth because they have been hardened by a world that can be heartbreaking and cruel. So, adults explain the attraction between teenagers as nothing more than immaturity, just a crush or maybe puppy love. But for Jamie and Lenny, it was more than that. It was a raw and simple feeling that touched their hearts.

One word. That was it.

"Yes," she answered, then leaned in, and kissed the special boy who made her heart feel something it had never felt before. Something beyond words.

Minutes later the ride was over, and the duo was locked arm-in-arm on to the next adventure. As Lenny had planned, the evening would end with winning his heartthrob a stuffed animal. And with inside knowledge from his cousin Jackson, who worked and traveled with the carnival one summer, how could he fail? Jackson had divulged every sneaky trick, every sleight of hand, every dishonest illusion the shrills pulled on their easy marks, so Lenny felt as though he was prepared for all their conniving deceit. He knew that the basketball free throw hoop was bent to be oblong and smaller than regulation, and the balls were overinflated to make them bouncier. He was aware that the milk bottles in the knock 'em over toss were filled at the bottom with ten pounds of lead, and the softballs filled with cork to make them ineffective. And the ring toss, well, Jackson explained that the rings barely fit on the bottle necks unless the shrill was using his own larger rings to demonstrate how easy it was to win. Even the tips on the balloon darts were filed dull, and the air balloons filled to thirty-percent capacity. Given all the deception, the challenge was choosing the one game where a player had a shot at beating the odds. For Lenny, that game was the coin toss. Fortunately, Jackson had worked that game and knew that the dishes were sprayed with canola oil to make them as slick as a used car salesman. To counter the oily surfaces, Jackson said a player would have to covertly spit on the quarter, and then make a toss with a very high arc. Instead of skipping off the plates like a flat rock on a pond, the quarter would drop from the heavens and stick as though it was landing in sludge. The only challenge left would be to pick out a stuffed toy hanging underneath the canopy.

Lenny had an advantage beyond the knowledge of how to beat the game. There was a large and active crowd of all ages tossing quarters from every direction when he and Jamie arrived, and the mob gave Lenny the opportunity to prep his coins without being noticed. The adults weren't good at playing the game, and their frustrated kids were especially bad. The pitchman kept making his sales spiel by encouraging the youngsters to keep trying, and the exasperated parents kept shelling out the quarters. Lenny licked both sides of his first quarter and shouldered in between two parents to make his throw. The coin hit off center on the plate and spun to the ground. On his second try, he came close, but the coin refused to remain on the dish. He felt certain he would be lucky on his third attempt. After all, the third time's a charm and instead of licking his quarter, he covered it in spittle. It was a gross tactic, but it worked. Jamie squealed as she picked out a big white rabbit with floppy ears. And Lenny felt awesome, like a hero who saved his girlfriend from an evil villain, so he decided to give it another try. This time she picked out a stuffed dog that resembled Rin Tin Tin. Tommy loved the television show that featured the German Shepherd, and Jamie knew he would be beyond excited when she brought it home. As the couple left, Lenny noticed the pitchman working the game, giving him a nasty look as he removed the soggy quarter from the plate. And Lenny couldn't help himself. He gave the game jockey a knowing smile and a "I got you" wink of his eye.

It was late and other than Jamie's dizzy spell on the Tilt-A-Whirl, it had been a perfect evening. After arriving back at the Food Stop, Lenny was rewarded with a long kiss and words of deep appreciation.

"Lenny, I had the best time of my life. Thanks for taking me to the fair," she said.

"I had a really good time too," he responded.

"I guess I'll see you Monday at school," Jamie said while loading the stuffed animals in the Rambler.

"Oh, I almost forgot to tell you. Johnny and I are coming to work on your mom's car in the morning. Is that okay?" he asked.

"Oh my gosh, yes! Are you sure you and Johnny have time to work on it?"

"Yeah. It's no problem. Johnny wants to go fishing after we finish, so we should be at your place around 10:00."

"See you tomorrow," she said. To be sure, it was a magical evening.

Twenty-Six

A DIRE WARNING

The restoration of a 1960 pea green Chevy Corvair began at nine-thirty on a Sunday morning in early November. The boys arrived with their usual tools along with a brand-new AC Delco battery and cables, and a used alternator Johnny found at a junkyard in McAdenville. The two shade-tree mechanics had yet to diagnose the problem, but both had a pretty good idea that the battery and parts would get the job done. As for the two girls, the silence between mother and daughter seemed to give way to respectful words when, earlier that morning, Jamie told Ann that help was on the way. The news that Ann's car might soon be back on the road seemed to trigger a truce—all because of two remarkable boys. Lenny and Johnny never visited sick children in the hospital, nor made donations to the local food bank, but their charity of restoring someone's car who couldn't afford the repairs was no less admirable. It would never be written about in books, but it would be written in the hearts of those who were blessed, even on the heart of Ann Russell. The boys had unloaded their tools along with the car parts and were about to pop the trunk lid to access the engine when Ann emerged from the trailer.

"Thank heaven you boys are here to fix my car!" Ann said in good spirits. "I'm Jamie's mom, Ann, and I've heard a lot about you both."

"Yes, ma'am, Ms. Russell. I'm Lenny Robinson," Lenny replied. Not knowing what Jamie had told her mother about their relationship, he was cautious about alluding to any kind of boyfriend-girlfriend liaison. He was tongue tied anyway when he saw Ann scantily dressed in nothing but a raggedy short robe that left more skin exposed than covered. "And this is my friend, Johnny Steele," Lenny continued.

"Hi, Johnny. I'm Ann, and it's very nice to meet you," she remarked while looking unsteady, rocking to and fro from too much early morning booze.

"Okay," Johnny shyly answered while staring down at his boots. As was customary, he extended his hand in greeting and never looked up. If he had, he would have seen that both of her hands were busy holding a Bloody Mary and a Marlboro cigarette. Never one who bothered with Southern gentility and good manners, Ann ignored his extended hand and took another sip from the plastic tumbler.

"Well, now aren't you the shy one," she said as she leaned to one side attempting to get a better view of Johnny's face. "It's okay. I promise I won't bite you."

"Okay." Johnny had always struggled socially, and no one could ever accuse him of dominating a conversation. However, given his uncanny focus and ability to repair anything mechanical and with his above average I.Q., the odds were favorable that he had Asperger's syndrome. Unfortunately, there were no doctors in Belmont who could recognize the disorder, so most people just thought his non-social behavior was a case of timidity.

Jamie was in the bathroom preening her feathers and didn't realize that the boys had arrived early until she heard Tommy yell from the kitchen. "Lenny and Johnny are here!" After one last touch of makeup and one more brush of her hair, she hurried out the door. She was surprised and embarrassed to see her mother barely covered in the untied robe. Life was difficult enough without her friends witnessing her mother drinking, smoking, and dressing, pretty much, au naturel.

"Momma, I'll stay out here and keep an eye on Tommy until you get dressed," Jamie said feeling embarrassed.

"Oh, these young boys don't care how I'm dressed. They may even enjoy a little peak at a full-grown woman," Ann laughed, took a long drag, and smiled as she exhaled the smoke from the cigarette. So much for the mother-daughter ceasefire. Jamie was livid.

"If you want your car fixed, you'll go inside and stay there until we get it done. We'll let you know when we finish, and you can come out then." It wasn't a shout, but Jamie's voice was stern and loud. So much so, Johnny looked up from his boots.

"Fine," Ann took another drink of her Bloody Mary, turned, and sashayed back inside the trailer.

"I'm sorry, guys, for all the drama. She's been under a lot of pressure lately, so she tends to drink too much to deal with it. If you can get her car running again, it'll help her not worry so much," Jamie said.

"Don't worry, Jamie. We'll get it running. Won't we, Johnny?" Lenny asked.

"Okay," Johnny haltingly answered.

The engineer who decided that the Corvair's engine should be in the rear trunk compartment was either drunk, or just hated auto mechanics. Working on a motor squeezed inside such a cramped area turned out to be a nightmare. Both boys were good with their hands, but not having access to a portable car lift gave rise to a lot of busted knuckles and bruised noggins. Just the same, they used all the tricks of the trade and installed the battery and alternator, and even replaced the plugs and points for good measure. It took almost three hours, but they had Ann's little car purring like a kitten with an occasional cough. Lenny and Johnny were good, but they weren't miracle workers. This was the best they could do with limited resources. Jamie was excited when the smiling boys came back from the test drive. After they parked, she stood outside the car, watching as they cranked the engine several times to run a final test of their work. The smiling boys exited the car with the mission accomplished.

"Momma is going to be so happy. I can't thank you all enough." Jamie was grateful to have her mother's car repaired but, selfishly, she was glad she would no longer have to share the Rambler. "And I'll pay you back, just let me know how much I owe you."

"You don't owe us anything. We like fixing cars; we were glad to help out," Lenny answered, feeling a warmth inside that comes from blessing others. Johnny felt a measure of self-worth as well, although he was more obsessed with fixing what was broken than feeding his ego.

"I can't let you guys do that. I didn't pay you anything the last time when you fixed my car, so I need to pay you something for fixing the Corvair," she insisted.

"No, we won't take anything from you or your mother, but we would like to go fishing to the same spot we went last time," Lenny replied. "That'll be payment enough for me and Johnny."

There was someone who was as excited as the teenage boys about going fishing, and his name was Tommy. He had been listening to the conversation and was standing nearby with his Zebco rod and reel, and tackle box. "Can I go with you and Johnny?" Tommy asked Lenny, hoping the two would let him tag along.

"Sure, you can, buddy. Just ask your mom if it's okay," Lenny answered.

"Let's go inside and let Momma know her car is fixed. We can ask her about you going fishing too," Jamie said in a very upbeat voice.

It was a simple plan, so Tommy turned and made a beeline for the trailer's front door. Jamie followed closely behind, optimistic that Ann would be in a good mood knowing that her car was repaired and more than willing to let Tommy wet a hook and line. Unfortunately, the siblings found their mother on the sofa, passed out from too many highballs and still wearing the wide-open robe. Upon seeing Ann's exposed body, Jamie ordered Tommy outside while she covered her mother with a blanket. She had seen Ann unconscious from an alcoholic-bender many times at night, but the clarity from the sunlight made this time different. It was the only explanation as to why she was so affected by her mother's visage. Perhaps it was the sadness of viewing her so helpless and weak with no one to protect her. Seeing a face scarred with abuse, regrets and guilt would touch the heart of most anyone. Jamie may have been ashamed of what her mother did and may have called her out for being an unfit parent, but she still loved her mother and knew that the bond between them could never be broken no matter how much they fought. Maybe it was a test, she thought. Perhaps God wanted to find out if her love, the most precious thing she possessed, would overcome her shame.

"Why do you do this to yourself?" Jamie broke down and cried. She knew her mother had not become an addict overnight but simply wanted to run away from her bad decisions after her divorce from Billy. A sip now and then led to an occasional bender which morphed into a steady diet of vodka which helped medicate her anxiety and depression. But the alcohol invited the darkness into her soul every time she got drunk. The emotional heartbreak of seeing her mother so broken by her failings, and the heartfelt joy from the two boys that fell from the sky stirred her feelings in a very powerful way. She reached down and picked up the spilled drink and tried to soak up the wet stain on the carpet with a dish towel. Not wanting the boys to see her crying, she went to the bathroom and composed herself before returning outside. When she walked out the front door, she immediately saw the beaming fishermen standing at attention like three soldiers, ready with rods and reels to go catch a record-breaking bass. She laughed at the sight of their anticipation.

"Well, I guess I know what you guys want to do," she said with a grin.

"Yeah, we're ready to go. But do we need to tell your mom what we did to her car, and let her know that she needs to think about getting some new tires? Johnny and I can probably find four over at the junkyard in McAdenville," Lenny gladly offered.

"No, she's not feeling well, so I'll let her know," Jamie answered. "Let's walk down to Raymond's and get some bait, and then I think I'm going to come back here and stay with Momma, if you and Johnny don't mind taking Tommy with you."

"Heck no. Tommy's our good luck charm! He has to come with us." Lenny said while looking at Tommy's smiling face.

"All right then. Grab your fishing gear and let's go," Jamie quipped.

It was a brief walk to the bait store and Tommy carried the conversation by talking nonstop about the monster fish he was going to catch. Upon arriving, the boys left their gear at the entrance and followed Jamie to the back of the store. She was surprised to find Maw wearing a petal-covered brimmed hat shaped like an upside-down flowerpot, and a vivid turquoise dress imprinted with white and dark blue flowers. The colorful hat and ankle length outfit were very dressy for someone who would spend the day dipping minnows and catching crickets. But then, Jamie realized what day it was, and that Maw had yet to change from her Sunday-go-to-meeting clothes. She had, however, left her reverence to not dip or smoke back in God's house. With a dip of Bruton and an unfiltered Camel in her mouth, she looked more like the little woman Jamie expected to find.

"Hey, baby girl! And there's my little boy," Maw dropped her cigarette in a spittoon on the floor and grabbed Jamie and Tommy in one of her group hugs. She then turned to Lenny and Johnny. "Come here, Lenny, and give Maw a big hug." Jamie was surprised that the tiny octogenarian had the mental acuity to remember Lenny's name but was even more taken aback by Johnny's reaction when she called his name and summoned him over. Unlike his usual shy response of lowering his eyes and blindly extending his hand, Johnny made eye contact, opened his arms, and stepped into her warm embrace. Maw held him for the longest time. And for a second, Jamie was certain she could see an aura of light surrounding the two, as though something spiritual was taking place before her eyes. Even though she had been bound by logic all her life, she could feel the presence of a divine goodness close by.

"Are youins goin' fishin'? Maw asked.

"Yes, ma'am. Me, Tommy, and Johnny are goin'," Lenny answered while his eyes caught a glimpse of the sign on the wall behind Maw. He paused for a second to read her latest insight that blended fish tales with Biblical principles. She had always believed it was sinful to disappoint the Man Upstairs, so her brand new poster read, "God, Help Me Not Lie About the One That Got Away."

"Didn't youins use wigglers the last time youins went fishin'?" Maw asked.

"Yes, ma'am, we did," Lenny answered.

"Well, I think youins will catch more if you use minnows this time. The bass are runnin' the bank after shad right now, and youins can catch em', and some bluegill and crappie too if you use minnows," Maw advised.

"We don't have a minnow bucket to put 'em in, Maw," Lenny responded.

"I've got an old Styrofoam bucket youins can have. I'll put you some extra shiners in it so youins will have plenty." Maw's generous offer sent a wave of excitement through the boys, but Jamie remained quiet, troubled by an unexplainable feeling of harm.

"Are you fishin', Jamie?" Maw asked.

"No, Maw. Momma's not feeling well, so I'm going back home to stay with her," she answered.

"I needs to talk to you after I get the boys fixed up. Can you stay fur a few minutes?" Maw asked.

"I'd be glad to, Maw."

Maw dipped the boys an extra two dozen minnows in their bucket and refused to take any money for the bait. If

Raymond had known she was giving out free shiners, especially to Jamie and friends, he would have lost it. Of course, with Maw being the matriarch of the Bates family, she would have told him to calm down and shut up. Once the three fishermen were out of sight, Maw pulled Jamie over by the bait cooler.

"What is it, Maw? You look worried."

"Are you and Tommy still wearing the necklets I gave you?" Maw asked.

Maw's question caught Jamie completely off guard. "I'm still wearing mine, but Momma threw Tommy's away. She got mad about him having it because she said it was from you."

"Why wus she mad about me givin' him a gift?" Maw asked.

Jamie didn't want to answer the question, but somehow knew that Maw would know if she was lying. "Don't get mad, Maw. But she said you were a witch and that you were trying to practice some kind of magic on us."

"I wus just tryin' to protect you and Tommy."

"Protect us from what?" Jamie's eyes crinkled.

"Protect you from the evil that's been killin' all these people we've heard about. I know this sounds strange but, I believe the evil that's doin' these murders is involved in black magic, in cahoots with the devil."

"Really, Maw?" Jamie said with an incredulous stare.

"Let me tell you what I thinks is goin' on," Maw said. She freshened up her snuff with a small dip and lit another cigarette in preparation to tell her story.

Maw began with a history lesson on the Appalachian Mountains, and how for thousands of years the art of magic had been passed down from generation to generation by the Cherokee and Catawba tribes, along with a mixture of Irish, Scottish, and German settlers. She explained that those who practiced magic back then were called witches, even though most were Christians. Those same practitioners had faith in the Bible not as a spell book, but as an instruction manual on how to deal with the Devil. The Good Book was needed because there were others that were wicked and practiced black magic by worshiping Satan. Those unrighteous disciples knew they had to make offerings to the Devil, to give something in exchange for the dark power they cherished. Maw clarified that the offerings could be anything from reading the Bible backwards, to the taking of a human life. Maw's alarming dissertation continued for thirty minutes, covering everything from graveyards at midnight to conjuring demons. Her final words were about the source of a person's faith placing them on the path of light or darkness. That message was delivered with certitude, the same certainty that sticking your finger on a hot iron will get you burned.

Jamie was stunned at the depth of Maw's understanding, the way she spoke with authority like an insightful historian. She had learned a valuable lesson to never stereotype anyone just because they spoke with an accent. "Maw, I'm blown away by everything you've told me, but I still don't understand why Tommy and I need protection," she said.

"It's 'cause I believe Raymond has crossed some bad people. And I believe these people are led by someone who has a pact with the devil, and they may come here to get revenge on him and on me 'cause they know I'm his momma. And 'cause I'm right with the Lord and practice magic too, they may think I'm a threat to them," Maw answered.

"I'm still confused, Maw. What does all this have to do with me and Tommy?"

"It's 'cause I care about you and Tommy, and they'll try to hurt anybody I care about, not just Raymond. But thar are other reasons why I'm worried about you."

"Why?" Jamie asked with a troubled look.

"These devil worshippers believe innocent children have power that devil worshippers can tap into 'cause children are pure and ain't learned to be sinful—a little one can be a worthy sacrifice to Satan. That's why I'm worried about Tommy."

Jamie's first thought was that Maw needed to be committed for mental evaluation at Broughton Hospital in Charlotte. But the threat to her brother, real or imagined, soon brought about a feeling of outrage. "Geez, Maw. I don't believe in any of this stuff!"

"I know it sounds unbelievable, Jamie, but you have to trust me," Maw pleaded.

"I've gotta go. I need to get home to Momma," Jamie turned and started walking briskly away.

"Jamie, please. One more thing," Maw loudly begged. "I think you have some special powers you need to know about."

Those words sounded as unbelievable as Maw's witchy stories but a little voice inside her head implored her to stop and listen. "What do you mean I have special powers?" Jamie asked while slowly walking back in Maw's direction.

"Have you ever knowed things were gonna happen before they did?" Maw asked.

"What do you mean?" Jamie's anger was turning into curiosity.

"I's think you know what I's mean. You know things are gonna happen in five minutes or in five days before they do. You have a gift. *The sight*. I's can feel it in these ole bones. I's knowed it the first time I's saw you," Maw answered.

Jamie had never thought about dreams being premonitions or omens, but Maw's far-seeing words prompted her to close her eyes as though she was trying to pull a file from a cabinet in her memory. "Sometimes I can sense stuff like that. Like I dreamed that Tommy was going to break his arm a week before it happened, and I can always tell when he's lying. And one time when I was little, I told Momma that Billy was cheating on her before she knew about it. And there's been other times when after my grandfather died, I would see him in my dreams. Pop would always warn me about something that was going to happen."

Jamie felt a sense of relief as she told Maw about the many other events she predicted before they took place. She always felt like she was the one that should be committed to a mental institution whenever these supernatural occurrences happened, not that she possessed a special gift. Beyond the clairvoyance, Jamie also talked about being able to feel the pain and joy of others as though there was an emotional echo in her body. Maw said that was part of her gift and to embrace it. She also said that God's home wasn't just some mansion in the clouds, but in everything that lived and breathed, including everything in nature. She encouraged Jamie to have faith, to walk in the light, and call on the Lord to be her protector. Maw ended with an omen when she said that life wasn't about being cursed or blessed or having good or bad luck. Life was about the eternal battle between good and evil, but not to worry because the Man Upstairs had a plan and purpose for her life. As for Jamie, if God had a plan for her, she had no clue what role she would play. She left Maw at her bait station and headed home feeling bewildered and unsettled.

Twenty-Seven

LIAR, LIAR, BIBS ON FIRE

In life, everyone is driven by something. For Deputy Sheriff Joe Griffin, that something was solving the homicides in Gaston County. He had two interviews scheduled for the morning and had high hopes he would get a break in the cases. His first meeting was with Doug Dutton and the second with Zelbert Rubley, Dovena Rubley's husband.

As for Puck Dutton, his something in life was making moonshine just like his daddy, and his daddy's daddy, and all the Dutton daddy's going back two hundred years. Stealing pigs was the other tradition passed down by a family that never felt encumbered by the law. But at one time Puck tried to sever his limb from the family tree. After getting married, he saw himself as a faithful husband and ample provider. He even got a regular job on the rail crew at CSX Railroad to begin his new life. And life was good until his wife, Effie May, better known as Dixie, opted for a romantic escapade with the now deceased Bodean Suggs. For Dixie, her infidelity was most likely whimsical, a fanciful attraction to Bo's loins and his redneck 007 mystique. Of course, when your husband looked like a hobgoblin, it was an easy fall from grace.

After the divorce, Puck moved out of their rental house and returned to cooking whiskey and thieving while his bitterness for his ex-wife and her dead boyfriend continued to fester like a foul-smelling wound. All the sneering and gossip by the town folk about his checkered past just made it worse. Not wanting to have contact with anyone, Puck had gone underground and became a specter. No one knew where he spent the daytime hours nor slept at night, and it took Deputy Sheriff Joe Griffin almost a month to track him down and arrange a meeting. That rendezvous would take place at the Phillips 66 gas station near Ranlo. Deputy Griffin had been standing outside his cruiser, waiting for Puck to arrive when he heard the unmistakable sound about a quarter mile away. The thunder-like rumble of Puck's Ford announced that he was nearby and had never bothered installing a new muffler. Joe would have issued him a ticket for the noise violation, but he was focused on something much more important. He was desperate and frustrated with his progress on the murders and didn't want to alienate a valuable source of information. After Puck arrived, it took a minute for the smoke from the burnt oil to dissipate from around the truck, but when it did, he emerged, and the deputy motioned him over.

"Over here, Mr. Dutton. Over here." Joe waved his hand back and forth to get his attention.

"Hey, Shuriff. I got word that's you'd want to see me," Puck skipped the handshake, reached into his front pocket, withdrew an unopened pack of Camels, and nervously smacked the package against the palm of his hand. Satisfied that the cigarettes were ready for use, he opened the pack, lit one, and placed another behind his ear.

"Yeah, I had a hard time tracking you down," Joe confirmed, mesmerized at the lit cigarette wedged between Puck's two bottom teeth and the one unlit smoke resting on his ear. Not to be ignored was his whiskey breath, the camo cap pulled down to his brow with the bill bent to the clouds, and his raggedy overalls smudged in dirt and small blotches of blood. "I couldn't locate where you worked, and no one seemed to know where you lived. You're a hard man to find."

"You know, I's not workin' regular right now. I'd be down on the river whar I trap beavers and run some trotlines. I's lives in a ole shack on the bank, so there haint no phone or 'lectricity or nuthin'. I'd be hard to find if you'd don't know where'd I be," Puck said.

"And where exactly on the river is your shack?" the deputy asked.

"Up there on the South Fork of the Catawba. But you kan't find my place unless you'd knowed whar you'd be goin'." Puck's dark, elf-like eyes were positioned below a singular eyebrow that looked like a wooly bear caterpillar. He was very uncomfortable with the questions and his shifty eyes were darting back-and-forth as though looking for an escape route.

"It looks like it may start raining soon, so why don't we get in my patrol car so we can stay dry. I won't keep you long. I just have a few questions about the Suggs brothers' murders," the deputy said as he glanced at the dark clouds.

"I's dun't mind gettin' wet, Shuriff. Sides that, I's gots some places I's needs to go this mornin' and I's dun't have much time," Puck responded like a convicted felon, as though the cruiser was a jail cell and getting inside was a life sentence.

"Well, I mind, so, let's get inside and I'll try not to keep you very long. And one more thing, I'm a deputy, not the sheriff," Griffin insisted.

Deputy Griffin questioned his judgment to use the cruiser as an interview room the moment they stepped inside and closed the doors. In the open air, the odor of sweat, smoke, and whiskey that clung to Puck's thin boned body was mostly washed away in the wind. With no breeze and only a few feet between them in the cooped-up front seat, the smell became ripe, like a dead roadside possum. Joe felt trapped and came close to losing his breakfast until he cupped his hand over his nose and mouth and instructed Puck to get back out. Once out, the men gathered at the car's hood and the deputy began the questioning.

"The reason I wanted to talk to you Mr. Dutton is because your name came up in our homicide investigation of the Suggs brothers. How long have you known the Suggs, and in particular, Bodean Suggs?" Deputy Griffin knew that Puck was familiar with the brothers and wanted to test his truthfulness, so it seemed like the perfect time for a little cat and mouse maneuver.

"I's dun't know Bodean Suggs. Sides that, how did my name come up?" Puck asked.

"Your name came up because of the affair your ex-wife was having with Bo Suggs," Joe answered.

"Why don't you talk to Dixie 'bout that? Puck's red face and ears divulged his embarrassment.

Even though the deputy had yet to speak with Dixie, he decided to use a little deception, to lie and see how Puck responded to the pressure. "I've spoken to Effie May already, and she said that you talked about killing Bo Suggs on several occasions when they were having the affair. She said you were angry enough to kill them both."

"She's lyin' 'bout that. All I know'd 'bout the Suggs is whut I hear. You know that they make moonshine. And I haint never said nuthin' 'bout killin' either one of them." Puck acted dumbfounded by the accusation and started fidgeting like his drawers were filled with ants.

"Don't you make illegal whiskey yourself?" the deputy sternly asked.

"Do I's make illegal whiskey?" Puck began breathing harder and shuffling his feet.

"That's what I asked," Deputy Griffin said while Dutton stared at his pickup as though he wanted to get away. The deputy knew that Puck was lying. All the telltale signs were there. Repeating questions, the happy feet, and his wild hand gestures. The only giveaway missing was a Pinocchio nose, although Puck had a hook nose that looked crafted by Gepetto's hand.

"No! I's trap beavers, muskrats, and otters on the river. And catch catfish to makes my money. I's never made no shine. That'd be agin' the law." Puck had wedged another smoke between his two bottom teeth and the cigarette was bouncing up and down faster than Ringo Starr hammering the hi-hat.

"I don't believe you, Mr. Dutton. My ATF contact with the revenue department said that they've been watching you for years. That you're one of the biggest moonshiners in Gaston County. My contact said that your granddaddy, Popcorn Dutton, was the biggest moonshiner in North Carolina and he's the one who taught you how to make whiskey." Joe hadn't spoken with anyone with ATF, but when you are playing the cat and mouse game, you may as well make up a whopper to see how your suspect reacts.

"That's a lie! All my granddaddy taught me to do wus traps and fish on the river. If I's made a little whiskey on the side, it wus for me," he said defensively.

"You just said that you didn't have a whiskey still. And now you said you do. Which is it?" Joe's forehead furrowed with doubt.

"I's dun't have no still no more. I's just meant I's used to." Puck's face was flooded with confusion.

Joe had Puck on the ropes and decided to keep throwing punches from any and everywhere to see if he could rattle him into unintentionally incriminating himself. "Mr. Dutton, where did all that blood on your overalls come from?"

"It come from a hog I's kilt this mornin'. One I's kilt to put in my cousin's smokehouse," he answered.

"Did you know Cooter Jones? He was a moonshiner like you and had hogs that he stole from other folks. He would sell or butcher them just like you. And he was killed just like the Suggs brothers." Joe threw an uppercut punch of a question and waited.

"Do I's know'd Cooter Jones?" Puck repeated the question.

"Are you hard of hearing, Mr. Dutton? You heard what I said!" the deputy had always trusted his instincts and he knew this man was lying.

"I's dun't know no Cooter Jones. And I's dun't steal hogs frum nobody." At this point, Puck started easing away from the cruiser in the direction of his pickup.

"I spoke with Alma Jones, Cooter's wife, and she said before her husband was killed, he told her that you wanted him dead because he stole back the hogs he sold you. Because you owed him money for the hogs and wouldn't pay him." The deputy was in step with Puck as he was backing away.

"That's a lie! I's never owed Cooter no money! I's paid him for them hogs when I's furst got 'em frum him," he said while back peddling even faster.

Finally, the deputy had the opening he wanted. "I thought you said you didn't know Cooter. And now you're saying you knew him and bought some pigs from him. Why are you lying to me about the Suggs brothers and Cooter? Did you have anything to do with their murders?"

Deputy Griffin's direct questions and stern voice had sent Puck scampering toward his pickup with Deputy Griffin following closely behind. "I's gots to go, Shuriff. I's can meets some other time if you wants to."

After scrambling in the Ford and starting the engine, a loud roar and a huge cloud of smoke billowed from the chassis, forcing Joe to step back a few feet to avoid the ear-splitting noise and noxious fumes. Puck sped out of the station's parking area with a long trail of black smoke in his wake. Deputy Joe Griffin was left behind to wonder if he had pushed too hard, if he should have treated him with kid gloves instead of bare-knuckle fists. But it was too late to relive the past, so before leaving for his next appointment, he entered the gas station, purchased a bottle of Pepto Bismol, and took a big swig. With a stomach churning from the intense confrontation with Puck and his rank body odor, Joe needed the relief.

******

It was only a fifteen-minute drive from Ranlo to Benson's Welding and Fabrication in Belmont and Deputy Griffin had arrived early. After parking the cruiser in front of the windowless red brick building, he killed some time, making notes about his encounter with Puck until a white 1957 Chevrolet Bel Air pulled up beside him. Inside was a woman with a mound of jet-black hair stacked above a pair of dark sunglasses looking his way. Joe returned the gaze and then his eyes found the catchy words painted in black on the car's front fenders...*White Lightening.* He chuckled, wondering if the car's name implied it could outrun revenuers or the good ole boys who drag raced on Lassiter Mountain. Or maybe both. After the two stepped from their vehicles, they met at the entrance to the welding shop and Joe initiated the conversation.

"Hi, I'm Deputy Joe Griffin," he said with a smile. "Can I help you with anything?"

"Hi, Deputy. I'm Dovena. It's nice to meet you," she returned the friendly greeting.

"Are you Dovena Rubley? Zelbert's wife?" the deputy asked.

"Yes sir. That's me," she acknowledged.

"I thought you and I were scheduled to meet next week at your house, Mrs. Rubley?"

"We were, but Zelbert wanted me down here when you talked to him. He said you could see us both at the same time so you wouldn't need to talk to me next week. He said it would be more convenient for you. And please call me Dovena, or Dovey if you want to. That's what my friends call me."

Joe was certain that Dovena's presence had nothing to do with her husband's thoughtfulness. It did, however, have everything to do with Zelbert wanting to control the conversation about the marks on her battered face. Ludean Suggs had already made it clear to the deputy that the source of the cruelty and pain was the meanest husband in Gaston County.

"Well, Dovey. It's very nice to meet you. And please call me Joe. No need for formalities as far as I'm concerned." Like any cop, Joe gave Dovey the once over and was surprised at her appearance. Long bodied and trim, she was clad in a faded gray ankle-length dress that had one time been as dark as her hair. She was fair complexioned and wore no jewelry of any kind. And on her high cheeks rested wraparound sunglasses that hid her dark eyes and a history of contusions and swelling from an abusive husband. Aside from the bruises that clung to her face, Dovey was good looking, smart, and well spoken. Like a professor at Duke, she was articulate and delivered every word with perfect diction which made Joe wonder how the hell she ended up with a monster like Zelbert. And why she had an affair with an uncouth hillbilly like Bodean Suggs.

"You know that I'm primarily looking into the deaths of the Suggs brothers and need to ask you some questions about your relationship with Bo Suggs. Can you answer some questions about that?" Joe asked as he watched Dovey nervously glancing over her shoulder at the entrance to the shop.

"Joe, I'll answer any question you ask until Zelbert comes out that door. When and if he does, I can't openly talk to you about anything because of what he'll do."

Deputy Griffin promised Dovena that there would be no more one-sided fights. That Zelbert wouldn't lay a hand on her, and if he tried, he would spend the remainder of his life in the county jail if he was lucky, and if he wasn't, he would be buried at the dump in Dallas with all the other county trash.

"Let's start with Zelbert. Tell me about how you met him and what kind of man he is," Joe began.

"Well, I need to tell you about my time in Chicago to explain how I met Zelbert. I had just turned thirty-five and was teaching there when things started to spiral out of control. I was married and my husband and I were deep in debt and struggling financially, and he was having a hard time keeping a job. He got desperate and got involved with drug dealers. He started selling the stuff himself to help us make ends meet, and his selling turned to using. After he started with marijuana, he got hooked on cocaine, then heroin. I was battling depression back then and started using heroin to help me cope, but my addiction got worse and worse every day. I eventually lost my job and just couldn't function like a normal person anymore. Not long after that, he was convicted of dealing and was sent to prison. That's when I moved back home to Belmont to live with my mother."

"That's when I ran into Zelbert. He and I grew up in the same neighborhood when we were kids and knew each other for years. When I came back, he offered to help me out until I made it through rehab over in Charlotte. We started seeing each other, and at first, he treated me with compassion and took care of all the bills. But as time went on, I realized that he had a bad temper and could be mean-spirited. And then I found out the hard way that when he started drinking heavily, the whiskey brought out the meanness in his fists. It woke up the devil in him. He became very controlling. Very jealous."

"Is that when you and Zelbert got married? After you got out of rehab?" the deputy asked.

"No, we're not married. I never divorced my first husband. I just moved in with Zelbert after I came back to Belmont," she explained.

The deputy had assumed Dovey and Zelbert were married, and her confession caught him off-guard. "Ludean Suggs told me that the two of you were hitched. I'm a little surprised that you would stay with someone like that."

"I know it doesn't make sense, Joe, but he wasn't always like that. And I feel like I owe him for helping me out when I needed it the most."

"You don't owe him anything, Dovey. If you'll just let me make out a report that he hurt you, I'll take him to jail right now!" Joe's gut told him that she wasn't staying with Zelbert because of a sense of gratitude.

"No! No! Please don't do that. You have no idea what he's capable of when he starts drinking. It's like the whiskey opens a door in his soul and there's some kind of evil inside."

"Is that how you met Bo Suggs? When Zelbert was buying whiskey from the Suggs brothers to fuel his drinking?"

"Yes, Bo would come around delivering whiskey when Zelbert was at work, and Bo just started staying around the house to visit after he stopped by. He was just being friendly, I suppose, and we just talked a lot at first and he paid attention to me. He really listened when I told him about Zelbert and how I was unhappy and scared. What I'm trying to say is that Bo was very understanding and always treated me with respect and kindness. But then, one thing led to another, and our relationship turned sexual. And then one day Zelbert came home early from work and caught us in bed."

"What did Zelbert do when he caught you?" Joe asked.

"He went crazy, yelling in a guttural way like he was possessed by a demon. He ran and got his shotgun out of the closet when Bo was leaving in his pickup. Shot at him several times. And then he screamed at me in that awful voice and beat me so badly that both of my eyes were swollen shut for a week. And he busted my lip and knocked out one of my teeth just to be sure I got the message." Dovey watched the shop door while recounting how she absorbed Zelbert's hate for a long time after she and Bo were caught. "Every time he got drunk, he would punch and slap me around and call me names you wouldn't call a mongrel dog. It got so bad one time he knocked me out cold."

"Did he ever say anything about killing Bo after that?" Joe asked as he felt his own anger building inside his core.

"Every day he said he was going to kill him. Every day he talked about how he was going to make him suffer. He even said he was going to dismember him for what he did," Dovena shook her head, still astonished at Zelbert's threat to deliver his brand of justice with a double-bit saddle axe.

"Did he threaten to harm you after he caught you and Bo together?"

"He told me every day that he'd kill me, and my mother, if I did something like that again. Or if I tried to leave him. I believe he'll do it, Joe. I'm terrified of what he has become."

"That's why you won't leave him. Isn't it, Dovey.? You're afraid he'll hurt your mother and you're protecting her."

Dovena never had the chance to answer the deputy's question. The shop's entrance door swung open and out swaggered the devil himself. And when he saw Joe and Dovena together, his temper turned hotter than the acetylene torch he had been using inside. It was a fearsome vision, a three-hundred-pound behemoth outfitted in a leather apron and gloves, and a heavy metal helmet that was swiveled upward on his bruin-like head. Below the mask were a flat nose, black eyes, and cauliflower ears pasted on a vile face that looked disconnected from anything decent and good. And underneath the apron was a spread-out body, paunchy and round sitting on a pair of stubby legs. His long arms were tattooed, and their bone-thin girth seemed out of place with his other dimensions. It was as though a kid had built him with pieces from a Mr. Potato Head game. But this hard drinking bully was anything but a toy. As for Joe, he was no Barney Fife. He was as stout and strong as a bear, but he was wary and on his toes.

"Are you Mr. Rubley?" the deputy's eyes narrowed.

Zelbert never answered nor looked at Joe. Instead, he leered at the woman he held prisoner because of her fear and vulnerability. It was palpable, the way the hate swirled around him.

"Rubley. You are Zelbert Rubley aren't you?" Joe stepped between Zelbert and Dovena to diffuse the tension.

"Yeah, I'm Zelbert Rubley," his face was screwed up tight with anger, but he spoke with a high-pitched voice like he had inhaled helium from a balloon. Joe wanted to laugh at the disjoint between his voice and physical size but kept the hilarity inside to avoid aggravating the monster.

"I'm Deputy Sheriff Griffin. And I'm here to ask you some questions about your involvement in the murder of Bodean Suggs."

"Have you been talkin' to my wife?" Zelbert's jaw clenched in anger.

"Well, first of all, I know Dovena isn't your wife. And secondly, I did talk to her and now I'm ready to talk to you," Joe calmly answered.

"Whut did she tell you?" Zelbert asked as he tried to peer around Joe to assess Dovena's demeanor.

"She answered my questions and told me what I needed to know," Joe responded. "Dovey, why don't you go sit in your car until I finish talking to Zelbert," the deputy pointed her to the Bel Air. "Is there somewhere we can go inside and talk?" The deputy had enough probable cause to arrest Zelbert for domestic violence, but first wanted to question him about the murders of the Suggs brothers.

"I reckon we can find a place," Zelbert answered, seething at how Joe had become so familiar to his so-called wife that he was calling her "Dovey."

It was a world unto itself inside the shop. It was an open area devoid of any welding booths which allowed the spatter from the torches to fly in every direction. The incandescent particles against the dim lighting made for an eerie scene, as if you had stepped through hell's front door. And maybe you had. Joe quickly learned that passing too closely by the welders torching metal guaranteed that his arms would be singed and hairless. It crossed his mind that Zelbert was purposely leading him next to the workers to get even for his one-on-one meeting with Dovena. He was relieved when they finally entered a break room at the back of the shop where they found their seats at a four-chair kitchen table. Zelbert removed his helmet and gloves, and they began a stare down like two boxers before the bell.

"I ain't got no goddamn thing to say 'bout Bo Suggs or his bruthers for that matter," Zelbert snapped.

"You'll talk to me here, or I'll take you into custody and you'll answer questions at the Sheriff's Office. It's up to you." Joe responded calmly, but with a measure of sternness in his voice to let Zelbert know the consequences if he failed to cooperate then and there.

"You've aw'ready talked to Dovena, so I'm sure you know 'bout them Suggs and whut they were doin'. Why dun't you tell me whut you want to know so I kin git back to work," Zelbert fired back.

"She said you caught her and Bo in bed together and shot at Bo when he was in his pickup trying to get away. Were you trying to kill him?"

"Damn straight I wus tryin' to kill him. He wus trespassin' in my house and screwin' my wife!"

Joe decided to skip all the mind games he had played with Puck. Besides, Zelbert didn't seem to have any intellect anyway. "Did you kill Bo Suggs?" Joe growled.

"Whut if I did, Deputy?" Zelbert leaned forward as if challenging Joe's authority.

"Did you? Because if you did, you'll be arrested and tried for murder," Joe answered while moving even closer.

"Are you gonna 'rest me, Deputy?"

It was obvious that Zelbert was hellbent on getting in a physical confrontation with Joe. And Joe wanted to accommodate him by driving his fist into his wicked face, hoping one punch would send the evil back to hell. But the deputy knew he needed backup before throwing a right-cross or attempting to place him in handcuffs. "Wait here, Mr. Rubley.

I need to get something out of my patrol car. I'll be right back."

Joe backtracked briskly through the shop and to the entrance door. Once outside, he instructed Dovena to go by Zelbert's house and pick up clothes and anything else she would need for a night or two away. And then to stay with her mother. After learning that Zelbert was being arrested for domestic abuse, her face turned white from fear and apprehension, knowing that the deadly storm cloud that loomed over her life would take out his savagery on her and her mother.

"No, Joe. Please don't do that. He'll kill me and my mother if you do that!" she begged. Dovena wasn't worried about tomorrow; she was worried about what Zelbert would do in the next five minutes.

"He knows that you and I talked, Dovena. If you go home with him now, odds are he'll either kill you or beat you within an inch of your life. He's about to blow his top and I don't have a choice. He's going to jail and you're going to your mother's or some other place where you'll be safe. I'll make sure he stays in jail without bonding out. That'll give you and your mom plenty of time to find a safe place to stay until he's in prison. He's an animal, Dovena. I'm certain he killed Bo and maybe his brothers too," Joe explained, knowing he had no other options.

Joe radioed for assistance as he watched Dovena and *White Lightening* disappear in the distance. Within five minutes, three deputies the size of grizzlies arrived to help place Zelbert under arrest. He didn't go willingly. His deep and throaty voice returned as he hurled insults at the brotherhood of bears and fought them like a wild animal himself. After wrestling him to the break room floor, it took two sets of bracelets to restrain his flailing arms. Joe then read Zelbert his Miranda rights and the four officers escorted him past the gawking welders. Zelbert never stopped cursing and threatening the deputies even as he was forced into the patrol car. Five minutes after leaving, he calmed down enough for his baby voice to return as he began to plead his case from the back seat of Joe's cruiser.

"I love Dovena. I let her live with me when she was broke and in rehab. I told her she could stay with me for free," Zelbert sounded remorseful.

"No, she didn't live with you for free. You charged her a bloody nose and busted lip for rent, you piece of shit! That's what it cost her to live with you!" Joe wasn't interested in hearing Zelbert's lies.

"It was the moonshine, Deputy. The Suggs made bad whiskey and it infected my head and made me act crazy. It was the shine's fault."

Joe knew the liquor didn't cause Zelbert to do something he wouldn't do sober. It just made him do it worse. "You're an animal, Zelbert. Wait a minute, I take that back. Animals don't do to their own kind what you did to Dovena. I don't want to hear any of your excuses. Just shut up and behave. We'll be at the county jail soon."

Zelbert reclined in the back seat and became as quiet as a rock. Catatonic really. That's when Joe's mind began to churn, wondering if it was the alcohol as Zelbert said, or if you could pass hate from one generation to the next. He had seen the sins of the father passed to many sons whom he had arrested over the years, and he knew that it was hard to escape from a culture of crime without an education...but Zelbert was just pure evil as though spawned by the devil. As Joe continued driving, his thoughts shifted to Dovena—about how fate had delivered her a life of abuse, and a culture of hate that was so contrary to her gentle spirit. He questioned how a loving God would ever allow that to happen. But he knew that it wasn't Jehovah who led her into that darkness. Fear, isolation, financial dependency, a belief the abuser would change, were all explanations he had heard before from women subjected to domestic violence. It broke his heart because he knew the abuser rarely changed, and often the woman who felt trapped by her circumstances paid for leaving the relationship with her life.

There was no softness in Zelbert Rubley, and Joe wanted to make sure he did hard time for what he had done.

Twenty-Eight

A BAD FEELING

Deputy Griffin made sure the arraignment date on the court docket had been delayed which left Zelbert Rubley locked up for the past three days, although the jail guards would swear he had been there for three years. The jail was a foul, noisy, and oftentimes violent place and could never be confused with a Howard Johnson Hotel—especially with a three-hundred-pound guest spewing insults, spit, and threats to whip the guards' asses whenever they walked by. Of course, the jail guards were partially responsible for Zelbert's anger since they kept poking the bear by calling him Mickey Mouse to mock his high-pitched voice. As for Joe's whereabouts, he avoided all the unpleasantries of the cell block. He was in a conference room at the Sheriff's Office waiting on a call from Special Agents Tim Hobbs and Ellison O'Neal with the State Bureau of Investigation in Harrisburg. The phone call was their regularly scheduled update on their investigations.

"Hello, this is Deputy Griffin speaking."

"Hey, Joe. This is Tim and Ellison. If it's okay, we're going to put you on the speaker," Tim said.

"You bet. I'll do the same on my end. By the way, Sheriff Myers is tied up right now, but he may join us in a minute," Joe said as he prepared to take notes.

"Sounds good. Do you want us to start out with our update?" Tim asked.

"Yeah," Joe agreed.

"Hey, Joe. This is Ellison. The Medical Examiner just issued his final autopsy report on our two campers, Mike and Elizabeth Walters, minus some final lab work on Elizabeth. So, I'll start with a high-level re-cap on the victims and the results from his examinations. By the way, I'm sure you already know some of the information I'll share with you, so forgive me if I'm a little redundant. Anyway, the couple were newlyweds who lived in Charlotte and had just returned from their honeymoon before their camping trip. Their parents said they loved the outdoors and had left for a weekend of bivouacking and canoeing on Ramsey Creek the day before they were killed. Nothing out of the ordinary about their trip. However, their wounds and injuries were anything but ordinary. The M.E. believes that Elizabeth was incapacitated first by the compound fractures in her arms and legs. He thinks that Mike tried to protect her and fought the killer given the defensive wounds on his arms and hands. And get this. He said that Mike died first from the loss of blood from the slashes and stab-like wounds on his body and was in a moderate stage of rigor mortis while Elizabeth had minimal stiffness in her muscles. Rigor was by and large absent from her body."

"What's the significance of that, Ellison?" Joe prepared to jot down the answer.

"It means that the killer probably targeted Elizabeth. He could have killed her instantly, but he wanted to torture her for some reason. She was still alive for several hours after her limbs were broken and while she was severely beaten. It was as though the killer had a vendetta or something against her. But everyone we've talked to said that she was a sweet young woman and that everyone who knew her loved her. No enemies whatsoever."

"What about the sexual assault? She was completely nude when I found her and our county M.E. said it appeared that she had been raped," Joe questioned.

"The pathologist said she wasn't sexually assaulted, so that wasn't a motivating factor in her death. Although, given how she was killed, I wonder if the killer had some kind of issue with women," Tim joined in.

"It's weird that you say that Tim. I arrested a really big guy named Zelbert Rubley a few days ago for beating the woman that lived with him. Tortured her for years. I'm also pretty sure that he killed Bodean Suggs because he caught the woman living with him having an affair with Bo and made threats about killing Bo and her. As for the other Suggs' brothers, they may have been collateral damage or maybe he killed them just for being a Suggs," Joe explained.

"Do you think he had anything to do with the Walters?" Tim's brows knitted.

"I can't connect the dots from him to the Walters. Although I would have never thought about a connection before we began this call. It's something I can investigate if Rubley is willing to talk to me. He's pretty pissed off right now, so I don't know if he'll cooperate or not," Joe spelled out.

"What about Doug Dutton? He's the man that found the bodies. Have you talked to him about any involvement with the Walters or Suggs?" Ellison asked.

"Yeah, I met with him the other day. The guy is as scrawny as a sapling. Probably doesn't weigh a hundred pounds and is barely more than five feet tall. He's decrepit and not strong enough to pick up an empty bucket. I just don't see how he could have committed any of these murders," Joe confidently answered.

"He could have had help though. Couldn't he?" Tim poked for confirmation.

"He could have, but he's a recluse. A real loner. I don't think he has any friends or family that would help him do this," Joe answered. "What about the toxicology results? Anything unusual there?"

"The initial tox report showed a small amount of THC in the blood of Mike and Elizabeth. They most likely smoked a joint sometime before their deaths. And there was a substance in Elizabeth that the initial testing couldn't identify. The pathologist said it had the characteristics of some kind of poison, but it's going to take a more in-depth lab analysis to identify it. It may take another six to eight weeks to get the results," Ellison answered.

"I've got a bad feeling about all of this. Originally, I thought the Walters' homicides were just random. An opportunity killing by someone who stumbled onto them in the woods. But with no sexual assault and with the M.E. thinking that Mike was killed first, and then Elizabeth tortured, I'm not so sure anymore." Joe's voice was filled with doubt.

"What about the Jesse Jones homicide, Joe? Do you think there's any connection in his death and these homicides?" Tim asked.

"Well, Cooter had a moonshine still and was making homebrew like the Suggs. Also, he was trying to cook crystal meth in his barn, although I don't think he knew what he was doing—a real upstanding citizen! Plus, his injuries looked similar to the wounds on the Suggs brothers and Mike Walters, although it was hard to tell a lot because we found him in a pen and the hogs had been eating on him pretty badly, even while he was alive. We're still waiting on the final autopsy results on that one," Joe answered.

"Man, that's nasty. All of this seems like a bad dream. Doesn't it?" Ellison's mouth twisted in disbelief.

Special Agent Ellison didn't expect an answer. They all knew these murders were a nightmare. They also knew that witnessing crime scenes and victims such as these could leave scars on their spirits. Forever. It could become maddening if you let it. But these men were professionals with a job to do, so they spent the next thirty minutes discussing any possible psychotic links between the murders. Most of the physical evidence had been tagged or tested, and the officers were left with nothing but conjecture as to the psychosis of the killer or killers, so they decided to do what all good investigators do when blinded by a crime. They agreed to go back to square one and take another look at the field documentation, interviews, and medical reports in case they had overlooked something in their initial reviews. It was a long shot, but sometimes the obvious can be obscure when your psyche is damaged by the brutality one human can inflict on another. All agreed to conference again in a week.

Twenty-Nine

THIS CAN'T HAPPEN

It was Wednesday evening around midnight in Paradise Point. Unlike Saturday nights when the discordant sounds of hard drinking, cursing, and fighting reverberated throughout the fish camp, on this moonlit night you could only hear the chatter of the frogs and crickets, and the muffled sounds of gnashing teeth drifting through the pines and oaks. Raymond knew that his bait shop business was covering operating expenses, but he also knew that the real money was in moonshine, marijuana, and cockfighting. And in the mind of a depraved moron, dogfighting seemed like a natural extension of his business empire. Raymond figured he could make more cash in one night of dogfighting than robbing a bank. Plus, he could pick up some extra income by selling doobie and hooch to the old men that gathered around the ring. So, in the spirit of hillbilly capitalism, he had built an outdoor dog pit deep in the woods behind the store and was hosting a mid-week trial to gauge the local interest in the cruel sport. It was a respectable turnout of ignorant men who searched for their honor and status from the win-loss record of their canines. Bad men who lived vicariously through a dog, who drew their masculinity from the strength and aggression of an animal that was simply trying to survive. Bad men who used puppies, kittens, and rabbits as training bait. Bad men who taped the mouths shut or broke the teeth of grown dogs they used to teach their cross-bred champions to kill. Bad men with no hearts. All these men were mean and despicable, but Raymond was even worse for opening the door for this to happen. Maw would be heartbroken.

In Raymond's mind, it had been a fine evening and he was wrapping up by collecting his cut of the cash from the heavy gambling. Meanwhile, the dogmen gathered their winning animals along with the carcasses of those that lost. All in all, CEO Raymond Bates seemed joyful, as though the stock in his IPO had exceeded the Wall Street bankers' expectations. Grinning like a mule eating briers, his teeth were exposed as he shook hands and encouraged his patrons to buy a jar of shine or a nickel bag of marijuana to take home until they could return. His last patron, Elrod Jackson, accepted his offer and purchased two Bell jars of white lightning before leading his pit bull, Badass, out of the trees.

Raymond's plan was to clean up the empty jars strewn around the dog pit, but he had a more pressing task, so he left all the kerosene lanterns but one and started weaving his way through the thick woods to the Paradise Point community outhouse. The initial nervousness from his grand opening along with the excitement of his overwhelming success had his stomach churning like the dangerous waters off the Outer Banks and, other than going in the woods like a bear, the outhouse was his closest point of relief. It was an uneventful two-minute walk until the high-pitched singing of the cicadas abruptly stopped. Feeling uneasy, he turned in a circle while adjusting his head side-to-side and after spotting nothing, reasoned that he was responsible for disturbing the treetop insects. But then he heard a rustle of leaves and the snap of a dead branch on the ground. Startled by the sound, he turned again, held the lantern outward chest high and did another scan in every direction. It was a sinister vista. The tall trees looked as though they were hiding something other than the cicadas, something malevolent, something that was watching his every move. Raymond raised the lantern above his head and barked at the would-be intruder.

"Who is it?" Nothing. Just silence. "Hell, Raymond, you're getting' worked up for nuthin'. It wus probably an armadiller scratching fur sum grubs," he said to himself, laughing at being scared by a possum in a tank.

No one had ever accused Raymond of being brave. Most said he was a big fraidy cat scared of his own shadow. True to his character, he was still unnerved by the disturbing sound and decided the best way to drown out the annoyance was singing a little refrain of his favorite song...*Don't Come Home A' Drinkin' (With Lovin' On Your Mind)*.

Raymond had never been married, and he often fantasized about Loretta Lynn crying every night because he never came home, and when he did, he was drunk on his own whiskey. He wailed the lyrics until he arrived at the outhouse, opened the door, and stepped inside.

It was a typical one-seat structure made from 2' X 4's, sheets of plywood, tin, and a unisex door carved through and through with a crescent moon and star. Inside were the usual spider webs, dirt dauber nests, cockroaches, and fetid smell. Raymond turned to face the door, slid the suspenders off his shoulders, dropped his corduroy trousers, and eased down on the rough plywood seat. Needing something to calm his nerves, he pulled a pack of Pall Mall cigarettes from his shirt pocket, lit a smoke, and took a deep draw. He would have skipped the tobacco had he noticed the missing roof pipes that would normally vent the methane gas from the tiny space. But even with the lantern, it was too dark to notice, too dark to even read the year-old edition of *Field & Stream* next to the seat. So, he reached to his trousers and pulled out a flask and sipped on his latest batch of homebrew while smoking and dreaming about spending his newfound money. And dream he did until he heard another odd noise just outside the privy. It sounded like the deep growl of one of the dog-on-dog combatants.

"Elrod, is that you? You come back for another jar of moonshine? Or how 'bout sum weed? I's got plenty and will gives you a special deal," Raymond laughed. "Is that Badass I's hird out thar? That's one mean dog. He sounds like he's lookin' for 'nuther fight."

Another snarl, only this time it was a little louder, and a little closer. A sound filled with ill will and darkness. "Okay, Elrod. You gots me. I'm gonna kick your ass when I's gets out for tryin' to spook me," Raymond chuckled with a faint smile on his face, although he wasn't prepared for what happened next.

It was a high-pitched screeching sound like someone dragging their fingernails on a schoolroom blackboard. But this noise was emanating from the tin metal roof of the outhouse. It was an impossibility, Raymond thought. You would have to be over seven feet in height to reach the rooftop. And then suddenly, the sound changed to something else, something like a cat sharpening its claws on a nearby hickory tree. Only this wasn't Felix the Cat nor Sylvester. This animal was using over three hundred pounds of body weight to help drag its claws downward and deep into the plywood sides of the outhouse. It was a terrifying impression.

"Dammit, Elrod. It's not funny enymore," Raymond's face turned crimson, and his breathing became labored. For a minute it was quiet, no aggressive growls, no screeching from above, and no gouging noise from splintered wood. But then Raymond heard something much worse.

"Raaaaaymonnnnd." It sounded like a ghostly voice calling his name in the swirling wind.

"Damn you, Elrod. That's enough."

"Raaaaaymonnnnd." Again, it whispered, but more eerie this time.

"Hot damn, Elrod. I's said that's 'nuff," Raymond yelled as his nose caught wind of a smell much worse than the outhouse pit. It was an odor of death and rot. To make his circumstances even worse, he heard someone or something stirring the leaves on the ground as it circled the small structure.

With his Fruit of the Loom's and pants still at his ankles, Raymond rose, leaned forward, placed his hands on the door jamb and peered cautiously through the star carved through the outhouse entrance. He was looking for Elrod, but instead of finding a friendly face, he discovered an abomination staring back. It was the same glowing red eyes that terrorized the Suggs brothers. Like the Suggs, Raymond wasn't much of a believer, and for most of his life the devil had been no more real than a pair of horns and a tail on a Halloween costume. Maw had warned him otherwise. On many occasions she had preached about the eternal fight between good and evil. But he had rejected her sermons as supernatural mumbo-jumbo. Sometimes the hard lessons are best, but not in this dire life and death situation. Now he wished he had listened to his mother. He fell back onto the seat and cracked his skull on the pine wall behind him. Immediately, he sprang to his feet while struggling to regain his balance. Trembling. Taking short, erratic breaths.

"Who are you?" he screamed, frantically trying to pull up his trousers.

Mental paralysis is an odd thing. Your mind is frozen, unable to function, powerless to control your nerves so you can fight back or run for your life. It is as though you are hovering outside your body, watching the horror occur to someone else. That is exactly how Raymond Bates felt when the outhouse door was ripped from the hinges and tossed aside like a toothpick. He never flinched when he felt the squeeze of the demonic hand clasp his throat, lift him from the outhouse chamber and stare at his frightened face. Nor did he feel the pain when his arms were ripped from his body and tossed to the ground like chicken bones. It would have been best had his mental faculties never returned, but unfortunately, his lucidity did rebound for a moment as he was held airborne, bleeding out on the leaf litter below. At that second in time, he had the most curious thought. Life is an uncertain thing he mused. One minute you're on cloud nine building your business empire, and the next you're knocking on the gates of hell. Satan was waiting to welcome him home.

Inside the mobile home, no one heard the horrific drama taking place outside. Although one of the residents was awake and in need of a toilet. Not wanting to wake his sister, Tommy quietly rose from the mattress beside her bed and shuffled to the bathroom. Once there, he flipped the wall switch for the ceiling light only to be reminded that the commode was out of commission. Jamie had made a makeshift sign with a picture of an unhappy face and taped it to the closed lid on the seat. It was more of a reminder for her alcoholic mother than her little brother, although Tommy understood the dressing-down he would have to endure if he ignored her warning. Normally, he would pee on the driveway in the middle of the night, but his upset stomach demanded a trip to the outhouse. Barefooted and shirtless, his only protection was his Batman pajama bottoms and the water pistol Chuckie gave him on their Halloween trip to Spencer Mountain. A handgun is always a good idea when you're out at night in a rough neighborhood, even if it only shoots H2O. After grabbing the flashlight off the kitchen counter, he slipped through the front door, and slowly walked down the footpath while humming and fanning the light and pistol at the surrounding trees. It was spooky, but he continued until the flashlight's illumination found the outdoor structure. Or what was left of it. Surprised that the building had been flattened, Tommy stood frozen, thinking about what to do next. It was an unnecessary decision.

Thirty

WHY?

The sun was scarcely peeking over the horizon when he whispered, "God why are you doing this to me?" It was a justifiable question, especially when you're the son of a Southern Baptist preacher. Plus, when you are baptized in the Holy Water at age six and grow up in the church, you expect to be blessed. And when your faith is resolute, when you know the words to *Amazing Grace* and raise your hands to Heaven during worship, you expect to be shown mercy. "So, why are you punishing me, he pleaded?" He looked upward for an answer from the sky. None came.

Being the lead investigator from the Sherriff's Office regarding the recent homicides, Joe Griffin had been dispatched to Paradise Point, and after viewing the bodies at the outhouse, he was filled with despair, wondering why God was stealing his heart, piece by piece. In a haze of confusion, his eyes were blank, and his movements slow as though he carried the heavy burden on his shoulders. After finally reaching the front door of the mobile home, he gingerly knocked, halfway hoping no one would answer. But they did. The rapping sound awakened Jamie from what had been a night of unbroken sleep. Glancing downward at the mattress on the floor, she noticed that her little brother was missing and assumed he was up and responsible for all the commotion. Rising rapidly, she rubbed the sleep from her eyes, did a quick search of the trailer and arrived at the door right after her mother. Jamie knew several days earlier that something bad was going to happen. Maw told her that she could feel it in her bones when she had a foreboding premonition. Jamie felt her omen in her heart. She just didn't know that the bad news would arrive at her doorstep.

Ann, dressed in a bathrobe, opened the door to the solemn face of Joe Griffin.

"Are you Mrs. Russell?" the deputy asked, his strong voice had turned as soft as a whisper.

"Yes, I'm Ann Russell. What's going on?" Ann asked as she peered through the dim light at the man standing in the doorway.

"I'm Deputy Joe Griffin with the Gaston County Sheriff's Office. You're Tommy's mom?" he asked with an empty stare.

"Yes," she answered as she turned to see Jamie standing at her side in her pajamas.

"Is it okay if I come inside?" Joe asked. "I need to talk to you about your son."

"Yes, please come in," Ann rubbed the sleep crust from her eyes.

Ann and Jamie led Joe to the cramped living area where mother and daughter found seats on the sofa just a few feet from where the deputy settled on the armless straight-back chair. Jamie didn't wait on the deputy to begin the conversation. "Where's Tommy?"

"Mrs. Russell, I don't know how to tell you this, but Tommy was found early this morning, just before dawn. One of your neighbors found him on the ground near the outhouse in the woods," he leaned forward as he answered.

Ann appeared confused and was unable to speak, although her voice wasn't needed. Jamie took care of the questions for them both. "Where is my brother now?" Jamie's voice trembled.

"A medic with the fire department checked all his vital signs and couldn't hear a heartbeat nor detect any breathing, so they started CPR on him immediately. An ambulance arrived about ten minutes later to take him to the Regional Medical Center in Belmont," Joe explained.

"What happened to him? Is he going to be all right?" Jamie appeared frantic. She recognized the swollen eyes of a hardcore lawman, a man who had been crying and felt tears beginning to well in her own.

"We don't know what happened to him other than there's some contusions and swelling on one side of his neck. I can't tell you anymore about his condition other than that." Joe knew his words were a bald-faced lie. He knew the condition of the six-year-old boy when his body was covered in a white blanket and loaded on a gurney by the ambulance techs. He just didn't have any heart left to tell the truth.

"Momma, get dressed. We're going to the hospital," Jamie barked. Ann didn't flinch. She heard her daughter's words, but her mind was thick with confusion, and she continued to sit motionless as though in a coma. "I said get up and get dressed," Jamie yelled this time as she pulled her mother from the sofa. Both rushed to their bedrooms leaving Joe in the living room wondering why life was so unfair.

Ann was as sober as a deacon on this Sunday morning, but her mind was awash with disorder, making the simplest task a challenge. Fortunately, Jamie was there to help her put on a button-up blouse and jeans. She had dressed her mother before, but on those occasions, she was drunk and had all the dexterity of a two-year-old. After Jamie speedily threw on a T-shirt and blue jeans, the kind deputy helped load her mother in the Rambler. Joe explained that he had to remain on scene for additional personnel to arrive and apologized for not providing an escort to the hospital. He then stood in the middle of the roadway for fifteen minutes after the taillights disappeared in the distance. He couldn't help but think about his father's words from a sermon he preached around the time he joined the Sheriff's Office. His words about the Lord having a walk for us all. Eight brutal deaths left him questioning why God had chosen this path for him. Numb and disillusioned, he felt untethered from anything good.

The Rambler's engine was early morning cold, and it coughed and sputtered as they sped past the Belmont city limits sign. In her panic, Jamie never thought about the location of the medical center and made a quick stop at an Esso gas station to get directions from a grumpy attendant. Within minutes, they arrived at the medical facility. Unlike the multi-level Charlotte Memorial Hospital with its unclear signs, multi-deck parking and one-directional streets, Belmont Regional was a mere one-story facility that offered street-level parking and simple-minded signage. Jamie parked the car in a visitor's space and she and Ann hurried through the double doors at the hospital entrance. A straightforward placard sent them scrambling to the emergency medicine department where they stopped at the registration station. Jamie appeared desperate, meanwhile, Ann stood beside her daughter, looking hollow-eyed and feeble as though she didn't understand why she was there. A grandmotherly woman standing behind the glass partition at the station recognized their presence and sense of desperation.

"Y'all look like you could use some help," she pleasantly smiled. "How can I help you?"

"My brother, Tommy Russell, was brought here this morning from Paradise Point. We're here to see him and find out what's going on," Jamie answered while supporting her mother.

With the flip of a switch, the woman's demeanor turned somber like she had been asked an impossible question. "Yes, he was brought here by ambulance about an hour ago. I need to get Dr. Fowler for you. I'll be right back." The elderly clerk pivoted and passed through the swinging door that led to the treatment bays in the back. Even though it seemed like she was gone forever, she returned in minutes, and oddly, introduced herself as though she wanted to make a personal connection. "My name is Ruby Suddeth. Is this Tommy's mother?" she asked while looking past Jamie at Ann.

"Yes, this is our mother, Ann Russell," Jamie answered. "Where is my brother?"

"I'm going to take you to the back to meet with Dr. Fowler. He's going to speak to you about Tommy."

Ruby motioned for Ann and Jamie to follow and led them down a narrow passage to an open space that served as the emergency room. The spacious area was bisected with curtained trauma bays filled with loud moans and the antiseptic smell of iodoform. At the end of the bays was a small, fixed wall office with several waiting room chairs used by family members while the attending physician explained the diagnosis and treatment of their loved ones. Ruby asked Jamie and Ann to have a seat and said the doctor would be right in. Ann followed orders by taking a chair and staring into space while Jamie paced back and forth like a caged lion. Within a few minutes, a young man who was halfway through his first year in emergency medicine walked through the doorway. He was small-boned and lean with a boyish face, peach fuzz skin, and brown tousled hair in need of a trim. He looked more like a high schooler on his way to dissect a frog in biology class than an ER physician saving lives. At least his plastic name tag, loose-fitting scrubs, and dangling stethoscope gave him the gravity of a real doctor. Immediately, he made one-way eye contact with Ann and began the dialogue.

"Mrs. Russell, I'm Ronald Fowler, the doctor that was on duty when your son was brought here. You are Tommy's mom, aren't you?" he asked. Ann remained apathetic as though she never heard a word, so the doctor turned to Jamie for an answer.

"In case you haven't noticed, she's in shock right now and doesn't understand what's going on. I'm Jamie, Tommy's big sister. Where is he?" Jamie was starting to feel a measure of anger, frustrated at the subterfuge around Tommy's whereabouts.

"Can I get you and your mother something to drink. Our coffee machine in the breakroom makes a pretty good cup of coffee." Fowler was an intern, a minor league doctor working his way up to the big show. While he did possess the experience to suture a laceration or drain an abscess, he had no mastery dealing with emotional wounds. The offer of coffee was his attempt to be consoling, but Jamie was not interested in a cup of Sanka. Instead, she was interested in his puffy red eyes. It created a feeling of despair as she felt the butterflies fanning her stomach.

"We don't want any coffee. We just want to know where Tommy is!" Jamie's message was loud and clear.

"He arrived by ambulance this morning under a pediatric code blue. It was around five-thirty at the time, and he wasn't breathing, nor did he have a heartbeat. I did chest compressions and tried intubation to help him breathe. We also utilized a defibrillator but were unable to revive his heart. We didn't order an x-ray to confirm the injury, but it appeared that a severed spinal cord most likely caused his death. He was—"

Jamie interrupted the doctor's discourse before he could finish his sentence. "What do you mean, his death? Where is he?" Jamie's trembling voice was firm and direct.

Again, the tears welled in the eyes of Ronnie Fowler, a doctor, yes, but also an older sibling who knew about the devotion and love for a little brother. He felt heart-sick at not being able to do more and there was no amount of medical training that could have prepared him for this. "He's in one of the bays outside. I can take you there now. I know you don't want to hear this, but the medical examiner's office will come by shortly to pick up his body. Given the circumstances of his death, they'll have to do an autopsy."

Like Ann, Jamie became despondent as she helped her mother from the chair and the two followed Fowler to the last treatment bay at the end of the hall. Unlike the other curtained bays, this area was a fixed wall space that afforded a level of much needed privacy. After entering the room, Ann was still unable to clearly think and recognize the white sheet covering her son. Jamie, meanwhile, started feeling overwhelming panic and closed her eyes as though not seeing would make it not so. She wanted to leave, drive home, and find her brother watching The Flintstones on television, not here in this room lying on a gurney. Summoning all her courage, she led her mother to the bedside and pulled the sheet down from his face.

"Jamie. Wake Tommy up and let's go home," Ann was still unable to comprehend what had happened.

"Momma, he can't wake up no more."

The expressionless face of the little boy Jamie had nurtured and loved was more than she could bear. It was as if time had stopped, and her life had no meaning. She held him in her arms and cried uncontrollably, brokenhearted and hurting all over.

Thirty-One

SORROW IS INDIFFERENT

If the public was paranoid about the deaths of five old moonshiners, the unexplained loss of a six-year-old boy catapulted the Belmont population into a collective panic. Local news outlets picked up on Tommy's death and speculated on how he might fit into the scheme of the recent murders. The national press, however, gave Tommy little mention, preferring to focus on the sensational way the others were killed—especially when Raymond Bates was found armless and stuffed down the outhouse pit. It was a very personal and excessive execution according to all the TV experts, and when combined with how the other homicides were carried out, the coverage sent viewership through the roof. Of course, every reporter within one hundred miles was sniffing around and interviewing everyone from the sheriff to the night manager at the Dairy Queen as though the homicidal maniac liked to stop by for a banana split after dismembering his victims. It wasn't hyperbole to describe the situation as a circus.

    Meanwhile, inside the Russell mobile home, things were as quiet as a tomb as Jamie and Ann had withdrawn from the outside world. Ann continued her destructive path by drinking herself into drunken stupors while Jamie sat on her bed in the dark, dwelling on what happened, hoping that she was having a bad dream and would wake up and find Tommy next to her on the mattress. The uncertainty of life without her little brother was taking its toll. Fortunately, or not, their misery was periodically broken by the endless stream of church ladies from First Baptist. Stranger after stranger appeared at their trailer with enough food to feed all the inmates at Gaston Correctional. In a zombie-like trance, Jamie would answer the door, accept the food, and wait for their awkward clichés. The well-intentioned ladies wanted desperately to help the distraught mother and daughter, to speak comforting words to ease their sorrow. Unfortunately, their voices proclaiming that *Tommy's in a better place now,* or *his death was part of a greater plan,* and the customary *there's a reason for everything* made Jamie indignant and mad. She was angry because a guardian angel wasn't there to protect him, resentful because the thought that God sponsored the death of her little brother fostered hate in her heart, not solace and peace in her soul.

Jamie was grateful, however, for the good people at Hope Baptist Church. This local church was located adjacent to the elementary school in Belmont and its members had worked quietly behind the scenes to fund the unavoidable expenses associated with Tommy's memorial. Led by Linda Foster, Tommy's first grade teacher and mother to Jamie's friend Lisa, the church had asked its congregation and the surrounding community for donations to help the family cover the funeral cost. Linda, who attended the church, also convinced the elders to gift a grave plot in the church cemetery so Tommy could have a proper burial. And not to be left out, Maw's church, the Church of the Holy Ghost, had taken up a love offering to help with the Russell family's day-to-day expenses. Given their lack of financial resources, all the benevolent gestures were greatly appreciated by Jamie and Ann.

Beyond the charitable churches and generous community, there had been two others that opened their hearts. One was named Lenny. Jamie's boyfriend had never talked about his feelings for Tommy, but he had been faithful by coming by to see Jamie and Ann every day since the tragedy. Oftentimes, unable to control his emotions, he cried because he cared for the little boy and was heartbroken. And in some way, his own grief helped ease the hurt they were feeling and alleviated their feeling of abandonment. And on his last visit, he went beyond consoler to counselor.

Jamie asked him to find Ann's hidden vodka and empty the spirits down the kitchen sink. He gladly complied.

The other good Samaritan was Deputy Joe Griffin. For the past few days, Joe had been stopping by Raymond's Bait and Tackle to interview Maw and anyone else in Paradise Point who might know of someone who wanted Raymond dead. It turned out to be half of Gaston County. While Joe was in the vicinity, he always came by the Russell household. At first it seemed odd since his only encounter with Jamie was the morning of Tommy's death. Yet something continued to whisper her name in his soul; an unexplainable force drawing him to her side. In his heart, he felt that a strong substitute father might be the solid ground needed for her recovery. At least he wanted to be strong. After all, he was a cop and a Southern male—showing feelings had always signaled weakness to fellow officers. But on more occasions than not, he couldn't hide his hurt and he cried as though Tommy was his own son.

Jamie was touched by his tenderness but was also glad he had been a source of information and answered many of her questions, although in her mind, some of the deputy's suppositions were impossible given her intimate knowledge of her brother. Even though there was a clear sky and full moon making a flashlight unnecessary on that terrible morning, Joe proffered that Tommy may have fallen, thereby causing his injury. Jamie dismissed that notion as nonsense. Her brother could climb a tree lightning-fast and perch on a limb like a squirrel. In her mind, tripping in the woods had nothing to do with his death. It had to be something more sinister than an accident. She also took the opportunity to query Joe about the details of Raymond's demise, thinking that there may be a link between the two deaths. Joe offered little help for that theory, although he did promise to let her know when Tommy's autopsy results were available. Ron Hinkle, with the Medical Examiner's Office in Gastonia, would issue that report, whereas

Raymond's dismembered corpse was sent to Mecklenberg County to be examined by the forensic pathologist. Deputy Griffin expected both reports and death certificates would be available within the next week which would allow Tommy and Raymond to be laid to rest. For now, Jamie was left with sadness and despair, wondering if she could die from a broken heart.

Thirty-Two

"HAYELL" AND BACK

It was a struggle, but Jamie managed to dress her mother in a black, slim fit knitted dress. A little tight in the hips for a funeral, but it was all she had in a somber color. Even more of a challenge was styling the uneven layers of the shag hair that bordered her face. It was an amateurish coiffure, but Jamie never claimed to be a hairdresser and it was the best her hands could muster up. Ann was still desensitized to life, a ghost really, unable to return to normal. Her anguish had forced her daughter to continue her motherly role, although Jamie's new child would soon be forty-one. In a way, it was a good thing. For the time being, the new responsibility forced Jamie to set aside her bereavement for Tommy and to think about someone else; although the recently released autopsy report had her mind refocused anyway. Deputy Griffin had stopped by the trailer earlier in the week and covered the results with Jamie while Ann sat nearby in a trance. It was a hodgepodge of medical terms referencing the transection of the spinal cord causing spinal shock which impaired the nerves that controlled Tommy's heart. The M.E. provided no explanation for the injury other than the contusions indicated that forceful trauma was the cause. The report was meaningless to Jamie. In her mind, this was no accident. Tommy had been at the wrong place at the wrong time and was murdered for his untimely presence. In her heart, she would never find peace until the killer paid for what he did. Her mind was still spinning while she clothed herself in a dark gray maxi skirt and smoky gray V-neck. The outfit would have to work since it was the closest thing she had to funeral attire. Not bothering with her hair or makeup, she led Ann out the door and secured her in the Rambler. Not one word was spoken on the drive to

Hope Baptist. The only sounds were the grinding gears and sputtering engine.

With Jamie's permission, Linda Foster made all the arrangements with the funeral director, including a graveside last goodbye for family and close friends. As for the chapel ovation, Tommy would be eulogized by Roy Holsomback, the senior pastor for the past thirty years at Hope Baptist. Unlike other churches in Belmont with young pastors on staff, Pastor Roy was in his late sixties with platinum, slicked-back preacher hair and shiny three-piece suits. Preferring to motivate the sheep by fire and brimstone, he fancied preaching from the Old Testament and never minced words when it came to God's retribution. Every Sunday he made sure the congregation knew that the penalty for sin was being struck down by the right hand of God, followed by a one-way ticket to *"hayell"*, where you would be introduced to the Lord's devilish counterpart. To hear ole Roy tell it, God had a quiver of lightning bolts and was itching to unleash them on all the sinners in the community. Some of those who liked to take a snort on Saturday night squirmed a little on Sunday mornings, swearing that they could feel the electricity in the pew bench when Roy was on a roll. The elders were certain that the senior pastor was hurting membership and were encouraging him to retire, hoping to find a first-rate preacher that focused more on God's son than sulfur and fire raining down on Sodom and Gomorrah. Or Belmont. Unfortunately for Ann and Jamie, the two associate pastors at Hope Baptist had scheduling conflicts and weren't available for Tommy's service, so they were stuck with hell and damnation.

Jamie pulled the Rambler in a reserved parking space at the side entrance to the church. She had seen the buildings across the cemetery from the elementary school parking lot but didn't appreciate the size and scope of the campus until viewing it up close and personal. The mega church auditorium, with a burgundy brick facade, was accented with tall stained-glass windows traced by borders of limestone. The superstructure was topped by a steeply pitched symmetrical roof which held a prominent spire crowned by the churchly cross that reached for Heaven.

   Jamie didn't have to worry about going astray. Lenny was already there, standing next to the Nova waiting for his girlfriend and her mother to arrive. And he wasn't alone. Alongside stood Johnny, dressed in a wrinkled white shirt and a frayed navy-blue suit that was two sizes too big. The suit and necktie most likely belonged to his father. The too-long sleeves covered most of his hands, and the pants' cuffs were gathered at his shoes. The clothes were unimportant. Jamie didn't know he was coming, and his presence hit her hard. Even though their friendship was new, she knew that Johnny had a special connection with her brother, a kind of childlike innocence between two boys that had fished together and talked endlessly about cars. She saw Tommy in Johnny's boyish face and it reopened her sadness. She began to cry when she stepped from her car. Lenny hurried to where she was standing and held her while fighting off his own tears.

   After a few minutes, both teenagers gathered their composure and helped a despondent Ann from the car. With Jamie and Lenny on either side, they escorted her inside and walked down a narrow hallway that led to the chapel with Johnny following closely behind. Once inside the sanctuary, they were met by Linda Foster who delivered her condolences and placed their pieced together family on the front row bench. At floor level, below the raised pulpit and within a few feet of their pew was a small casket bordered by two pastel flower sprays on easels. It was a surreal scene, although the perfume from the red roses and lilies resting on the coffin reminded everyone that this was no dream. Meanwhile, in the back of the auditorium, solemn voices whispered reverent words of consolation that Jamie and Ann never heard. It was probably best since those attending speculated about what Gaston County had done to deserve the rage of a serial killer. The old men and women milling about in the large foyer were certain that damnation had befallen the county because church members had not prayed long and hard enough for a guardian angel to protect them—as though Gabriel was on a beach vacation and an extra minute of prayer would have brought him back early. All in all, it was a remarkable turnout, especially given the Russell family's lack of kinship with the community. Other than friends from Belmont High, these were all strangers, people Jamie couldn't identify even if they were wearing name tags. Although, there were two individuals walking from the foyer into the sanctuary that she did recognize, Maw Bates and Joe Griffin. Jamie rose and met her dear friends halfway down the aisle. With eyes tightly closed, she tenderly embraced Maw, seeking a measure of peace in her arms. Turning to Joe, she hugged and thanked him for coming. The fresh tears were inevitable. However, neither Maw nor Joe was prepared for the beseeching words from a brokenhearted girl.

"He's not coming back, is he?" Jamie looked at Maw and Joe, hoping for a miracle.

Maw answered for them both, "No, baby girl. I's wish he could, but our little boy can't come back." Joe wasn't prepared for the question, and it hit him hard. But Maw, she was an emotional wreck having lost Tommy, and her only son, Raymond. The little woman buried her face on Jamie's shoulder, and they held each other tightly until Maw withdrew in tears.

"I don't understand why anyone would want to harm an innocent boy," Jamie stared at Maw's eyes, still unable to accept what befell her brother.

"I's don't know, baby girl," Maw answered. "But maybe with Deputy Joe's help, we can find out."

Wanting her special family to sit together, she clutched Maw's right hand and Joe's left, and asked them to join her.

"Momma, Lenny, and Johnny are sitting with me on the front row. Come sit with us."

"Awright, baby girl. You know I's wants to be with you," Maw answered while Joe nodded yes.

The service began with a special thanks from Pastor Holsomback to those attending in support of the grieving family. His introductory remarks were followed by two traditional hymns. The first anthem was, *Turn Your Eyes Upon Jesus*, sung solo by the lead soprano in the church choir. It was beautiful. If you closed your eyes and opened your heart, you could hear the heavenly angels singing with her. Her sweet voice made the tears flow from even the nonbelievers sitting near the exit. The young vocalist then asked those attending to stand, take a hymnal from the pew book rack, and turn to page 133. Accompanied by the Steinway Baby Grand, she led the congregation singing, *Sweet, Sweet, Spirit*. Until today, Jamie had never seen the inside of a church nor heard good, decent people sing about God's promise. She felt overwhelmed listening to their voices fill the sanctuary. And although she didn't understand what she was experiencing, it was a powerful, beautiful feeling—like Heaven was reaching down and stirring her spirit. For the first time since Tommy's death, she felt an indescribable peace within her heart.

Unlike his lengthy Sunday morning sermons, Pastor Roy kept the eulogy under twenty minutes. Everyone was surprised at the brevity other than Leroy Cook who was hoping Roy would wrap it up even sooner. Leroy's golf game had been on the skids lately and he wanted to hit a few practice balls before their tee time. Perhaps it was best the pastor didn't have time to wander from the reason they were there, to get sidetracked on everyone going to *"hayell."* Instead, he spoke about the joy of Heaven and how the love of a child was one of the truest gifts from God. He also mentioned how the little ones were always welcomed into the arms of Jesus. It was comforting for Jamie to hear those words, but it was Pastor Roy's comments directed to those attending the funeral that appealed to her heart; his special charge about each person having an irrevocable call in life, a purpose for which they were created. He preached about never being promised a life without troubles, but a life where we face and defeat our enemies.

At that precise moment in time, Jamie had an epiphany, a resurrection of who she was. She was the avenger who would unravel the mystery and identify and punish the evil person who stole her brother. It all made sense. All the hours in her youth when Ann left her at the library, all the hours spent reading the novels by Agatha Christie and Truman Capote. And she was especially mesmerized by the short stories written by Sir Arthur Conan Doyle. The profound effect these mysteries had on her psyche now seemed like a revelation and by the end of the service, Jamie's mind had withdrawn into the breeches of her new calling. It was probably best that her mind was zoned out. While leaving the sanctuary she never heard the well-intentioned voices speak of how it was best that Tommy never suffered.

Jamie's single-mindedness continued at the graveside farewell. She was silent, barely acknowledging Lisa and Chuckie, two friends who cared deeply for Tommy. And when the casket was lowered and the last flower tossed into the grave, she chose not to hang around and share fond memories. Instead, she gathered her mother and left. Having her brother made life better, less like a prison where others control your life and more like a wide-open world of possibilities. When you are poor, when your family crest is the Goodwill logo, you need that sliver of optimism that makes life worth living. And now it had been taken away. It would be a struggle to gain it back. But she had something more important to do before she could fully recover. Her unfailing devotion to Tommy had not ended with his death and she would never find peace until she found who took the most precious thing from her life.

Thirty-Three

COMPELLED BY DESTINY

The Church of the Holy Ghost was located down a dirt road in the shadows of the piney woods. It was a whitewashed concrete block structure with unadorned windows, and shingles so old they sagged over the eves. Unlike the piety of the big houses of worship in Belmont and Charlotte, this tiny parish had an unrefined culture of its own. In other words, it was a sweet old backwoods church that its women parishioners loved, and its male membership needed. This was *as mean as a snake* world for the uneducated men who attended the church. Men who wore do-rags and hardhats and worked in the quarries, mines, and plants. For those hickory tough men, Sunday mornings were the only time that hard world softened. It was an enraptured feeling when they listened to the Gospel, sang the spirit-lifting hymns, and raised their bruised hands to the rafters. And the women, well they were the spiritual compass that always pointed their menfolk to the little church to be refreshed, even if they had to drag them there sometimes. In truth, were it not for the mothers and wives, most of the men would have never made it to the Promised Land, nor fished the River Jordan. No, the church had never seen a starched shirt or evening dress, but on this Saturday morning, the memorial service for Raymond Cletus Bates had the men dressed in their best overalls and work boots, and the women adorned in their homespun dresses and Sunday-go-to-meeting shoes.

  Jamie was running late and arrived just minutes before the service began. Maw, hoping she would be there, saw her in the back of the chapel and motioned her to the front pew. Given Jamie's limited wardrobe, she was wearing the same maxi skirt and gray top she wore at Tommy's memorial, although she was probably a little overdressed when considering the other clothing styles in the church. After sitting down, Maw clutched Jamie's hand and gave it a reassuring squeeze.

"I's glad you come, baby girl. I's glad you come," Maw whispered.

Before Jamie could respond, the powerful voice of Pastor Dewey Guthrie echoed throughout the small chapel, waking any man who may have worked the night shift at the iron works plant. The pastor, of course, was dressed for the occasion, wearing his Sunday garb of a light blue suit with wing-like lapels, a white dress shirt, and a blue extra wide necktie with a knot as big as his fist. Pastor Dewey wasn't a fashion hound nor was he an articulate man, but his preaching could make a grown man cry and he was bestowed a special gift from the One Most High. He was more disciplined than an Airborne Ranger at Ft. Bragg. He believed in laying out the ground rules for any memorial service he pastored, so he let everyone know from the get-go that Raymond had been cremated so there would be no laying of hands on the casket. Dewey was disappointed. He knew about Raymond's awful reputation and had hoped to have all his body parts present since he thought it easier to pray a corpse into purgatory than an urn filled with ashes. The pastor next spelled out that Betty Sue Wright, playing the upright piano, would accompany all stanzas of *Amazing Grace* and *In the Garden*. The hymns would be followed by a thirty-minute eulogy delivered by himself. Lastly, he reminded everyone that the church ladies, who could cook a blackbird and make it taste like Kentucky Fried Chicken, had brought dinner (which is lunch to all the Yankees up North). The fine meal would be served in the church basement after the service. All things considered; it was a sound plan.

Pastor Dewey stuck to his schedule and finished the service in the allotted half-hour. He had to adlib a little to stretch the time since Raymond didn't have many attributes he could praise in a house of worship. So, he stuck with the usual refrain used by preachers around the world when eulogizing a despicable person..."Raymond was a good man." He also threw in a few, "Raymond tried not to overcharge people at the bait shop," and, "People said that Raymond loved animals," proclamations that were lies. The pastor would have skipped all the subterfuge, but Maw was a longstanding, God-fearing member at the Church of the Holy Ghost and Dewey had to come up with something nice to say. Maw was pleased with how he led the service. He only held and shook his Bible twice at those in the pews, never tried to heal anyone, and only mentioned going to "*hayell*" one time. After ending the service with a prayer for any member who might be backsliding into sin's wicked grip, he announced that the dinner fare of meatloaf, green beans, potato salad, and cornbread was waiting downstairs. The church sisters would have brought the always popular deviled eggs, but Pastor Dewey wouldn't let anything inside the church named after Satan. Of course, the pastor saved the best for last when he revealed that sweet potato pie and peach cobbler would be available for dessert. All these Southern delights would be washed down with a jumbo glass of sweet tea.

    Grief is always part of losing someone you love, and oftentimes, so is the impact that sadness has on one's wellbeing. Five pounds had been subtracted from Jamie's bones since Tommy's death, five pounds she couldn't afford to lose, and Maw knew that her body would gradually shut down if she didn't start eating soon. Maw encouraged her to stay and join her for dinner. Jamie reluctantly agreed and once downstairs, Maw pointed her to a table in the corner and took care of filling both of their plates at the serving line. She loaded barely enough food to feed a jaybird on her plastic dish, but on Jamie's plate, she loaded on a slab of meatloaf and two helpings of green beans and potato salad.

"Dang, Maw! That's enough food to last a week for me. There's no way I can eat all of that. And you brought me two desserts!" Jamie said when Maw delivered her dinner.

"Dun't wurry, baby girl. You kin take whutever you dun't eat home with you," Maw smiled, took a seat across from Jamie and prayed over their food. She then started nibbling at her pone of cornbread and stared at Jamie as though she could read her mind.

A connection had begun to develop between the old woman and young girl since Maw gave Jamie the history lesson about the mountains that day at the bait shop. It was a different kind of kinship as though they could read each other's thoughts. Jamie began the conversation with a question she knew they both were thinking. "What's going on, Maw?" Jamie anxiously asked. "I know you can feel it. You know that something is out there."

"It's been out there as long as I's can remember. It's like it stays hidden for a while, like it's sleepin', and then it wakes up and comes out again. I's kin remember when I's wus little and we lived up on Big Ridge Mountain when 'bout every five or ten years, people near us wuld start gettin' kilt. Or a baby wuld turn up missin'. And nobody could ever catch who wus doin' it. My momma said that the evil wus comin' from over at Spencer Mountain to kill our menfolk or take one of our babies 'cause we made somebody mad about somethin'," Maw answered.

"Oh my gosh, Maw. I went to Spencer Mountain at Halloween with Tommy and Lenny. And a couple of friends went with us too. We went inside a really old, abandoned house at the top of the mountain. We were pretending it was haunted so we could have a little fun and scare each other."

Maw dropped her cornbread in the middle of her green beans, grabbed her purse and pulled out a pack of Camels. Pastor Guthrie didn't approve of smoking in the church any more than deviled eggs, but Maw tamped an unfiltered cigarette on the table to pack the tobacco, lit it anyway and with a trembling hand raised the smoke to her lips. Jamie's words had hit a nerve and Maw refused to exhale to allow the nicotine time to ease her apprehension.

"Whur on Spencer Mountain?" Maw nervously asked.

"I don't know exactly where we were. Lenny was driving and all I heard was something about going north on Highway 29. I do remember that the old house was down a dirt roadway back in the woods." Jamie stopped eating and gave Maw her undivided attention.

"There wus a witch that lived up there years ago. Folks said she didn't have no husband, but she had a son and daughter. People said that she wurshiped the devil and practiced black magic, and that she could raise a monster frum unholy ground and use it to get rid of her enemies. It's a bad place, Jamie. You shouldn't have gone there." Maw took a deep draw from her cigarette, hoping the nicotine would continue calming her nerves.

"Something strange did happen when we were there," Jamie responded.

"Whut happened?" Maw appeared confused.

"Well, Tommy didn't want to go inside the house, so we left him in the car. After we'd been inside for a while, we heard him screaming and we all ran outside to see what was wrong. He was terrified. He said an old woman was looking in the car window at him. He said she had crooked teeth and looked like she had lights in her eyes. It was weird because there was an old painting over the fireplace in the house that kind of looked like the woman he described. Oh, and right before Tommy screamed, one of our friends who was outside on the balcony said he saw a pair of red eyes near the car. He said the eyes were glowing," Jamie answered, transfixed by the pale look on Maw's face. "What's wrong, Maw?"

"Oh, Jamie. You shouldn't have gone there. Could you tell if there were any graves 'round the house?" Maw's eyes narrowed.

"Yeah, there was a small graveyard with some real old tombstones. It was right off a path that led to the house. We didn't think anything about it, but there was one odd thing," Jamie answered.

"Whut?" Maw leaned forward in her chair.

"One of the graves in the cemetery looked like the ground had been dug up not long ago. Like someone was buried there recently," she answered.

"Did you hear any strange noises?" Maw took a deep toke and waited for the answer.

"What kind of noises do you mean, Maw?" she asked.

"Noises like an animal howling, or a person cryin'. Any kinda sound that didn't seem normal," Maw answered while exhaling a plume of smoke.

"Nothing like that. But we did hear a loud noise when we were upstairs in the house. It sounded like it came from below us somewhere. Oh, and there was one more odd thing," Jamie continued.

"Whut wus that?" Maw's brow was furrowed, anticipating Jamie's answer.

"Well, when we were upstairs in one of the rooms, it got really cold when we walked in. It was so weird because we all felt it," she explained.

Maw wasted little time lighting another cigarette off the one she had been smoking. After dabbing the butt on her uneaten food, her eyes softened, and her shoulders sagged. "The evil that kilt Raymond came from that mountain. That evil kilt my boy," Maw quietly said. Jamie just stared. In that rare moment, she understood that a mother's hopes and dreams about her son being a decent man never goes away, but neither does her love when that same son chooses a hellish life of crime. It was a heart-felt lesson for a teenage girl.

"You don't think it was an accident like Joe said, do you Maw? Do you think it killed Tommy?" Jamie already knew the answer.

"It wusn't no accident, baby girl. That evil thing kilt our little boy too," Maw's soft face turned hard.

"Will you help me find out who did it, Maw?"

"We'll work together and find out, baby girl. We'll do it together," Maw responded and clutched Jamie's hands.

What were the odds of an eighty-year-old mother and a sixteen-year-old big sister teaming up to discover the truth? What an unlikely twosome. The tales of the Sherlock Holmes and Dr. Watson of Paradise Point had begun.

Thirty-Four

THE GAME IS AFOOT

The trailer was as quiet as a graveyard, still missing the sound of a little boy's voice. But, for the past four months, life had been inching back to normalcy. Jamie had returned to the routine of schoolwork which kept her mind busy, and her schoolmates and teachers had been supportive in ways she never imagined. Without a doubt, going back to Belmont High had been therapeutic. So had her return to the Food Stop. Mr. Morton had continued his kindness as expected. The Coach had encouraged Jamie to come back to work by offering her an open schedule that could flex with any hours she wanted. Even the customers at the store recognized the teenage girl who had been through so much, and there was never a shortage of sympathetic words nor an extra quarter or two for tips. The additional cash was certainly needed. Money was getting tight, and although Ann had returned to a part-time schedule as an in-home caregiver, she continued to spend more on Smirnoff than milk and bread and never stopped fading in and out of confusion. Her mental lapses proved to be unimportant since the old woman she cared for was even more disoriented. The elderly matron was suffering from severe dementia and never knew if Ann was in the room or on Mars. As for Jamie, when she wasn't in school or working, she was at the public library in Gastonia. She was a prisoner by choice; held hostage in the pursuit of her brother's killer, and the library reference room was where she started her journey. Meticulously, she combed through and read the newspaper articles on the microfiche reader regarding the recent string of homicides. Beginning with the observations of the reporters who researched and wrote articles about the crimes seemed logical to her problem-solving mind. And she thought she discovered a pattern in the murders but needed more information to confirm her suspicions. A reporter named David Brewer with *The Charlotte Times* appeared to have the best sources with the police authorities and the medical examiner's office, so Jamie contacted him first and asked if he wanted to interview the sister of the little boy killed in Paradise Point. Initially he declined, but Jamie talked about Tommy's death not being accidental, and being a newshound always looking for the next big story, he agreed. Besides, he was burned-out writing about the Tet Offensive in Viet Nam and had a reporter's hunch that Jamie might have some juicy stuff that may have been overlooked by the other journalists. Both decided to meet at the restaurant at Howard Johnson's off Interstate 85 after Jamie wrapped up her last class at school.

Jamie was running late and arrived at HoJo's a little before four o'clock. She was worried that David may have grown impatient and left, but she easily spotted him in a corner booth finishing up a double scoop of butter pecan ice cream. The young reporter had a head full of unkempt brown hair, was short-bodied and somewhat fattish, although his girth was easily explained. When you spend hours sitting on your tuchus tapping the keys on an old Royal typewriter, it's easy to balloon-up, especially when you're drinking sodas by the dozens to stay alert. All of the arriving early and staying late did, however, earn the twenty-four-year-old the respect of the old guard at the *Times*. His senior editor, Paul Hunter, thought he had a gift for writing and was always supportive of his willingness to dig deep to find the truth. The boss was also a trusted mentor, although he loved to poke fun at his young protégé by calling him Soda Pop. All the older beat reporters were a little jealous. In the beginning, David was given all the fluff pieces on lost puppies and tree-bound kittens, but on one occasion he was assigned a story about a mother and five-year-old daughter that were senselessly murdered by an abusive husband. His vivid depiction of the stone-cold killer was a raw look into a heart of darkness, an evil that had no sense of decency or love. His powerful news piece that portrayed this monster frightened all the perfect people who were warm and safe in their perfect homes. David's penchant for investigating murders and the fallout misery was the genesis of his not so flattering pet name. This young man wrote about horror stories and the old guys nicknamed him Dr. Death.

   David waved Jamie over his way and after the introductions, both gave the other a good once over. Being young and well-favored, Jamie had the look of high school on her face, but David couldn't help but notice something else beneath her dark eyes. It was the look of someone who had been to hell and back and refused to give up. It was the look of determination. Jamie was equally affected by David. At first, she thought he seemed geeky. Perhaps it was the wrinkled dress shirt and horned rimmed glasses that swayed her opinion. But then she noticed a pair of lively green eyes, a freckled nose and a little boy's grin that stretched across his mischievous face. And then it hit her. He reminded her of Tommy. Even his mannerisms were similar. She couldn't help but wonder if David was a peek at the future had her brother been allowed to bloom. The gawking ended when Jamie responded to a waitress who asked if she wanted something to eat or drink.

   "No, no thanks. I'm good," Jamie shook her head.

   "*The Times* is picking up the tab, Jamie. So, you may as well have something," David smiled.

   "Well, the ice cream sure looks good. But you don't have to bother. I can go to the stand in the front and get it myself," Jamie remarked politely.

   "Don't you dare get up, sugar. I'll take care of it for you. Do you want a cone or dish? And what flavor do you want?" the waitress asked.

"A scoop of chocolate in a cone would be great," Jamie's mouth twisted upward.

David had learned from his senior editor that news journalism is straightforward. And if you want to be an effective journalist, you have to be affable. If you can't make a personal connection with a stranger, you'll never get the inside skinny from a tight-lipped source. For David, it had become as natural as a pig rolling in the mud. And after a quick glance at the waitress's name tag, he called her by name, complimented her beehive hairdo, and changed Jamie's order.

"Better make it two scoops, Brenda," he said with a grin. Much like Jamie, David grew up in a world where the naysayers kept telling him he would never amount to anything. That's life when you're part of a blue-collar household that struggles to pay the bills. His family knew all about being broke on Monday when payday didn't come around until Friday, and college was never an option. No, he knew he was destined for a lifetime of minimum wages working for the man. But David, like Jamie, had a plan to break the mold—he was smart. His drive to excel in high school translated into academic credentials that opened the door to a scholarship at UNC in Chapel Hill. And when you love solving a puzzle or a good mystery, you typically end up in criminal justice or journalism. A part-time stint writing articles for the *Daily Tar Heel* made the Hussman School an easy choice. After graduation, he was hired by the *Times*, and the rest was history.

"Let me grab something and we'll get started." David leaned to his side and pulled a handheld audio recorder from his satchel and placed it on the table. "If it's okay, I would like to record our conversation?" he asked with a half-smile.

"Yeah, that's fine," Jamie answered and then finished the last bite of her ice cream.

"Now, listen. If there's something you want to say off the record, let me know and I'll turn the recorder off. Does that work for you?"

"Yeah."

"All right, then. Why don't you tell me about your family? And your little brother, of course."

Jamie's narrative was not one of being poor, disenfranchised, nor weak. It was a story about the relationship between two siblings. About how when she was ten years old, she became his surrogate mother due to her own mother's failings. She spoke about her pride when Tommy took his first steps, and of having a lot of sit-down talks about the difference between right and wrong. And she reminisced about having an easy hand if she ever had to spank him, and about cradling him when he was flush with fever. Even though the Russell's were as poor as the poor could be without being destitute, she was rich in the boundless love of her little brother. Her sincere words and the soft look in her eyes pulled David into all her sweet memories. But her story turned dark when she relived the morning when Tommy was found in the woods. From that day forward, she lost the future and was left with only anger and sadness. Anger because her brother didn't deserve to die, and sadness because she couldn't shed the emptiness inside. She had no answer for her internal distress other than avenging Tommy's death by making her tormentor feel her pain. It was a plain and simple message and David clearly understood what was driving her emotions.

"Jamie, what do you know about these homicides?" David questioned.

"All I know is what I've read in the newspapers at the library and seen on TV, and what Deputy Griffin was able to tell me," she answered.

"You told me on the phone that Tommy's death was no accident. Do you still believe that after what you've read and seen?" he slid the recorder closer to Jamie.

"I know it wasn't!" she answered forcefully as her jaw tightened.

"I spoke with someone at the M.E.'s Office in Gastonia about Tommy and they are pushing the scenario that he somehow accidentally fell and fractured his neck," David explained.

"That's a lie. That's not what happened," Jamie retorted.

"They're explaining it that way because he wasn't dismembered like Raymond Bates. They believe that if Tommy was murdered, his injuries would have reflected the same kind of brutality that was inflicted on Bates. They are explaining it that way because all of the other victims were savagely killed, and Tommy wasn't," David continued.

"I don't care what they're saying. I know my brother was murdered." Jamie's face turned red with anger and her voice was so loud it caught the attention of Brenda who was standing at the counter. Jamie wanted to tell David that she was certain about Tommy because she could sense it in her heart. But she also knew that trying to explain something beyond reason, something that couldn't be seen or felt was not a good idea. Especially to a fact-based reporter. She decided to keep her sixth sense to herself.

"Calm down, Jamie. Take a deep breath; I'll get you a glass of water." David was about to rise from the booth to find Brenda when Jamie insisted that it was unnecessary.

"I'm sorry. I just get so mad when I hear people saying those things about him," Jamie said in a more soft-spoken voice.

"No need to apologize. I completely understand where you're coming from, and I understand your frustration. But I want you to listen to me carefully. I don't believe Tommy's death was an accident either. For the past three months, I've done a lot of research digging into the records at *The Gazette* and *Times*. Those records go as far back as 1760, and there's been a pattern of these kind of murders in Gaston and Mecklenberg Counties for the past one hundred years. When I dug into the archives, I lost count of how many adults were killed. Kids and babies disappeared. Oh, and there was a disproportionate number of teenage girls that vanished into thin air. Much higher. And no one was ever caught. Not even one legitimate suspect was ever identified. There's no way that kind of pattern could be a coincidence," David spelled out his case with a look of confidence.

"Why do you think all these people were killed?" Jamie's eyes widened.

"I don't know why yet. But I do know the one thing they all seem to have in common and that is illegal whiskey. Most of those killed were either moonshiners or they distributed the booze. That's the connection I've been able to figure out so far," David answered.

"But Tommy wasn't a moonshiner, so why was he killed?"

"I think he was in the wrong place at the wrong time, and he saw something he wasn't supposed to see. I believe he saw the killer when Raymond Bates was murdered. And the killer couldn't allow a witness to live that could identify him," he answered.

"So, what are you going to do now?" she asked.

"I'll do my job and keep digging." David turned the recorder off and returned it to his satchel and picked up the tab in preparation to leave.

"Would you keep in touch with me, David? Will you let me know if you find something that could explain what happened to Tommy?"

"Anything that's not confidential we can talk about. But if I share information with you, I need something in return." David felt certain that given Jamie's grit, she wasn't going quietly into the night.

"What's that?" she winced.

"My gut tells me that you're not going to let this go, so if you uncover something, you've got to share that with me. Can you do that?"

"Of course." Jamie gladly agreed to David's terms. Before leaving, he gave her his business card and she shared her phone number at the trailer and encouraged him to call the Food Stop if no one answered at home. The game truly was afoot.

Thirty-Five

SUMMER OF CLUES

After a while you become numb. That was Jamie's mental state when the school year ended Friday afternoon in May of 1968. Her grades had withstood all the distractions and she qualified for the Honor Roll and was invited for membership in the National Honor Society. But she was thrilled that school was out so she could devote more time to searching for the monster that killed her brother. Given the demands of school and work, most of her time had been devoted to gathering information.

Unlike law enforcement that focused on present day interviews and research, Jamie believed that the answers to the murders were hidden in history. David Brewer had sent her down that path with his remarks about the killings going back for a century. So, her plan was straightforward. Gather all the facts historically available, and then begin the process of painting the picture with a palette of clues from the documents. Her searches were exact and thorough, and she had plenty of help from the public servants who recognized her name and the trauma of her loss. She had developed more contacts than the FBI had informants…Sue at the Register of Deeds, Joyce at the Gaston County Court House, Henry at the Gaston County Police Reports, Mary Beth at Gaston County Genealogy, and Bobbie at the Clerk of Superior Court, to name a few. Those sources along with her investigative work at the library had yielded three accordion file folders so thick with evidence it would make a trial attorney beam with pride.

Beyond her digging into the past, she remained diligent by trying to stay in touch with David Brewer and Deputy Griffin. Regrettably, since David's leads had dried up and the homicides had stopped in Gaston County, her phone calls to him had been more "How have you been doing?" rather than "Do you know who did it?" conversations. Besides that, he had been sidetracked covering deaths halfway around the world. May was the deadliest month of the Vietnam War for U.S. forces and someone had to write about the unpopular news. Dr. Death was the easy choice for the assignment.

And Deputy Joe, well initially he didn't mind reassuring Jamie that the Sheriff's Office "was doing everything in their power" to find the guilty culprit. But after months of Jamie's weekly inquiries, he had grown tired of making excuses and started treating her calls like poison ivy. Joe genuinely cared about her and, in truth, just didn't want to hear her disappointed voice when he explained that nothing had changed. The deputy did, however, introduce her to Priscilla Osborn who managed the archive records at the Sheriff's Office. All the individuals she had met in her quest to understand what happened were important, but there were only two close friends named Lenny and Maw that had her back.

From Belmont High, Lenny followed Jamie in her Rambler back to the mobile home in Paradise Point. Upon arriving, he parked the Nova and waited for her to check on her mother. Once inside, she found Ann alone, sitting on the sofa in her bathrobe holding a tumbler half-filled with Smirnoff. Unlike her past reactions, Jamie didn't bother snatching the drink from her mother's hand. She had grown tired of playing a DUI cop and was fatigued from searching the trailer like a revenue agent. Besides, Ann had found ways to circumvent her seizures anyway. She had learned that stealing booze from the liquor cabinets of her elderly companions stricken with dementia was as easy as apple pie. So, Jamie had given up on exorcising all of Ann's personal demons. Moreover, she had her own devil perched on her shoulder that kept twisting her mind with bitter thoughts and she needed to let her resentment go. She did so by allowing her animosity to wane, and by forgiving her mother for all her misgivings, including taking away the amulet Maw had given Tommy for protection. No, Jamie wasn't proud of her Momma, but she was still her Momma and she decided to allow her love to be stronger than her anger.

"Momma, you need to get up and eat something. I'll open a can of tomato soup and heat it up for you. I'll get you some crackers too." Jamie pulled on her mother's free hand to help her rise from the sofa, but Ann jerked back, resisting her daughter's attempt.

"Leave me alone, Jamie. I'll eat something in a little bit. I just want to sit here a little longer and look at some of Tommy's pictures. The shoe box with the pictures is on my bed. Go get it for me and leave me alone for a little while and then I'll eat some soup." Ann's slurry voice and glassy eyes confirmed that she had been drinking vodka as though it were water and was severely intoxicated.

"Fine. I'll get the pictures for you and then I'm going to see Maw down at the bait store. Lenny is waiting outside. He's going with me." Jamie turned to walk to the bedroom and her mother made a request that could only come from a lonely, confused drunk.

"You should have told me that Lenny was outside. Why don't you tell him to come inside and have a drink?" Ann coyly smiled and jiggled the ice cubes in her tumbler.

"Geez, Momma. You just stay where you are, and I'll be right back." Jamie hurriedly returned with the box, gave it to Ann and stepped outside to catch up with Lenny.

"Hey. Momma's been drinking again. Let's drive your car down to the store and then come back here so I can check on her," Jamie remarked with a grim look on her face.

"Sounds good," Lenny responded.

Thirty seconds later Lenny parked the Nova and the teenagers stepped inside the entrance to find Maw's Bait and Tackle store bustling with customers. It was Maw's idea to be watchful and cleanse the store of any negative vibe still hanging around after Raymond's demise. Renaming the store was step one. Step two was posting signs throughout the premises that were inked with verses from Chapter 6 in Ephesians. In Maw's mind, the Bible was filled with all kinds of armor that could stand against and cast out any maleficent spirits left by her pagan son. And her strategy seemed to be working. People loved her friendly management style, and the beginning of summer had every wannabe fisherman looking for advice on fishing gear and supplies. Rods and reels were in short supply and anything, artificial or alive, that could send a bass to the taxidermist was leaving the bait shop in droves. And Pabst Blue Ribbon, well that was popular as well. Maw would have given up the liquor license, but in her mind, it didn't make sense. Unlike Raymond, she wasn't breaking the law by cooking moonshine and figured beer was close enough to the Bible's take on wine to pass the smell test. It was an easy decision. The hard part for Maw was trying to manage the business while being pulled in every direction. She was recommending a Hellbender fishing lure to one customer and pointing another to the Vienna Sausage when she spied Jamie and Lenny headed her way.

"How's my baby girl doin'?" Maw asked with a big smile. "And how 'bout you, Lenny. You doin' good?" Maw's eyes twinkled as she reached for Jamie.

"Hey, Maw. Yeah, I'm doing okay," Jamie answered as she released Maw from their usual hug.

"Me too, Maw. I'm hangin' in there," Lenny replied as Maw gave him the same warm welcome. "Looks like you're covered up with business around here."

"Yeah, everyone wunts to go fishin' this weekend with school out and all. I's needs sum help round here, and nobody wunts to work in the store. I's reckon they's all fat and happy gettin' their government money and dun't wunts to put up with a crusty ole woman like me." Maw shrugged her shoulders and shook her head.

"Maw, you know that's not true. Anyone would want to work for you," Jamie countered.

"Well's, how 'bout you and Lenny? As much as you two love to fish, I's bet you'd love workin' here," Maw's offer caught Jamie completely by surprise.

"You know we would if we could, but we can't leave Mr. Morton at the Food Stop in a bad way. He's been really flexible with my hours and needs us both there," Jamie answered.

"Well's, if youins change yore mind, jest let me know," Maw grinned as she placed a pinch of snuff between her lower lip and gum.

"Maw, you said you wanted to tell me something when I saw you earlier this week. What's going on?" Jamie asked with a quizzical expression.

"There'd be two things. I's got somethin' for you, and I's been talkin' to the ladies from church and I's got somethin' to tell you," Maw answered and motioned for them to follow her to the back of the store.

Maw led Jamie and Lenny to a small room in the back corner. Inside the crowded enclosure were a single bed, an old cotton recliner, and a tall handmade rosewood cabinet that was resting against the wall. She unlocked and opened the cabinet's armoire-like double doors that were held closed by a metal latch secured with a padlock big enough to protect the gold at Ft. Knox. This was the private space where Maw took breaks when tired from working, and in that space, she also stored her precious jars, bottles, and cans filled with everything from herbs to stump water. A porcelain mortar and pestle used for grinding all the gnarly roots were on the top shelf, and the bottom shelf held an assortment of charms from hair clippings to fish bladders. No, you would never find these rare trinkets in the *World Book Encyclopedia* unless the book added a section on Appalachian hoodoo. But Maw was superstitious to the bone and fought evil with a mixture of religion and magic.

"Here," Maw reached inside the cabinet and withdrew two necklets identical to the ones she previously gave Jamie and Tommy. "Baby girl, give your momma one of these to wear, and Lenny, you take the other one for yourself."

"Thanks, Maw. We really appreciate you looking out for us," Jamie said as her mouth curved into a smile.

"Yeah, thanks Maw," Lenny echoed his gratitude.

"Jest wait a minute. I's got somethin' else for you both," Maw said as she bent down to reach the bottom shelf. As she rose and straightened her body, she handed Jamie and Lenny two rusty horseshoes.

"Baby girl, you take your horseshoe, wrap it in aluminum foil, and hang it upside down over your front door. And Lenny, you do the same with yours," Maw instructed.

Both kids had looks of incredulity on their faces. "Why?" Jamie asked.

"Cause the horseshoes will keep any haints or the devil from comin' inside. It'll stop 'em from hurtin' you and Lenny," Maw explained.

Jamie agreed to follow Maw's instructions while Lenny remained as quiet as the magical rocks in Maw's cabinet. He knew his father wasn't superstitious and would never allow a horseshoe to be nailed over their home's front door. If the threat wasn't something his father could see or feel, it wasn't real. Lenny thanked Maw just the same. "Yeah, thanks Maw. I really appreciate it," Lenny said with a dumbfounded gaze.

"Maw, what did you want to tell us about the ladies at your church?" Jamie asked.

"All the ladies think these killings are 'bout a moonshine war that's goin' on. And Clarice, one of the ladies at the church, is Ludean Suggs's aunt, and she said youins should go talk to her. She thinks that Ludean knows who's behind all this," Maw explained.

"Wasn't Ludean's husband killed with his brothers?" Jamie's eyebrows rose.

"Yeah, he wus kilt. But Clarice said that Ludean's husband was a moonshiner and that Ludean knowed bout everythin' that wus goin' on. Clarice said that youins could find out a lot if youins would go see her. I'd go too, but I's can't leave the store," Maw answered.

"Do you have her phone number, Maw?" Jamie asked.

"I's can look it up and youins can use the phone here at the store to call her if youins want," Maw offered.

"If you can find her number, that would be great. We need to go back by the trailer and check on Momma, so I can call her from there," Jamie replied.

After arriving back at the mobile home, Jamie asked Lenny to wait in the car while she went to check on her mother and call Ludean Suggs. Once inside, she found Ann asleep on the sofa with photographs of Tommy strewn across her torso, and the ice from her tumbler spilled on the floor. As Jamie stared at her momma, she couldn't help but wonder if Maw's magic horseshoe would keep the vodka out of the trailer. After all, some of the most evil spirits come in a bottle. She shook her head at such a foolish thought and then dialed Ludean's number on the rotary phone. Mrs. Suggs answered after the first ring, and after listening to Jamie's reason for calling, insisted that she and Lenny come to her house right away. Even though months had passed since Buck's death, Ludean was still in sorrow's grip, adrift on a sea of what might have been. She was feeling unloved and lonely and the thought of ending her one-way conversations by speaking with someone else was thrilling. She had just enough time to finish cooking a snack before the teenagers arrived.

******

It had been sunny for several days and the dust enveloped the Nova like an unwanted sandstorm. Lenny had spent two hours washing and Turtle waxing his car the day before, and he cringed thinking about how it would look after driving on the dirt road to Ludean's house. Considering the reason for the trip, complaining to his girlfriend would have been a bad idea, so he remained silent and focused on dodging the numerous ruts sprinkled along the driveway. After Lenny parked, Jamie jolted from the car and headed for the front door while Lenny took a moment to assess the layer of dirt on his Chevy. Meanwhile, Ludean had seen the kids arrive from the kitchen window as she was scooping the last pieces of their snack from the iron skillet. A possum had been hanging around the chicken coop behind the house and Ludean finally caught the sneaky critter pilfering eggs. She immediately held court and executed a death sentence by firing a .22 caliber long-rifle in its skull. After skinning the critter and carving out small parts of meat and fat, she added her special ingredients which included a covering of cornmeal along with heavy doses of salt and pepper, and then fried the parts in rendered pig fat to make some tasty rinds and cracklins. Jamie's nostrils flared when Ludean opened the front door. The aromatic smell of hot grease and cracklins was unavoidable. Ludean's warmth and friendliness was as hard to overlook as the aroma from the kitchen.

"You must be Jamie. It's so nice to meet you," Ludean smiled, "Come on inside."

"It's nice to meet you too, Mrs. Suggs," said Jamie as Lenny skipped up the front porch steps and stopped beside her.

"Call me Ludean. I dun't like all that furmality stuff," Ludean answered and motioned the teenagers to the kitchen. "You two sit down and I'll get you somethin' to eat."

"Oh, no thanks, Ludean, nothing for me." Jamie responded while waving her hand side to side.

"Well then, Lenny, you sit down here," Ludean slid a chair away from the table and pulled Lenny by the arm and gave him a gentle downward push onto the seat. Lenny was as hungry as a bear coming out of hibernation, so he gave little resistance to Ludean's offer. She turned, grabbed a pan of deep-fried possum parts off the counter and placed it on the table with a couple of paper towels. She then fixed Lenny a large glass of sweet tea and told him to join her and Jamie in the living room when he had his fill. Then Ludean turned her attention to Jamie.

She was captivated by how similar they looked at how she could be mistaken for Jamie's mother. Long black hair, dark eyebrows, high cheekbones, and full lips were their most similar features. Jamie's likeness momentarily sent Ludean back in time, reminiscing about how much she wanted a baby, a little girl. But it just never happened. It was God's will she thought as the years passed by. As immoral as Buck was, maybe God just wanted her to hold on to him as though he was the only soul on earth.

"Have a seat, Jamie, and let's talk," Ludean pointed to the sofa, and both sat down within arm's reach of each other. And for the next thirty minutes, Jamie listened while Ludean shared the most interesting story.

Ludean felt the need to chronicle the past so her theory about what recently happened to Buck, and the other murder victims made sense. It was an uncomplicated explanation of how she was a good woman who deserved a good life but fell in love with a whiskey man who operated an illegal business in the mean world of moonshiners. Even though she tried to convince Buck to change his ways, his demon was the liquor and he clung to it like a mother clutching a newborn baby. And over the years while Buck dodged the revenuers and avoided hard time in prison, Ludean became a captive in her own home. She endured a life of cleaning the house, cooking his meals, taking care of the laundry, and nurturing the garden and animals. It was a mind-numbing routine that consumed her days while her nights were spent praying for Buck's safe return home. And for the next thirty years, that was their story.

Jamie carefully listened to every word and from those words learned a valuable lesson. Buck never deserved Ludean's love, but she gave it anyway because he needed it. Jamie couldn't help but think that the same could be said about Ann; a mother who made many mistakes in life, but desperately needed the love of her daughter. It took Ludean a half hour to relive those three decades. Unfortunately, everything she shared about Buck was common knowledge in Gaston County. That was until she revealed an important secret. Buck and his brothers had recently started selling marijuana and heroin as an add-on service for their moonshine customers, and anyone else who wanted to get high. Their source for the illegal drugs was none other than Raymond Bates. Jamie knew that Raymond trafficked in weed, but the heroin was a complete surprise.

"So, you see, Jamie, thur wus a whiskey and drug war that wus goin' on between all the shiners and dope dealers in the county. Buck tole me that someone wus out to get him cause of the fightin'. He thought he wus in danger. But Beaver and Bo wunted to keep sellin' the whiskey and dope to everybody 'cause the money wus so good."

"So, it sounds like everything was related to the booze and drugs?" Jamie looked at Ludean for confirmation.

"It wus mostly the drugs, but Buck tole me that some of Puck Dutton's customers had started buyin' whiskey from him 'cause he was sellin' it cheaper than Puck. Buck said that Puck weren't right in the head, and that he wus the one that skeered him," Ludean answered.

"What about the other man that was killed? The one that was found in his hog pen. Do you know anything about him?" Jamie had learned about the details of Cooter Jones' demise from David Brewer and wanted to probe Ludean for any additional color.

"Cooter Jones and Puck Dutton has been feudin' fur a long time over money and pigs. Cooter used to run whiskey for Puck but decided to build his own still and go out on his own. Some peoples say he wus tryin' to build a meth lab too. Everybody knowed that Puck wus mad at Cooter fur all that stuff," Ludean cocked her head to the side as though everyone knew about the ongoing feud.

"And Tommy? What about him?" Jamie's eyes narrowed.

"I think Tommy jest stumbled onto the person that was killin' Raymond Bates. People say that Raymond wus kilt cause he wus movin' in on somebody else's territory. I dun't knowed who's territory it wus, but I dun't think Tommy wus supposed to be kilt," Ludean answered.

"And Beaver and Bo were just collateral damage?" Jamie asked.

"I believe they wus both kilt 'cause of that, but Bo culdn't keep his pecker in his pants and wus messin' 'round with Dixie Trotter or Dixie Dutton I reckon. Dixie wus Puck's wife and people said Puck wanted Bo dead when he found out. But so did half the husbands in the county," Ludean grinned. After hearing some footsteps coming from the kitchen, she paused and looked over her shoulder to find Lenny walking into the den. "Hey, young man. We'd been so busy talkin', we furgot you'd be here."

"Yeah, I've been kinda busy eating all the pork cracklins and rinds you fixed. They sure were good!" Lenny said with a big smile.

"Well, I'm glad you'd like them, Sugar, but they weren't pork cracklins," Ludean shook her head to affirm her answer.

"Oh, yeah?" Lenny said with puzzlement on his face.

"No, Sugar. Those were possum cracklins. I kilt a possum last night that wus tryin' to get my chicken eggs. I skint it and cooked it before youins got here," Ludean said with pride.

Much like when Deputy Joe realized he had been eating something akin to a big rat, Lenny was completely caught off-guard by the surprise. His face immediately drained of color, and he held his breath in an effort to keep all the cracklins and rinds in his stomach. Jamie couldn't let the opportunity pass by without ribbing her boyfriend.

"Lenny, I had no idea you loved possum so much," Jamie laughed, knowing Lenny's palate would never be the same after eating an animal that hung upside down by its tail.

"Yeah, that's very funny. I'm going to go outside and wait until y'all get through talking," Lenny did an about face and hurried out of the den.

Ludean and Jamie laughed like two schoolgirls and made jokes about Lenny's reaction until the revelry abruptly stopped. The mood turned dead serious when Jamie made one final request from her new friend. "Ludean, do you know where Puck Dutton lives?"

"Why do you wunt to know that?" Ludean's face instantly turned grim.

"I want to talk to him," she answered.

"About whut?" Ludean's forehead furrowed.

"I want to find out if he knows anything about what happened to Tommy."

"Oh, Sugar. That's not a good idea. Buck tole me that Dutton wus dangerous. If you start askin' him questions about anythin', he might hurt you or do somethin' worse," Ludean said with a somber voice.

"I wouldn't go to talk to him by myself. I can get Deputy Griffin to go with me. Or maybe the reporter I know who works for *The Times*. I know he would go. He wants to talk to Dutton too. And Lenny, he would go with me for sure," Jamie tried her best to sound reassuring.

"Promise me you'll be careful, Jamie. Promise me you'll not do anythin' to get yourself hurt."

"I promise, Ludean. I'll be careful." Jamie gave Ludean her word.

It was an imprecise map, but Ludean did her best to sketch the directions based on passing comments she recalled from her late husband. She gave Jamie the drawing and invited her to stay a little longer so they could talk about subjects much less dire. Jamie knew that staying would help curb Ludean's loneliness, but Lenny was waiting so she thanked her for her help, apologized for leaving so soon and promised that she would come back to see her, or at the very least call her on the phone. After an affectionate hug, Jamie stepped out the front door to find Lenny with a face as white as a sheet as he stood next to his car. It could have been the thought of what he had eaten or perhaps it was the deep-fried grease that made him queasy. Whatever the reason, Lenny had thrown-up at the edge of the woods while bracing himself on a white oak tree.

"Jeez, Lenny, you look like a ghost. Do you want me to drive?" Jamie amusedly smiled.

No one drove Lenny's Nova, but Lenny. Well, maybe he would let Jesus drive it, but only after he had given the Lord a crash course on how to handle a Hurst four speed shifter. "No, no. I'm fine. I can drive," Lenny answered quickly.

Both kids stepped into the car and waved to Ludean who was standing on the porch watching them leave. Jamie was quiet, staring out the car window as Lenny left the dirt road and turned onto an asphalt thoroughfare. Her mind was restless thinking about the conversation she had with Ludean. She now knew for certain that there was a serial-angle to the murders and her next challenge was how to leverage her newfound knowledge. A phone call to David Brewer was first on her list. Her promise to share any new information she uncovered had not been forgotten.

Thirty-Six

LOOKING FOR ANSWERS

David Brewer was unavailable, and so was Deputy Joe Griffin. That left only Lenny and Maw. Jamie had a lot going for her, a lot of strengths that would emerge from a Myers–Briggs personality test. But patience wasn't one of them. She was dead set on finding Puck Dutton's shack and talking to the hermit as soon as possible. And she had the perfect tour guide.

Maw knew the hills, hollers, and river as well as anyone and could get them there. And Lenny, well, he would come along for protection. He had a .22 semi-automatic rifle that was given to him on his thirteenth birthday, and he could knock a distracted squirrel out of an oak tree at fifty yards. The rifle was in the Nova's trunk along with a box of long-rifle shells. He was ready for action.

The only thing left was a good plan—they had a plan all right but finding the shack and knocking on the front door wasn't very strategic. First, Lenny and Jamie would pick up Maw at the bait store around five in the afternoon after they got off work at the Food Stop. Normally, the teenagers worked until closing on busy Saturdays, but Coach was upbeat given how well the store was doing against his new competitor up the street. Even Trigger had been exceeding expectations by raking in the quarters, so he gladly gave his blessing for their early departure and told them to be careful. As for Maw, one of the church ladies from the Holy Ghost had agreed to help by keeping an eye on things at the bait store until it closed at eight. Maw was sure that The Spirit had a hand in finding her a substitute on such short notice.

Lenny followed Jamie and the Rambler back to the mobile home in Paradise Point. He had talked Jamie into driving her car on their trip to Puck Dutton's instead of taking the Nova. It was something about his car being close to empty and his big V8 only getting about five miles a gallon. In truth, it had rained earlier in the day, and he didn't want his car covered in mud from traveling down a backwoods road, nor did he want muddy shoes, nor cigarette smoke smelling up the interior. Jamie really didn't care which car they drove; she just wanted to get there before a dark sky made finding their way difficult. So, within seconds after arriving at the trailer, Lenny transferred his rifle to the Rambler, hopped in the front passenger seat, and off they went to the store.

Maw was waiting outside and after Jamie parked, she wanted to climb in the backseat with her nonfiltered cigarette, but Lenny quickly exited the car and insisted she sit in the front so she could navigate the way for Jamie. It was an error in judgment. Maw immediately rolled down her window attempting to funnel the smoke out of the car as they began the journey. It didn't work. The wind carried the fumes along with the hot ashes to the back seat where it landed on Lenny's face. He started to complain but Maw pulled two Moon Pies from the deep pocket in her jacket and offered them to the teenagers as though she was apologizing for her bad habit. Jamie declined the offer, but Lenny had skipped lunch at the Food Stop, so he accepted Maw's apology by eating them both. A few minutes later after a little small talk, Jamie noticed that Maw seemed to be feeling especially playful given the lop-sided grin that refused to leave her face.

"What are you so happy about, Maw?" Jamie asked.

"Whut kinda outfits does youins got on?" Maw continued to survey their white shirts and green bow ties, causing her mouth to twist upwards into a full-blown smile.

"Oh, crap. We forgot to change. It's our Food Stop uniform," Jamie explained while removing the bowtie from her collar.

"Well, thar you go, baby girl. You wouldn't have to wear stuff like that if you worked at the Bait Shop," Maw snickered.

"I know. And who knows? Maybe one day I can. But until then, how about taking a look at the map Ludean gave me and just telling me where to go as best you can."

The trip was thirty minutes of zig and zags with many instructions to turn back around and go another way, but Maw finally got them to an isolated location down a dead-end dirt road. It was a malodorous spot. Too lazy to drive to the county landfill, the local rednecks dumped their garbage off the road in the tall weeds, and the rummaging racoons did a fine job ripping the bags open and digging through the rotten food. Maw could see an obvious trail that weaved through the trash and onto an old logging road that disappeared into the nearby trees. She instructed Jamie to park the Rambler on the opposite side of the road and be sure to lock the doors. Needing a nicotine boost to calm her nerves, Maw pulled a can of Bruton from her pocket, placed a pinch next to her gum, then exited the car. She huddled with Jamie and Lenny to lay out the way to their destination.

"The only way to get to whur we needs to go is through the woods over thar. You kin get thar by boat, but this here is our only way. It's 'bout a half-mile walk to the river where Ludean said the shack is. Thar should be an old road that'll lead us thar, but it's probably covered up a lot over the years," Maw's jovial mood had turned as serious as Pastor Dewey preaching about the torments of hell. Lenny could sense the tension and his expression turned as sober as Maw's.

"Maw, I didn't say anything about it, but I brought my rifle to take along just in case we need it," Lenny said while pointing at the trunk of the car.

Lenny wasn't the only one packing heat. Maw wryly smiled and reached into the pocket of her canvas jacket and pulled out a silver two-barrel derringer. She held up the small gun to allow Lenny and Jamie to inspect her weapon of choice. "You best bring the rifle, Lenny. And I'll bring Miss Daisy along jest in case we need her." Maw sensed that they may encounter danger and had the best intention by bringing the tiny pistol. But she knew she would need to be at point-blank range for Miss Daisy to be effective...close enough to smell the breath of the monster she wanted to kill. "We'd better git goin'."

The tract of land had been clear-cut by Jemison Lumber Company around ten years ago, and even though the old road was still visible, it had been over-seeded with red maple, white ash and hickory trees that were mature enough to have switch-like limbs. Through the middle of the overgrown road was a meandering trail used mostly by deer, bears, and raccoons. Like two lost puppies, Jamie and Lenny followed Maw on that path into the deep woods. This was a harsh place where the law belonged to nature and the three pathfinders moved like shadows, hoping to avoid the teeth and fangs of anything hidden behind a tree, in the leaves or under a rock. The trail was choked with briars and underbrush, and even with the heavy weight jacket and chaps that Maw was wearing it was a difficult hike. Unfortunately, Jamie and Lenny were still dressed as though they were at the store bagging groceries. Nevertheless, on and on they trudged.

Up the ridges, down the ravines, and through the thickets, briars and bogs they traveled until Jamie's and Lenny's clothes were unsuitable for the Salvation Army drop box. Lenny was not happy about the abuse of his outfit, but he was getting even more annoyed at his girlfriend because of the strap-like welts on his arms. Jamie avoided the hazardous tree branches and vines by sticking so close to Maw's backside that the whiplashing limbs passed her by while Lenny tried to parry them with his rifle. Maw was unaware of all the drama taking place behind her. The little eighty-year-old wonder just kept pushing through the foliage like an unfazed porcupine. After slogging through one last patch of pines, an old shack surrounded by century-old oaks and the glassy water of the South Fork Catawba River came into view.

"We's here," Maw said while pointing at the crude structure and scanning left to right, "This is the place. I's dun't seed nobody 'round though."

All three paused momentarily, surprised by the unusual view. They had expected to see a well-built cabin, but not one that looked constructed by a carpenter who was stone-blind from drinking too much whiskey. It was a windowless, ill-proportioned hut made from unpainted sheets of plywood that were capped by a rusty corrugated tin roof that was sagging from the rotting rafters. The small hovel rested on concrete blocks about two feet off the ground which was, in all likelihood, a safeguard to keep the cottonmouths from taking up residence inside. Truth be told, the owner didn't have to worry about snakes, nor muskrats, nor beavers moving in. Any critter or reptile within range was immediately dispatched with a double-barrel shotgun as evidenced by the animal hides that were salted, nailed to the shack, and then cured in the sun. The other oddity was the lack of any outbuildings, sheds, or outhouse. In fact, the only other structures were a four-post empty pig pen and a lopsided six-piling pier that teetered on falling into the river.

"Look over thar. In the river," Maw's eyes crinkled at the corners, and she pointed at the water's edge.

"Are you talking about the dock over there?" Jamie asked, looking in the same direction.

"Yep. If'n this is Puck Dutton's place, he's probably gettin' here by boat. He shor ain't comin' the way we just came. We kin look 'round and knock on the door to be sure, but I dun't think anyone's here."

Even with the risk they were taking, Maw seemed confident and Jamie appeared fearless. But Lenny looked spooked. Taking no chances, he put on the proverbial white hat and loaded his rifle with ten bullets before following Maw and Jamie to the shack's front door. Upon arriving, Maw's demeanor instantly changed, as though she was feeling the same anxiety that had been eating Lenny up inside. That apprehension had now found a place in her gut.

"Oh, Lordy. I's wus 'fraid of this," Maw's eyes widened as she glared at an inverted cross crudely carved into the top of the door.

"Is that what I think it is?" Jamie asked.

"I'm fraid so, baby girl. I'm fraid so. We probably should get outta here," Maw did an about-face in preparation to leave.

"No, we can't leave yet. We just got here," Jamie wasn't going anywhere. She slid behind Maw and started rapping on the door. "Is anybody at home? Mr. Dutton, are you here?" Jamie knocked so hard this time it forced the unlatched door to swing open. After leaning forward and peering inside, she confirmed that indeed Puck wasn't at home. "Maw, let's go inside and take a look around. We came all this way and need to check out this place. Lenny, you wait outside and keep a lookout for anyone who may show up," Jamie ordered. Lenny gladly complied while Maw questioned Jamie's judgment.

"That's a bad idea, Jamie. This place is evil. I's can feel it. We needs to leave," Maw's voice was filled with tension.

"I'm going inside. You can stay outside with Lenny if you want to," Jamie ignored Maw's warning and stepped inside the gloomy enclosure.

Maw felt like her relationship with Jamie was a divine appointment, an opportunity to protect her, to make a difference in the life of a young girl. She had no intention of letting her go into the darkness alone. "I's comin' in with you."

It was a one-room squalor, illuminated only by the slithers of sunlight that carved its way through the gaps in the plywood siding. Once inside, Jamie and Maw allowed their eyes to adjust to the poor lighting. On one wall was a brand-new Army cot, a military-style folding stool, and a wooden box topped with open cans of beans and potted meat. Against another plywood wall were a kerosene camping stove, two lanterns, and a Johnson rod and reel that was enveloped in spider webs. Since the shack was so close to the river, it seemed odd that Puck hadn't used the fishing gear. But Maw identified the reason why when she spied two crank-style portable telephones on the floor.

Puck thought it was too hard to catch a largemouth on a plastic worm, so he had jury-rigged the magneto components of the phones so he could drop the wire leads in the water and shock the stunned fish to the surface. Then, of course, it was easy to net them. Maw said it was called "phoning up the fish" and described anyone doing it as despicable. Of course, since she was in the bait business, her condemnation was not surprising.

She and Jamie continued their appraisal by pivoting around and viewing the wall that supported the entrance door. In that location they found several boxes of Mason jars and around a dozen one-gallon jugs bunched in the corner. Maw felt certain that Puck had a nearby still and used the jugs and jars to store his corn liquor, so items like that weren't unexpected. In fact, at this point in their inspection, they had seen nothing out of the ordinary, nothing unanticipated. But then Maw found something that caused her to recoil with jitters when she surveyed the final wall. It was a handmade table constructed of 4' x 4' legs and a particle board top that was covered with a bizarre assortment of devilish sacraments. Cowrie shells used to cast and break spells, black candles for rituals, mandrake roots, and jars filled with formaldehyde and animal parts were some of the strange paraphernalia. And just above the table were six inverted crosses and a pentagram carved into the wall. Maw knew that this shack was a temple devoted to the unholy one; that all of these Satanic offerings and symbols were used for worship and appeasement, and it made her skin crawl with apprehension.

"We needs to leave this place. Now!" Maw ordered their departure and pulled Miss Daisy from her pocket. Jamie could sense the wickedness that Maw was feeling, but before she could follow her orders, they both stopped, thinking they could make out a voice echoing from the riverbank.

It was Lenny. He had heard a sputtering Johnson outboard coming their way and was sounding the alarm.

"Someone's coming," he yelled as he sprinted to the shack. Lenny stuck his head through the doorway. "There's someone coming in a boat, and he's waving a gun!" Lenny exclaimed.

Jamie and Maw burst outside in time to see a five-foot-five gremlin drifting up to the dock in an old V-hull boat powered by an even older outboard engine. It was Puck. And he was pissed.

With his high-pitched, screech owl voice, no one could understand what he was screaming. Well, Maw did recognize his blasphemous words that were breaking the Second, or Third Commandment, depending on whether your expert was Pastor Dewey or Pope Paul VI. To her, the numeric order and religious experts were unimportant. Puck was still taking the Lord's name in vain which added another strike to all his other demonic depravities.

Puck tied up the boat, and Jamie, Maw, and Lenny needed to act quickly. All three scrambled like kids who just egged a house on Halloween night. Fortunately, they had made it to the deep cover of the tree line when Puck reached the shack. At that moment, they heard the shots from his .410 double barrel.

"Keeps movin'," Maw barked as she led the way through the woods, "He might be followin' us!"

The hike back to the Rambler took half the time as the trip to the shack. And the drive to the Bait Shop gave Jamie time to think about her decision to ignore Ludean's warning. In hindsight, expecting a cordial sit-down with Puck Dutton was foolish, and more importantly, it placed her friends in a very perilous situation with potentially lethal consequences. She felt sick about what she had done and apologized profusely to Maw and Lenny. Her confession was instantly dismissed. Both assured her that, even now, they would do it again. Maw was adamant that the knowledge they learned about Dutton was worth the risk. She was convinced that Dutton's shanty was the operational headquarters for Lucifer, Inc., and that Puck had struck a bargain with the devil that would make Doctor Faustus green with envy. The illegal whiskey and drugs were merely means to fund the evil. Over and over, Maw kept quoting Scripture about how an ungodly man diggeth up evil until she divulged some suspicions that caught Jamie and Lenny by surprise. Maw was certain that it was a short trip by land or boat from Dutton's shack to the location where the young campers were murdered. She believed the folding cot and chair in the shack may have been part of the couple's camping equipment. Just based on the filthy condition inside the shack, the gear was out of place. It was simply too new and too expensive for vermin like Dutton. Plus, she could feel it in her bones.

The unrighteous hermit was now their number one suspect.

PART III

A MIGHTY FINE PLAN

Thirty-Seven

CAN'T GET NO REST

The mobile home was a run-down junk heap and would never be mistaken for the Biltmore, but it had been a place where Jamie felt safe, and a refuge where she shared her love with Tommy. But now the trailer felt uneasy, as though there was something disturbed within its walls. Jamie had been sensing that disquieted presence, and on every occasion, like a little kid, she wanted to look in the closet or under the bed. Beyond the anxiety, the unexplainable feeling had fostered a number of unnerving dreams, and for the past several weeks, she had been unable to soundly sleep. Oftentimes, she would wake up in the middle of the night when she heard a plaintive whisper. At other times it would be a wishful dream about the future, a life with Lenny, a family with kids, and a big house filled with laughter. It was a beautiful fantasy, but the vision was always taken away by some malevolent force.

Out of all the bad dreams, one kept coming back again and again. The scene was inaudible, but she could see Tommy's lips moving and the agitated look on his face. It was strange because he was always glaring and pointing at the shadows. It seemed like her brother was reaching out from the grave, as though he wanted to tell her a secret or reveal someone's face. Not understanding Tommy's message was frustrating for Jamie, especially since Maw had told her that she had the *sight*. If Maw was right and she could see and comprehend things before they happened, why wouldn't her clairvoyance show her the answer when she needed it the most?

Jamie needed a reprieve from the trailer and Lenny was the perfect antidote. His phone call asking for a date to the movies was just what the doctor ordered. Paul Newman, starring in *Cool Hand Luke*, was playing at a walk-in theater in Belmont called the Regency, and Lenny's plan was to pick Jamie up at Maw's store that evening at six. It was Monday, Jamie's normal day off at the Food Stop, and she wanted to show Maw how much her love and support meant to her, especially after the botched mission to Puck Dutton's shack. Filling in for a sick employee at the Bait Shop was the perfect way to do just that. And Maw was thrilled to have Jamie around, and so were the Guin twins. Throughout the morning, Terry and Jerry followed Jamie around like two bloodhounds trailing a rabbit. Maw finally got so annoyed she ignored that important command about loving your neighbor and told the twins to get the hell out of the store. They did, but not before Jerry asked Jamie on a date to go water skiing followed by a trip to the Dairy Queen. She declined by mentioning she had plans with her boyfriend.

Throughout the day, there was a steady flow of customers, but on a few occasions, traffic slowed which afforded Maw and Jamie time to huddle up and plan their next move to bring Puck Dutton to justice. Both agreed that protection would be needed on the next excursion and decided that a guardian angel toting a .357 Colt Python would be the perfect choice. Even someone who wasn't right in the head like Dutton would never challenge a lawman bullet coming from Deputy Joe's cannon.

The plan was simple. Jamie would contact the deputy and give him an update on what they had discovered including information about Puck's demonic ties to the unholy one. As for the shack's location, that would be kept in her back pocket to be used as leverage. She didn't think of it as bribery or extortion, but she wanted to make sure she tagged along, and that knowledge was her ticket back to the river. Maw wanted to join in, but after the last trip, she doubted her stamina and speed, and asked to sit this one out.

The only missing piece was Lenny, and Jamie was confident he would happily round out their trio. With Tommy at his final destination in Heaven and Ann still chasing away her loneliness with booze, Lenny had become something more than a boyfriend. At a time when she needed someone to console her, to support and love her, he was always there. In fact, he was her crutch, and she was drawing closer to him not just in an emotional way, but with a more fervid physical attraction. No, Jamie wasn't a lovesick teenager who couldn't control herself, but she wondered if Lenny felt the same sexual pull she did. Never once had he made a move to touch her in an intimate way, not even an accidental brush against her breasts. Even so, she could sense his desire and wondered what it would be like to, just for a moment, be brainless and forget her inhibitions, and let her carnal desire take control. But the promise of pregnancy from unprotected sex waded into that logical brain and she thought about the terrible shame she would have to endure at school. Being ostracized and branded a slut were certainties along with the heavy decision between abortion or teenage motherhood. It was a lively discourse playing out in her mind, but she never had the chance to finish the debate.

The round-bellied Billy Joe Farley interrupted her daydream when he stopped by the check-out counter with a fishing lure in each hand. Billy Joe was heading out on the river and needed advice on which lure caught the biggest bass. Was it the Blue Belly Crawdaddy or the Tiger Orange Water Popper? Jamie had never used an artificial bait in her life, and didn't know a Crawdaddy from a Popper, but blue was her favorite color, so she highly recommended the Crawdaddy. Being a good salesperson, when Jamie heard Billy Joe's stomach growling, she also recommended some saltines and sardines for his day on the water. And so, that was her day...dipping minnows, renting boats, restocking the Deviled Ham, and endorsing the Crawdaddy until the last one sold out. At the end of her shift, she gave Maw a long hug before stepping outside to meet her boyfriend. As much as the upcoming movie with Lenny was needed, her day at the bait shop was good medicine too, a welcome escape from the sadness at the trailer. After hopping in the rumbling Nova, the kids exchanged smiles, and within minutes were turning onto Highway 74 to Belmont.

Jamie marveled at how smoothly Lenny pulled and pushed the stick shift. It was as though he was King Richard on turn three at Daytona. Although the Hurst shifter wasn't the only thing that caught her attention. His face was easy on the eye, and she stole a glance between second and third gears. He noticed her attentive eyes and raced the engine, slid the shifter into fourth gear and returned her gaze with a Steve McQueen grin.

"How do you do that?" Jamie shook her head in amazement.

"Do what?"

"Shift the gears like that. When I shift my car, it sounds like I'm grinding metal," Jamie answered.

Lenny was flattered by the compliment but paused for a moment before responding. If he were truthful, he would tell Jamie that she handled her column shifter with the dexterity of a drunk clodhopper. But a little white lie was called for. "Oh no you shift great. It's the transmission, that's the problem. The trannie just needs some work." Jamie knew Lenny was lying, but his words were a testimony of how much she meant to him. And she loved how considerate he was of her feelings. It had been a good day and the positive energy put her in the mood for a little music. She asked Lenny to pop in his eight-track tape of *Gimme Some Lovin'* by *The Spencer Davis Group*. He obliged and both teenagers belted the chorus. Little did they know, the song was foretelling things to come.

The Regency was a beautiful theater that opened in the 1930s. And even though it lacked the marble flooring, statuesque columns, and ornate ceilings of the movie palaces in Charlotte, it had something much better. There wasn't a bad seat in the house. Lenny and Jamie scanned their options and chose the next to the last row from the top since there were no other patrons nearby. And for the next two hours, they had a cozy little neighborhood where they could snuggle and watch Cool Hand Luke be cool. And he was. The movie was an entertaining mix of humor and drama, and the two hours spent inside the theater seemed more like two minutes. Once outside, the teenagers discussed a number of different scenes as they walked back to the car. It was a lively conversation covering everything from how many boiled eggs a person could actually eat in an hour, to what Luke could have done to avoid capture after escaping from the prison camp. Jamie wasn't a fan of the movie's ending, but Lenny enjoyed the flick from start to finish. He even remarked about how Luke's unbreakable will reminded him of Jamie. Instead of returning the compliment, she made a cutesy remark about Luke's good looks. Even though he had no reason to be envious, Lenny felt a little rejected, as though he had to compete against a Hollywood star to win favor with his girlfriend. In reality, Jamie was just teasing him, and he had no reason to be jealous. But he was. A little.

"I guess he's okay for an old man," Lenny sneered.

"Don't tell me you're jealous of Paul Newman," Jamie smiled and teasingly poked at Lenny's side.

"No, I'm not jealous of him. I think you've got a crush on him, though." In retaliation for Jamie's attempt to rouse his envy, Lenny slipped behind her, held her tight with one arm and tickled her ribs with the other hand.

She squealed, twisted, and turned, and delivered a famous line from the movie, "What we've got here is failure to communicate, Lenny! A failure to communicate!"

"Yeah, I'll give you failure to communicate all right!" Lenny laughed as he moved his fingers upward under Jamie's armpits.

"Okay, stop! I give in!" Jamie broke free from Lenny's hold, and defensively walked backwards to the car, unable to stop grinning.

"You hungry?" Lenny asked as he followed in her footsteps.

"A little bit. How about you?" She asked.

"I'm starving. Let's go by the B&W and get something to eat."

"All right, let's go!" she enthusiastically agreed.

Their playful banter continued until they arrived at the B&W and Lenny backed the Chevy into his favorite spot. After he shut off the engine, Jamie's demeanor turned quiet as though something had instantly changed. And it had. Everything about the place reminded her of Tommy and how much he loved the drive-in. His excitement was unforgettable, especially when he saw the restaurant's bright lights, smelled the food's aroma wafting in the air, and when his burger and fries arrived with his favorite chocolate shake. Her melancholy sensation was inescapable, but it was more than just the pensive feeling. At one point, she was certain she felt someone's presence in the back seat. There wasn't anyone there of course, but she did feel a chill that triggered enough adrenaline to jog her heart and twist her stomach.

"Lenny, would you mind if we went somewhere else to eat?" Jamie's voice cracked with emotion, and she appeared confused.

"Heck no," he answered, recognizing her uneasiness. "Are you okay? You look a little pale."

"Yeah, I'm fine. I'm just feeling a little queasy. I think I need to get something in my stomach. It's been a while since I've eaten." Jamie was reluctant to tell Lenny the real reason for her anxiety.

"There's a pizzeria just down the street, if that's okay?" he asked.

"Sounds good. I haven't eaten pizza in a long time," Jamie welcomed the offer.

Romero's Pizzeria was a small family-owned restaurant just off Wilkerson. Beyond the fact that people loved their pizza and calzones, the parlor offered the most affordable prices in town. That combination was a natural attraction to the local high schoolers, and Lenny and Jamie were greeted by a lot of friendly faces when they walked in the door. Booth by booth, they made the rounds to say hello and catch up on *who broke up with whom*, and booth-by-booth, the anxiety Jamie felt at the B&W faded away. Promptly after the couple settled side-by-side in their own corner booth, the waitress arrived with menus which Lenny dismissed. He had been to Romero's on many occasions and was familiar with the bill of fare. With the skill of a pizza connoisseur, he ordered the pepperoni pizza special and two Pepsi-Colas.

"Can you believe what Kenny just said about Chuckie and Lisa breaking up?" Jamie's mouth fell open although, given the couple's history, she really wasn't surprised.

"I forgot to tell you. I saw Chuckie about a week ago at the store. He said that he broke up with her, and that she was furious," Lenny answered.

"I wonder what caused the breakup this time?" Jamie asked.

"Well, Chuckie said that Lisa had been acting weird lately. That she would fly into a rage about anything. He said she would get mad about little stuff, unimportant stuff. He even said she threatened him when he told her about the split," Lenny's eyebrows rose.

"Wow! I've never seen her blow up like that. I hope nothing bad is going on with her," Jamie shook her head in disbelief.

"Yeah, me too," Lenny concurred.

"I'll try to get in touch with her to see if I can do anything to help out," Jamie said.

Jamie's eyes widened when the waitress delivered a pizza as big as one of the chrome wheels on Lenny's Nova along with refills on their drinks. The delivery was perfect timing. Jamie was hungry, but Lenny was famished, and the pizza slices would be consumed based on how fast he could shove pepperoni pie down his gullet. Since Lenny could eat as fast as a pig at the trough, the ratio turned out to be two slices for him, and one for Jamie. Lenny should have been a magician because Harry Blackstone couldn't make a pizza disappear any faster. Jamie was laughing on the inside, thinking Lenny might be able to beat Cool Hand Luke's fifty egg record. Within ten minutes there was only one slice left and there was no doubt about who would eat that last piece. Lenny paid the check, both waved goodbye to their friends, and minutes later, he and his girlfriend were in the Nova and on to the next stop on Lenny's itinerary.

Their fun night out would conclude at the secluded parking lot behind the elementary school. Since Tommy's death, Jamie and Lenny had been close, but not the kind of closeness that could take two horny teenagers to the brink of losing their virginity. But tonight was different. Jamie's earlier musing about Lenny's sexual urges still lingered in her head. And Lenny had picked up on a new energy from her that had been missing since Tommy's passing. He shared their next destination on their walk to the car, and not surprisingly, after getting in the Chevy, Lenny shared a couple sticks of Juicy Fruit gum. No reason to have garlic breath spoil the evening.

The Nova rumbled like a storm cloud when at rest, but when Lenny shifted into first gear and pushed his foot to the floorboard, the glasspack mufflers roared so loudly you had to communicate with sign language. The smell of burnt rubber, the g-force shoving her against the seat, and the speed of the car were new experiences for Jamie, and the power was exhilarating. Of course, Lenny was just showing off, but he was also in a hurry. And he was planning ahead.

Knowing how much music influenced Jamie's mood, he asked her to sort through his box of eight tracks and pick out her favorite. It was a smart move. A playboy move. She pulled out a Smokey Robinson and the Miracles tape with two of her favorite love songs...*The Tracks of My Tears* and *You've Really Got a Hold on Me*. She slid the tape in the player about the same time Lenny wheeled in the lot and parked in a far corner near a grove of giant oaks. Johnny had warned Lenny that his battery wouldn't hold a charge the last time the two worked on the Nova, but Lenny turned the car key to the accessory position anyway while Smokey kept singing about the tracks of his tears and the hold his girlfriend had on him. Meanwhile, Lenny was playing it cool, talking about the full moon and beautiful stars. A potential dead battery was the last thing on his mind. Jamie followed his lead with some idle small talk of her own, trying not to seem too eager, but after about twenty minutes, she grew tired of the conversation and made an out of character move on her own. Her daydream at Maw's store about losing her inhibitions and letting her body take control had won the argument. Of course, Smokey's sexy voice didn't help either when it came to maintaining her self-restraint.

"Do you want to get in the back seat, Lenny?" Jamie always wore her emotions on her face, so when she removed her Juicy Fruit and fluttered her eyelashes, Lenny got the message and sprang into action. Out the driver's side he flew and over to Jamie's door he scampered while swallowing his gum along the way. Being a gentleman, he helped her into the back seat, and climbed in behind. Initially, both sat upright while giggling and wiggling as they tried to get comfortable. And when they did, the kissing started. Long, deep kisses that sent their hormones into overdrive. Both could feel the warmth of each other's body and smell the fragrance of their cologne and perfume and, when they finally separated, both made a number of clumsy moves attempting to recline to a more intimate position. It was difficult. The Nova was built for speed, not convenience. Lenny and Jamie's attempt to lie down on a seat that was five by two in size, was like trying to wrestle a circus bear in a coffin. But Lenny had a history with that tiny seat. He had wrestled with Della on many dates, and he had a few tricks up his sleeve.

"Jamie, try sliding a little farther down," Lenny instructed.

"Okay. Is that better?" she asked as she pushed with her hands to lower her body.

"Yeah, but can you move over to your left a little bit more?" he continued.

"Is that better," she asked.

"Yeah, that's much better."

Lenny responded to Jamie's new position by contorting his body like a rubber band until he was on top of her, balancing on his elbows. Even with his backseat experience, he was still clumsy. One of his hands did manage to find her breasts and, when she didn't object, he slid the other down to her groin. Lenny's engine was getting more revved than the Nova's V8, while Jamie was finding it difficult to breathe and needed to come up for air. Not from her arousal, but from getting mashed into the roll and pleat upholstery. She decided that switching positions was the only way the petting could continue.

"Lenny, you're squashing me," Jamie implored. "We need to switch places."

Lenny's arms were beginning to numb from holding his weight anyway, so he was happy to accommodate her request. He began the transfer by lifting his torso high enough to place him eye level with the car's side window, just inches from the glass. He was not prepared for what happened next.

"Oh, shit!" Lenny blurted and, in a flash, ducked back down on top of Jamie.

"What is it?" she asked, pushing upward on his shoulders to see his face.

Uncertain of what he had seen, he peered out the window again. "Shit! He's still there!"

"Who?" Jamie's voice was filled with tension.

"Tommy! He's looking in the window." Lenny was jolted senseless. His breathing accelerated to the point of hyperventilation and his heart thumped wildly. He instantaneously withdrew to the opposite side of the car as though he could hide from a ghost.

Jamie bolted upright, snapping her head around to view what Lenny had seen. "Tommy?"

Lenny's eyes were still like saucers and his face was white from the shock. "I saw Tommy standing outside the car looking inside at us! I saw him, Jamie! I saw him!"

"Let me out," she demanded while struggling to squeeze past the folded bucket seat and out the door.

Once outside, Jamie stood beside the backseat window momentarily and then walked three times around the car as though she could catch up with Lenny's phantom. She was thorough, looking everywhere but finding nothing. Despite no ghostlike images near the Nova, she kept staring across the parking lot toward the Hope Baptist Church and the cemetery where Tommy was buried. She had not visited his gravesite since the funeral even though she felt a tug in her heart to go back. How could she have ignored that plea? How could she have dismissed her haunting dreams about Tommy? But now she couldn't. She knew in her heart that Lenny had seen her brother.

Lenny wasn't afraid of anything flesh and bone, but he was frightened of the supernatural. He had remained in the back seat, waiting, and watching as Jamie circled the car until he finally gained enough courage to climb out the passenger door. "Am I going nuts?" he asked, hoping his mind was playing tricks on him.

"I believe you. I believe you. I can feel him. He's nearby," Jamie was certain.

"Shit! I was hoping it didn't happen." Lenny wanted to get in the Nova and peel the tires all the way out of the parking lot. But he couldn't. Smokey was no longer singing. "Oh crap! The battery's dead. There's no way we can push it anywhere. We need to walk to the Pure station so I can call Johnny. He'll come give us a jump so we can get out of here. Come on, let's go."

"You go ahead, Lenny. I'll wait for you here," Jamie declined his offer.

"It's not safe for you to be here alone. You need to come with me," Lenny insisted.

"I'm not going anywhere, Lenny!" Jamie adamantly refused.

Lenny wasn't surprised by Jamie's refusal. He had a good idea why she wanted to remain. "All right. The keys are in the ignition. Lock the car and stay inside. You hear me? Stay in the car and I'll be right back."

Jamie watched Lenny disappear in the darkness and wasted no time ignoring his wishes. The clear sky and full moon provided more than enough light for her to cross the parking lot, step onto the flat terrain and scan for a recognizable landmark that would lead her to Tommy's grave. Belmont was a blue-collar town, and the Hope Baptist cemetery lacked the customary statues of winged angels and baby-faced cherubs found in cities where the dead had money. Originally a pasture, the cemetery also lacked any giant live oaks draped in moss that might point her in the right direction. All she had was the smell of newly turned soil, mowed grass, and decaying flowers, along with a confusing sea of low-level tombstones. It didn't matter. She could have closed her eyes and found his gravesite. Within minutes she had weaved her way through five acres of granite and found Tommy's ground marker with his name and short lifespan etched in the stone...Thomas Wayne Russell, June 12, 1961 to November 26, 1967. Christian people believe that when a person is interned, their spirit goes up or down. And non-believers are certain that there is no Heaven or Hell—that the dead simply keep to themselves, and their stories remain in their graves with them. But Tommy's story wasn't over, and he had no intention of remaining anywhere. His spirit had other plans and he needed to contact his sister. Jamie could feel his presence, and for a long time she spoke as if she was in the ground with him, trying to wake him up so he could tell her the secret. And for a long time, she cried.

Lenny was not surprised when he returned to the Nova and discovered Jamie missing. He knew she would be in the cemetery, and he had just enough time to find her and bring her back before Johnny arrived. It was an easy task. All he had to do was follow the sound of her sobs. He found her, down on her knees, still begging for the answer.

"Tommy, I know you're close by and can hear me. And I know you're trying to tell me something, but I don't understand what it is. Please, show me what it is," Jamie begged.

"Jamie. Jamie! We need to go. Johnny will be here in a few minutes with the jumper cables. We need to get back to the car," Lenny said with urgency in his voice.

"He's here, Lenny." Jamie looked at Lenny, her eyes flooded with tears.

"I believe you, Jamie. I know he is," Lenny whispered. Much like Jamie, Lenny could sense Tommy's presence, but his heart told him that her brother was doing much more than revealing a hidden truth. The little boy was trying to protect his sister. The question was...from what?

Unnoticed by Jamie's tearful eyes were several bare footprints in the burial dirt that was still not overgrown by grass. Prints that could have been made by a child. The tracks were not overlooked by Lenny. In order to protect her from further anguish, he reached down, helped her up and promptly turned her toward the school. He held her close to his side, consoling her, reassuring her that they would discover the truth together. Meanwhile, Johnny had arrived. Their slow walk to the car gave him time to jumpstart the Nova and depart before they returned. Johnny could hear the sadness coming from the cemetery and knew he couldn't stand to see Jamie so distraught. The only thing left was a quiet ride back to Paradise Point.

This was not the ending to the evening Lenny had in mind.

Thirty-Eight

DEAR LORD IN HEAVEN

It wasn't a torture rack, but spending hours sorting, scrolling, manipulating, and viewing microfilm in a 3' X 3' cubicle sure felt like it. Jamie's back and limbs were already sore from stocking the shelves at the Food Stop that morning, so when she left the public library that night at ten, she was exhausted, but satisfied that she had uncovered the necessary information to understand her brother's restless spirit. However, her day didn't end when she arrived back at the mobile home. With file folders and paperwork spread across her bed like a quilt, she spent another four hours cross referencing the historical and genealogical information from the library with the layers of birth, death, marriage, and deed records she retrieved from various county agencies in Gastonia. Her prior investigation had narrowed her research solely to Douglas Ubel Dutton and his family history. With the pieces she had uncovered on this enigmatic man, she was confident she could fit them together and solve the puzzle. But for now, her sleuthing would have to wait. She had an six-hour shift at the grocery store tomorrow followed by a four o'clock trip with Deputy Joe Griffin and Lenny. This newly formed crew was heading back to the river, and she needed some sleep.

Jamie had lost her edge. In the past she was the queen of schmooze, always ready with a timely compliment when carting a customer's groceries to their car. It was just good business. A little informal sweet talk always put an extra quarter or two in her pocket. But today she was distracted. Even her usual banter with Lenny was missing. And for good reason. All day she had been counting the minutes in anticipation of their rendezvous with Joe Griffin. When their shift finally ended, she and Lenny headed to the bathrooms in the back of the store. Unlike their last trip with Maw, they brought clothes more suitable for hiking and needed to change for the journey.

The South Fork boat launch was a public facility on the south side of Spencer Mountain. The popular launch featured two concrete ramps, a water side dock, and a large parking lot that could accommodate anything from a bass boat to a kayak. Deputy Griffin was there waiting with an aluminum flat bottom in tow behind his Dodge pickup when Jamie and Lenny arrived. It was his personal watercraft, not the one used by the Sheriff's Office for water rescue and flood emergencies. This trip was strictly unofficial business, and he was dressed in a pair of khaki pants, hunting boots, and a dark green polyester shirt with the sleeves rolled up to his elbows. It was probably against protocol since he was off duty, but he was wearing a dark brown Gaston County Sheriff's ball cap. Rounding out Joe's ensemble was the Colt Python resting on his right hip. Jamie and Lenny were looking for a uniform and couldn't find him after they parked the Nova and scanned the area. Fortunately, Joe found them.

"Jamie! Over here." the deputy yelled and waved his hand to get her attention.

"Is that the deputy?" Lenny asked, squinting his eyes to get a better look.

"Yeah, that's him," Jamie answered and returned the wave.

Joe looked surprised when two kids met him next to his truck. Lenny's presence was completely unexpected. "Jamie, you didn't tell me you were bringing someone."

"Joe, this is my boyfriend, Lenny Robinson. Lenny was with us when we found the shack, and I thought he could help us find it again, if I get turned around," Jamie had to bite her lip to tell that fib.

Joe and Lenny had a formal, but chilly handshake. And the deputy held on to his serious visage as he laid down the rules. "I'm off duty, which means we're just doing a little sightseeing on the river. If the department found out I was taking you two into a potentially dangerous situation, I would be fired. Immediately! Do you understand what I'm saying?"

"We understand," Jamie confirmed.

Lenny nodded. "Do you want me to get my rifle out of the Nova?" Lenny pointed at the car.

The way Joe winced you would have thought Lenny kneecapped him with a round from his .22. "Your rifle? You're not taking that along. Didn't you hear what I just said?"

Jamie stepped between the two and diffused the tension by taking the heat. "I told Lenny to bring it with us just in case," she answered. "Don't worry. It's going to stay in the car!"

Deputy Griffin's fondness of Jamie was special, more akin to a father's affection for his own child. But this trip was taking place because of his desperation to solve the murders, not because of his tender heart. After Puck hastily left their last meeting at the gas station near Ranlo, he still had a number of unanswered questions. And two high school kids were his way back to the gremlin so he could finish that interrogation. Joe had also grown tired of all the badgering from the press. Even Sheriff Myers had sniped at him for not making enough progress on the investigations. No, without a doubt, it was time for a different approach, and for now, the teenagers were his only option.

After the boat was launched, Jamie and Lenny did their part to get the journey underway by holding the watercraft to the dock until Joe parked the truck. When he returned, he ordered Jamie and Lenny to get onboard, don lifejackets, and sit on the front seat and let him know when they neared Dutton's shack. He then climbed onboard himself, sat down at the stern and within seconds, the twenty horsepower Evinrude was sending them winding in a southerly direction on the backwater of the Catawba River. With a light breeze and calm water, the ride was as smooth as glass, but in the distance, the sky was dark and threatening. A storm with low-banked, black clouds was headed their way from the southwest and Joe throttled the outboard faster, knowing that their time may be shorter than expected. For half an hour they traveled past steep rocky hillsides and low grasslands while swerving like a water snake around the giant boulders and fallen trees. Just like centuries ago, it was a primitive area, raw and wild where civilized men held no sway. But it was beautiful as well, although Jamie and Lenny never had the chance to take in the panoramic scene. They were too busy closing their eyes and holding their breath every time Joe swung the boat wide of disaster. They were worried, but so was he. Not about running into an obstruction but doubting the teenagers' claim about the shack's location. When he was about to call it a day and head back, Jamie squealed and flailed her arms with excitement.

"There it is! On the left over there," Jamie stood and pointed at a broken-down dock, a dock that was missing the hermit's boat.

"That's the pier!" Lenny yelled.

"Stop yelling. Y'all sit down and be quiet," Joe motioned downward with his hand.

Being a law enforcement officer, the deputy had planned to arrive undercover by ordering Jamie and Lenny to stay in the boat while he tiptoed up to the shack and surprised Dutton before he could slip into the woods. It was an uncomplicated plan, and he attempted to remain unnoticed by idling the engine, nudging the flatbottom against the pilings, and whispering instructions to Lenny on how to secure the mooring lines. Jamie was unaware of Joe's game plan, although she would have ignored it anyway. Being the quintessential teenager, "no" meant "yes" and "stay" meant "go". She had accomplished her objective by returning to the shack and she had no intention of remaining in the boat. Her window of opportunity presented itself when Joe and

Lenny were occupied tying the lines. In her world, the only thing that mattered was confronting Doug Dutton face-to-face, so she leaped on the dock and sprinted toward the front door. Meanwhile Deputy Joe was yelling at the top of his lungs. So much for the covert operation. If Puck was at home, he damn sure knew he had company.

"Jamie! Wait!" Joe stepped up on the dock and barked at Lenny to stay put.

Jamie had blasted through the shack's front door like the team leader on a SWAT unit. It was a dumb move. She possessed no special training and certainly carried no weapons. Thank heaven she had backup. The deputy entered closely behind with his hand on the Colt, ready to pull his service revolver from the holster.

"Dammit, Jamie! You shouldn't have done that!" Joe's veins protruded from his thick neck. His annoyance, however, was inconsequential. Jamie never acknowledged his presence. She was totally transfixed on something else that had grown in scope and size. "Dammit, girl! Didn't you hear me? Didn't you—" Deputy Griffin never finished his sentence. His eyes caught sight of what had gripped Jamie's attention. "What the hell?" he said astonishingly.

The setting sun and dark clouds made it difficult to see the satanic shrine, but thankfully, Joe found a lantern tucked away in a corner, checked for kerosene, and lit the scorched wick. The lamp cast a yellowish glow which exposed an altar that extended over the entire side wall in the room. Five jars filled with deer blood, fish bladders and other internal organs had joined the collection of sacraments that were seen a week earlier. And what appeared to be hair clippings bound together with yarn were another disturbing addition along with a dozen or so black votive candles. Insofar as the other areas inside the shack that were bare of any hellish symbols just days ago, all walls were now painted red with inverted pentagrams and crosses. Jamie couldn't help but remember Maw's words about idle hands being the devil's workshop and, in introspection, thought that the hands that built this place were anything but idle. While she was reflecting on the proverb, Joe was deep in thought about what to do next. He had expected to see a room filled with beaver traps and fishing gear, not a church built to worship unclean spirits.

"Dear Lord in Heaven. What am I looking at?" he prayerfully asked. Jesus didn't answer, but Jamie did.

"This is a place for evil of the worst kind." Jamie's eyes narrowed.

"It's just hard to believe that anyone could be into something like this." Joe picked up a number of the jars for a closer inspection. He was still tied to rational thinking, reasoning linked to science. So, his dismissal of supernatural phenomena wasn't a surprise. After all, he was a cop, and a cop would never accept an explanation founded in magic. No, this was the work of a certified fruitcake named Puck Dutton. Nothing more. Nothing less.

"Believe it or not, this bastard believes that Satan is God, and he is into this devil worship crap. Maw told me all about people like him who try to get power from using black magic," Jamie explained as they continued to sort through the devilish sacraments.

The rain had yet to arrive, but a mass of black clouds and sheets of lightning were now at the shack's front door. The ominous streaks of light along with the thunder and dark surroundings were enough to spook Lenny, but that wasn't all that had him on edge. He was certain he heard the leaves rustling behind a large oak nearby and was so scared he bolted out of the boat, ran to the shack, and burst through the door. Joe's butt clenched and Jamie jumped two feet in the air when he crashed inside.

"Dammit, Lenny! You scared the shit out of me. Is someone coming?" Joe was a God-fearing man, a preacher's son, and it was rare for him to cuss. But this place had him wound tighter than a two-dollar watch.

"I heard something behind one of the big trees," Lenny pointed in the general direction of the dock. "It sounded like someone was moving around. Like they were watching us," Lenny explained.

"Well, Dutton's boat is not here. So, if it's him, he would've had to walk here and he's too feeble for that. You probably just heard a raccoon or something. It's time we got out of here anyway. I'll come back tomorrow with some deputies and a search warrant. We'll seize all of the stuff in this place, and hopefully, catch Dutton. Right now, we need to leave so we can beat this storm back to the launch," Joe sounded more at ease, but still carried a twist of anxiety on his face.

Jamie was smart enough to know that cruising in a metal boat was the last place you want to be when lightning bolts are shooting from the sky. She was all in with Joe's plan. And Lenny had the heebie-jeebies; he was ready to leave before he entered the cabin. He grabbed the handle, opened the door, and froze from the hell born vision. Two eyes shining red in the gloom were staring back. Instantaneously, his mouth fell open and he slammed the door shut.

"What's wrong?" Jamie studied his face.

"I think I just saw someone looking at us. From outside," Lenny answered while glaring at the door.

"Stop with the funny stuff, Lenny. Open the door," Joe's voice was dismissive and curt.

Thinking his imagination may have gotten the best of him, Lenny opened the door again while, simultaneously, a flash of lightning illuminated the darkness. Jamie's line of sight was blocked, but Lenny and Joe had an unobstructed view of something standing a short distance from the shack. Their view was only a millisecond, but they were startled by an abnormally tall animal, seven or eight feet maybe, with desiccated lips and two rows of jagged teeth. The unblinking eyes were shocking and impossible to overlook. As the grumbling thunder shook the plywood walls, Lenny again slammed the door and he and Joe bumped into Jamie as they lurched backward in the room.

"What the hell was that?" Lenny yelled.

"You two move farther away from the door." The deputy shouted and shoved them back while taking hold of the Colt's handgrip. "I'm going to open the door and look outside." At times, Joe may have been bossy, the kind of authority figure teenagers love to hate. But tonight, his take charge demeanor was euphoric, especially when he pulled the revolver from his holster.

Ever so slowly, Deputy Griffin eased open the door while Jamie and Lenny peered around him, hoping to gain a better view of the thing waiting outside. With the night as black as coal, no one could see past their nose. But they knew something was there. The swirling air smelled damp and foul, and they could hear a guttural sound, an animal-like growl.

"Did you hear that?" Lenny was horrified.

"Be quiet!" Joe barked as he raised the Colt to eye level.

Seconds later, several cloud-to-cloud discharges revealed a glaring view of the thing outside. It was like nature turned a light switch on and off three times in rapid-fire succession. And with each flash from heaven, the thing moved closer. A mask of ashen skin more suited to a corpse and a thin layer of dark hair from neck to feet were now visible. And its black splayed nose and bat-like ears were certainly not human. But the features most striking were its massive shoulders, out of proportion stick-like arms and hands bigger than baseball mitts. As for the long-curved claws that tipped its bony fingers, those weapons were sharp enough to disembowel a wild boar. This thing, this creature was built for killing and was an immediate threat. Joe instinctively double-squeezed the trigger and the creature instantly disappeared.

At first, Jamie and Lenny appeared confused, rattled by the deafening sound and blinding muzzle flash inside the tiny room. But Joe brought them to their senses when he turned and issued his next order. "Stay behind me and don't let go," he yelled, and without looking, reached backward for Jamie's hand while she grabbed Lenny's.

The kids gladly obeyed and did their best to stick together down the path to the safety of the boat. Being enveloped in darkness made for a clumsy jog, but their attempt to get onboard and untie the dock lines was even more awkward. It was dangerous. Of course, all three kept looking over their shoulders which contributed to their lack of dexterity. Fortunately, the freakish thing remained unseen, and no one fell in the water. Joe cranked the engine. Lenny took up a position sitting on the bow with a spotlight, and Jamie relayed instructions to Joe regarding which way to go. Regrettably, minute-by-minute the storm grew worse and the hour-long trip back to the South Fork launch was nerve racking and without conversation. The howling wind chopped the water and swooshed through the treetops while the bolts of lightning highlighted the rock cliffs that were backdropped by the deep purple sky. Lenny flashed the spotlight at the riverbank, wondering if monsters were hiding behind the swirling trees. When the trio finally returned to the launch, the rain from the fast-moving storm had subsided which made loading the boat easier than expected. After Joe parked the truck, all three gathered for the debrief of their hair-raising trip.

Joe knew what he had seen, but he was a man who had to be sure about any and everything, a man who needed to test his eyes by touching the untouchable. As for Jamie and Lenny, they didn't get a clear look at the animal and would be unreliable witnesses in a court of law, but they had seen enough to know that the creature wasn't human. Joe's dismissal of the thing as something in nature or possibly Puck, or better yet an illusion, was met with a strong rebuttal.

"Look. I'm not sure what I saw at the shack. It could have been a deformed bear, you know, an animal that was trapped and injured in a brush fire. This kind of lightning we've had tonight has started a lot of fires in the woods. Or maybe it was Dutton. I just can't say for sure," Joe shook his head with uncertainty.

"Bullshit!" Lenny forcefully responded. "That was no bear. And it wasn't Doug Dutton unless he's an eight-foot-tall monster!"

"At this point it doesn't matter. I'll be back there in the morning, and this will all be over. You two need to go home. Stay there. And don't say anything to anyone about us being there tonight. Do you both understand?" It really wasn't a question, but a clear and concise order delivered with the sternness of a drill sergeant.

Jamie wanted to argue but didn't. She had plans of her own anyway, and Joe's directive didn't mean diddly squat to her. The wise move was to surrender today and take up the fight another day. "We understand. Will you let us know what happens tomorrow?" she asked.

"Yeah, now go home."

The teenagers turned, silently walked to the Nova, and climbed inside. Lenny was about to crank the engine when Jamie saw Joe trotting toward them, waving his hand. She rolled down the window, wondering what he had forgotten.

"I've been meaning to give this to you. I found it in the woods the morning Tommy died and figured it probably belonged to him," Joe explained as he reached through the window and handed Jamie the keepsake. She took a deep breath to stay her emotions and thanked him for his kindness.

Sometimes in life we find beautiful memories in the most unintended keepsakes. A forgotten song, a faded photograph, a flower pressed between the pages of a book... even a little boy's water gun.

Thirty-Nine

WE GOT HIM?

Last night was traumatic. The kind of trauma that sucks the energy from your body, leaving you physically tired and mentally drained. Jamie badly needed a boost of energy, so she made a pot of coffee strong enough to send a rocket to the moon. The mobile home was thick with the burnt-like smell, and she had been drinking cup after cup to stay alert. She had spent the morning leveraging her most unique gift...the ability to take disjointed information and join it together in such a way that it told a story. She had spent her day off from the Food Stop putting together a kind of road map, a Dutton family map to be precise. The labyrinth of documents she uncovered in her exhaustive research had grown too large for her bed and were now spread across the floor. Over the course of the day, she painstakingly pored over every detail including the history of Gaston County and confirmed that David Brewer was right about the homicides. It was chilling. The sheer number of unsolved murders in that bygone time were too many to count. But the exercise was also educational, especially digging into the past about the colonial land grants that dated back to the 1700's, and how the Dutton family received a number of those grants totaling over twelve hundred acres. The family didn't stop with that land grab. They acquired an additional five thousand through land patents and claims. Three brothers, Miles, Walter and Levi were noted in the court records around 1790 and their sister, Lydia Dutton, made an appearance beginning around 1800. Known as a ruthless woman that held no compassion, she rose to power by doing anything to eliminate the family's competitors. Nonetheless the brothers were different. They believed in being industrious, not heartless, and over the years founded or acquired a number of legitimate businesses for the family including a cotton mill in South Fork near McAdenville in 1867. According to newspaper articles, the family did well until the American Civil War when their holdings were crippled or decimated. It was then that the Dutton's fell from grace and started delving into illegal activities to support their lifestyles, and more importantly, to satisfy Lydia's hunger for power.

Their lack of morals was well chronicled by the press over the years, ranging from run-ins with the law to disputes with neighbors as nasty as the Hatfields and McCoys. The criminal reports also detailed the nefarious life of Douglas Ubel Dutton, aka Puck. The illegal manufacture and sale of intoxicating liquor, petty and grand larceny, indecent exposure, and a handful of DUI's were just a few of the arrests. The charges rarely turned into convictions, which made Jamie wonder if Puck had Perry Mason for his lawyer. All in all, the information made sense other than one missing piece from the genealogy archives. There was no record of Lydia Dutton's death.

After last night's adventure, Jamie was hoping to hear from Deputy Griffin regarding the department's morning assault on Puck Dutton's shack. Even though he never called with an update, she had her answer when she viewed the five o'clock TV news featuring a press conference with Sheriff Harley Myers. The segment began with the sheriff walking up to the podium with a little John Wayne hip tilt, the kind of swagger a lawman displays when he is confident, when he has caught his man. Myers commenced by standing at a podium and talking into a cluster of microphones about the coordinated effort between the Sheriff's Office and the Special Bureau of Investigation, and he thanked the North Carolina Marine Patrol for their assistance.

He continued by stating that the law enforcement team arrived around eight in the morning and found nothing left of the shanty but smoke and rubble. It had burned to the ground sometime in the early morning hours, he said, with the cause of the fire still unknown. Jamie couldn't help but wonder if the burning lantern they hastily left in the shack played some role in the fire. The place was nothing but good kindling anyway and it wouldn't have taken much to set it ablaze. Her curiosity was cut short, however, when the sheriff announced that a body had been found in the ashes. He went on to say that even though the remains were not yet identified, there was a strong possibility that the charred bones belonged to one Douglas Dutton. Even though the sheriff didn't outright state that Dutton was the killer that had terrorized the county, he wanted to pin the homicides on him, so he referenced his prior criminal charges. He also implied that all the evidence pointed to a turf war among moonshiners with Dutton playing an Al Capone role by trying to eliminate his competition.

After presenting more details about their investigation, he opened the floor for questions from those in attendance. That's when Jamie noticed a mop of brown hair she had seen before. It was David Brewer, an obvious firebrand among the gathering of deferential reporters. Leaping to his feet, he fired away with question after question regarding why the sheriff thought Dutton could be the killer, and if he was the culprit, whether or not the sheriff thought Dutton had an accomplice. Harley was annoyed by the difficult questions, but even more irritated by a story David had written a week earlier that began, "The trail of murders grows longer, and the Gaston County Sheriff's Office has been unable to identify any suspects." The newspaper article made the sheriff look inept and David wasn't adding to Harley's stellar reputation with the tough interrogation at the news conference. Brewer ignored the sheriff's feelings, however, and launched into another line of questions. He inquired about the father from Lowell who was reported missing by his family when he didn't return home from fishing over the weekend. The more he asked, the more Harley mumbled and bumbled until the sheriff shut David up by moving on to questions from some of the more respectful journalists. Like David, Jamie had doubts about Dutton. He was just too small and weak to pull off the murders by himself. She wondered if the missing father's disappearance could have played some role in this mystery.

Forty

A RESTLESS SPIRIT

They were five minutes into a fifteen-minute drive. Lenny had picked up Jamie at the mobile home and they were on their way to Lucky's Bowling Alley in Belmont. It was Chuckie's idea. He had a first-time date with Nancy Turner, a cute little strawberry blonde with a pixie nose and perfect teeth and had asked Lenny and Jamie to join them. Lenny was still scarred by the past thirty-six hours and had been silent since they left Paradise Point. His girlfriend, however, had been jabbering nonstop. The Channel 6 press conference with Sheriff Myers was eating at her insides like a cancer and she was verbalizing all the noodling going on in her pretty head. Meanwhile, Lenny was deep in thought, still disturbed by the events that took place at Dutton's shack. Jamie's recount of the press conference wasn't important anyway. What was important was their absolute unanimity that if Puck Dutton committed the murders, he did not act alone. Lenny's psyche was still burned by what he saw outside the shack, and he believed that the creature played a supporting role. At the time that the bullets were flying, Jamie's view was obscured by Deputy Joe's thick body and Lenny's tall frame, so she never had the line of sight needed to see the supernatural thing that frightened her boyfriend. No, she was still cloaked in logic, holding fast to an explanation more rooted in humanism, a belief that the killer was a depraved human being that held no regard for another person's life.

"I've got a bad feeling about all of this, Lenny. I don't think it's over," Jamie forebodingly said.

"I don't think so either. I don't know if Dutton is dead or not, but I know the thing I saw outside his shack was real," his forehead furrowed.

"And what about Tommy? You think he's trying to communicate with us, right?" she asked.

"I don't know," Lenny answered, "but I do know I saw him the other night."

"I saw him again last night in my dreams. I can still feel him too. He's trying to tell us something." Jamie was emphatic and wanted to continue the conversation, but Lenny was wheeling the Chevy into a parking space at Lucky's, and they were out of time.

"Can we talk about it later?" Lenny asked while shifting the Nova to first gear, engaging the emergency brake, and shutting off the engine. Jamie agreed.

After Jamie and Lenny stepped through the entrance, they were instantly greeted by the sound of roaring balls and crashing pins. And Lenny was greeted by the familiar voice of his good friend.

"Roscoe!" Chuckie shouted so loudly a startled bowler on a neighboring lane gave him a dirty look after rolling a gutter ball.

The fluorescent lighting made for an obscure view, but Lenny located Chuckie and Nancy a few lanes from the bowling teams that were busy smoking Marlboros, drinking Schlitz, and dreaming of making a seven-ten split. Chuckie, of course, wanted to arrive early so he could get in a little practice before the competition began but given the noise, it was too difficult to communicate from a distance. So, instead of yelling back at his friend, Lenny used a little sign language by pointing to the counter and waving at the snack bar to let him know they needed to check in, rent some smelly bowling shoes, and grab a little food. Ten minutes later, Lenny and Jamie arrived and after dropping their sodas and hotdogs at a nearby table, they stopped by the ball rack to select their perfect weapons for rolling strikes. Chuckie was anxiously waiting, and once they delivered their balls to the return, he gave Jamie a big hug and exchanged some kind of secret Masonic-like handshake with Lenny.

"Hey, guys," Chuckie said, "I want you to meet Nancy Turner. Nancy and I were in ole lady McCain's chemistry class. We were lab partners, but Nancy did most of the work," Chuckie laughed.

Jamie was struck by the difference in height. With Chuckie at six-three and Nancy barely breaking five feet, they looked more like big brother-little sister than two teenagers on a date. "Hi, Nancy. I'm Jamie Thompson and you probably already know Lenny."

"Oh, yeah. Everybody knows Lenny. Plus, we were in homeroom together." Nancy's mouth curved into a little smile, and she gave Lenny a church hug to avoid touching their unmentionables.

"Well, let's get the show on the road," Chuckie announced, "how 'bout Roscoe and I play the girls in the first game, and then we can switch partners?"

Being a star athlete, Chuckie was fiercely competitive and couldn't mask his drive to win. He figured he and Lenny would mop up the lanes with the girls in the first game and then he could choose Nancy or Jamie as a partner for the next ten frames depending on who was the better bowler. Unfortunately, things didn't go according to plan. Throughout the first game, Chuckie and Lenny took three giant strides, and inches before the foul line, heaved sixteen-pound balls down the lane with the speed of a cannon ball. No skill whatsoever. Just brute force that shook the acoustic ceiling tiles and rattled the re-setting machine at the pit. Simply put, it was a bowling pin explosion. There was only one problem. Their powerful technique produced far too many splits and way too few strikes. When it came the girls' turn, they took three small steps, barely swung, and released their little six-pounders as though they were holding a baby bird. Chuckie and Lenny were getting annoyed watching their balls head for the gutter, then miraculously, turn back and roll into the pocket between the one and three pins. Their squeals, jumping about, and hugging just made it worse every time they made a strike. Not surprisingly at the end of the game, Chuckie was unable to declare a winner. Of course, he knew the girls had won and Lenny chuckled when his friend announced that he had forgotten to write down their scores on several of the late frames. Otherwise, it was close, real close, he said.

"So, why don't we split up this time? I'll play with Nancy, and Roscoe, you and Jamie can play together," Chuckie said, thinking he had chosen the best partner.

"Works for me," Lenny agreed.

"Me too," Jamie concurred.

Chuckie gave Nancy a side hug, leaned down and delivered a peck kiss on her lips for good luck and whispered something about having no mercy against their sleazy competitors. It was a tight match with a lot of trash talking and laughter until the third frame when an angry former girlfriend appeared from the shadows. Red-faced and full of rage, her mouth was twisted, and eyes glossed over and transfixed. Her hair was Medusa-wild, thickly curled and sticking out in every direction. Jamie didn't recognize who she was when she hurriedly passed by, walking in a straight line toward Chuckie. He never saw her coming.

Chuckie was lifting his sixteen pounder from the ball rack when she fronted him and delivered a hard openhanded slap that sounded like the crack of a bull whip. Stunned and confused, Chuckie dropped his ball on the hard floor, and luckily, regained his wits in time to block another blow headed for the other side of his face. Enraged that her second attempt failed, Lisa went to a place of mental darkness where she no longer had control of her body. Like a whirling dervish, she unleashed a barrage of fists and feet, and blood curdling screams that reverberated downward from the low-set ceiling. She sounded more like a crazed killer than a resentful girlfriend. Instinctively, as though he was tackling an opponent on the gridiron, Chuckie bear-hugged her arms to slow her attack. Being immobilized, however, didn't stop her from trying to use her gnashing teeth to bite his forearm. It was a crazy scene, and more than one beer was spilled by the horrified bowlers on the next lane over. After recovering from the initial shock, Lenny jumped in to help, but he and Chuckie still struggled to restrain her violent body. In the nick of time, a burly member of the Burgess Iron Works team lent his muscle. All three wrestled Lisa to the pinewood floor and held on tightly until she calmed enough to reclaim her senses. It was like someone flipped an off switch and she became a different person.

"What's going on? Get off me." Lisa stared in disbelief.

"You attacked me!" Chuckie retorted.

"Attacked you? How did I even get here?" Lisa looked heavenward and pushed the trio away so she could rise.

"Don't you remember coming here?" Lenny glared.

"No, I don't, but I need to leave now." Lisa gazed suspiciously around the alley, still trying to recover her bearings.

After realizing Lisa must have had some kind of psychotic episode and blacked out, Chuckie offered to drive her home—even though she had slapped him into Mecklenberg County. Of course, Nancy put the kibosh on that offer. She had no intention of riding in Chuckie's Mustang with a hellcat in the back seat. It didn't matter. Lisa refused help from anyone, left in a huff, and disappeared as surreptitiously as she arrived.

After all the unexpected excitement, Nancy became nervous, wondering what Chuckie had done to spark such fury. She asked him to take her home immediately and he agreed, although he really wanted to finish their competition. He and Nancy were up a few pins, and to him, winning that final game was worth the dirty looks from the other bowlers who witnessed the melee. But he reluctantly agreed, and the stunned couple was out the door in less than a minute. It was a bad situation all right, a situation that got worse when they arrived at Nancy's house and discovered they were still wearing their rental shoes. Jamie and Lenny were taken aback as well and decided to leave, although not before turning in their footwear.

When they settled inside the Nova and pulled away from the parking lot, Lenny expected to hear Jamie's psychoanalysis about what the hell had gotten into Lisa, but instead, she resurrected their conversation about Tommy. "Lenny, I want to go back to the elementary school parking lot where you saw Tommy," Jamie implored.

"You want to go back?" he incredulously asked.

"I think if he is trying to contact us, he may do it there. He's buried in the cemetery, you know, and I feel like he's restless," Jamie answered.

"All right. We'll go, but if we haven't seen anything in an hour or so, we'll leave. I've got to get home by ten." Lenny told a brazen lie about being on a timeclock. He was still spooked from viewing the thing at Dutton's shack and wasn't thrilled about the possibility of seeing the deceased Tommy again.

It had been an unusually warm day, and when combined with the cool evening, a thin layer of fog had formed and now enveloped the school parking lot. The light from the half-moon peering through the tall oaks appeared uneven and grotesque, and the shadows from the cemetery tombstones rounded out the ghostly setting. It was the perfect location for a horror film. Jamie made no mention of the ambience. She just pressed Lenny to park the Chevy on the cemetery side of the lot which put them within feet of the closest grave. Lenny acquiesced, even though he was as nervous as a possum in Ludean's garden. He was so jumpy, he insisted that both car doors were locked before shutting down the engine. Jamie didn't argue, although she wondered if he thought Tommy was going to show up and hop in the backseat.

And so, they waited, and talked, finally getting around to the crazy incident with Lisa at the bowling alley. Jamie had the *Elementary, my dear Watson* explanation for her friend's bizarre behavior. She knew that Lisa was bipolar and took antipsychotics to treat the disorder. For some reason, Lisa must have gotten off her medication which unlatched her brain and sent her into a rage. Chuckie just happened to be the unfortunate recipient of her anger. With skepticism, Lenny listened to Jamie's version of what happened. It all sounded logical, but he had felt the abnormal strength in Lisa's body and had seen her contorted face up close and he sensed that something else was at play other than a seventeen-year-old missing a dose of lithium.

The conversation then shifted to a number of other subjects as the teenagers relaxed in the bucket seats and talked about everything from their work schedule at the Food Stop to the need to repair the Rambler's transmission. After an uneventful hour and a half had passed, Lenny apologized for having to leave while Jamie, although disappointed, confirmed her understanding with a kiss on his cheek. The Nova came to life with a roar, Lenny turned on the headlights and then checked the rear-view mirror. He was about to put the stick shift in reverse when he immediately shut down the V8, twisted his torso toward the backseat, and stared over his right shoulder out the car's rear windshield. After a moment, he turned back to the steering wheel and re-started the car. And again, he turned off the ignition switch, turned and gazed through the rear glass. He was fixated on a streetlight, a mercury lamp atop a telephone pole located near the south corner of the elementary school. The lamp was at least one hundred feet from the Nova in a parking area reserved for the teachers. Whatever Lenny had seen caused him to be really frightened—so terrified the color disappeared from his face.

"What do you see?" Jamie asked as she studied his expression.

"Look right under the streetlight," Lenny pointed toward the Nova's back window.

The little boy was surrounded by a radiant glow, barefooted, shirtless, and wearing Batman pajama bottoms. He wasn't moving, yet he was pointing at something behind his back. And even at this distance, Jamie could tell his eyes were fixed on her. His image lacked perfect clarity in the misty air, but Jamie and Lenny knew who it was.

"Tommy!" In the blink of an eye, Jamie opened her door and was about to spring from the car when Lenny grabbed her arm and restrained her.

"Wait a minute," Lenny pleaded.

"For what?" Jamie was obviously upset with Lenny holding her back.

"Let's get out and go together. Who knows, he may want to tell us something at the same time," his left eye twitched with trepidation.

Lenny's suggestion made sense, although he was frightened at seeing Tommy again and wanted Jamie with him for support. She agreed and the two stepped from the Chevy, held hands, and slowly made their way toward the school. Initially, Jamie was thrilled at the opportunity to reunite with her brother, to tell him how much she loved and missed him. But with each step taken, his apparition became vaguer as though he was dematerializing little by little. Jamie became worried and started walking faster, pulling her unsteady boyfriend along. Her rapid pace just sped up the vanishing process and Tommy had completely disappeared when they arrived. Jamie was brokenhearted, but it would be a lie to say Lenny wasn't relieved.

"Where are you, Tommy?" Jamie shouted. So frantic to find her brother, she scampered to the school windows and started peering in the lunchroom.

"Tommy? Hey, buddy. Where'd you go?" Lenny joined in although he was praying that Tommy had more important things to do than reappear. Unfortunately, his prayer was unanswered, and things went from bad to worse when he turned around to check on his car.

"Holy shit! He's standing next to the car," Lenny's voice was sharp and loud. His eyes bulged and he pointed at Tommy standing next to the Nova, resting his hand on the passenger-side door handle.

So shocked to see him again, Jamie was unable to utter a sound. But, unlike Lenny, she wasn't afraid. She sprinted for the car, hoping her little brother would be there waiting when she arrived.

"Jamie, wait for me." Lenny's heart was beating wildly, his voice was weak and, by now, he was sweating profusely. Tommy's reappearance surprised him in such a raw way he was panic-stricken and having muscle spasms. Unable to move or shout, all he could do was whisper, "God, help me."

Lenny's support was unneeded. Tommy had again faded into the darkness before Jamie arrived at the Nova. Frantically, she circled the car and then dashed for the cemetery in search of her brother. Nothing. So, she retraced her steps back to the school and then made her way to his gravesite. She found nothing. Scared and confused, she returned to the Chevy, leaned over the hood, and cried.

Devastated and broken, Jamie just needed to know. Feeling certain the answer was hidden somewhere in all the documents she had uncovered in her research; she couldn't understand why Tommy wouldn't just tell her what happened. His disappearing act was a real mystery! If he would only remain long enough to tell her his secret, everything would be fine.

Forty-One

PLAN B

Dawn arrived and it had been another restless night for Maw. The little woman had been unable to sleep soundly since her son's death and the news about Puck Dutton's alleged demise made her insomnia even worse. After phoning Jamie, the two friends agreed to meet at the bait store at the end of the day. Much like her baby girl, Maw was still having dreams and premonitions about some kind of danger close by and neither she nor Jamie believed that Dutton went up in flames with the shack. Beyond the imminent threat they felt, identifying the monster that killed Raymond and Tommy was top priority, and Jamie was anxious to tell Maw about her supernatural encounters with her little brother. And for good reason—other than Lenny, Maw was the only one who would believe her. Anyone else would recommend a stay for her at one of the fine mental health centers in Charlotte. Of course, the same could be said for Maw. If being a yarb doctor, granny witch, and fortune teller didn't get you into Broughton Hospital, nothing would.

Her five-hour shift at the Food Stop flew by, and Jamie said goodbye to Lenny on her way out the door. Under normal circumstances, she would have invited him to join their meeting, but he was still fighting the jitters from his second encounter with Tommy, not to mention the monster-like thing he saw at Puck Dutton's shack. Jamie knew he would be even more of a wreck if exposed to a discussion about witchcraft, demons, and the living dead. Their date tomorrow night would be the opportune time to debrief him and sugarcoat any scary details to protect his fragile psyche. In the meantime, she had arrived at Maw's Bait and Tackle, entered the store, and found the good-natured little woman at the cash register. Jamie listened as Maw was telling a lame joke to the last customer of the day as she rang up his bobbers and hooks.

"Tell me, Ray-Ray. Do you know why it's so easy to weigh fish?" Maw asked with a sheepish grin.

"No Maw. I don't," Ray-Ray answered, shrugging his shoulders.

"Because they have their own scales!" Maw guffawed while Ray-Ray looked puzzled, as though he had been asked to explain the theory of relativity. The punchline soared right over his head.

"Never mind. Thanks for coming in, Ray-Ray. Tell Marlene I's said hello." Maw turned to Jamie, gave her a warm hug, and suggested they talk in the room where she took her work breaks and stored her witchy potions and charms.

After Maw did a quick walk through the store checking for any stray customers, she locked the entrance, and she led Jamie to the small room in the back. After arriving, Maw settled on the old recliner, lit a Camel, and took a dip from her can of snuff. In the meantime, Jamie sat on the bed and worried about Maw looking so frail and tired.

"Maw, are you okay? Jamie asked. "You look like you're exhausted."

"Yeah, baby girl. I's okay. I's guess I's still getting used to runnin' the store by myself. And I's haven't been sleepin' good since Raymond and Tommy were kilt," Maw explained.

"Well, you need to get some rest," Jamie's voice was filled with concern.

"Don't worry 'bout me, baby girl. Just tell me whut's goin' on with you and Lenny," Maw took a deep drag off the Camel and leaned back in the recliner.

Jamie began a lengthy dissertation of what happened. Maw listened patiently, lighting one cigarette off another as Jamie talked about Lenny's first contact with Tommy at the elementary school. She continued with a recount of the frightful trip to Dutton's shack with Deputy Griffin, and the maniacal actions of her good friend at the bowling alley. But Tommy's encore appearance at the elementary school seemed to grab Maw's attention more than anything else. There was a pause when Jamie finished that story, and the room was silent as though the two were absorbing the beyond-belief words in their spirits. Both Jamie and Maw took deep breaths, fought back the tears, and looked at each other's eyes.

"I don't understand why this is happening," Jamie's voice was trembling.

"It's always been here. The evil thing I's mean. It's up on the mountain whur youins went. It's been there since before I's wus born, and it ain't gonna stop 'til somebody stops it," Maw answered.

"What about Tommy? The pastor said that God had taken him home, so, why is he still here?" Maw could see the anguish on Jamie's face.

"I's think Tommy wunts you to know whut happened to him. You said he was standin' with his hand on the car, didn't you?" Maw took two quick draws on her cigarette.

"Yeah. When we saw him last night, he was next to Lenny's car. Like he was trying to get inside," Jamie answered.

"I's think Tommy wunts somebody to go back to that house on the mountain—maybe the deputy. He can't rest 'til we know what happened to him and the answer is up there," Maw looked heavenward as though seeking confirmation from Tommy.

"But there wasn't anyone there. The house was abandoned," Jamie appeared bewildered.

"That don't mean nuthin', Jamie. Evil can be anywhere, even in an empty house. And Puck Dutton used to live there. Did you knowed that? Sides that, I's don't think he's dead. I's dun't believe whut the sheriff said bout him gettin' kilt when that shack burned down." Maw and Jamie could feel a supernatural energy in the room, and both glanced up at the bulb hanging from a loose wire in the ceiling. At first the light flickered, and then it pulsated as though the power company was playing games with the electric dam on the Catawba. "You can feel it, can't you?" Maw took a long pull on her cigarette and waited for Jamie's response.

"I can, Maw. It's like someone is in the room with us." Jamie could feel a spike of adrenaline and glanced around for the source of her anxiety. "I'm going back to that house no matter what. I think Lenny will come, and I'll ask Deputy Joe to come as well."

"It's too dangerous for you and Lenny to go!" Maw objected.

"I told you, Maw. I'm going back even if I have to go by myself!

"Awright, awright. I'll go with you and Lenny, and we'll ask the deputy to go with us. Do you and Lenny still have the necklets I's gave you?" Maw's eyes crinkled.

"Yeah, I've got mine and I think Lenny still has his."

"Good! And how 'bout the deputy? Do you think he would go up thar with us?" Maw exhaled a cloud of smoke.

"I don't know," Jamie nodded her head. "I can ask him."

"Tell him that Puck Dutton is alive, and you know whar he is on the mountain. But you'll have to show him how to get thar. Like you did when you took him to the shack on the river. He'll go if you tell him that," Maw said with conviction.

Jamie didn't know if it was a little white lie or a whopper, but she agreed to coax Deputy Joe with the promise of Puck's whereabouts. Normally, their meeting would have ended at that point, but Jamie still had unanswered questions. So, for the next hour, one generation spoke to another as though they were twins. Jamie fired away like she was a prosecuting attorney and Maw was on the witness stand—conjuring demons, black magic, and pacts with Satan. Something given for something taken. If money or power was sought, a soul, a life, even a trade of sex would be the heavy price. Maw's assertions were incompatible with a logical mind, and under normal circumstances, Jamie would react to her beliefs with a raised eyebrow and quick dismissal, but her earthbound logic was left at the elementary school when she saw her brother. She accepted it all now, including Maw's contention that if the source of the wickedness was destroyed, the evil would end.

Forty-Two

WHAT A SURPRISE

Every choice has consequences, and Ann had chosen to drink herself into the grave. And at times Jamie felt guilty about not doing more to stop her. But you can't help someone who refuses to help themselves. Her mother continued to deny her alcoholism and refused a helping hand of any kind, even when Jamie begged her for the umpteenth time to join a treatment center or try medication to quell her addiction. She even considered ushering her mother to church in hope that a preacher could exorcise the demon booze from her body. But she knew it would take a straitjacket or Deputy Joe's handcuffs to get her in the front door, so that option was off the table. So, for now, Ann was living a hospice-like existence and Jamie was doing what she could to help her mother day-to-day while searching for the killer.

It was a blue-sky day, eight in the morning and Joe Griffin was leaning on his police cruiser in the parking lot at Maw's Bait and Tackle. True to her nature, Jamie had been relentless in her phone calls to the sheriff's office, and her mild coaxing to get the deputy to Spencer Mountain had evolved into hot box pressure and outright lies. "Yes," she said. "I saw Puck Dutton and his pickup at the Texaco station in Ranlo. I'm sure I did," she said.

Although he was skeptical about her story, he still acquiesced to meeting for two reasons. The deputy knew that if the body at the shack belonged to Dutton, identification would have been next to impossible since Puck wouldn't know a dental chair from a La-Z-Boy and had only two teeth in his head. As such, there were no records for comparison. So, on a hunch, the deputy requested an examination of the dental evidence from the skeletal remains with the records of the person reported missing over the weekend. A forensic dentist in Charlotte identified the body as belonging to Phillip Wells, the missing father from Lowell. Although no one knew for sure, the inexplicable presence of Mr. Wells at the shack was assumed to be the result of foul play, and his death just added another homicide to the long list of mysterious murders. The second reason for Joe's presence had more to do with three days of indigestion. He was still haunted by the creature at Puck's shack and confused how two 158-grain bullets didn't put the animal on the ground. His mind was still churning when Jamie pulled in and parked the Rambler in front of the store. At about the same time Maw appeared outside and all three convened at the hood of Joe's car.

"Maw. Jamie. How are y'all doing?" Joe asked with a hesitant smile.

"We be good, Joe. How 'bout you?" Maw answered and Jamie followed with an update of her own. "It's been rough, but we're hangin' in there."

"To be honest, I've been pretty stressed out with all the hours I've put in lately and the pressure to solve the case. But I really shouldn't be complaining. You two have been through a lot more than me," Joe's face softened with understanding.

"Well, we thinks we kin hep take away some of that pressure, Joe. If we shows you whar Puck Dutton is, you kin 'rest him so these killins will stop," Maw sounded confident.

Joe was working under a tight schedule, and he wasted no time getting to the point. "So, Jamie, based on what you told me on the phone, you saw Puck at a gas station in Ranlo. Is that right?" The deputy looked directly into Jamie's eyes for a hint of deception.

"Yes, I did," she answered with her best poker face.

"How did you know it was Puck Dutton?" Joe asked, forcing Jamie to come up with another fib.

"When I went inside to get a root beer, I heard someone in the store say it was Puck." Jamie replied with another deadpan expression.

"Uh huh," Joe wasn't buying her story, but wanted to get to the truth and turned his gaze to Maw. "Maw, are you sure that Dutton is hiding out on that mountain?"

"I's know he be up thar. Thar's whar you'll find him!" Maw was adamant.

"All right. I'll follow you up there, but neither of you can get out of your car. Once we get there, both of you stay put."

"I'm tied up this morning, so we'll have to leave around noon. I've got to be back no later than three o'clock," Joe spelled out the timeline.

Maw looked as though the deputy had confiscated her smokes and snuff. "I's can't go this afternoon. Bobbie Lynn Sims' momma died, and I's have to be at the funral this afternoon. How 'bout we go tomorrow?"

"This afternoon is it for me. We're in training classes for a week starting tomorrow. Besides, if Puck's involved in all this like we think he is, and if he's up there, he may not stay around very long. He may be long gone after today," Joe answered emphatically.

It was settled and Maw didn't argue about the plan. Jamie reassured her not to worry and promised that Lenny would go instead and make sure she was safe. When Joe heard that Lenny was coming along, he delivered a stern warning. No guns. Jamie knew it was a thinly veiled threat for her boyfriend, and that was okay because the danger they faced was without form and immune to lead. Thank goodness the deputy didn't know about the magical weapons Maw kept in her back-room cabinet. Otherwise, he would have banned those too.

Within minutes, Joe wrapped up their meeting with some final dos and don'ts and agreed to meet Jamie and Lenny at the mobile home at noon. He then followed Maw inside to purchase something to fill his growling stomach. With a hectic schedule, he had left home before eating his usual eggs and bacon breakfast, and right now, even Ludean's possum sausage sounded appetizing. Instead, he purchased a Pepsi, Hershey bar, and Butterfinger. A fine combination of corn syrup, phosphoric acid, and sugar. And lots of caffeine. Some stereotypical coffee and donuts would have been a healthier choice had they been available in the store, but the candy and soda would have to do.

Maw was down one employee due to illness, and Jamie agreed to fill in during the morning hours, although her thoughts about the return to Spencer Mountain had her so distracted, she struggled to accurately check out customers at the cash register. She daydreamed, wondering if she would be on the five o'clock news; the story of the brave girl who solved the murders and brought Puck Dutton to justice. It was a flight of fancy, but at least it kept her mind off Tommy because, even from the grave, his presence was always felt. Unfortunately, her lack of focus was causing missteps and customers were getting disgruntled about the overcharges on their lures and Pabst Blue Ribbon. After promising Maw to get her mind right, she finished out the morning with no mistakes. Jamie even sold Snake Beasley two Red Eyed Mr. Murder fishing lures which made her wonder if the name of the crank bait was a portent of their afternoon on the mountain. Of course, Snake asked the question every fisherman asks, "Will it catch anything?" And Jamie lied through her teeth by guaranteeing a monster bass on the first cast. She had no clue if the lure would catch a largemouth or a shark but after her deceitful story about seeing Puck Dutton in Ranlo, she figured telling one more lie wouldn't feel too unseemly. If you tell enough whoppers, it starts to feel normal.

******

There is no such thing as a routine call for a police officer, and domestic violence calls are the perfect example. The altercations are usually an emotional tinderbox, and most folks think a deputy need only arrive on scene, reprimand the couple for disturbing the peace, and make them kiss and make up—when in fact, nothing could be further from the truth. In reality, if the abuser is armed and liquored up, bad things are guaranteed to happen. And even if the officer stops the blowup and handcuffs the assailant, things can still go south in a hurry. As a rookie, Joe found that out the hard way.

While on a DV call, a young wife had a rush of forgiveness, and asked Joe to leave without arresting her abusive husband. When Joe refused and turned his back to leave, the little woman plunged a steak knife between his shoulder blades. Lesson learned. Beyond his rookie mistakes, over the years he had learned something else. He was an expert at trusting his gut. And as he headed to the Russell mobile home, he leaned on his intuition while considering his original list of suspects.

The obvious number one was Zelbert Rubley who was still incarcerated at the county jail. He knew Zelbert was a domestic abuser, a bully, a drunkard, and an asshole. He was a lot of bad things, but deep down in his soul, he knew Zelbert wasn't the killer. He knew because the county jail was a holding pen for those awaiting trial and was not designed nor intended to rehabilitate prisoners. And yet three days ago Joe had interrogated the big man and was shocked to find someone as gentle as a kitten. Contrite and begging for forgiveness, Zelbert had even warmed up to the jail guards who, at one time, ridiculed his squeaky voice by calling him Mickey Mouse. And Otis Burgett, well Joe was certain that even though Otis had a temper bent toward rage, it was all a disguise for a heartbroken man who had lost his wife and thought he was protecting his daughter from a child predator named Bo Suggs.

Joe had run into Clystine at the Quick Mart in Mt. Holly, and she said her father had changed and had not laid a hand on her since the deputy's visit. Not exactly the temperament for a serial killer. And Clystine had another welcome surprise. She had found a new dandy from Gastonia... Jimmy Don Belcher. Her young beau was as country as cornbread and would on occasion bend the law, but he had a good job at the rock quarry and thought she hung the moon. Her father had even given his blessing when Jimmy Don asked for his daughter's hand in marriage. Clystine promised Deputy Griffin an invitation once the wedding date was set. Turning a negative situation into a positive outcome was one of the perks of being a good cop. And Joe was thrilled.

He wasn't thrilled, however, about his last suspect. Puck Dutton was an enigma and that bothered him. A lot. How could someone with the strength of a ninety-year-old grandma commit these murders? And where were his whiskey stills? The ATF boys had scoured the woods after his shack burned to the ground and found no trace of anything. It just didn't make sense. As for physical evidence, there was none to link him to the homicides. And what about the occult angle? The altar at the shack had all the earmarks of Satanism which Joe knew nothing about and slapping the bracelets on the eight-foot monster he viewed in the dark wasn't included in his training at the academy. Everything about Puck had kept his psyche in an upheaval.

At noon on the button, the police cruiser arrived at the mobile home to a waiting Jamie and Lenny. Deputy Griffin was behind the wheel, but both teenagers squinted, trying to identify the officer in the passenger seat. Jamie knew she had seen his face, but it took a minute to register. It was Sheriff Harley Myers. She had seen his mug at the press conference on the five o'clock news a few days ago and wondered if he felt foolish about his statements regarding Puck Dutton and was looking for redemption. Especially when he was grilled by David Brewer about his fuzzy logic regarding the body. Perhaps apprehending the real culprit this time was the way to save face. But most likely it had everything to do with the upcoming election. Harley was in a tough race for Sheriff of Gaston County and a little airtime in front of the camera was always good publicity. After parking, Deputy Griffin remained in the car, stuck his arm out the window and motioned the kids over.

"All right, listen up. I think this is a wild goose chase, but we're going to follow you to the location of the house. But, once we are there, the two of you will have to stay put or retreat somewhere safe." Joe was all business in front of the boss.

"Lenny, we'll stick close behind you. If you get lost, pull over. Sheriff Myers knows a little bit about the area where we're headed, so he may be able to help get us back on track if you get turned around. Do you understand?" Joe asked.

"Yes sir. I sure do," Lenny answered.

Jamie and Lenny settled on the Nova's seats with Lenny's .22 rifle tucked away in the trunk. Jamie had forgotten to tell her boyfriend about Joe's warning, and it was too late to turn back and leave the rifle at the trailer. They had turned off County Road 29 and were winding down a dirt roadway traveling the final mile to the old homestead. Everything looked different in the daylight, not nearly as ominous as when in the dark. Even the leaf-bare apple tree where Lenny parked the car didn't seem quite so monstrous. No, everything appeared non-threatening until Lenny spotted Dutton's beat-up F100 about thirty yards away. Puck had partially hidden the pickup in an isolated clump of scrub pines covered in weeds and ivy. It was hard to miss since the small stand of trees was the only place within eyesight to hide anything. Joe and Harley took note as well, thinking Puck may as well put up a billboard sign pointing to his truck's location. The subterfuge really didn't matter. They had confirmed that Puck was likely nearby, and the threat level skyrocketed to the moon.

Joe parked the cruiser next to the Nova and all four exited their vehicles. Joe opened the cruiser's trunk and pulled out two sets of lightweight body armor made from silicon carbide. Used extensively by the military, the protective coverings were called "chicken plates." Not that Joe or Harley were cowards, but they were smart and knew that they could be walking into an ambush. The arrest warrant for Puck and the search warrant for the house meant nothing if the men failed to come home safely at the end of the day. So, they took deep breaths to muster some courage, squeeze into the protective vests, and check to make sure their handguns were loaded with all six rounds. Lenny and Jamie silently watched as the gravity of the situation sank in. It made them shudder.

"Sheriff, I'll take the lead when we go inside the house to look for Dutton. He knows the place and has the advantage, so I'm not going to knock or do anything to announce we're coming in. If he's here, he knows that already. As we move through the house, you stay behind me and cover my back. I'll give a yell if I spot him and you do the same," Joe holstered his weapon, turned to Jamie and Lenny, and gave them final instructions. "You two stay here. Do not come near the house! If you hear gunshots and we don't return, get in the car, and hightail it out of here. Get to a phone and call the Sheriff's Office and let them know where we are. Tell them we need backup." Joe said sternly before heading toward the house with Sheriff Myers.

The uneasiness continued to grow when Joe and Harley walked by the family cemetery on the winding path leading to the house. In the middle of the graveyard stood a weeping willow that should have been draped in lance-shaped leaves given the late-spring weather. Instead, its stone-like limbs were bare and completely covered with something very different than foliage. Crows. Hundreds of black, shining eyes staring downward, cawing incessantly as though beckoning a soul from one of the graves below. Unlike their cautious nature, the birds never flew away nor flinched when the men passed by. Joe and Harley ignored their presence and continued their two-man parade. As they drew closer, they couldn't ignore the stench that seemed to emanate from the house. It was like the old mansion was breathing, warning them to stay away. With guns drawn they continued on, up the uneven steps to the front porch where they paused at the front door entrance.

"Okay, Sheriff. Let's move slowly and stick together no matter what." Joe looked back to see Harley's face covered in trepidation, a look that said I wish I were back at the office sitting at my desk answering phone calls.

"Okay, got it," Harley answered hoarsely, his mouth as dry as desert sand.

Once inside, the two officers inched down the narrow hallway to the grand parlor that had served as a gathering spot for many generations of the Dutton family. And then on to another passageway that led to an open kitchen that had a stone fireplace on one wall, and a cast iron wood stove on another. The fireplace hearth and stove covered in dust were utilized to cook food in years gone by, while a more recent addition to the kitchen was currently in operation. It was a moonshine still. Making use of the ventilation pipe, a vat, coiled piping, and large wooden barrel were positioned next to the old stove. The entire setup was alarming, but more concerning was the steady drip of whiskey into a smaller barrel. Someone was there cooking whiskey. Joe pointed to the still, made a shushing gesture with his finger, and whispered next steps to Harley.

"He's here. Let's ease upstairs and check those rooms, and then go check the cellar before we start looking around the property. Stay close!" Harley agreed with a slight nod of his head.

Room to room they cautiously searched. Joe didn't have to worry about Harley sticking close by. The Sheriff kept bumping into Joe's backside as he repeatedly looked over his own shoulder for anyone sneaking up from the rear. When the men finished their search of the second level, they found nothing but spider webs and an old rocker in the sitting room next to the balcony.

"Let's ease downstairs and outside. We'll need to get into the cellar from the double doors on the side of the house," Joe whispered.

The instant a police officer assumes premises are safe before finishing a sweep is the moment things go to hell in a handbasket. Joe and Harley stepped outside the front door, paused on the porch, and exhaled deeply, trying to relieve some of the overwhelming tension. After adjusting their vision to the bright sunlight, the men stepped off the porch and walked side-by-side toward the batten doors that opened to the cellar. Their premature relief was a grave mistake. They were within fifty feet of the entrance with service revolvers in hand, hanging at their sides when the right half door swung open. Suddenly, Puck emerged from the cellar. It was evident by the surprised look on his face, he had no idea Joe and Harley were on site, searching for him in the house. Joe immediately shouted for Puck to drop the shotgun while Sheriff Myers became frozen with fear, never raising his weapon to respond to the threat. Dutton ignored Joe's command, shouldered the .410 and trained both barrels on the wide-eyed sheriff.

A blast of eight pellets found Harley's thighs. The big man fell to the ground like a sack of potatoes as Joe responded with deadly force.

Two rounds from his .357 pierced Puck's chest, one penetrated his jaw, and the final round missed its target and was embedded in the side of the house. Joe felt certain that the little man was mortally wounded as he watched him fall hard to the ground and writhe in pain.

All the commotion didn't go unnoticed. Jamie and Lenny were next to the Nova when they heard a faint echo of Joe shouting in the distance. The loud boom from his handgun, however, sounded like it was within feet of where they were standing. Both kids jerked as though a monster had reached out from under their beds and grabbed their feet.

"We need to go see what's going on," Jamie implored.

"We can't. Joe told us to leave if they didn't come back." Lenny countered.

"They may be shot. We can't leave without them!" Jamie turned and started running toward the house. Lenny was close behind, cussing, yelling at his girlfriend to stop.

Joe should have been angry for the teenagers' disobedience, but he wasn't. The deputy was on his way back to the cruiser, trying to support a wounded fat man and was struggling to keep him upright. All four met on the path at the cemetery and Joe tried to issue a mild rebuke over the sound of the cawing black birds still perched on the limbs.

"I told you two to leave if there were gunshots," Joe said, breathing heavily. Lenny never heard the deputy's reprimand and sprang into action by sliding under the unsupported side of Sheriff Myers. The sheriff's legs were useless, and Joe was exhausted from dragging the dead weight, and even though he wouldn't say it, he was thrilled that Lenny was there to help out. "All right let's go. You too, Jamie."

Jamie was ready to follow when something about twenty feet off the path in the graveyard caught her eye. It was a familiar name carved on a homemade headstone. *Miles Dutton* it read. She moved close enough to see another marker. *Walter Dutton*. And then one more. *Levi Dutton*. No birth inscriptions nor dates of death were recorded on the brothers' gravestones, just their names. She ignored a chill down her spine and was about to do more exploring when a shout from Deputy Joe snapped her from her trance.

"Jamie, get up here now!"

After reaching the cruiser, Joe asked Lenny and Jamie to take Harley to the hospital. Their remote location made it impossible for police cruiser's radio to reach emergency help, and with Lenny behind the wheel, his street rod was the best option available. It was a smart plan because unknown to Joe, Jamie had some basic first aid training and played an important role by applying tourniquets and bandaging the sheriff's legs before they departed. Once ready, the car turned in a half-circle as the rear tires spun dirt and rocks for fifty feet. Within seconds, the standby ambulance was on its way to Belmont. In the meantime, Deputy Griffin knew he had to return to the house. He knew it was improbable, but he had not confirmed that Puck was in hell spending all his time with his close friend, Lucifer. If the hermit was still alive, Joe felt certain he could carry the little man to the cruiser and drive him to the hospital. Slowly, he would drive. Very slowly.

Forty-Three

KEEP LOOKING BACK

There is nothing an elected official won't do for a vote because a shameless politician has no boundaries. It was eight o'clock the next morning and it was short notice for Channel 6 and the press core, but an important announcement was imminent. A wounded Sheriff Myers on crutches, hobbled up to the podium, leaned forward to the cluster of microphones and announced that the Catawba River killer, Douglas Ubel Dutton, had been apprehended. The sheriff explained in great detail how the arrest had played out, including how he had to draw upon his courage (mind you, the same mettle he exhibited when he turned into a frozen popsicle at the old mansion) when staring at a double-barreled shotgun that ultimately peppered his legs with lead. The life-or-death risk, he said, was worth it in order to bring Dutton to justice and keep Gaston County citizens safe. The sheriff did praise Deputy Joe Griffin for his bravery and strength for disabling Dutton with his service revolver, using a fireman's carry to get the felon out of the wilderness to his cruiser and then to Belmont Regional Hospital where the killer remained in critical condition and under twenty-four-hour watch.

Although not mentioned by name, the sheriff did allude to two concerned citizens who helped authorities with information about the location of the suspect. It wasn't surprising that the teenagers were kept anonymous since they shouldn't have been there in the first place. Jamie laughed while watching the RCA in the trailer, although her demeanor turned serious when the sheriff mentioned that the kitchen in the old mansion was the hub for Dutton's illegal whiskey business. Jamie thought the statement odd since there was no moonshine operation in the kitchen when they visited the house around Halloween. And then Harley talked about the meth lab discovered in the cellar and Puck's motive to eliminate his competitors by murdering them.

It all made sense until the reporters were unleashed to ask questions. David Brewer was the first and he started with the same doozy he asked at the previous press conference. "How could a man with the size and strength of Dutton commit the murders without help from an accomplice?"

Harley was annoyed by the question but prepared with an answer. "We intend to get to the bottom of it," he said. "We'll be waiting at the hospital if and when Dutton recovers to give him the third degree."

Lenny felt exhilarated. And why not? Even if he wasn't on the front page of the local newspapers, he had played an important role in the arrest of Dutton and helped Sheriff Myers arrive at the hospital in record time. It's not often you get to drive over 100 mph without the threat of a speeding ticket. But more importantly, he sensed he helped Tommy rest in peace by catching his killer.

Jamie was a different story. She was feeling the discord between flesh and spirit, sensing that something was off-kilter. Happy that Puck was off the street, but unlike Lenny, she still felt her brother's presence in her bones and knew he was not at rest. That disharmony consumed her thoughts throughout the afternoon until it was seven o'clock and time for the Food Stop to close for the day. The two teenagers had worked the late shift and Lenny wanted to celebrate with a trip to the Skyview Drive-In to see *The Dirty Dozen*. Jamie liked the toughness of Lee Marvin, and certainly loved his persona to accomplish the mission no matter the cost but, tonight, she had a mission of her own. Lenny was initially surprised and thought about arguing when she asked to return to the elementary school parking lot. But he had a change of heart when he started fantasizing about their back seat wrestling match that was interrupted by Tommy's ghost a week ago. Easy decision. A quick stop at the B&W for a burger and then on to the school.

There is nothing quite like the grapevine. Even when school is out for the summer the teenage gossip still spreads like wildfire. Word had gotten around about Lenny and Jamie's involvement in the arrest of Puck Dutton and the energetic kids at the B&W crowded around the Nova like a swarm of bees. Their friends wanted to hear the account of what happened, and Lenny was happy to provide the blow-by-blow. Of course, a little embellishment didn't hurt an already good story. Jamie just sat, listened, and smiled, wondering about the part where Lenny faced down the devil and sent him back to hell. Just the same, the adulation felt good.

After thirty minutes, their cheeseburgers and chocolate shakes arrived and the story telling ended. The crowd dispersed to spread their own version of the harrowing adventure, and after finishing their meal, the couple headed for the school. It's funny how their minds were in totally different places on the drive to the parking lot. Lenny, the typical male, was thinking it was an idyllic night given the muggy weather. The combination of the cool air from the car's AC and the warm temperature outside was creating a thick layer of condensation on the Nova's exterior glass. It would be a nice privacy screen for the monkey business going on inside. Even a curious cop trying to take a peek couldn't see him separating Jamie from her Food Stop uniform. Nor would the kids have a view of Tommy outside if he decided to show up. Naturally, Jamie's thoughts were diametrically different. She was dwelling on the uneasy feeling in her gut, not being disrobed in the Nova's backseat. Upon arriving, she asked Lenny to nose the car to the curb in a parking spot a stone's throw from the cemetery.

"Did you want to park here because you think Tommy may be nearby?" Lenny nervously asked as he turned off the ignition.

"I don't know. Since Puck has been caught, Tommy may never show up again. I just wanted to come here one more time to be sure. Is that okay with you?" she appeared apologetic.

"Of course, it is. Do you want to talk about anything while we wait?" Lenny responded.

"No, not really. Why don't you put in a tape and let's listen to some music? We can get in the backseat in a few minutes if that's okay?"

"Oh, sure, sure. I've got a new tape by the Classics IV I'll put in," Lenny smiled at hearing the magic word. Backseat.

It wasn't planned, but it was appropriate. *Spooky* was the first cut that played on the eight-track player and Lenny and Jamie burst into laughter when the upbeat music started. The irony of the lyrics changed the mood completely and both sang along and did some hand dancing in their seats. It was a wonderful diversion from the drama of their own ghostly location.

There was an energy to the music. A sexual energy that began to stir the teenagers' libidos. First a coy smile from Jamie. Followed by a knowing look from Lenny. And then a long, slow kiss that made their world seem small. Just the two of them. No one within a mile.

"Do you want to get in the backseat?" Jamie batted her lashes.

"Oh yeah!" Lenny answered and turned to make sure there were no dirty work clothes on the floorboard. He was about to scramble to the back when he saw some movement with his peripheral vision. His eyes drifted upward, and he panicked. Slowly, one by one, letters began to appear in the thick condensation on the outside of the car's back windshield. It was terrifying.

"Oh crap! Jamie, look!" Lenny's voice quivered and his heart jogged wildly.

Pulling at Jamie's shoulder, Lenny tried to get her to turn and focus on the letters being written by someone, or something, on the exterior glass. The scribe may have been unseen, but Jamie knew who was behind the eerie inscription. She recognized the handwriting. It was Tommy. Both watched until the lettering stopped.

rǝtƨ of

Jamie blinked once, and again. And then within inches of Lenny's ear, she screamed. "Tommy!" Lenny shot upward; the top of his head bounced off the headliner like a basketball. "It's Tommy," Jamie's voice was still animated.

"I know." Lenny's body wanted to go into a fight-or-flight mode, but his mind was more transfixed on the back window. "What the heck has he written on the windshield?"

"Retsof?" her eyes widened for a better look.

"Yeah, I can see that. But what does it mean?" Lenny was now confused and scared.

"I don't know." Jamie was beginning to grow anxious about the message, not knowing the meaning.

"We're getting out of here." Lenny was about to pee in his Food Stop pants.

"No, Lenny. Please!" Jamie begged, grabbed his hand, and tried to pull it away from the ignition switch.

Lenny ignored her plea, jerked his hand away, cranked the Nova and revved the engine so loudly he woke up all the other ghosts in the cemetery. He was about to shift the transmission in reverse and get the hell out of there when he stopped for no apparent reason. It wasn't something audible, not even a whisper, but he felt it, something psychic maybe, something pulling his eyes upward to the car's rearview mirror. He did his best to ignore the urge, to think about anything else. Nothing worked. That something kept telling him to take another look. And when he did, his face turned chalky white. Jamie was stunned when he turned the engine off, wondering why he decided to stay.

"Oh, no!" Lenny grimaced.

"What is it?" her face was covered with confusion.

"Lean over this way and tell me what you see," Lenny angled the rearview mirror so Jamie could view the back windshield.

foster

"Oh, god. It says "foster," not "retsof." Tommy wrote it on the outside and we were reading it backwards," Jamie was certain about the name. "Tommy was dyslexic, and he wrote his r's and f's backwards. It's foster all right."

"You don't think he's talking about Lisa, do you?" Lenny's eyes flashed with skepticism.

"She's the only Foster I know. And remember how crazy she acted at the bowling alley? How she attacked Chuckie, like she was possessed or something? And you said she was supernaturally strong. Don't you think she could be involved?" Jamie asked.

"I don't know. It's possible, I guess. But this is just too much. I need to go; I'm not feeling well." Lenny was flooded with fright and his stomach was churning like the spin cycle on a Whirlpool washer.

"Okay, let's get out of here," Jamie was agreeable this time for one reason only. The Rambler was parked at the Food Stop and after Lenny dropped her off, she would make a beeline back to the school parking lot. Once there she would wait for her little brother to show up with another clue. A terrified boyfriend wasn't needed for that spooky encounter.

Lenny exhaled a deep breath, and for a second time, cranked the engine. But he just couldn't resist the temptation. The little voice in his head kept saying, "Just take one last look in the mirror." It was a grave mistake.

"Oh, shit!" Lenny yelled.

Jamie's face was filled with dread as she turned to see what had startled Lenny.

And there was Tommy. Still bare-chested and dressed in pajamas, he was sitting upright on the back seat and pointing at the window. Lenny was stunned and desperate to escape from the car. So much so, he swung the front door open so hard it rebounded straight back at his legs when he stepped off the bucket seat. The hard impact sent him to the rough pavement where he rolled on his side and grabbed his knees. It would have been painful had he not been so juiced with adrenalin. He sprang to his feet and back peddled like a defensive back on the football field. With heart pounding, he stared at Jamie in the car. She was sitting calmly in the front seat as though she was back at the B&W drinking her chocolate shake. Lenny was surprised at her tranquil demeanor because Tommy had not gone unnoticed. She had just enough time to see a faint glimmer before he vanished.

"I saw him before he left," Jamie wistfully smiled.

Forty-Four

THE ANSWER

Jamie hadn't slept a wink all night. She had returned to the elementary school after Lenny dropped her off at the Food Stop and had spent hours in the Rambler waiting for Tommy to make another appearance. Even three trips walking through the cemetery and calling his name couldn't resurrect her little brother. Finally, she gave up, drove home, and spent the next few hours assembling more pieces to the puzzle. With no room left on her bedroom floor, documents held fast by Scotch tape were now papered to her walls. It's a painstaking process when you declare war without identifying your enemy. A month ago, her general research on Gaston County was the focal point. And then she began pursuing an odds-on favorite named Puck Dutton. But now she had zeroed in on another would-be adversary...Lisa Marie Foster. A message from a six-year-old ghost had sent her in that direction, and a trip to the Gaston County Court House was first on the day's agenda. Jamie wanted information from the genealogical records and felt certain her contact, Mary Beth Parsons, could help her out.

It was quite a balancing act. Jamie was driving the Rambler with the steering wheel lodged between her knees while holding a Styrofoam cup filled with hot coffee in one hand and changing the column shifter with the other. After staying up all night, she needed the caffeine although she was spilling as much on herself and the seats as she was drinking. Thank goodness it was a short trip. After parking the car in front of the multi-level building, Jamie headed to genealogy records on the second floor. Upon arriving, she opened the glass paneled door to the department, saw Mary Beth about to step away for her morning break, and waved.

"Mary Beth, you probably don't remember me, but I'm Jamie Thompson. You helped me with some records I needed for a school project I was doing on Gaston County," Jamie's mouth curved into a little white lie smile. Her research on the county was anything but a school project.

"Of course, I do, darling. Good to see you again," she countered with her own cheerful grin. Mary Beth was as southern as grits and red-eye gravy. Dyed black hair, bespectacled and deathly thin, the sixty-year-old grandmother had the metabolism of a hummingbird and could eat a chocolate pie and never gain an ounce.

"Good to see you too," Jamie smiled broadly.

"What can I help you with, sweetie?"

"Well, I'm helping a friend who is doing a project for her summer school history class on government records, and she's using herself as the example for the research. She knew I lived nearby and asked me to stop here and get whatever historical records you all have on her. Is there any way you could look her up?"

"Well, we ain't supposed to share those kinds of records with a stranger, but since she's your friend, I reckon I can make an exception for you. What's her name and date of birth?" She pushed her horn-rimmed glasses higher on her nose and grabbed a pad and pen in preparation to take some notes. Mary Beth knew she was bending if not breaking the county's privacy laws, but she also knew about Jamie's little brother and didn't want to seem uncaring by refusing her request.

"Her name is Lisa Marie Foster, and I don't know her birth date. But she's seventeen years old."

"That'll put her birth year at 1951. There won't be much on her 'cause she's so young. The only thing we'll probably have in archives is a birth certificate," Mary Beth grimaced and shook her head.

"Well, can you make me a copy of that, and I'll tell her she may have to use someone other than herself or come up with a different project?" Jamie asked.

"All right, let me go back and check our records," Mary Beth winked.

Mary Beth returned within minutes with a Xerox copy of the certificate. Jamie expressed her thanks although she was initially disappointed in the overall lack of information on Lisa. Once in the Rambler, she sat and more thoroughly reviewed the document which, at first, seemed completely ordinary. The child listed was *Lisa Marie Foster*...check. The birth mother was *Linda Gail Foster*...check. And the birth city was *Belmont*...check. As Jamie expected, the usual boxes were checked, and everything appeared unremarkable until two critical pieces of information caught her eye. The birth father was listed as *Unknown*. And the birth status was recorded as *Adopted*. Jamie now understood why Lisa always changed the subject when her dad came up in the conversation.

She wondered if Lisa knew that Linda wasn't her biological mother. If she did, she never talked about that either. Jamie was more confused than ever. Things just didn't add up and she couldn't make the connection between Tommy's message and Lisa being the centerpiece in the ongoing drama.

On the drive back to the mobile home she rolled down her window, hoping the warm breeze would clear her mind and allow the truth to become apparent. It didn't work. And by the time she parked the Rambler in front of the trailer, she had given up on finding any new evidence supporting Lisa's involvement. But then something strange happened. She rolled up the window and was preparing to step out of the car when a whiff of air blew across her face. Spine tingling, but it felt good. And then deep inside, she felt as though she was filled with a warm spirit that wanted her to revisit the birth certificate. She picked up the document off the front seat and covered it item by item but found no additional revelations. The only thing she had not covered was the application form that was stapled to the back of the certificate. Jamie had ignored it, thinking it was immaterial since all the vital facts were on the birth registration itself. But now she read every instruction, every line, every filled in space, and found nothing until she read the answer to the final query. It was a question answered by Linda Foster...LAST NAME PRIOR TO FIRST MARRIAGE: Dutton.

Jamie raised both arms in victory and yelled at the top of her lungs, "Yes! Thank you, Tommy!" Now it all made sense.

From inside the mobile home, Ann had heard Jamie shouting and peeked out the screened front door with a message of her own. "Jamie!" she yelled, "you've got a phone call. It's Lisa Foster."

Jamie sprinted inside, picked up the phone receiver, skipped the courtesies and fired away. Question after question Jamie asked until Lisa interrupted her barrage, and in a trembling voice, explained that she could have all the answers if she came to the old mansion on Spencer Mountain tonight with Deputy Griffin. It felt like a trap.

Forty-Five

YOU'RE RIGHT!

Maw smoked like a burning house, and that's how Jamie found her. Lighting one Camel off another while dipping minnows for Gator Hayden at the live bait tank outside the back of the store. Maw was a good-tempered woman, but today she was nervous and looked like she was on fire. The lead story on the Channel 6 morning news announced that Douglas Dutton had passed away at Belmont Regional while undergoing a second surgery to save his life. The male news anchor with a fancy suit, wavy hair, and teeth like the Cheshire cat said that since the killer was dead, life could go back to normal. He even encouraged the viewers to unlock their doors and send the kids back outside to play. Maw knew the darkness was still there and wanted to talk with Jamie. She certainly didn't have time to deal with a tightwad moron like Gator.

"Maw, I think you gave me two dozen instead of three," Gator held up his minnow bucket as proof, as though Maw had x-ray vision and could see through the metal container and count the darting minnows.

"No, Gator. I's counted out three dozen minnows when I's put them in your bucket. You stood thar and watched me," Maw retorted as the cigarette bounced up and down in her mouth. Everyone knew Gator would accuse his momma of cheating him if he could save a buck. So he kept badgering Maw until she eventually told him to pay for two dozen and git. She then turned to Jamie, skipped the usual pleasantries and hugs, and went straight to the point.

"I's knowed why you're here, baby girl. I's dreamed about you last night. We both knowed that Puck Dutton ain't the killer." Maw exhaled a cloud of smoke and her whole frame tremored. "I's not right 'cause that ole witch put a curse on me. I's found some graveyard dirt under my bed last night. And thar wus some sulfur mixed in with it. I's dun't knowed how she got it thar, but I's as weak as a newborn and I's runnin' a bad fever."

"You need to see a doctor, Maw. Your face is super red and you're sweating badly."

"I's the only doctor I need to see, baby girl. I kin stop this spell, but it'll take a few days. I's just need some rest 'til then. Now, tell me whut you found out."

"It's my friend, Lisa Foster, and her mother. They're the ones, Maw. Not Puck Dutton. Lenny and I saw Tommy last night at the elementary school and he wrote "Foster" on the car windshield. He knew Linda Foster. She was his first-grade teacher. That's what he's been trying to tell us all along. He's saying that they're the ones responsible." Jamie said with excitement.

"It's gots to be a Dutton. It can't be a Foster. Tommy must be tryin' to tell you somethin' else."

"She is a Dutton. I checked with the courthouse this morning and found out that Linda Foster's maiden name is Dutton. She was a Dutton before her first marriage. She's the one we've been looking for. And I think her daughter is involved in some way. She called me earlier today and told me to come to the old house on the mountain, and to bring Deputy Joe with me. She said she had all the answers I was looking for and to come after dark."

"If you go, you may not come back," Maw took a deep draw on her Camel and shook her head. "This Linder Foster may be the witch that's tryin' to poison me. And she may be waitin' on you up thar to try to kill you."

"I don't care. I'll call Joe and tell him what I found out and ask him to come. Lenny will bring his rifle with us," Jamie scowled with determination.

"That rifle wun't do no good unless the bullets are fixed. If you wun't change your mind, you and Lenny have gotta stop by here before youins go. I've got somethin' that'll help. I love you, baby girl, and I's would go, but I's too weak to help out."

"I know you would, Maw. We'll stop by. I promise."

Forty-Six

NIGHTFALL

Deputy Griffin said it was a lot of malarkey. Even though he had seen some kind of paranormal creature at Puck Dutton's shack, Jamie's unearthly story about encountering Tommy's ghost was dismissed as the hallucinations of a distraught big sister. And Jamie's tale about the Fosters was rooted in nonsense. It was a desperate attempt to find justice when justice had already been served with the death of Puck Dutton. Besides, he had met Linda Foster on a visit to the elementary school and she looked nothing like the green witch from *The Wizard of Oz*. Everything, including Jamie's reference to demonism and black magic, was immediately dismissed as a figment of her imagination. And then came the stern warning. "The old house is still considered a crime scene, and if you go there, you'll be arrested." In one ear and out the other, Jamie was going back to Spencer Mountain no matter what he said

But first, a trip to Maw's Bait & Tackle was needed. It was around seven o'clock and the sun was dropping from the sky when the Nova rumbled into the parking lot. After killing the engine, Lenny turned and gave Jamie a knowing look, a reassuring gaze that no matter what happened, he was there for her. She set her eyes on him, wondering what she had done to be worthy of his love and devotion. The teenagers stepped from the car and walked inside the store to find Maw at the register, ringing up the last customers of the day. The Guin twins, Terry and Jerry, had stopped by for Cokes and Little Debbie cakes and, although Jamie ignored their indecent stares, her boyfriend didn't. With eyes narrowed and face contorted, Lenny leered back with a look that made even Jamie shiver. The twins got the message, picked up their snacks and quickly left the premises while

Maw slowly ambled from around the counter. Now struggling to stay on her feet, she was growing weaker by the minute and badly needed medical attention, but in her mind, all she needed was Jesus and another puff on her cigarette. Her face was even brighter red, and she was still soaked with sweat.

"Maw, you look worse now than earlier today," Jamie looked shocked.

"You dun't worry 'bout me, baby girl. The Good Lord, He'll sho nuff look out for me. 'Sides that, I's got some herbs I's fixin' to mix with stump water that'll help me get better." Maw held close to her heritage and had the promise of Heaven if she didn't recover. She wasn't about to see a fancy doctor in Belmont, no matter how bad her condition.

"We're just worried about you," Jamie reiterated.

"I's be fine. Now, do you or Lenny have somethin' to put some water in?" Maw asked.

"The only thing we have is Tommy's water pistol. It's out in the car," Jamie answered.

"That's perfect. Lenny, would you get it for me?" Maw asked. "And bring in your rifle bullets too."

"My .22 rifle shells?" Lenny asked with a bewildered look.

"Yep! That's whut I's need." Maw responded while nodding her head.

Lenny turned and headed out the front entrance while Jamie helped Maw to the back room in the store. Maw sensed Jamie's apprehension and had her sit on the chair next to the bed.

"I's knowed whut you're thinking, Jamie. I's knowed you'd be scared. But you've gots to be brave and keep thinkin' 'bout Tommy. Just keep rememberin' him and have faith in yourself. I's be prayin' for you, and you'll have a power with you much stronger than whut that ole witch has. If things get bad, you've got to have faith." Maw encouraged.

Jamie's eyes welled with tears as the two held each other tightly. Lenny appeared at the doorway in time to see their embrace and wondered what was going on.

"Is everything okay?" he stared.

"Everythin's fine, young man. Git on in here and let me show you whut I's got," Maw waved Lenny inside the room.

Maw unlocked and opened the door to the cabinet that housed her medicinal concoctions and special weapons against evil. Jamie and Lenny watched as she reached inside and withdrew a quart jar filled with a clear liquid. To the kids, it looked like ordinary water, but Maw had put the Bell jar in the hands of Pastor Dewey on Sunday and asked him to bless it. The Church of the Holy Ghost wasn't St. Peter's Basilica and Pastor Dewey wasn't a Roman Catholic priest, but he knew all about fire and brimstone, and he quoted Second Thessalonians when he purified the rainwater and promised the devil a one-way ticket back to hell. The preacher was certain that Jamie's enemy could not withstand the power of the holy water when he returned the glass jar to Maw.

Maw handed Lenny the jar and pointed to the rear entrance to the store. "Now, Lenny. You take this out back and fill up the water gun. Bring back inside whutever you dun't use. Dun't pour it out."

Lenny followed Maw's orders, although he spilled more water on himself than he funneled into the small hole in the water pistol. He returned inside with drenched hands and a gun loaded and ready to fire, or more accurately squirt. There he found Maw instructing Jamie on how to use a most unusual knife. It was jade, with a ten-inch fixed blade like a Bowie knife and a handle in the shape of a cross. The green knife, Maw said, was effective against witches, warlocks, and demons. Maw had one more power play to combat the evil waiting at the house. She asked for the .22 caliber rounds for Lenny's rifle and carefully dipped each lead tip in the holy water and rolled it in a powdery white ash. Her advice on how to use the weapons came straight out of her handbook on how to incapacitate and kill demons. The holy water would disable their foe, and then the bullets or knife would be used to finish the job.

"Shoot it in the neck or head to kills it. Do you's understand?" Maw asked while looking Lenny directly in his eyes.

"Got it," Lenny confirmed.

"And Jamie, stab the witch in its black heart. Can you do that, baby girl?"

"Yes," Jamie answered.

"Now, are you two wearing your necklets I's made for you?" Maw tapped her neck as though she was wearing one herself.

"Yeah, we're wearing them," Jamie and Lenny answered together.

"Awright. Don't take them off! And remember, long as that witch is alive, so is that demon."

The kids had a tingle on the back of their necks wondering if the demon Lydia Dutton conjured up was the monster at Puck Dutton's shack.

Maw might have been an Appalachian witch down to her bones and believed in backwoods magic, but her faith was what sustained her. She thought everyone was God's children and deserved to be loved and protected, and she had one last request in preparation for the trip. She told Jamie and Lenny that they carried their Heavenly Father's name in their hearts, and that they belonged to Him. And after making a circle by holding hands, Maw said a prayer asking for protection from God and His band of angels and ended with a strong "Amen!" There was nothing left for Jamie and Lenny to do but face their fears.

Few words were spoken on the winding drive to the old house. The hills and hollers knew about the malevolence on Spencer Mountain, and so did Lenny. His head was still spinning with the image of an eight-foot monster as he downshifted to third gear on the final slope up the steep hillside.

Meanwhile, Jamie had withdrawn to a quiet place in her mind, wondering about Lisa and Linda Foster. Was there an unholy partnership between her friend and her foster mother, or was she being used by a wicked old witch? Jamie would soon know the answer.

Once Lenny and Jamie reached the plateau, both caught sight of a Mercedes Benz 300SE Cabriolet parked next to the apple tree a short distance from the house. Lenny knew cars and was aware that the black convertible's price tag meant it was owned by someone with money. Someone like Linda Foster. Lenny shifted the Nova to first gear, killed the engine, and cut off the headlights. Jamie noticed his hand shaking when he pulled the key from the ignition.

"You okay?" She gazed at his face.

"I've got a really bad feeling about this. But I'll be all right." Lenny was experiencing a surge of primordial fear and his heart was beating wildly. He was short of breath, like a caveman about to take on a saber-tooth tiger.

"I'm scared too, if we stick together, we'll be okay. Maw gave us things we can use to protect ourselves. And if it gets too dangerous in the house, we can run back to the car and get away from here." Jamie was on edge as well, but she was determined to go inside.

The teenagers exited the car and Jamie watched as Lenny stepped to the back and opened the trunk. He reached inside, pulled out a flashlight and aimed the beam inside the rear compartment to locate his Browning rifle. After loading eleven rounds into the magazine tube, he pulled the breech bolt rearward to chamber the first round. Meanwhile, Jamie picked up the water pistol, glass jar filled with holy water, and the jade knife from the passenger-side floorboard.

Before beginning their walk to the mansion, they paused at the front of the car and Jamie placed her special weapons on the hood. She then reached for Lenny and hugged him in a way she had never done before. A long, tight hug as though it may be her last chance to express her love and appreciation. The warm feeling from the embrace washed away Lenny's trepidation and filled him with resolve. It was a powerful infusion of courage, and the old Lenny was back. Yes, he was back until he walked by the graveyard on the narrow path to the old house. When his jitters returned, he was thinking about whistling and looking the other way and, if it was up to him, he would have. But Jamie had seen a large gathering of crows perched on the limbs of the willow tree, so she grabbed his arm and pulled him to a stop. It was a clear, moonlit night, and although artificial light wasn't needed, Lenny aimed the flashlight upward and illuminated hundreds of eyes glowing in the dark. It was an eerie scene. Instead of being deathly quiet on an overnight roost, the birds were looking downward and shrieking loudly, like they were on guard and had caught sight of an unwanted trespasser. Lenny lowered the beam to the ground and discovered why the crows were so alarmed. An unmarked grave had been freshly unearthed as though someone had been raised from the dead.

"Look," Lenny waved the spotlight at the gravesite.

"Weird but look over at the house. You can see some dim lights on in the windows," Jamie squinted.

"Yeah, I see them. Let's keep going," Lenny said.

Both kids could see the front door standing open. And the awful stench, it was still around, wafting from the open doorway. It smelled like a decomposing corpse and their nostrils flared as they stepped on the rickety porch.

"Ugh! It smells worse than the last time we were here. Look at all the flies swarming around the entrance." Lenny whispered.

They both knew the evil inside was the source and Jamie felt an unusual power inside her core, a fearlessness that fueled her determination to kill the frightening things waiting for her. Unfortunately, Lenny was not feeling so brave. His anxiety had returned full force, and his hands trembled.

"Just stay behind me," he said. Ready for a fight, Lenny inched through the doorway with the rifle tucked under his right armpit and the flashlight in his left hand. Jamie followed closely behind with the jade knife in one hand and the Bell jar in the other. Much like a gangster about to rob a bank, she had the water pistol tucked below her belly button in the waistband of her jeans.

The flashlight was helpful lighting the narrow foyer, but not needed when Jamie and Lenny entered the grand room. You could smell and hear the crackle of burning pine in the large fireplace and the languid flames and embers created a chilling mix of light and shadows that prompted Lenny to shoulder his rifle. His eyes scanned left to right and immediately shifted to the row of tapered black candles on the fireplace mantel and the old portrait mounted above. He was stunned.

"Look at the picture above the fireplace!" His jaw dropped and his eyes widened in shock. Jamie was as aghast as Lenny.

The woman's corpse-like skin was now bright and youthful. No longer lined with wrinkles, her face was completely void of liver spots, and appeared as vibrant as the complexion of a sixteen-year-old. And her spider web-like hair was now thick and blonde and her lips full and supple. All things considered; it was a miraculous transformation. But her eyes had not changed. Both held an expression of malevolence. With the same reddish tint as before, she appeared to be staring back, sizing up Jamie and Lenny in preparation for their battle. Lenny's face had changed as well. His jaw tightened and his eyes darted from side-to-side. He had seen enough and was ready to move on to another room.

"Let's check out the kitchen. I see some light coming from that end of the house," Lenny nervously whispered. Jamie agreed.

They pivoted and quietly moved down the dark corridor that led to the kitchen. Upon arriving, Lenny poked his head in and out of the doorway several times to get a visual of anyone, or anything, hiding in the shadows. Nothing. Not even the resident rats were present. Satisfied that the room was clear, they slowly eased inside, and much like in the grand room, heard the crackle and pop of the dancing flames in the hearth. The blaze from the burning logs smelled like sulfur and smoke and created enough light to reveal unrecognizable words and signs scrawled in red on three of the four kitchen walls. Most disturbing, however, was the satanic altar. Similar to the shrine at Puck's shack, the rectangular table was decorated with a half-circle of black candles fronted by several small locks of raven hair tied together with red yarn, along with several items that made Jamie cringe with dread. Three Polaroid photographs taken of her and Lisa on a school trip to Charleston were laying on the table. Jamie's face was marred with an inverted red cross while Lisa was disfigured with what initially looked like the gender symbol for a female, but instead of the plus mark below the circle, there was an upside down cross. Jamie's alarming look made Lenny shudder.

"I think we should leave. We should wait until Joe can come back with us," Lenny was starting to lose it. He couldn't help but think they were about to encounter the god of the underworld.

"I'm not leaving—at least not before I check out the rest of the house!" Jamie fired back.

Lenny felt a trace of anger at Jamie's refusal to get out while the getting was good. But this wasn't the time to consider any weaknesses he might have. Besides, he was in too deep to turn back now. He was afraid, as would be any sane person, but he was no coward. After pulling back the breech to make sure a bullet was still chambered in the rifle barrel, he turned to his girlfriend to pledge his loyalty. "All right. I'm with you. Let's keep looking around."

After searching two storage rooms on the mansion's main level, Jamie and Lenny returned to the formal parlor, readying themselves for the trip up the long flight of stairs. Both froze at the bottom step when an odd noise drifting from the sitting room caught their attention. Jamie had heard something similar at Maw's. It was a relaxing, not a care in the world sound from the runners on a rocker on the store's front porch that she remembered. But, in this old house, the faint squeaking was wicked and unnatural. The creepy sound made her weak at the knees.

Lenny recognized it as well. It was the old handmade rocking chair they discovered in the sitting room when they explored the house with Chuckie and Lisa. Back and forth the sinister sound continued, as though someone was patiently waiting for them to arrive. Jamie was afraid but she also seemed relieved, at peace knowing that regardless of the outcome, she would know the truth. And, if Maw's magical weapons worked, she would have her revenge. And if they didn't, hopefully Maw still had God's ear and he would send the Archangel Michael down to bail her out. As for Lenny, his face was as pale as the moon, and he was heaving for breath.

"Lenny, you don't look good. Why don't you sit down on the stairs for a minute?" Jamie gravely said, worried that Lenny was fading fast.

"I'm okay. I don't need to sit down. I just need a minute to catch my breath." Lenny shook his head in denial.

Creating doubt is always an effective strategy, especially when at war with two kids who are emotionally immature and lack the annihilation skills of a Navy SEAL. These untrained teenage soldiers had a small caliber rifle, a green jade knife, and a squirt gun. And a jar of holy water. Not exactly the weapons you would choose for a battle with a powerful foe. And yet, they were walking up the creaking stairs, still willing to set aside their fears to end the nightmare. Once they reached the top of the stairwell, they could see fingers of candlelight shining from each room down the narrow hallway. And they could hear the sound of the squeaky rocker inside the sitting room growing louder. But then suddenly, it stopped.

"Jamie, I know you and Lenny are out there. Lisa told me you were coming. Why don't you take off those nasty necklets that ole woman gave you? Those things are worthless and won't help you anyway. Just take them off and we can talk." It was impossible to miss that syrupy accent and Jamie was certain the voice drifting from the room belonged to Linda Foster. Much like a siren, she was trying to tempt them away from the safety of their charms.

When Lenny peered inside the doorway, he could see a dozen votive candles arranged in a quarter circle on a second altar table situated in the middle of the room. The altar was similar to the one in the kitchen but lacked the disfigured photos of Jamie and Lisa. After placing the flashlight on the floor outside the door, he raised the rifle to his shoulder and exhaled a deep breath to steady his hands. Focused on what lay ahead, he stepped inside the room with his shooting eye trained down the barrel. He wasn't worried about an attack from the rear because he knew his girlfriend had his back. And Jamie had already prepared for their encounter. She had opened the glass jar of holy water, stuffed the lid in her back pocket, tightened her grip on the blade, and stepped inside behind Lenny.

The atmosphere was warm and hypnotic. A humid breeze whispered through the open balcony doors foretelling a storm on the horizon. The light wind caused the candles to flicker, creating soothing shadows meant to dull the teenagers' senses and make them vulnerable. It was a spell. A bewitching spell that was meant to impair their reaction time and it was working. Lenny was experiencing head spins like the first time he and Chuckie cracked open a bottle of Southern Comfort. And then he started feeling drowsy and struggled to keep his eyes alert. But not Jamie. She was clear-headed and wide awake. And the second Lenny started lowering the rifle, she woke him from his stupor.

"Lenny, snap out of it!" Jamie barked while shaking his shoulder.

"I'm okay! I was just feeling a little dizzy." Lenny's eyes rapidly blinked as he attempted to re-shoulder the Browning and clear his woozy head.

"Why don't you two come over here so we can talk? And where's Deputy Griffin? I thought he was coming with you." Her voice was alluring, sweet and musical as though her seductive words were being sung.

The rocker was located just inside the double doors, facing away from Jamie and Lenny toward the opening to the balcony. If standing in front of the chair, a person would have a direct line of sight to the cursed ground below and could conjure an unclean spirit from the cemetery. But Linda Foster wasn't standing. She was sitting in the chair, slowly rocking back and forth. Squeak. Squeak. Squeak. Squeak. Jamie and Lenny could only see her from the rear and were stunned that her thick, flaxen hair now appeared gray and brittle. Needing a better angle to make sure it was her, they inched along with their backs to the wall until they had a clear view of her face and body.

Her once smooth skin was now lined, pitted, and covered in age spots. The forty-two-year-old who once looked like a high schooler, now appeared ready for the grave. Although her clothing was a different story. Dressed to the nines, her long-lived body was covered in a full-length Yves Saint Laurent black dress and her feet in Moya Bowler pumps. And even though she was dripping with jewelry; it couldn't mask her hideous appearance. What a dichotomy! Jamie was more startled than Lenny, although they both shuddered when they saw her eyes. Those one-time baby blues had turned reddish-brown, almost as dark as the crows' perched outside on the willow tree.

"Well. now. You two look like you've seen a ghost," she smiled and sighed deeply. Her breath reeked of the stench emanating from the house and her mouth was filled with uneven yellowish teeth.

"Who are you really?" Jamie cringingly asked.

"Who am I? Well Jamie, you know me by Linda Foster, the schoolteacher. But over the years I've been known by many names. Although when I was born, my mutha named me Lydia. My real name is Lydia Dutton. I think you already figured that out, didn't you?" The old woman continued rocking as her smile faltered.

"It's not possible. You'd have to be hundreds of years old." Jamie shook her head in disbelief. She wanted to stick the blade between Dutton's ribs but, more importantly, she wanted to know the truth about what happened to Tommy.

"I am old, little girl. I bargained for my soul with the master a century ago when my brothers were weak and unwilling to do what we needed to survive. So, I took over the family's business and made the hard decisions—including the ones about our competition. My long life and young appearance have been sustained by a dark power that I've appeased in many ways over the years. Sex. Devotion. Sacrifices. Many things. But, as you can see, my immortality is fading. I need to pay the master again to regain my youth and power," she licked her thin lips and smiled.

"I don't give a damn about how you look or your power. All I want to know is what did you do to my brother?" Jamie's eyes burned with hatred.

"Oh, I liked Tommy. He was a good student. Smart like you. But he was in the wrong place at the wrong time. He saw me when my business associate was taking care of Raymond Bates. I told my partner to make it fast and painless so the boy wouldn't suffer."

"What business associate?" Jamie asked with an incredulous stare.

"Oh, you'll meet him soon enough. Now, why don't you drop those weapons," Dutton pointed her finger at the blade and jar, and then the gun.

"Don't do it, Jamie. You neither, Lenny!" A loud, high-pitched voice echoed off the walls. "She made me call you. I didn't want to do it." It was Lisa Foster. She had been standing in a corner of the room, hiding in the shadows beyond the dim candlelight. Jamie could make out her face, swollen and red, as though she had been crying.

"Lisa! You knew your mother was behind this?" Lenny shouted.

"That bitch is not my mother. She killed my mother when I was a baby. And now she wants to use me to fulfill some kind of bargain she made with the devil. She's trying to offer me up as a sexual sacrifice to the monster that does her killing!" Lisa began to wail. "And she's planning on killing you and Jamie, and Deputy Griffin! And Maw Bates too!"

The only nightmare Jamie could see was the one sitting in the rocking chair, although Lenny began to sweat heavily, praying that Lydia's business partner wasn't the creature he had seen at Puck Dutton's shack. Without a doubt, it was a convoluted web of horror he and Jamie were in, and neither fully understood the ramifications. But Jamie wanted to know the truth. All of it. And she was prepared to do anything to understand what happened. Lydia Dutton seemed more than willing to give her a history lesson to help her appreciate her current predicament. In fact, she seemed to enjoy it.

She smugly lifted her chin and began the story by explaining her nefarious motives, as though she was proud of her criminal enterprises. The old witch especially enjoyed destroying her competitors while, at the same time, creating misery and death in her wake. The Revolutionary and Civil Wars were the main culprits, she said. Her family lost everything twice. What the British didn't destroy, Sherman's army did when the family farm, cotton crops, and businesses were burned to the ground in Charleston.

After the Dutton family moved to Spencer Mountain in 1866, Lydia became head of the family and diversified into other business endeavors, including illegal whiskey and opium. But shortly after arriving, she found herself ill with cholera and on her deathbed. And to save her life, she renounced God and made a bargain for her soul. Her pledge of undying loyalty was required, and for that she was forever joined with the devil. And thus began the never-ending payments to demonstrate her faithfulness…payments in exchange for immortality and a demonic minion who would do her bidding. If rival moonshiners encroached on her territory, they were disemboweled. If anyone decided that there was easy money selling illegal narcotics in her backyard, they would be dismembered. The beast was her muscle. Yes, especially when exacting revenge on Bo Suggs, the man who destroyed Puck Dutton's marriage. The beast did all of that, including killing the young campers when they discovered one of Puck's riverbank stills. The monster enjoyed torturing the newlyweds before finishing them off, she said.

For over one hundred years, she remained young while making the payments required to renew the bargain. And now a carnal installment was needed, and unlike in the past, the monster wanted someone other than Lydia. Someone undefiled. Linda Foster knew the day would arrive when that debt would be due, so an infant was adopted to pay the price. An innocent girl named Lisa.

"You piece of shit! You killed my little brother over moonshine and drugs?" Jamie released all the hate that had been welling up and stewing since Tommy's death.

"There was way too much money at stake, and he was killed because he could identify me. I couldn't take that chance," she said with a cruel grin. "Besides, I made sure he had a nice funeral and that he was buried at the church cemetery."

Jamie screamed louder, "Did you know that he didn't stay in the ground? He came back and told me you killed him."

"No, I didn't know that. But that doesn't matter now anyway. You're going to be joining him soon. There's a burial plot next to his that has your name on it!" Lydia cackled.

"You asshole!" Jamie bellowed.

Easily within range, Jamie splashed the old woman's face with the holy water from the jar. The ensuing wail sounded as though it came straight from hell. Lydia lurched from the rocker, fell to the nasty floor in her designer clothes, and started flopping around like a fish out of water. She wiped at her singed face with both hands and rubbed her dark eyes. Jamie and Lenny stepped backwards, shocked by her violent reaction. It was, however, a temporary setback. Lydia cocked her head toward the balcony doors and let out a blood chilling scream.

"Asmodeus!" It sounded like a distress call to Hades. Lydia's summon for her stooge was answered by a deep throated animalistic noise from the balcony. Was it a grunt or a growl? It was difficult to identify the sound among the chaos. Lydia was still loudly sobbing and rolling on the floor, and Lisa was tugging at Jamie's arm, shouting at the top of her lungs.

"Run!" Lisa warned them but it was too late to get away. Outside on the balcony, the teenagers could see a pair of unblinking eyes glowing red in the dark. Lenny's worst nightmare had arrived.

As though announcing its presence, the night air from the balcony became livelier, swirling around the room. The breeze whipped the candle flames about as Lenny widened his eyes and braced his feet in preparation to empty the rifle on whatever stepped inside. He knew it was close. He could smell its rancid breath. Slowly it moved. Deliberately, as if this thing was intelligent and wanted to assess its adversaries. After ducking its massive body under the door frame, it took one giant step and was inside the room. It paused to allow its nostrils to flare and sniff the air for fear. Swaying back and forth like a cobra, it stared at Lenny with its demonic eyes, inviting him to join the party. Lenny was stunned. Seeing the monster at the shack from a distance was scary enough. Seeing it up close was harrowing.

Just the same, he rallied his mettle and accepted the challenge. It was an act of courage, but Lenny had forgotten one critical piece of information...Maw's instructions on how to kill the beast. Use the holy water to incapacitate it, she said, and then aim for the neck or head for the kill shot. It's hard to remember instructions when you're staring at an eight-foot beast with razor sharp teeth and deadly claws. It was obvious the creature had not lost its focus on Lenny. Staring back, it was swishing its six-foot tail like an irritated tomcat, annoyed at having to bother with this insignificant boy and his pop gun. The lapse in memory aside, Maw's guidance wouldn't have worked anyway. Jamie had emptied the holy water from the jar in the witch's face which left none to disable the beast.

Lenny was left with very few options and didn't want to wait for the animal to pounce, so he did what any panicky person would do. He fired all eleven rounds in the monster's hairy chest. Streams of hot gas spurted from the bullet holes and the demon swiped wildly at its wounds. The room was absolute bedlam. The beast was howling in pain, and Lydia had resumed crying from her own burns while trying to yell commands to the monster. Meanwhile, Lenny was cursing himself for forgetting Maw's instructions while clumsily trying to reload the rifle. Lisa, was hysterical, screaming and running from the room like a ten-year-old in fear for her life.

The only one who had kept their wits was Jamie. The opportunity to avenge Tommy was glaring at her from the floor. Lydia was still disoriented and trying to lift herself when Jamie jumped on top of her like a football player piling on. She straddled the old woman and pinned her arms with her knees and prepared to deliver the coup de grace. After clasping the knife with both hands, she raised it above her head and began the downward thrust to finally end the one-hundred-year terror. It was a fine plan save one small detail. The beast.

The bullet holes from Lenny's Browning had completely healed and the monster was back in action. With the flick of its wrist, the knife was slapped from Jamie's hands and sent flying across the room. With the other paw, it wrapped its bony fingers around her neck and lifted her as though she was a rag doll. It could have been over in seconds. The same snap of her neck the monster delivered to Tommy would have ended her life. But the creature had a morbid curiosity about this young girl who fought like a wild animal; it wanted to inspect her soul. So, it held her mid-air, face-to-face, and stared into her eyes. Jamie was so close she could see the yellow drool leaking from the corners of its foul mouth. It continued the inspection by cocking its head side-to-side and huffing its awful breath so hard it ruffled her hair. Never to back down, she spit on its face to buy a few seconds of distraction while flailing away with one hand and reaching into her waistband with the other.

That little boy's water pistol was a fitting surprise for such a big, powerful demon. In rapid fire succession, Jamie started squirting the water directly onto its face. The monster reacted by roaring like a lion and madly rubbing its searing hide. The burns from the holy water were extremely painful, but not agonizing enough for Jamie to be released from its grip. The odds of her surviving were not good. She needed a Lone Ranger, and she needed one now.

It would have been easier to flee than to have your bravery tested under these crazy circumstances, in this life-or-death struggle. Quitting requires no inner strength. But someone decided to stay and fight. The veil of smoke from the burns made it difficult for the beast to see, but Jamie had a clear view of her hero. Courage had a name…and his name was Lenny Robinson. In all the commotion, he had crept behind the beast with the jade knife he retrieved from the floor and was preparing to strike. With both hands, he tightly gripped the blade and raised it above his head. When the monster finally spied him sneaking up from behind, it made one last attempt to defend itself with a powerful swing of its sharp pointed tail. It was too late. Lenny had plunged the knife deeply between its shoulder blades and the sitting room turned deathly quiet. Instead of a blood curdling howl, the beast made not one sound, not even the whisper of a groan. It just dropped to the floor with a thud while releasing Jamie on its way down. She quickly bounced to her feet, squealed, and looked for Lenny to deliver a celebratory embrace. Her legs turned to Jell-O when she saw him in a fetal position lying on the floor. His rush of adrenaline was no longer capable of masking his pain. He grabbed his left thigh with both hands, swallowed his breath and loudly moaned. Her heart stopped when she knelt beside him.

"That damn thing got me with its tail." Lenny was badly cut. The creature had slashed him when it felt the blade piercing its spine. Fortunately, the gash had missed his femoral artery and massive bleeding wasn't an issue, although several superficial veins were sliced and needed immediate attention.

"I need to make a tourniquet, Lenny. Take off your shirt," she ordered.

Any other time, being ordered to get undressed by your girlfriend would be a teenage boy's dream come true. But this wasn't the back seat of the Nova and hanky panky was the last thing on Lenny's mind. He gladly shed his gray plaid shirt which Jamie ripped into a long, four-inch-wide strip. Being careful, she wrapped the tourniquet around his thigh and tied a snug knot hoping to stop the flow of blood. She did allow him a modicum of modesty by not confiscating his tee shirt but teasingly warned he would be bare chested if she needed extra bandages. Once on their feet, they realized they were by themselves and had to come up with a new plan of action.

"Geez, that thing is huge!" Lenny scanned the room. "Where is Lisa?" His eyes were as big as saucers.

"And Lydia?" Jamie replied with her own question. During all of the confusion, the witch had somehow slipped from the room. "We have to find her. I'm not leaving until that bitch is dead." Jamie's eyes narrowed. "Do you have any bullets left?"

"Yeah, I've got about twenty more rounds," Lenny confirmed.

"Good! Reload and I'll get the knife out of the beast. Then we'll start on this floor and work our way down." Jamie was clearly in charge of their mission.

Lenny was consumed with thoughts about what was waiting for them in the dark, worried that his injury might place them both at a disadvantage. As for Jamie, her confidence was soaring after facing down Lydia and her monster. She was determined to finish the job, but she knew she wouldn't have gotten this far without him. And if they didn't make it out of the house, she didn't want to leave anything unsaid.

"I love you, Lenny," Jamie's face softened, and she fought back the tears.

"I love you, too." Expressing his feelings had always been difficult, but he tenderly returned her sentiment and wondered what he had done to be worthy of her affection. He may have been afraid, but he would walk through fire for that girl, and she knew it.

After getting to their feet, they resumed their formation with Lenny taking the point and Jamie guarding the rear. Carefully, the teenagers cleared the upstairs level by moving from room to room and were headed downstairs to the parlor when they heard a savage scream.

"Help me! Somebody help me!"

"Lisa!" Lenny said with alarm.

"Sounds like she's in the cellar," Jamie concurred. "The doors are on the side of the house, so we'll have to go outside to get to it."

"All right. Just stay behind me. I'm going to take a shot as soon as I see the old hag. If by chance Lisa is double crossing us, I'm going to unload on her too!" As a precaution, for a third time, Lenny pulled back the breech to make sure a bullet was still in the pipe. They were ready.

Forty-Seven

AT CLOSE RANGE

The ground level batten doors were swung open, permitting two kerosene lanterns in the cellar to forebodingly illuminate the entrance. No one was hiding their presence. It was clearly another invitation, and Jamie and Lenny were unnerved by the boldness of their adversary.

"It's a trap," Lenny looked to Jamie for one last dose of courage.

"Well, it may be a trap. But why don't we go down and find out?" Jamie's eyes glistened. She was ready to write the final chapter to this frightening story.

The cellar smelled dank from the trapped moisture within its dirt floor and walls. But, more so, it smelled of rotten eggs and cat urine. This was the previous home of Puck Dutton's meth operation, and the remnants of the lab were scattered all over the ground. Everything from propane tanks, pots, and funnels to containers of drain cleaner and paint thinner. Any and everything that would cause you to stumble and fall. Lydia knew exactly what was in this cave and chose the location to give her a strategic advantage.

Maw's amulets were doing their job and the black witch had given up on her magic spells. Something less mystical was required, something natural, and the residual ammonia smell from the methamphetamine along with tripping hazards from the junk was the answer. As intended, the odor burned the teenagers' eyes, making it difficult for them to see. With his leg still aching, Lenny felt dizzy and rubbed his eyes while hobbling down the uneven steps, slowly, warily, ready for a surprise attack. Meanwhile, Jamie followed within inches. She was experiencing the same eye irritation and dizziness while trying to peer over his shoulder but was ready to thrust the knife and squirt the water pistol at anything that moved. But there was no anticipated ambush from Lydia. No, there was no trap at all. However, after stepping off the bottom stair there was something Jamie and Lenny never thought possible.

Their eyes regained focus in time to see the beast swaying, hissing, holding Lisa with its bony fingers hooked tightly around her throat. In its outstretched arm, she was dangling, kicking wildly, choking, unable to make a sound. Jamie and Lenny were stunned. How could the beast still be alive? And then, Jamie remembered Maw's warning, "You must kill the witch if you wunts to kill anything she's conjured up." But how could it have slipped from the sitting room without the teenagers noticing? It must have made an incredible leap off the balcony in order to arrive at the cellar before they did, Jamie surmised. That was the only explanation, although all the mind work about the beast and witch was unnecessary. Her high-priced dress was filthy and tattered, and her face was covered with dirt from the sitting room floor but there, next to the beast, stood Lydia, rocking back and forth in sync with her henchman.

"Drop the gun, Lenny! If you drop it now, you and your bitchy girlfriend can walk away. I may even let Lisa go with you. If you don't, none of you will see another sunrise," the old witch smirked, looking confident as though she had the upper hand.

"Don't do it, Lenny!" Jamie screamed and stepped from behind her boyfriend, flashing the blade and waving the water gun.

"Last chance. One word to Asmodeus and Lisa will be dead, and you two next," Lydia's voice grew in timbre.

"We're not going anywhere, you old bat," Lenny yelled, shouldered the rifle, aimed at the beast and emptied the magazine in seconds.

There was good news and bad news after the final bullet left the gun's smoking barrel. Lenny had avoided hitting Lisa, but he had also missed the monster. Completely.

Perhaps the witch had found a spell that affected his vision, an incantation that finally overcame Maw's powerful necklets. Or maybe his vision was still blurred from the lethal odors from the meth. Regardless of the reason, all eleven rounds ended up in the wall. In retaliation, the demon tossed Lisa aside and charged at Lenny and Jamie, hellbent on eliminating the danger they posed to its master. Lisa hit the dirt gasping for air as Lenny frantically attempted to pull the remaining nine rounds from his pocket and reload. It was too late. He was sent flying by a bestial backhand and landed on top of Lisa who was still struggling to breathe. With an empty rifle, Lenny was no longer a threat, and the monster was now transfixed on Jamie. Its claws were just feet from slashing her face when all hell broke loose.

This mountain was a place where the law wasn't to be found, and yet there he was. No one saw or heard him slip down the cellar stairs. Not Lydia, Jamie, Lenny, nor Lisa. Not even the beast. It was as though he fell from the sky. The triple squeeze of the Colt's trigger and deafening sound confirmed he was no illusion.

Deputy Griffin knew telling Jamie to stay away from the old house was like telling a bear to stay away from honey. The deputy would have been more effective talking to a telephone pole. He was a decent man and there was no way he would look the other way when he sensed she may need his help.

"Roar!" The sound could have been mistaken for rage, but it was a howl of pain. Joe leaned on his police training regarding use of deadly force and centered two .357 magnums in the demon's chest and a third between its eyes. The thing reacted like someone cracked a two-by-four across its head as it catapulted to the ground. The dust exploded from around its body, and it was motionless, seemingly dead. With four against one, the odds were now in the favor of the good guys and Lydia was livid.

"You bastard!" the witch screamed.

"Show me your hands and drop to your knees!" Joe ordered loudly.

"I'm not getting to my knees, you son of a bitch. You killed my boy!" Lydia yelled back.

"If this thing on the ground is your boy, you are one screwed up mother," Joe remained calm and kept his revolver aimed at Lydia's torso.

"No, you bastard! You killed Doug!" she angrily screamed.

"Puck was your son?" The deputy appeared confused and momentarily lost his focus. Even with her coffin-like face, he recognized the woman as Linda Foster, the woman in her forties much like Puck Dutton, so in his mind, her claim made no sense.

Joe Griffin did not know that Lydia Dutton had lived for a century beyond her deathbed, retained her youth because of a pact with the devil, and birthed or adopted a number of babies to use as pawns in her criminal activities. Puck just happened to be one of her favorites and she had always come to his rescue, to be his protector, and his avenger when he had been wronged.

"She's a witch, Joe. She's the one who killed Tommy and all the others!" Jamie shouted in anger.

"I'm taking her in, and she'll stand trial for what she's done."

Lydia was calculating her next move and going nowhere. She knew the beast would recover. All she needed to do was create a diversion to give it a few more seconds. Slowly, she began to sidestep toward the cellar entrance as though she wanted to escape. It was an effective illusion. Everyone was facing away from the demon with eyes fixed on her. Everyone's eyes but Lisa's.

"Behind you!" Lisa's voice box was back, and she screamed at the top of her lungs. She had seen the beast rise from the dirt, its murderous teeth gnashing and red eyes glowing. Joe never saw it coming. The beast cocked its head, rolled its eyes, and dropped its snapping jaws to deliver a vicious bite to his left shoulder. Its sharp teeth pierced his trapezius muscle and snapped his clavicle like a matchstick. The sharp crack of the bone sounded like a round from Lenny's rifle. Even with his body high on adrenaline, the pain from the horrific wound was excruciating. The deputy grimaced and expelled a deep moan. He was badly injured, and his left hand and arm were now useless, but he continued the fight.

A quick about-face had him so close to the beast, he could feel and smell its nasty breath. Reflexively, he emptied the Colt's last three rounds in its grisly mug. Lenny reloaded his rifle in time to fire an additional nine rounds at the monster's heart. He didn't miss this time. He couldn't. He was within two feet of his target. The beast reacted with a loud howl, backhanded Joe across his face, and staggered backwards a few feet. It next clawed at its chest as though trying to extract the slugs from Lenny's rifle. The small caliber bullets that had been soaked in holy water and white ash caused the excruciating pain while the holes from Joe's larger ammo were treated like mosquito bites. The beast looked like a walking steam boiler with hellish gas shooting out from the bullet holes in its chest. Joe spit the salty blood from his mouth and even though he was stunned, he was not unconscious. He was on his butt, however, frantically trying to use his only good hand to reload the Colt with bullets from his utility belt. Lenny was out of ammo, although he had found a rusty axe resting against one of the meth vats and was getting ready for another round of combat.

Given all their chaotic fighting, Joe and Lenny had completely forgotten about Jamie and Lydia, although the two females had not ignored each other. Jamie was small, petite really, and yet she appeared possessed and filled with rage; she didn't hesitate to pounce on her much larger adversary. And Lydia may have looked old and weak, but her strength belied her appearance. She was strong and the two were going at it like wild cats. It was primal, a street fight on a red dirt floor and their violent grappling had them wrapped in a cloud of dust. No, there were no Queensberry Rules that prohibited head butting and hitting below the belt or striking anywhere else for that matter. There was some of that going on for sure. But most of the fighting was biting, kicking, and gouging. Joe and Lenny were momentarily in a trance-like state watching the savage explosions of feet and fists and listening to the neurotic screams and animalistic growls. Their distraction was a big mistake. The beast had regained its senses and was about to mount another attack.

Perhaps the creature sensed that Joe was crippled and defenseless, or maybe the smell of the blood oozing from his gaping wound triggered the response. Or maybe Lydia gave her servant specific instructions on dismembering Joe, a little motherly revenge for the deputy taking her son's life. Regardless of the reason, the thing chose Joe as its first victim. It was within two steps and had its arms raised, swaying, preparing to strike with its massive claws. Joe knew he was vulnerable and had a sinking feeling he would never see another sunrise.

Undoubtedly, the deputy's life would have ended then and there were it not for Lenny. The teenager had slipped behind the creature, and with all his might, dropped the axe on its long tail. Lenny enjoyed it. It was payback for the slash in his thigh. Another deafening howl was followed by a back fist that sent Lenny crashing into several propane tanks in the corner of the cellar. His brave maneuver gave Joe just enough time to load two shells in the gun's chamber and fire twice at the creature's chest.

The beast dropped to its knees from the force of the slugs and let out another demonic groan. It was angry and irritated at this annoying human who kept putting holes in its hide with that damn .357. For sure, it had an enraged disdain of the deputy's heroism and its inhuman eyes glowed like a fire. Easily within striking range, it raised its claws preparing to deliver a death blow to the deputy's face and throat and would have done so had Lenny not come to the rescue. Again. The young boy had picked up the monster's severed tail from the dirt, clutched it like a knife and jumped on the creature piggyback style. His strength was fading but he mustered the energy to reach over the creature's shoulder and bury the tail section in its heart. He then hung on for dear life as the beast twisted, turned, and howled in pain. Howls not from the stab wound, but from its contact with Lenny. He had forgotten about the holy water he spilled on his hands when he filled the water pistol at Maw's store. Once he remembered he began to give the monster a massage, a Lenny-style rubdown all over its neck and chest. The beast's wail reached a new crescendo.

  At this point, the entire cellar was filled with hostility. Between the wails from the beast, the growls and howls from Jamie and the old witch, the groans from Joe, the cursing from Lenny, and the screaming from Lisa, the place was sheer pandemonium. There was so much confusion and chaos, no one noticed that during their struggle, Lydia had struck Jamie with a steel pot she had found in the rubble from the meth lab. The blow to Jamie's forehead rendered her dazed, giving Lydia time to rip the necklet from her nape and gain the upper hand. Much like when Jamie straddled Lydia in the sitting room, the old woman had pinned Jamie's arms and was choking the life from her body. Deputy Joe was too weak to help; Lenny was riding the beast like a rodeo cowboy, and Lisa was scared witless, still hiding in the dark corner. For a second, the thought of seeing her brother and being with him forever fluttered in her mind like a sweet dream. But the most unlikely savior had a different plan. Jamie's eyes were cloudy, but she could see the indifference and cruelty in the witch's face turn to disbelief and panic. That expensive Yves Saint Laurent dress was ruined when the tip of the blade penetrated the fabric. Whether it was out of anger or revenge really didn't matter. After all those years of being submissive, Lisa had found her courage along with the jade knife and came out of hiding. Calmly, she walked up behind her mother and drove the sharp blade in her back, through her heart and out her sagging left breast. A slight tremble, a twitch maybe, and then a demonic scream that sounded like a thousand unclean spirits leaving their host.

"You bitch!" the witch bellowed.

An open casket funeral would not be needed for Lydia Dutton. She had returned to ashes and dust. One hundred years of decomposition occurred in one second, leaving Jamie's sweaty face coated with her remains. The beast called Asmodeus exploded into powder as well, and found itself back in hell with its master. It was over and Jamie was exhausted and limp, unable to rise without regaining her wind. And Lenny was on his back as well, wide-eyed and confused. One minute his arms were folded around a bucking beast and the next his adversary was gone. Maw was right. If you kill the witch, you'll kill her monster. With regard to Lisa, other than screaming like a banshee and delivering the death blow to her mother, she had expended little energy in the fight. However, that important blow ended the reign of Lydia Dutton, and Lisa was still clear headed enough to recognize that Joe was going into shock.

"We need to get the deputy to the hospital," Lisa broke the temporary pause with a quick call to action. A secondary dump of adrenaline helped Jamie and Lenny to their feet, and after a lightning-fast hug, the three kids marshaled enough strength to get Joe out of the cellar and into his car.

Lenny dreamed about being a police officer when he was a kid, and he finally had the opportunity to experience it first-hand. He had no idea how fast he was traveling when he drove Deputy Griffin's patrol car. He did know, however, that within minutes of leaving the old mansion, the speedometer needle had disappeared off the dashboard display. Fortunately, the wannabe cop figured out how to engage the siren and roof top emergency lights. Otherwise, he may have run over every slowpoke car and truck in Gaston County.

Joe never knew what was going on. He was unconscious and bleeding profusely on the back seat, at peril of not surviving the trip. But just like a good lawman, Lenny radioed ahead to let Charlotte Memorial know he was on the way. It was a smart move. The emergency room doctors and nurses were waiting when they arrived, and with little fanfare, they saved Joe's life and addressed Lenny's laceration. The deputy's shoulder wound was infected with a powerful toxin from the creature's saliva, and the medical staff worked overtime to develop an effective antibody treatment to restore his health. What they couldn't recover was the deputy's memory. Joe could tell the nurses nothing about the clash with Lydia Dutton and the beast, and the doctors said the poison from the bite most likely affected his temporal lobe and wiped out his short-term memory. Jamie and Lenny believed he was somehow affected by one of Lydia's hoodoo spells while doing battle in the cellar. After all, he wasn't wearing one of Maw's special charms.

There was someone else who enjoyed the trip to Charlotte. It was unwritten, but it was a hard and fast rule cast in stone. No one drove the Nova but Lenny. But this was a dire situation, so he had handed the keys over to Jamie. She had dreamed about holding that steering wheel as it trembled from that V8 power, of pushing that accelerator to the floorboard, of rolling down the windows and feeling the wind in her hair. After her brush with death, she needed that kind of jubilation. And her wish came true. She was still somewhat loopy from her fight with the witch but managed to keep up with the patrol car while grinding through the gears. Had it not been for the police car's wailing siren, Lenny would have heard his girlfriend rearranging his transmission. Although, under the circumstances, he would have been forgiving and simply called Johnny for help with the repairs. As for the Mercedes 300SE, well it was supposed to be third in line behind the Nova, but the car never made it to the hospital. Instead, it vanished into thin air—along with Lisa.

Epilogue

WHAT WE BECOME

He listened. With arms crossed and eyes glazed over, Sheriff Harley Myers heard every gruesome detail from Jamie and Lenny. His occasional "uh huh" or "um-hum" and total lack of questions was a clear indication of his disinterest. Nonbelief really. And even if he did believe their story, to go public would take away his heroism in bringing the real culprit, Puck Dutton, to justice. Once a politician, always a politician. Never to be deterred, Jamie contacted David Brewer from the *Charlotte Times*; he at least asked detailed questions about the encounter. But at the end of the day, Brewer said his editor would never let the unbelievable story go to print.

Right after Lisa Foster disappeared, people said she was in Florida, working as a beach lifeguard in Miami and living the dream. After being abused for seventeen years by a black witch, she deserved that happiness. Jamie and Lenny hoped the story was true but couldn't help but wonder if she had vanished in the night with plans to take up where her mother left off. South Florida had a reputation as an enclave for those who practiced Santeria and voodoo. Greed, sex, and power have always been irresistible sins. All that was needed was a pact with a fallen angel.

Joe Griffin spent four weeks in the hospital. Four days in a coma, two trips to ICU, and three surgeries later left him a different man than before. Still a cop, but different. He never could recall what happened that night at the old house when he saved the day. And his memories were vague at best when he tried to recall the night at Puck Dutton's shack, the night he fired two rounds at the monster standing outside the front door. He remembered none of that, but he never forgot a little seventeen-year-old fighter named Jamie. That fondness never went away until after he passed away as a proud grandfather of three precious girls.

Like a little mouse that peeked out from its hole, that young boy, Johnny Steele, went on to be the crew chief for Petty Enterprises. He stopped staring at his boots and helped make Number 43 the fastest car on the NASCAR circuit. He had found heaven on earth helping The King become the most successful driver in the history of the sport. It doesn't get any better than that.

And Maw, well she didn't live long enough to be at Jamie's wedding, but she did attend her graduation from Duke. Occasionally, God gives us an unexpected gift in the most unlikely package. Maw would say, "God works in 'sterious ways," and Jamie was certain He did. The little old woman had loved Jamie and taught her that in every seemingly hopeless situation, there is always hope if you look to Heaven. Maw lived those words and when Jamie's life was falling apart, there Maw was, dipping snuff, smoking cigarettes, quoting Scripture, and giving advice. Jamie delivered a beautiful eulogy at her funeral and wondered if Jesus had a can of Bruton and a pack of Camels waiting for Maw when she arrived.

Lenny struggled coping with the aftermath of Tommy's death and the images of the beast Lydia conjured from hell. Tommy's return as an apparition, and the episodes at Dutton's shack, and the old mansion on the mountain gnawed at his soul whenever it entered his mind. Unfortunately, Jamie was a reminder of all that pain, and over time, they felt more like comrades-in-arms than soulmates. Not surprisingly, they grew apart and took different paths in life. While at school at N.C. State, Lenny met a beautiful girl named Diane and they married and had three wonderful kids. Of course, everyone liked Lenny and he rose to a prominent role with Kimberly-Clark Corporation and retired as a happy husband and doting grandfather. What a wonderful ending for this unlikely hero.

For about a month, Jamie went back to the cemetery, hoping that Tommy would reappear. She badly wanted to say a final goodbye, to apologize for not protecting him from harm. And she wanted to tell him that the witch responsible for taking his life was dead. He never returned to hear those words. But her life continued with a focus on school by immersing herself in her high school studies. That hard work paid off with an academic scholarship to Duke University. There she excelled and in four years received her undergraduate and graduate degrees in the fields of Neuroscience and Clinical Psychology. Given her uncommon life and special gift, it was an appropriate career choice. As expected, she set up her practice in Charlotte, and over the years used her *sight* to help law enforcement solve some seemingly unsolvable cases. While in Charlotte, she met a fellow psychologist, convinced herself that she loved him enough to get married and have two daughters and a son. Her mother, Ann, never met her grandchildren. She lived long enough to be at her daughter's wedding but passed away from cirrhosis of the liver before the grandbabies were born. Jamie tried really hard to move on from her days in Paradise Point. She had escaped in body, but after fifty years, her spirit kept returning to that haunting place. Some people say that time can erase any amount of pain, that the years have a way of diminishing our memories so any horror from our past is scarcely remembered. For Jamie, it was a big lie. Sometimes the scars are on the inside and the sorrow and emptiness never go away.

An excerpt from

Message from Boo

By

R.G. Johansen

16

The Chevy cast a veil of dust as it slowly traveled on the dirt road. This was a far cry from the high-speed, mortared streets of Atlanta. The remote roadway continued on, winding peacefully through a stand of unbroken pines. Finally, the gentle curves gave way to a straight byway that passed a deep ravine that was green with a network of kudzu. The violet blooms from the creeping plants filled the air with the sweet fragrance of late summer in the country. The vines extended out and up, smothering the ground and trees in a choking reminder, a reminder that the inviting smell of the flower may often conceal the malevolent intent of the creeping vine.

   Their journey to the Rimmon farm finally ended eight miles into the wilderness. They had arrived at a gabled old cabin nestled against a wooded hillside. Both men stopped and turned to survey the property after they stepped up on the boarded porch. The bottom land in front of the house extended for several hundred yards, halted only by an upland hill dotted with pines, oaks and maples. The property was a testament to the pioneering ingenuity that built the log-sided farmhouse, and the fertile soil bespoke of the hard labor that sowed the sun-drenched crops.

   It also spoke of rural hardship and dispossession. The cabin's oak bark roofing shingles and squat stone chimney were of the same natural materials used by settlers in the region decades ago. Much as the settlers used a crossbred mule for tilling, so did Virgil Rimmon. Their style and quality of life quietly declared their independence, that everything on the farm was put there by their hearts and hands, mixed with their love and caring for the land. It was simply enough. After the detectives finished their examination of the property, they turned and walked across the rickety planks to the cabin's front door. An eerie high-pitched squeal followed each of their steps. It was a baneful warning.

Victor used his hands to shade the low rising sun from his eyes as he gazed through the screen on the half-hinged door. John gingerly knocked with his right hand while shading his own face with his left. That's when he noticed the ceiling on the front porch was painted an odd shade of blue. The unusual paint on the ramshackle structure triggered a memory deep in his mind. Rebecca's grandparents were from the Lowcountry in South Carolina, and she once told him that they painted their porch ceiling blue to keep the spirits from entering the house. John simply dismissed the weird superstition as coincidental and began another series of raps on the door frame. Finally, the elderly Mr. Rimmon silently emerged from a back room in the cabin. Speaking no words, he stepped through the doorway past the detectives while motioning them to follow. At the side end of the porch, he methodically placed three of his crudely made chairs in a small circle and asked the detectives to sit down.

As John seated himself, he couldn't help but stare at Mr. Rimmon. His heavy skin was tan and weathered. The acute wrinkles on his forehead, cheeks, and neck followed the conformation of his face, much as the deep furrows he had farmed conformed to the neck of his land. He was old in time, yet young in spirit. This man with hickory hands and silver-white hair was pushing eighty years, yet he was a man that still possessed great physical strength. And when John gazed into Rimmon's sharp blue eyes, he sensed that his spirit held that same vigor. But today, his gritty resolve was clouded with confusion. His one and only son had been killed and he didn't understand why.

"I'm Virgil Rimmon, Frank's daddy," he said in a subdued voice. "Y'ald be the police from Atlanter?"

"Yes sir, Mr. Rimmon. I'm Detective John Williams and this is Detective Victor Lechman," John responded while shaking the farmer's calloused hand.

"Hootie tole me y'ald be 'round today, so I's been 'spectin you," Mr. Rimmon said with a troubled expression. "If' y'all need to ask questions 'bout Frank, I'll tell y'all what I know. My wife h'aint takin' his dyin' too good, so I'd be grateful if' y'all leave her be."

John and Victor gratefully accepted the offer and began the inquiry. Virgil was more than cooperative. The only problem was his speech. By degrees, he answered their questions in that twangy backwoods drawl placing his accents on whichever part of the word struck his fancy. At first, John was having a hard time understanding him. But after about twenty minutes, he had broken the imperfect code and was starting to appreciate the rhythmic dialect. He even began introducing a few doublewords in his own sentences, and without thinking, began to blend his nouns and verbs as though they were of liquid.

"Chief Goodwin tole us that Frank was a doctor-man practicin' in Atlanta. Did Frank ever say anything to you about a patient, or anyone else for that matter that might wish to harm him?" John asked.

"No, Frank was a rubbin' doctor so I don't know why any of his patients would want'a hurt him. 'Sides that, he'd only come 'round 'bout once a year. Never talked to me 'bout his payshunts. Jest stay'd long enough to visit his maw a'spell and then he'd leave," Mr. Rimmon answered.

Victor finally heard two words he understood, "What do you mean by a rubbin' doctor?"

"He'd be a bone cracker. A kirepracter. As fur as I know'd, he'd didn't make no enemies doin' that. The boy never done nothin to deserve to die like that," Mr. Rimmon's voice trembled. The tears in his eyes spoke loudly, a father should never have to outlive his son. His attention was fixed on the barn as his hands wiped the drops from his cheeks.

John could feel an immense need in Rimmon's voice. It was as though the weight of the world bore squarely on his shoulders. "Is there anything you can tell us that might help us find the person who killed your son?"

Suddenly, the teardrops were supplanted by a vision of anger as Rimmon's face reddened with hate. "I know'd who kilt my boy."

"Who killed your son?" John asked as he slid to the edge of his chair, awaiting the answer.

"Last night he come down from the mountain over thar," Mr. Rimmon said as he pointed to the wooded hills. "I know'd he was comin' cause the dogs were a'howlin', and the cows low'd and low'd cause they wus skerd. I looked out the window and seed all my chickens run up to the porch and that's when I seed him comin'. Ridin' a coal-black rig bein' pulled by a coal-black horse, he come from over yonder. H'it were dark...real dark, but I knowed it was him. When he stopped his rig by the barn I could tell."

Mr. Rimmon paused to catch his breath. His account of the evening had stirred his heart to an off course, galloping pace. His brief moment of rest allowed John enough time to view the barn from the porch in an attempt to understand what the farmer had seen.

"Mr. Rimmon, your barn is some two to three hundred yards from this house and I don't think there was a moon out last night. How could you recognize anyone, let alone see anything from this distance?" John asked.

"I knowed sir, cause I'm a preacher-man on Sunday. And any preacher-man knowed that only the devil can bring with him that kind'a stench. The air was foul. I smelt it. It were the smell of death and it come callin' on my boy last night. The devil come callin'."

Rising briskly from his chair, Victor closed his notepad with a loud slap. "Well, that will about do it. I haven't understood much of what you said, sir, but I think I got the gist of it." Victor turned back to face John. "John, what say let's zip back to Atlanta, get a warrant on Mr. Lucifer, zip back here, run up the mountain, and place the ole cuffs on the unholy one." Victor's impatience and disbelief in Mr. Rimmon's story was apparent in his face and gestures. It was also apparent that Mr. Rimmon didn't appreciate Victor's disgust with his account of the strange events.

"I don't care whut you think, mister. That thar's the truth!" Rimmon's eyes narrowed.

Sensing that Victor's vehemence would hinder the investigation prompted John to take quick action. Much like his strategy with Chief Goodwin, he asked Victor to leave him alone with Rimmon and to begin the review of the crime scene in the barn by himself. John knew that his absence would allow him to continue the questioning without being interrupted by any outbursts of emotion.

John's strategy worked, although a half-hour of additional questions provided him very little additional information. Mr. Rimmon's knowledge of his son's activities for the past few years was vague at best. John did learn that Frank had left his parents and the town of Dallas about ten years ago to pursue his chiropractic education and career in Atlanta. Evidently, Frank wanted out from under his father's puritanical thumb. It didn't take John long to understand why. Mr. Rimmon had begun to give him a fire-and-brimstone sermon on how mankind should live by a strict and rigorous religious doctrine.

Virgil was one of a vanishing breed of homespun country preachers on Sunday, and a hardworking farmer during the week. Intent on quoting the Scriptures, Mr. Rimmon spoke of nefarious pacts with the devil and how his son had become God's rival because of his incessant quest for knowledge and power. The Book of Isaiah was his divine reference as he recited the consequences of making a covenant with Hell. After John realized he was making little progress, he rose from the split-bottomed chair, preparing to walk to the barn. He concluded that Rimmon's tale of his son's death was an explanation espoused of grief intermixed with a pulpit view of life, not one based on logic and reality. Excusing himself, John thanked Mr. Rimmon for his cooperation, stepped off the porch, and proceeded to catch up with his partner.

A subtle, uneasy feeling embodied John as he walked across the grassy pasture toward the barn. It was farfetched, but Rimmon's story still hit him hard. Unlike Victor, he hadn't dismissed it as the ravings of a lunatic preacher. Perhaps Mr. Rimmon opened up a mason jar filled with moonshine and had a few snorts. Or maybe it was a simple case of an old man with dementia, distorting what he really saw. John just didn't know what to make of it. He did know, however, that as he approached the aging barn, he began to feel numbness in his hands and feet. It was as though his body was being restrained from moving forward by some unknown centrifugal force.

His vast experience of viewing grisly murder scenes refused to counter this powerful apprehension. The terrible numbness in his body instantly turned into a wave of nausea as he approached the barn's open double doors. Suddenly, he gasped for air. It was as though he was being suffocated by the foul breath of death wafting from the rafters. It was a stench so bad it caused him to shake as the odor drew closer. With all his senses now ignited, he convinced himself to take two more steps. But then the thought of turning back crept into his mind. *Victor can handle the details on the corpse.* He thought. *I need to turn around and get away from here.*

John followed his instincts, yet as he turned about, he found himself face to face with something much worse than a decomposing corpse. It was a muscular, black bull. Yes, he was almost nose to nose with two thousand pounds of mean-spirited beef. The animal had been grazing in the pasture surrounding the barn and had taken notice of this out-of-place stranger.

It's eyes, dark with danger, had been carefully appraising John's movements. The agitated bull shook its wide head, side to side, as though it was warning John to go the other way. John stood as motionless as a pillar of salt while he hastily considered his options. The choice became as clear as the cloudless sky above. Chances for survival with a decomposing stiff were infinitely better than those with a hostile ox. He made one more about-face and quickly sprinted inside the barn.

Gloomy slithers of sunlight carved their way between the gaping planks on the side of the barn. The lack of illumination created a lurid setting given the brightness of the outside world. With hands protected by latex gloves, Victor was busy turning the suspended body, ignoring the stinking breeze and absence of light when John came rushing in.

"Look out, John!" Victor yelped, as he watched his partner draw near.

John failed to see the animal carcass laying in his path. As he stumbled over the unseen remains, he wildly grasped for any hilt of balance. His hands found only the loose, rancid skin of a disjointed cow as he fell clumsily to the ground.

"What the hell!" John exclaimed as he recoiled to his feet from the fall.

"Say hello to Elsie," Victor laughingly said.

"Here... catch," he said, tossing John a cylinder-shaped flashlight.

John caught the flashlight in both hands and, nervously, thumbed the switch to the on position. Quickly, he aimed the beam toward the ground. The artificial light did its job by helping his myopic eyes focus on the bulging heifer. It was ghastly. A metamorphic night had converted the cow's serene face into one of sunken terror. John stared in disbelief as a swarm of flies buzzed in and out of the animal's vacant eye sockets. As he fanned the light up and down the swollen carcass, he also noticed that the cow's tongue, udder, and reproductive organs were missing.

"Damn, why would anyone mutilate an animal this way?" John asked, as spasms once again found his belly.

"Let me tell you something, pal. We've got the work of a big-time Satanic cult here—a big-time cult! They cut out the animal's parts so they can use them in their rituals," Victor responded with an authority of both excitement and disgust.

"Even the cow's sex organs?" John inquired as he reeled from the nausea.

"Especially those. These Satanic cuckoos believe the sex organs contain power. They believe that the release of sexual energy is one way they can reach a higher level of consciousness. By taking the sex organs, they think they can add power to their rituals. And I'll bet you dollars to doughnuts that the cow's blood has been drained."

"Remember, Rimmon said he heard the cows bellowing last night. That's when this must have happened," John remarked, as he continued to shine the beam up and down the carcass.

"Maybe, maybe not. These fruitcakes usually use an electric prod to stun a large animal like this. Knocks them right off their feet. Then, they'll spray the face and neck with Freon so the cow's alive, but not alive. Usually no sound. The commotion the old man heard last night could have been caused by something else."

"Great, this is just great," John said.

"Come over here, John. Take a look at this. The cow's not the only one missing a sex organ." Victor's voice was painted with disgust.

Between the side stalls, in the hub of the barn, the naked body of Frank Rimmon hung upside-down, tethered by a hemp rope that was tied to a large timber that supported the roof. With both feet bound together, the six foot, two-hundred-pound body drooped laxly as though without bones. John couldn't help but notice Rimmon's bluish arms as they dangled toward the wheat-strawed ground.

And Victor was right. A dangling penis was AWOL. Just like Pierce, Rimmon's severed organ was nowhere to be found. Victor pulled John's attention to another part of Rimmon's anatomy by spinning the body around and pointing to the buttocks. An inverted cross of crimson had been smeared on his right cheek. He also instructed John to take note as he pried open Rimmons swollen eye lids, providing him a palpitating view of two dilated orbs, milky white in color. They were just like Pierce's bleached eyes. Finally, Victor pointed to the ghastly mouth that spoke without speaking. It was agape, in a grinning bow of horror. The question of whether the death of Pierce and Rimmon was related had been answered with an awful certainty. The stink, the cross, the eyes, it was all there, and not one drop of blood could be found.

The detectives were persistent. For almost two hours, the vein-like beams from their flashlights jittered up and down the corpse, and then on the ground underneath. Other than the obvious, they came away with nothing other than a case of Hootie's heebie-jeebies. Both men seemed unable to train their light on Rimmon's abhorrent features any longer. Besides that, they were growing exhausted from their search in the difficult light inside the barn.

"Victor, let's step outside. I need a breath of fresh air," John said as he wiped the sweat from his forehead.

"Yeah! So do I. This is all like a bad dream," Victor nervously replied.

The bright sun restored their sense of balance. It made them momentarily forget that humanity could be capable of committing this kind of evil. Yet, both men were unaware that this temporary reprieve would soon be lost, unaware that they were destined for a long, horrible ride on a wicked carousel that would have them questioning everything. For now, it was best they didn't know. They had too many unanswered questions regarding Rimmon. Both agreed that the situation called for technical support—lab technicians, pathology, the works.

They also agreed that Victor would continue the investigation at the barn, while John contacted the necessary personnel. The only problem was that the Rimmons lacked even the most rudimentary conveniences, including a telephone, and the detective's mobile radio could not reach the station from this remote distance. So, John had to leave the farm. It was a preordained trip, anyway, given his previous desire to leave the premises. As he walked to the car, he cautiously watched for the menacing bull that had earlier impeded his path. No bull this time, although his path was still blocked. Now, it was a pint-sized matron, the mother of Frank Rimmon. She confronted him squarely in the middle of the open pasture. Threadbare in dress, decorated only with a pair of silver-rimmed spectacles, she seemed restless, troubled as if her life was completely off-center. Her voice, bodefully quiet, seemed sapped of the strength it normally possessed.

"I'm Alma Rimmon. I seed you on the porch with my husband. Are you gonna find who kilt my Frankie?" she asked as tears stained her sullen cheeks.

"Mrs. Rimmon, we're going to do everything in our power to find out who did this," John responded but his words lacked the commitment being sought by a tormented mother.

"Promise me. Promise me ya'll find who did this. An eye for an eye," she said, her voice now trembling.

John frantically searched for the perfect words to say to a grief-stricken mother. With knowledge that hundreds of murders go unsolved each year, he hesitated to make such a vow. Yet, he knew it would bring her solace. With all of life's sorrow and confusion, the promise would be the perfect words she needed to hear, the commitment she so desperately wanted. In the darkness of her son's death, it would be her light of justice.

"Yes ma'am, we'll find who did this. I promise."

With pledge in hand, she seemed more at ease. John took the opportunity to ask her some questions regarding her son. From odd bits of information, he learned that on previous visits, Rimmon had spoken to her about an invisible torment, of changing his ways and, most importantly, of meeting his Maker. Frank Rimmon's words to his mother were a self-fulfilled prophesy. Finally, Mrs. Rimmon confirmed her son had arrived unannounced last night, and that she nor her husband knew of his presence until they discovered his body this morning.

CPSIA information can be obtained
at www.ICGtesting.com
Printed in the USA
LVHW050042301222
736159LV00012B/980